JEM SPEARS

A COURTSHIP IN QUARANTINE

A Courtship in Quarantine

An International Love and Misadventure novel

www.jemspears.com

This is a work of fiction. All of the characters, organizations, and events portrayed in this novel are either products of the author's imagination or are used fictitiously.

Printed in the United States of America.

Spear Stone Press | Cincinnati, Ohio

First Edition

Editor: May Peterson

Cover by Ana Grigorio-Voicu

ISBN 978-0-9963034-9-1

Library of Congress Control Number: 2025913906

Also by Jem Spears

The International Love and Misadventure Series:
Starlight and Cinnamon

Author's Note

I have no doubt you'll notice that I've taken liberties. I first read about the quarantine hotels popping up in Italy in the summer of 2020, followed by stories of similar facilities in places like South Korea. I hadn't heard that Aotearoa New Zealand had also done so until months later, when I was already nurturing the seed of a meet-cute: what if two quarantined strangers got to know each other by passing notes through their shared suite doors?

So I needed a country that had these quarantine hotels, that spoke English, and was invested in the health of their citizenry. I also needed it to be a little disorganized and a little stricter, so I let myself fiction and made some things up, including the timing of certain restrictions. In reality, Aotearoa New Zealand's early response to the pandemic was one of the most comprehensive and effective in the world.

I'm relying on our collective fuzzy memory of worldwide chaos and uncertainty during that time to suspend your disbelief just long enough for Mattie and Raphael to get together. Since March 2020, time has felt softer. Allow me to reshape it slightly, in service to this story. I'll be gentle. And as a reward, there will be kissing.

For everyone who's had to search for their found family.

Content Guidance

This book contains emotional abuse and manipulation, mention of past physical abuse (no details), mention of disordered eating, stalking, panic attacks, gaslighting, fatphobia, ablism, mention of bugs (though the characters never see any), politics, and graphic sex.

Contents

North Island

Aotearoa New Zealand

PART ONE

Day 3 of Quarantine
Monday, March 23, 2020

Greetings, fellow prisoner,

I knew that New Zealand required all non-national travelers to stay at one of their "quarantine hotels" for 14 days after arrival, and I assumed that my various devices and hotel TV would easily hold my interest for that long. But it's only Day 3, and I already find myself utterly uninterested in looking at another screen. Eleven days of further isolation without entertainment or enrichment could easily foment in me a slowly increasing madness on par with *The Yellow Wallpaper*.

Luckily, hotel stationery still exists. And they've even furnished me with two brand-stamped ballpoint pens. We are truly blessed to be imprisoned at such a luxury establishment. Here I am, writing a letter on paper for the first time in—I'd rather not say. My hand is already cramping, let's leave it at that.

So I have a proposition for you: if you would like to participate in a real-life, physical letter exchange with me, the unfamiliar Englishman in the adjoining room, in an attempt to prevent brain rot or simply stave off boredom, you can write me back tonight.

For additional context, I was the man in the face mask who sat next to you on that 13-hour flight out of Los Angeles three days ago. It feels like forever ago to me, so I won't take it personally if you don't remember. I can't imagine I made much of an impression, being asleep most of the time. Perhaps you'll give me the opportunity now.

If, as of tomorrow morning, there's no return letter from you, I'll be a proper gentleman, respect your wishes, and leave you alone for the rest of our internment. You have my word. Simple as that.

Though it does feel irrationally exciting, like passing notes in class: the most mildly forbidden thing we can do.

—R

***

Hello R,

I remember that masked man who sat next to me on the plane three days ago. He's the same guy I saw walking around the Auckland airport when we landed. Then he got on the same bus as me, to go to the same quarantine hotel as me, and was escorted to the same hallway as me. A month ago, if I had seen you in all those places, I would have immediately found alternate accommodations, because that's stalking. But the coronavirus has taken it out of our hands, and I can't fault you for it.

This does feel like passing notes. How many times did the hotel tell us we're not allowed anything in or out of the room except via their personnel? Eight? A dozen? It was so many times. And yet, why give us stationery and pens if they didn't want us writing letters, hmm?

Did you not bring any books with you? I always bring my e-reader with its many, many titles, but I also can't help packing an embarrassing number of physical books as well. What if the battery dies? What if I drop it in the tub, or pool, or ocean? Always have a backup book. Tell me what you like to read and I'll consider loaning you one of them. It'll have to wait until day eight of our isolation, once we test negative and can go out on our balconies. I'll just toss it over to yours.

What brings you to New Zealand, R? It was the quarantine hotels, wasn't it? You heard about this paradise of seclusion, thin carpets, windowless bathrooms, and cleaning your own room for two weeks and just had to experience it for yourself. And look! Bonus! A set of exquisite plastic pens embossed with this fine establishment's seal. I, for one, never want to leave.

Strange to think we didn't tell each other our names, but I like your idea. If you don't mind being pen pals with an unfamiliar American woman, write to me whenever you'd like.

—M

p.s. If you see a woman trapped within the vines of your wallpaper, send her to me. She and I are sisters.

Day 4
Tuesday, March 24, 2020

Text Message
between Matalina, Corinne, and Daphne
10:05 a.m.

Matalina:

> I would stage a prison break for some decent coffee.

Corinne:

> Well, you have two willing accomplices on the outside.
> Tell us what you need.

Daphne:

> We can bring you coffee, Mattie!

Matalina:

> And how will you get it to me?

Corinne:

> Impersonate a nurse?

Daphne:

> rope. basket. balcony.

> I mean impersonate a nurse. Do you have a balcony?

Matalina:

> Yeah but I can't use it yet.

Corinne:

I bet the nurse thing is sounding pretty good right now.

Matalina:

lol don't worry about it. So the guy I told you about from the plane is in the next room over, and there's a door between our rooms. He wrote me a letter on hotel stationery saying hey. Wants us to be like pen pals. Is that weird?

Daphne:

Yes.

Fuck him.

Corinne:

Wait fuck him like "fuck that guy, he's a creep" or "take him to bed"?

Daphne:

8===> (o)

Corinne:

Ooo Daphne going old school with the emoticons

Matalina:

His eyes are striking, and he cuts a nice figure, but we're literally quarantined in separate rooms for the next 10 days soooo

Daphne:

I said what I said.

Corinne:

"He cuts a nice figure" lol ok Jane Austen.

Matalina:

> Daphne wants me to sleep with a guy whose face I haven't seen, and Corinne is judging my turn of phrase. Such friend. So help.

Daphne:

> yes.

Corinne:

> You're a writer, write to him. It's as risky as DMing. He can lie as well with a pen as he could with a keyboard. And you don't need to tell him personal info.

Matalina:

> He signed his letter R, so I signed mine M. I like hearing what you each have to say and trying to find a middle ground between batshit crazy and annoyingly practical.

Daphne:

> love u too sis

Corinne:

> Call me practical again, I dare you.

***

Hello M,

I am absolutely in New Zealand for the quarantine hotel. The cleaning basket's hand sanitizer smells like kiwi fruit, and I can only imagine the craftsmanship that went into this bespoke item. To think I've been here a mere four days and all my dreams have already come true.

Beyond that, I'm here for work. They're trying to get everyone into the country before the borders close, which seems inevitable at this point. I figured I can use this time in isolation to catch up on work as well as the binge-able shows I've been too busy for. Do you have any suggestions? The algorithm doesn't seem to know me at all and apparently my friends only watch shit.

What is so important that it has you braving a plague to travel here? I saw you move through the airport with the practiced ease of someone who is either a professional traveler or has navigated this particular airport a number of times before. You can lie, if you like. As long as you make it interesting. I love a good story.

Besides everything on my tablet, I brought one physical book: *That Scarlet, Beating Heart*, by Peter Fortstaff. Work wants me to read it before I join them. I started on the plane, but it's too dark for me. I honestly don't know what to do with it. But if you were to loan me a book, I wouldn't read this one, and that's probably not the best way to start a new job.

I've been here once, in the before-times. New Zealand, I mean, not "in the position of having to read a book I have no interest in while being confined for two weeks in the beginning of what is most likely a pandemic." If you're looking for any recommendations for activities and whatnot, I can provide at least two that will definitely be on any "must-see" list you'd find online. I do try to be helpful.

—R

p.s. The woman in the vines only comes out at night. I'll set an alarm to catch her and send her over.

***

E-mail
From: Luke Maston, getoffmylawn@tepidemail.com
To: Raphael Callan, raffinityraccoon@wormwood.gb.ww.co
Subject: she's at it again

12:40 p.m.

Well, well, well. Raphael Callan. Welcome to Aotearoa! As a lifelong Kiwi, I can tell you with certainty: there's usually less plague.

A few days ago, I packed my bags and left Lena and Cassidy and mum at our house, drove fifteen minutes, and arrived on set to absolute mayhem. Payton is finally panicking that the rest of the cast and crew will be caught outside the country when the borders close. I have a feeling this won't be coming together anytime soon. Sorry you had to fly here and quarantine for what will turn out to be nothing. You can stay with me and the girls once Payton realizes they can't film here and you can't leave. Sleepovers every night, bro!

You can bring your new friend, too. Of course you'd try to start something with a masked woman, that is some tragically romantic shit if I ever heard it. I hope she writes you back. And that she isn't a soul-eating demon like your ex, who BY THE WAY

is spewing about you across the internet. There's enough of an overlap between her ForEverette fans and your Pro-Raphaelites that her nonsense is just confusing people and not turning anyone against you, except her die-hards, who always wanted you to, uh, die hard. She messaged me a couple times and I never wrote back. If she thinks I'm going to turn my back on you in favor of her, she's got another thing coming. I've got you.

Luke

***

Email
From: Raphael Callan, raffinityraccoon@wormwood.gb.ww.co
To: Luke Maston, getoffmylawn@tepidemail.com

Subject: RE: she's at it again

1:11 p.m.

What a warm welcome I've received in your country, where I get cotton swabs jammed up my nose at regular intervals and threatened with fines and arrest if I so much as open my hotel room door without permission.

Still better than Los Angeles, though. And London. I'll take any number of Covid tests over the public's unrelenting attention. I only agreed to this project sight unseen because it took me out of the eye of the storm and into the quietude of New Zealand forests. Has it gotten worse for you recently, too? Has the constant stream of staged encounters and genuine harassment driven you to the woods? My quarantine may be forced, but it's also a reprieve.

As far as I'm concerned, Edie Everette can shout into the ether of the internet as much as she wants. I blocked her everywhere I could. I'm shocked she hasn't tried to text from a burner phone or email from another account. If you don't want to block her like I have, that's fine, but I don't want to hear about it. She's taken enough from me. I won't let her have another minute. Oh and stop calling her a soul-eating demon. The demons don't deserve the comparison.

The woman next door wrote back, offered to loan me books that she brought. I don't know her name, but she signed her letter with an M. I sign mine R. She's already seen the top half of my face and didn't seem to recognize me, and I didn't want to take the chance that knowing my name might jog her memory. I've Googled "Raphael" recently and I'm in the top five hits. She's smart. If she realizes who the internet says I am, our dynamic will change. You're reading this shaking your head like I'm full of shit, but I haven't been able to find a date that wasn't starstruck or a part of the entertainment industry in...I want to say a decade.

I am not looking forward to this project. I started reading *That Scarlet, Beating Heart* and all I can do is hope that the screenplay is more of a loose interpretation. My character is an entitled brat. Your character isn't any better. Do we really owe Payton so big a favor? I can't believe I agreed to this. Let's not do that again.

They're sending the script today. Tell me it's amazing. Tell me it's nothing like the book. Tell me there's still a chance to back out of this disaster.

Raphael

Day 5

Wednesday, March 25, 2020

R—

I can't believe you got the kiwi-fruit-scented hand sanitizer. They gave me "clean linen," which, historically, smells neither clean nor of linen. Ten bucks it was named by a man who's never done his own laundry. And now I have to suffer for it.

You know in the movies when an organization has an impossible mission and they call up the retired, grizzled mastermind and say, "You're the only one who can help us, take this one last job and it'll set you up for life, and we'll never ask you for anything ever again"? It me. I'm the retired, grizzled mastermind. I'm also the one recruiting me, and my "one last job" is my brother's wedding in two weeks.

I've been told that my belief that family *shouldn't* treat one another badly isn't normal. But I wouldn't put up with a stranger treating me like shit, so why would I have even lower expectations for the people who say they love me?

It's hard to kick the habit of assuming "relatives" and "family" are the same thing, and it took me until my thirties to realize my siblings and parents might be related to me but are certainly not family. So I made myself a deal: the last of my siblings is getting married, and if I attend, I will have fulfilled every familial duty to them all, and I can walk away with a clean conscience.

I could complain about this for pages and pages, but I'll leave it at that for now. TL;DR: I'm here for my brother's wedding, and if

I attend, I will give myself the gift of never seeing any of my toxic relatives ever again. Hence, "braving the plague."

I know that Fortstaff book. If your job wants you to read it, it's probably because they idolize the main character, who is insufferable. I mourn those hours I spent reading it. That could have been episodes of *Schitt's Creek*, or *Dickinson*, or any of the books in my to-read pile. I heard it's going to be adapted into a movie. My heart goes out to all the not-assholes that have to work on it.

It's too late for me, but there's still time for you. Save yourself and throw the book right into the trash. Or if you want to be dramatic, wait until you can open the balcony door and throw it, just throw it as hard and as far as you can. Tell your bosses that you read a chapter and didn't bother with the rest. Glorifying being a dick is literally the point of the book, so they'll be happy that you understand it like they do. It'll work, I swear.

Also, quit that job. Unless you've been very clever in these letters and have hidden the fact that you're an absolute par (am I using that right? I'm not up on British slang), the culture there is going to grind you down to powder.

Thank you for offering to recommend activities, but I've also been here before. And the few days leading up to the wedding are already packed dawn to dusk with related events, and my flight leaves the morning after the wedding. No time for anything fun. Well, besides the next ten-ish days in this room. What does it say that I'm here for a wedding and my favorite part will be the two weeks in isolation? Please excuse me, I have to go rethink my entire life.

—M

***

Dear M—

I feared this book would be terrible. I felt it in my bones, just looking at the cover, that pretentious title, who's praising it. It's getting tossed. Burning it seems unachievable in our current state of confinement, but I need it gone this moment. Maybe I'll keep it in the sink and let the water soften its spine until I can throw it out the balcony door and watch it splatter against the road in a wet, pulpy mess.

I would love to quit the job, but I owe someone there a big favor and can't get out of it. Thankfully, my best mate is working there, too. He tells me it's bedlam already, and he is an agent of chaos, which means that either he's in his element—and I can ride it out in his wake—or it's incompatible with his energy—in which case, it'll be that meme with the fire and the pizzas and the troll.

Yes, you used "par" correctly, and no, I'm not one. I think.

As someone who is familiar with the trope, I feel I must point out that the "one last job" usually leads to the character's death and not a Happy Ever After. Assuming you've already considered this, and have decided that death is an acceptable outcome, your relatives must be much worse than you say. If you wanted to tell me more about them, I'd love to hear it. I'm imagining *The Crown*, but without feeling torn because I'm English. It will be just a terrible and entertaining story. I can't wait.

On a more serious note, fuck your relatives. Is that too bold of me? I absolutely agree that people who say they love you shouldn't treat you like rubbish. I've also had problems with that in the past. I'm looking forward to you finding the peace that comes from leaving them behind. Life's too short to allow shitty people to steal your time, so strive to be with the people who truly love you.

I noticed you snuck in bingeing recommendations, thank you. My laptop figured out that I'm not in the US or UK, so my streaming options are limited, but I'll check them out if I can.

What do you do for work, that you can enjoy fourteen days of quarantine before a weekend of hell?

Yours,

R

**

Email

From: Raphael Callan, raffinityraccoon@wormwood.gb.ww.co

To: Luke Maston, getoffmylawn@tepidemail.com

Subject: That Terrible, Bloody Novel

3:01 p.m.

I read the script. And some of the book. I'm beginning to understand why Payton is doing everything outside of legitimate channels. "Authenticity" my ass, I bet Miramar didn't want anything to do with it.

You and I are going to have to tank this production before it gets started. So far, my ideas include shutting down the country, faking Covid, and actually getting Covid. I would also accept calling in bomb threats, faking my own death, and faking amnesia—forever, if that's what it takes.

When your girls are teens, they're going to watch this film, and they'll never forgive you.

Think about that whenever you consider that I might be exaggerating just how damning and damaging this story is. Think of Lena and Cassidy at thirteen and fifteen, watching this, watching you in this, knowing you voluntarily took that role. I wouldn't want to be in your shoes, mate.

—Raphael

***

Text Message
between Matalina, Corinne, and Daphne
4:41 p.m.

Corinne:

What kind of goodies do you want?

Matalina:

Romance novels and snickerdoodles. Scented candles, scarves, wine, fresh fruit, vintage sunglasses, notebooks, croissants, and what the heck are you talking about?

Corinne:

When we smuggle you a care package.

Matalina:

I really don't think the nurse thing will work.

Corinne:

Don't worry about that part. We're gonna try something else.

Matalina:

Well in that case, my list stands. Actually make it 2 notebooks. This free stationery only has like 6 pages and we're going to run out soon.

Daphne:

ooOOoo, Mattie and R sitting in a tree

Corinne:

You're really writing to each other that much?

Matalina:

There's not much else to distract me from work, and I don't feel self-conscious saying anything to him because we don't know each other. I don't know if I could say any of it to his face (or half his face, because mask). Writing a letter feels more intimate yet oddly freeing. I could easily lie to him about anything but I don't want to. I want to show him me and see what happens.

Daphne:

she's got it bad.

Corinne:

Yeah she does.

Matalina:

Haven't seen his face!

Corinne:

Well it sounds like you've seen his heart.

Daphne:

and the heart is the dick of the soul.

Matalina:

Daphne lol

Corinne:

Daphne is right. The heart is the dick of the soul, now get out there and work his heart-dick with a letter.

Daphne:

YES RIN-RIN!

Matalina:

You two are gonna get me in trouble.

Corinne:

We're gonna get you laid, and that will make you happy, and that will steel you for dealing with your relatives.

Daphne:

Oh! Oh! Make him your wedding date!

Matalina:

Daph. Be serious.

Daphne:

I am, it's perfect. Kyle and Celeste have you down as solo. Bring a date to fuck that shit up. It'll feel so good. Then you can work R's dick-dick like you worked his heart-dick and blammo, bad relatives out, sexy new bf in.

Corinne:

Why am I agreeing with you? Is something wrong with me? Is something right with you??

Daphne:

Sometimes I know my shit, Rin.

Matalina:

Ok I'm not going to entertain that suggestion until I've at least seen his face. Day 8 we get tested. If it comes back negative, we can use the balconies.

Corinne:

So you both step out on the balcony, see each other...

Daphne:

and then make out.

Matalina:

No make out, Daph. Still no contact with anyone until Day 14.

Daphne:

lol good luck, you'll be so horny by then.

Matalina:

You're not wrong.

Corinne:

Poor Matalina.

Daphne:

poor, poor Matalina

Matalina:

Yep. Poor me.

Day 6

Thursday, March 26, 2020

Dear R,

Happy Ever After, huh? Maybe come balcony time, I'll toss over a romance, the absolute opposite of *That Scarlet, Beating Heart*. Did you actually read any more of it, or was my excellent description enough to convince you it belongs in the garbage? What's this I'm feeling now? Is this...is this what it feels like to wield power? The power to dictate which books are awful, and someone actually listens?

I would be such a bad dictator. I'd be excellent at fulfilling the role of a despot with my despotic decisions, but I would be a bad person. Hmm. Can you think of any examples of book-opinion-based dictatorships, and tell me how they turned out? I imagine they all ended in death by 1,000 paper cuts.

Speaking of paper cuts (nailed it), I'm a freelance writer. This brings to mind technical manuals and employee handbooks and brochures and other not-bestselling-novel projects, all of which I have, actually, worked on.

But a lot of it is proprietary and I can't talk about it. No offence. *waves fingers in your face like a Jedi* *Forget that last part*!

So I don't actually have two weeks free from work. I'm just able to do it from my computer. I envy you. Now that you've chosen the path of light, you've freed up all that time it would have taken you to trudge through that book. It sounds like you still have work, but at least your misery won't be compounded. I noticed you didn't actually mention what you do. Keep your secrets, R. I'll find out before the end.

I'll say a little more about my relatives, since you seem interested, but I'm running out of space. On this page, but also in my life (nice segue?) when it comes to allowing people who don't really care about me to usurp my time and energy. But I have a whole lifetime of shared memories with these people, so I can't in good conscience just abandon all that without trying one more time (one *last* time) to have a relationship with any of them that doesn't include insults, criticism, or attempts to change my fundamental nature. If there are any benefits to keeping them in my life, several decades hasn't been enough time to recognize them.

I'm definitely keeping my sister Daphne, though.

She and our friend Rin have some sort of plan to smuggle me a "goody bag" and I've requested notebooks. If they come through (one of them is good at ideas but not execution, the other is, as you've described your friend, an "agent of chaos," and they're trying to break into a quarantine hotel, so, I put their chances at about 8%), I'll toss a notebook over with the romance book, so our dwindling stationery won't be an issue.

Later,

M

***

Email

From: Luke Maston, getoffmylawn@tepidemail.com

To: Raphael Callan, raffinityraccoon@wormwood.gb.ww.co

Subject: Project Burn It Down

10:35 a.m.

I won't bring up your ex again. It's hard to remember that the most harmful stuff she did was real, so I can only imagine how gaslighted you've been feeling. And she's made you look the villain, and it's maddening. Is there anything she might do that you'd want me to tell you about? Or that you'd want me to jump in to defend you? At this point, I would settle for her finding her soul mate and being happy forever, if it meant she left you alone for good. Never thought I'd wish her well, but, here we are.

On a happier note, tell me more about M. You don't want her to figure out you're Raphael Callan but you do want her to get to know this "R" character you're playing at. I don't think this will turn out how you expect. But tell me why you want it to. What makes her special?

I was waiting to see how everything played out here until I decided to burn it all down, but you're right, I guess we can start now. Suggestions?

***

Email
From: Raphael Callan, raffinityraccoon@wormwood.gb.ww.co
To: Luke Maston, getoffmylawn@tepidemail.com
Subject: RE: Project Burn It Down
11:02 a.m.
To start, arson is not an option. I just want that to be very clear, and in writing, for legal purposes. No destruction of property. Can you talk to the writer, assuming it's not Fortstaff himself? Payton? Have you noticed any violations that would cause the production to shut down if the proper authorities were notified? Are you sure there's not a family emergency that requires you to be called away and to take me with you?

The first thing that attracted me to M was that she was my row-mate on our flight. She didn't recognize me and she was personable. We were two of the only people who wore a mask, but her eyes are a beautiful, deep blue, and I could tell when she was smiling beneath the mask, which made me smile. She worked on her computer most of the time and we only said a handful of sentences to each other, so it wasn't until she wrote back to me three days ago that I realized she's also smart and clever and playful. She's going through similar toxic-people shit that I have, and we seem to be of the same mind about it.

I'm enjoying getting to know her, and that's enough for me right now. Also, "R" isn't a character, it's me. I plan to tell her who I am, but in the meantime, I'm still telling her who I am. One opinion, one observation, one fact at a time. I want to savor what it feels like to talk to someone who doesn't think they already intimately know me based on roles I've played and interviews they've seen. It's an odd feeling, that freedom.

She said her friends plan to smuggle her a goodie bag. Where's my friend to smuggle me a goodie bag?

-Raph

***

Dear M,

Toss me that romance novel. Whatever it is, it'll be an effective palate-cleanser after abandoning *That Scarlet, Beating Heart*. I read more than half of it and it was more than half too much.

I can't seem to remember everything you said about being a freelance writer, for some reason, but something else stuck out for me: what kind of writer packs an e-reader and a dozen physical books, but no notebook? Suspicious, that. In fact, I can only think of one person so confident and terrible that they don't need a notebook. I know exactly who you are.

You're Peter Fortstaff. You're catfishing me for your next novel, no doubt a bestseller, but still absolute rubbish. Should be ashamed of yourself, seducing a stranger like this. You wicked man.

Probably still helpless against your charms,

R

***

R—

Okay first of all, I know you haven't seen my entire face, but I'm not a white man. Second, if I had Fortstaff's income, I would send my brother an expensive but impersonal wedding present and skip the ceremony altogether. Oh, my relatives will never forgive me? Let me wipe my tears with a fistful of $100 bills.

Third, I'm not sure I could force myself to write a novel's worth of crap, even if it meant fame and fortune. If I did, I would definitely do it under a pen name, though, so you've got that right. I have written things not to my taste, that comes with the freelance territory. But I would never write something that would further stigmatize or endanger marginalized groups of people, even for fame, even for fortune. I am not Peter Fortstaff.

Fourth, thank you for sending me the woman in the wallpaper. Her bulging eyes and torn nails are uncannily similar to my own. You don't think that means anything, do you?

Also I wasn't aware I was seducing you? Pivoting quickly to a related topic:

You and I are going to have a two-member, quarantine-style Romance Book Club. I might need your number so we can text about it when we run out of stationery, if my friends' plan falls through. I'm enjoying our letter exchange but needs must.

Oh, I definitely brought a notebook. I just didn't want to rip pages out of it. I would, if it came to it, but if Rin and Daph bring me new ones, then I get more notebooks for free. I'm smart like that.

Temp check: normal. How are you feeling? Infected?

I've been in the country six days and besides Daphne, no relative has contacted me. I'm fourth of six siblings, and you would be forgiven if you assumed that the fourth child should skate beneath the radar of overbearing parents, but you would also be wrong. Daphne and I were the two that never fit in, though she was always forgiven for it because she's the youngest and also a lesbian. Any behavior our relatives deem unacceptable is blamed on either or both of those characteristics.

Would I like an equivalent that would let my own "unacceptable" behavior slide? Sure. Is there anything in the world that would be an acceptable excuse to my relatives? Not a damn thing. I think it's because they take me seriously, but Daphne will always be the baby, so her opinions will always be misconstrued as naïve.

In truth, Daphne is fierce, and you'd do well not to cross her. But my parents and siblings have always tried to protect her innocence while, at the same time, trying to manipulate every fiber of softness out of me. Someone says a mean thing to Daph? Everyone comes to her rescue. Someone says a mean thing to me? Everyone tells me to suck it up.

It doesn't help that I tend to confront inappropriate behavior when I see it. I've never been one to keep quiet if I see someone being a bully, or saying something sexist, or racist, or vile, or harmful. And it's never the bullying that people have a problem with, but the fact that I call it out. My relatives say I "make a scene" or "stir the shit," but if they didn't want me to say something, they should have dealt with it before it got to the point where I had to. And it embarrasses them.

Anyway, I don't mind talking about it, but I totally understand if this is more intense than what you were expecting.

My relatives weren't always like this. Well, they were. But I have good memories, too. We traveled a lot, which was fun. One of my brothers taught me morse code; another used to take me down to the creek to catch frogs. My father and I had a game hiding a tiny plastic spider where my mother would definitely find it and freak out, over and over again. I guess it just feels like none of that is enough to allow them to make me feel like shit as an adult. Maybe this is what it means to grow up?

—M

Day 7
Friday, March 27, 2020

Text Message
between Matalina, Corinne, and Daphne
9:23 a.m.

Matalina:

uhhh he said I was seducing him???

Daphne:

WHAT

Corinne:

lol wtf

Matalina:

I convinced him not to read that awful Fortstaff book, and then he thought I didn't bring any notebooks and said only one writer was incompetent enough to not have a notebook, so I must be Fortstaff, catfishing him, seducing him. Also, please include one more notebook so I can give it to him to keep our letters going.

Corinne:

Mattie's so thirsty she's ready to fall in bed SORRY I meant in love after four letters with this guy.

Daphne:

wholly approve.

hole-y approve.

Cinnamon also approves.

Matalina:

Then how can I disagree? Pure Cinnamon roll.

Daphne:

Hey, that was her name before it was a meme.

Matalina:

Will she be at the wedding too?

Daphne:

lmao no. I love her, she doesn't deserve to suffer. The relatives were at our wedding, that's the only time they get to see her. I've tucked her away in San Francisco where they can't touch her.

Corinne:

Daph, you may be the smartest of us all.

Matalina:

Seconded.

Daphne:

aaaaand the motion is passed, I'm the smartest of us all. For my first act as emperor, I decree Mattie and R should hook up.

Matalina:

I'm trying, Daph. Keep you posted.

***

Dear M—if that is your real name—

You've convinced me you're not Fortstaff. Mostly because you did, in fact, bring a notebook. And if you have a plan to get more, free notebooks? Very writerly. A very not-Fortstaffian thing to do. If you decide you can share from your meagre store, I would certainly appreciate a notebook myself. I imagine your friends riding by your balcony on bikes, throwing items as best they can like paperboys. I hope their plan is better than that.

If this isn't a seduction, I'm curious what one would look like. Though it's bad form for me to have assumed you were single. Or interested. I'm about to say something narcissistic, but before I do, I want you to know that I know it is: I am attractive. Though it occurs to me that I can't have enamoured you with my good looks, since I've been masked every moment you've seen me. Oh god. Have a made a fool of myself? I'm going to just move on. Maybe you won't notice.

As for the book club? I'm in. I'll send you my number when I run out of paper. Wait, that won't work. I can knock on your door and tell you through it. Or across the balcony. Dazzled by my intellect yet?

This letter is exposing some of my worst shortcomings. I don't have enough paper left to start over, so I guess this is the one where I let you see my most annoying flaws and hope you still want to write to me.

You've told me a little about your sister Daphne, who sounds like a good friend. You also mentioned Rin, so tell me about that friend next. I want to know the kind of people you surround yourself with to make up for the fact that your relatives are apparently monsters.

My parents, younger brother, and older sister are generally decent people, but while I don't have first-hand experience with the need to keep "relatives" and "family" separate, I wholeheartedly agree with the sentiment. Because of how I look, and my profession, a lot of people think they're entitled to my body, time, and thoughts because they project what they want me to be instead of accepting—or even taking the time to find out—who I really am.

It took me a long, long time to feel comfortable even voicing my boundaries. At least now I'm more discerning regarding what jobs I take, since being charming and interacting with people are part and parcel of that, which is the perfect storm for harassment. More than one person has told me this will affect future job offers. Men are supposed to like physical attention from women, right? Even from strangers. But for me, that's a red flag. If it wouldn't be acceptable for a guy to act that way towards a woman, why is it acceptable for a woman to ignore a guy's boundaries?

I have the greatest of sympathies for pregnant people in public: so often touched without their permission, because people feel entitled to that person's body.

I didn't mean to end this letter so grimly. To answer your questions: I do not feel infected. Temperature normal. Maybe we'll get through this thing unscathed?

Yours,

R

***

Dear R,

You know full well that M is not my real name. Though I have a feeling I'll be telling you what it is before we're released from quarantine.

I don't know what Daph and Rin are planning, but a bicycle drive-by sounds right. Usually they include me in their shenanigans, and I try to steer them to more effective and less dangerous actions. Without me, they come up with things like "impersonate a nurse" and "try to throw things onto a third story balcony." I'm going to end up with exploded fruit and wine-soaked notebooks, aren't I? Sigh. And they were so excited about it.

I'm single. Might be interested. Depends on what you have to say. If you've been honest about yourself, of course. We'll just have to see where it goes.

I was going to be sarcastic and say "You must have had such a hard life, being so beautiful," but then you went and wrote about the problems it's actually caused, and I feel like a jerk. Yeah, it's a little narcissistic to admit it, but when there are physical and emotional consequences of it, it's also true.

I mean, obviously the problem is not how you look, but the patriarchy, which taught us that pretty things are only valuable insomuch as they're pretty.

You said that people feel entitled to you because of your profession, so I want to emphasize something: You have to do what's right for you, which includes making your work place somewhere you feel safe and don't worry about being harassed. If that means you'll get fewer job offers, then those are jobs you wouldn't have felt comfortable doing anyway. So it's like a preventative measure.

That's what I'm trying to do with my relatives. I know that this wedding is going to be uncomfortable for me, but I promised myself it's the last time I'm going to let them make me feel that way.

Also, your description of your profession makes me think you might be a sex worker, and if that's the case, I fully support that, and I want you to feel comfortable talking to me about it.

If you want to hear more about my friends, you'll have to tell me more about yours. Who is this chaotic friend you'll be suffering workplace harassment to spend time with? And who is the person you owe a favor to, though I can't imagine being friends with someone who would ask you to do something you hate and then force you into it by saying it's a favor you owe them. Are you sure that one is a friend?

Please describe to me what an upbringing in a loving and decent home looks like.

Yours,

M

***

Text Message
between Raphael and Luke
12:32 p.m.

Raphael:

M just asked if I'm a sex worker. So. Things are going well.

Luke:

"No it's the OTHER oldest profession."

Raphael:

I flirted with the language to describe acting without actually saying it, so I'm pretty sure she's correct.

Luke:

Just tell her you're an actor. She's going to find out. Or are you never going out on that balcony? Or, if things go well, do you want her to never see your face?

Raphael:

We get tested tomorrow and will know by tomorrow night if we're allowed outside, which is such a small thing but feels huge after being stuck in here for a week. We'll probably see each other the day after that.

Luke:

You walk outside, hear a gasp, and realize she's also outside and recognized you.

Raphael:

Not ideal.

Luke:

If you like her, you have to be trustworthy. If she finds out from someone else, it'll feel like you were trying to trick her. Trust. Can't have a relationship without it.

Raphael:

I will tell her. Tomorrow. How goes it on your end?

Luke:

Fuckery abounds. I know we haven't come up with a plan yet, but we may not need to. They're doing an ace job of it themselves. Let's not owe anyone any favors ever again. And let's not honor any we've made in the past.

Raphael:

What happened to being trustworthy?

Luke:

For people you love, it's necessary. For everyone else, fuck 'em.

Raphael:

Never been so glad you love me.

Luke:

I do love you, bro. That's why you should listen to me about M.

Raphael:

I am. Text if anything noteworthy happens. Love you too bro.

***

Dear M,

Are you sure that hearing about my drama-free childhood wouldn't make you more unhappy? Without getting into detail, I suppose it's like always being surrounded by people who are your friends and who support you and wish for your success. It sounds like you've cultivated that life in adulthood and know how important it is. My childhood wasn't without its issues—no one's is—but I know how lucky I am that my family acts like family.

While I'm appreciative of your support, I should clarify that I am not, in fact, a sex worker. I can see how you might make that assumption because I'm an artist, and without specific details, describing either profession sounds a lot like the other. Though sex work must also demand artistry, I'm not that kind of artist.

My friend Luke is by far the best thing about working on this upcoming project. I love the man like a brother, and we have each other's backs. He's always doing these enormous pranks, the kind that make you think, "What dedicated person had the time and energy to do all of this?" But he also puts that level of time and energy into showing his friends how much he cares about them, from getting them out of a rut to throwing an elaborate surprise party. I'm looking forward to seeing what kind of mischief Luke will dream up on this already-chaotic job.

I suppose I shouldn't describe the person to whom I owe a work favor as a friend, precisely. He gave me a chance when nothing in my life was going right and he changed my entire trajectory. I truly do owe him. But he's not infallible, and sometimes his ideas are shit, and it just happens that it's for one of his shit ideas that he asked for my help. Luke already tried talking him out of it, but his charms have thus far failed. I'll try my hand at it when I can see him face to face. I'll need to employ the full impact of my rakish good looks on this one.

So. Perhaps you're interested in me. This is a good start. Let's go on a date, then. *Stepbrothers* is on the hotel TV tonight at 7. Maybe we can watch it together, in our separate rooms? I desperately need some comedy. I know we've joked about *The Yellow Wallpaper* but the isolation is actually starting to get to me.

Fingers crossed our tests come back negative tomorrow. I can't wait to go outside. Fresh air. Birdsong. Maybe it'll rain. God, I would love to just stand in the rain. Would also love to see another person in the flesh who isn't dressed like they're handling hazardous materials.

Until then,

R

***

Dear R,

I've forgotten what air smells like when it doesn't smell like my own breath. Or cleaning supplies. Or hotel food (which, have you noticed, is pretty good? Further proof that NZ is more civilized than the US or UK, if only slightly).

Supportive family sounds amazing. People who accept you as you are instead of trying to re-mold you into something better.

You know, it worked on me for a long time, their attempts to change me. It was easier to comply, to act and react how they wanted. I became good at it, and I got their love (not love, I know that now) in return. But eventually, with time and distance, I wondered why I abandoned who I was simply to make them comfortable. They're clearly not worth it.

Relatedly, the joke's on you, I'm always dressed like I'm handling hazardous materials. Wait. Is that why I have trouble getting dates? Meanwhile, you've only seen me in one outfit, you have no idea I dress like a Victorian widow, or Sophia from *Golden Girls*, so you ask me out. It's all making sense now.

I would love to watch *Stepbrothers* with you tonight in our separate rooms. In case you want to live-text me as we watch, I've included my phone number at the bottom here. Look at that. You asked me out, and I gave you my number. You're doing well, R. I wish we could get popcorn. I'll add it to my list of items I'd like Daph and Rin to throw at my window in their ill-thought-out plan to bring me joy. They mean well.

Luke definitely sounds like the guy version of Daphne, so your friendship makes sense to me. I want to go on adventures with you both. Okay, mostly him. You're probably fun too, or you wouldn't hang out with him. I can only imagine the kinds of pranks he's going to play on your upcoming project. Please, whatever happens, text me about his current tomfoolery while I'm out and about doing wedding stuff.

I have to get some work to my editor before the movie tonight, which means I'll be spending the next few hours fucking around online before emailing her the best my isolation-brain can do at 6:59 p.m.

Meet you at our TVs at 7,

M

Day 8

Saturday, March 28, 2020

Dear M,

I didn't want to distract you from your work yesterday afternoon, or I would have told you I won't text you yet. Would I like to text you now? Yes. Did I want to text you the moment I got your letter? Yes.

But I'd like to wait until we meet face to face, so you can decide whether you want me to have your number. This may sound strange, but, since I'm the one who initiated contact with you, I want you to have more control over what happens next. That means seeing my face, checking out my social media, etc. Plus, what's one more day? We'll be here another six. I think we have time.

I do want to text you, though.

It's been a while since I saw *Stepbrothers*, but I think it holds up. I heard you laughing at parts I usually don't—you have a great laugh, it was a such a welcomed sound in this lonely room—and it gave me a better appreciation of those scenes. Comedy is difficult to do well.

Speaking of, those ASB commercials are pure gold. Ben and Amy are my new favourite couple. The "cold feet" one made me cry. He loves her so much. Hashtag relationship goals.

So today's the day we find out if we're allowed fresh air for the next week. I haven't had any symptoms, and my temperature is normal, so I've set my expectations far too high. This morning, I thought I heard birds outside, welcoming the dawn, and I walked to the balcony door and—don't tell anyone—I unlocked it. I took a deep breath and grasped the handle, knowing I could open it with the slightest movement, but I stood there, still, with my eyes closed. Then I locked it again and walked away.

Hope is utterly necessary for me. If I had opened the door, it would mean I gave up on the hope that I will be able to do it lawfully later tonight, and tomorrow, and every day until I get out of here. Going to sleep with the door open tonight. Fairly sure I'll wake up to find birds have settled in as my roommates. I'm at the point where I don't see anything wrong with that.

I've never met a Victorian widow, so I'm intrigued by these outfits you mentioned. Unless it includes a full helmet, I think it will be different enough from the hazmat suits of our jailors that it counts as "seeing another human being."

Adventures with Luke are...memorable. I can't wait to see how your friends try to send you groceries and supplies and compare that to what he would do. When I asked him to similarly bring me contraband, he laughed. Granted, he's already on-site at the project and elbow deep in shit, so I forgive him. I'll have to live vicariously through you.

Yours,

R

***

Text Message
between Matalina, Corinne, and Daphne
11:20 a.m.

Matalina:

I think I know who R is.

Daphne:

!?

Corinne:

Out with it, woman.

Matalina:

He must be an actor. Like, a famous one. He said he's an artist, and described a vague "project" that I'm thinking is a film. I can't think of a good reason to be that elusive unless he's always had to be, because he's a celebrity.

Corinne:

And?

Daphne:

Yeah? Who is he?

Matalina:

Okay so here's the thing

I don't want to know.

Corinne:

Dammit Mattie.

Daphne:

I'm rolling my eyes so hard right now.

Matalina:

I think it might be easy for me to figure it out, but I want to give him privacy and hope he tells me on his own. Plus there's the problem of what do I even do if that's the case??

Daphne:

You know what to do! We have a plan!

Matalina:

The plan was I'd get to know, over a series of letters and maybe some in-person, distanced conversations, a handsome, random man, not a potential celebrity. That requires a totally different plan, Daph.

Corinne:

Why does that require a different plan? Why can't you get to know him the way he wants you to get to know him? Instead of fan-girling before you even know who he is?

Matalina:

Let's not pretend there's not a significant obstacle to overcome. I'm not thin. And guys like R? They don't date women like me. Name one male celebrity who has found happiness with someone heavier than he is

Daphne:

Matalina Redgrave, you

you make me so angry

I cant typr straight

Corinne:

HE wrote to YOU, you stupid, stupid dummy!

Daphne:

ong i just

Corinne:

Don't you dare do this to yourself.

Daphne:

ducking impostee syndrome thats what

Matalina:

I'm not gorgeous. I haven't excelled at anything besides anxiety. I like writing letters to him because I can pretend to be a better version of myself.

Corinne:

Bullshit. I bet you're giving him your most genuine self. So if he walks away from this incredible person because you can't be mistaken for a store mannequin, FUCK THAT.

Matalina:

I'm not saying I don't have worth. I'm saying it's possible I don't have a chance.

Corinne:

You can have anyone on the damn planet. HIM. It's HIM who has to worry! How dare he be famous? And make you think you're not good enough for him??

Daphne:

i am TELLING CINNAMON

Matalina:

Um. I honestly don't know who to be more afraid of right now, Rin or Cinnamon.

Daphne:

BOTH

Corinne:

That's right, the problem is not "ohhhh this person I have a crush on might be well known by a lot of people and somehow that translates to my body isn't good enough for him" but rather "Oh shit did I just piss off Rin?"

So listen to me closely. If he turns out to be famous, or if he turns out to be just a regular, hot guy, you absolutely deserve him. Full stop.

Matalina:

Ok, ok, thanks, Rin. I hear you. I won't know for sure whether my hunch is right until tomorrow, unless I see him tonight after our tests come back. Hoping we're both negative. Then, balcony, and I can see his face.

Corinne:

Then you tell us immediately what's going on.

Matalina:

Promise.

Corinne:

And throw that fat-phobic self-doubt in the bin where it belongs. I don't want to hear you talking about my friend like that again.

Matalina:

I'll try. I have to jump on a video call soon, so I gotta get ready. Sorry for freaking you out.

What's the plan for the "goodie bag" and can you add some popcorn to it?

Corinne:

Text when your test comes back negative, and I'll give you instructions.

Matalina:

Not ominous at all.

***

Dear R,

I don't know about birds, but you'll definitely get weta, so unless you like enormous, flightless crickets burrowing into every crevice of your room, your clothes, your luggage, your bathroom...keep the door closed. By all means, go out on the balcony, but shut the door behind you. They're not dangerous, they won't hurt you, but. Giant insects. Not my choice of roommate, but I don't know how you roll.

Oh god, please don't let them into your room, they'll make their way over to mine.

It's totally fine that you didn't text. I appreciate that you recognize there's a bit of a power imbalance between us and are trying to level it. As you say, we have another week here, so there's time.

Your laugh is nice, too. It felt weird to hear joy from a real-life person. I can't hear you through the walls otherwise. Or maybe you've been quiet deliberately. I have NOT tried to be quiet, so if you've heard me definitely not modulating the volume of my voice while I'm on a call, I'm sorry for disturbing the tomb-like quiet of your room.

That commercial was so cute, it almost made me want to open a bank account.

So. You talked to Luke about me, huh? Or at least told him that your neighbor has friends who are maniacs. I may have mentioned you to those maniacs as well. They think this whole thing is very romantic. They're inappropriately invested in my love life.

Yes, Victorian widow. Lots of layers, each a mystery, what's it all hiding? Could be anything. I'm a walking secret.

The solitude is getting to me, too. I let myself stand by the door and be still, then trailed my fingers along the walls as I walked slowly around the room, measuring my confines in breaths and strides, finding the flaws trapped under the wallpaper, the nicks and tears, spots on the ceiling, stains on the carpet. Then I shut off all the lights and did it again in the dark.

It's not as desperate as it sounds.

Okay, it might be as desperate as it sounds.

I'm really hoping both our tests come back negative.

And...they just took my swab for the test. They're coming for you next. Fingers crossed.

—M

***

Email

From: Raphael Callan, raffinityraccoon@wormwood.gb.ww.co

To: Luke Maston, getoffmylawn@tepidemail.com

Subject: Is it too soon to like her?

3:47 p.m.

M and I went on a date last night. We watched *Stepbrothers* on the hotel TVs in our separate rooms. It was surprisingly intimate. Knowing she was just a room away, enjoying the same movie I was. I heard her laugh. She gave me her number to live-text each other during it, but I couldn't. I don't want her to have my number yet, in case her attitude towards me changes when she finds out who I am. Given her letters so far, I want to believe it won't affect anything.

She told me she dresses like a Victorian widow, "lots of layers, each a mystery," and I want to solve each of them. I don't know how I can feel this way after less than a week of just exchanging letters. Maybe it's the isolation?

She also said that you sounded like someone she'd want to go on an adventure with. So she's not perfect.

Give me an update on the production. This whole email can't be about M.

M also said I shouldn't keep my balcony door open because of weta. Is that really something I need to worry about? I think she might be exaggerating.

—Raph

***

Email
From: Luke Maston, getoffmylawn@tepidemail.com
To: Raphael Callan, raffinityraccoon@wormwood.gb.ww.co
Subject: RE: Is it too soon to like her?
4:00 p.m.

Look mate, you like her. It doesn't matter how or why, you just do. People meet online all the time, and at least this way you already know what she looks like. And she seems to like you, so, you're doing well for yourself, considering the state of you.

Bring her here so I can meet her. I need someone who will encourage my harmless pranks and charming defiance, not the wet sock you've become recently.

I'll give you one guess who wrote the screenplay. It's Payton. Who is still trying to find people to fill an alarmingly high number of positions on the crew and a smaller but still worrying number of cast roles. Crew members tell me they're short a bunch of equipment, too. I'd say it feels like a grammar school production, but our productions were much better organized than whatever is happening here. It's hard to believe Payton is the same guy who made *Crosshatch Fugue*, and I can't tell if he's lost some of that genius, or if maybe he only succeeded in the past because he surrounded himself with competent people who are conspicuously missing on this production. I hate to say it, but given the subject matter of *That Scarlet, Beating Heart*, I'm leaning towards the latter. Was he always an asshole, and we gave him a pass so we could get on with our careers, too?

Oh and they're changing the title. Now it's *Broke*. That's it. *Broke*. Why not go a step further, just call it *Rubbish?*

Weta are harmless and endearing creatures and you absolutely do not want them in your room. They probably won't leave the comfort of their trees, but do as M says. Keep the door shut.

Wish you were here,

Luke

***

Dear M,

I received your last letter moments after they swabbed my nose for traces of the coronavirus, but they must have damaged some brain cells in the process, because I haven't been able to concentrate on anything since then. I've had flu tests before and I know they have to get pretty far in, but this seemed aggressive on a personal level.

Yes, I talked to Luke about you. He said you seemed like a better partner for pranks than I am, and he confirmed that I do not want a weta infestation. I'm not a fan of even small insects, so inviting large ones into my room is not an option.

I have heard you talking, but it's indistinct. Don't quiet yourself on my account, I find it comforting.

Your friends are inappropriately invested in your love life, but I find myself increasingly invested in it, too.

Forgive the torn page, it's my last one, and I meant to ask earlier if I could buy a few blank pages of your precious notebook. Otherwise, I have half a page after this, and that's the end. I'm a desperate man now.

—R

***

Dear R,

By all means, here are some blank pages. The notebook isn't so precious I won't tear a few out to continue our correspondence. And don't try to slide any money under the door. You can pay for them by giving them back to me with writing on them. Or sketches, or whatever you like. This is my last piece of hotel stationery too. To think we once thought this place the height of luxury! Damn their cheapness.

So what I'm getting from your letter is that, when I talk to my friends about you, I have to keep my voice low, or you'll hear. Okay. Got it.

I'm also hearing that you might have a crush on me. I'm not surprised. I, too, would be hard-pressed to resist the charms of someone half-glimpsed after thirteen sweaty hours on a plane, who spoke too loudly in the next room, with obvious emotional issues, friends that don't understand personal boundaries, and a wardrobe that would make the most conservatively dressed people wonder why I'm such a prude. Yeah, that checks all my boxes, too.

You, though. An exemplary seat mate on said plane. Doesn't have the TV volume too loud. Knows how to form complete sentences and, for the most part, spell words correctly (no points off for American vs English spelling). Likes romance novels. Listens to my advice. You, sir, seem like a catch.

So.

What's wrong with you?

I'm a woman who's been on the internet her entire life. I know about cultivating a personality for show. And one of the signs of that is a lack of annoying qualities. So tell me. Tell me the most annoying things about you, or tell me which of the other things about you you've embellished. If you're interested in me, I need to know: who is the real R?

—M

***

Dear M,

When I meet someone for the first time, I mimic their voice back to them. I can't help it. It's a mix of nerves and curiosity, trying to get the accent and tone right, especially if I've never heard its like before. This mimicry is off-putting. Then I try to charm my way out of it, so I come across as insincere, like I just had a private joke at their expense. I think fart jokes are hilarious. I am absolute shit at budgeting and any other financial skills, because I grew up well-off and never had to learn. I know that's a problem.

I need close relationships, but I also have trust issues, which complicates everything. Now that I've written it down, I realize it's not something I'm comfortable talking about right now, so I'll continue to my other shortcomings.

Thanks to Luke's bad influence, I'm ready and willing to jump into a physical fight, and I can hold my own in it. The willingness is annoying, not the skill. Though the skill does feed into the willingness. Conversely, I'd rather avoid all other kinds of confrontation, specifically emotional ones. That stems from struggling with my sexual identity as a teenager—surprise! I'm bisexual.

I'm trying to understand all the ways I'm privileged, and use it to fight inequality, but more often than not I feel woefully inept.

And many more! But that seems sufficient for now. See? I'm a real person, like everyone else. But I know what you mean about cultivating a personality for show, so I don't mind sharing these things with you, to demonstrate I'm sincere.

Thank you for the blank pages, I'll put them to good use.

They just called to say my test came back negative. Weta beware, here I come!

Yours,

R

***

Text Message
between Matalina, Corinne, and Daphne
8:15 p.m.

Matalina:
Negative for coronavirus!

Daphne:
yay! no Rona!

Matalina:

So far. R also tested negative. You know what that means!

Daphne:

KISSING TIME

Matalina:

Almost! We can see each other on our balconies now!

Corinne:

Ok, here's the plan. Did you bring any bright scarves?

Matalina:

I have a sage colored shawl?

Corinne:

That'll work. Go out to your balcony and tie it on a railing where we can see it. What floor are you and what's the street your room overlooks?

Matalina:

Third floor, second to last room. Ballard St. Scarf tied. You two are going to paperboy my balcony, aren't you?

Daphne:

ooo there's an idea

Matalina:

Also, let's use our code names. I have a feeling we should conceal our identities.

Corinne:

Gotcha. We'll be there at dawn.

Matalina:

DAWN

Daphne:

wait DAWN

Corinne:

YES. DAWN.

Matalina:

Not sure I need wine that badly.

Corinne:

You will be there or there will be consequences.

Matalina:

ok, I'll be there then.

Daphne:

uh can I sit this one out?

Corinne:

No, Daph. It'll be fine. I'll buy you breakfast afterwards.

Daphne:

Can I have waffles?

Corinne:

Sure.

Matalina:

Do I get breakfast too?

Corinne:

You'll get what we give you and you'll be happy about it.
This is going to be so much fun.

***

Dear R,

Your list caught me off guard. I wasn't expecting something so...genuine? Personal? And a couple of them might warrant a deeper conversation, if you wanted to talk about them. I'm also bi, but it was never something I had to reconcile. Daphne was always gay, and we were thick as thieves. And I never really cared what anybody else thought of me in that regard, which is, as you mentioned about other things, an immense privilege that I know a lot of people don't have. Nothing on your list was heinous enough to ghost you. No red flags.

Yet.

I also tested negative! I didn't see you outside when I stepped out, but I didn't stay there long either. It wasn't the rain that bothered me. To be honest, after a few deep breaths of cool March air, I found the entire experience overwhelming. Lots of sounds. Lots of smells. Lots of smells of food I want that aren't on the menu.

Maybe I'm just hungry.

I love that the prize for having a negative test result is clean sheets. I mean, I'm sure people who test positive also get clean sheets, and having to put them on by ourselves isn't exactly a five-star experience, but, it feels like a reward at this point.

I have become so easily delighted.

Daph and Rin told me to be outside at dawn for their drop-off. I still have no idea what they're going to do. I asked if they were going to paperboy the stuff, and Daph seemed surprised and intrigued by the idea. If you hear a ruckus out there, I implore you to stay inside. These endeavors of ours have a way of incriminating even the most innocent of bystanders.

Cheers to not being infected,

M

Day 9
Sunday, March 29, 2020

Email

From: Raphael Callan, raffinityraccoon@wormwood.gb.ww.co

To: Luke Maston, getoffmylawn@tepidemail.com

Subject: These are our people

8:31 a.m.

Eighth morning waking up in New Zealand, and my body still isn't in sync with the clock here. I awoke at dawn, unable to pretend to sleep any longer. I shuffled to the in-room coffee maker to brew my daily cup of Gross The Sleep Out Of You, aroma of burnt coffee filling the cramped room as the machine sputtered out its dark liquid in the most vulgar fashion. As is routine by now, I dumped three creams into the coffee and yawned my way to the glass door, stirring the toxic elixir as I went.

The wide street below was still in shadow, but in the soft blue-grays of the opening day, not the impenetrable dark of midnight. It's a quiet road, to the back of the hotel, with single-family homes on the other side behind a tall concrete wall, and no cars driving past at this ungodly hour. Yet there was movement. Two white, blinking lights, slowing as they came alongside the building. Curious, I opened the glass door and stood in the doorway, the metal track cool on my feet, mug warm in my hand.

The lights slowed more as they approached our rooms, and I could make out the silhouette of two bicycles. Closer still, and I saw who rode them. I heard the gears and chains and two people talking in loud whispers.

"I think that's it," one of them said. The person from the bike in front: long, dark hair under a pastel helmet, a flash of meagre light reflecting in her glasses. Dark clothes, appropriate for the kind of clandestine work they were undertaking. She braked to a stop, the second cyclist following suit.

"That doesn't look like a green scarf," whispered the person on the second bike. Short blond hair, no helmet, in a light-colored dress and jumper. "That scarf looks white. Must be the wrong room." American accent.

The first woman snorted. "Don't be daft, Daph. Third floor. Second room to the end. Shawl tied to the railing. It's hers." Kiwi accent. That must be Rin, then.

"Yes, and—oh! Hello! Are you R?"

Yeah. They saw me. I wish I could say I at least had the coffee cup covering the lower half of my face, but, I didn't. I CAN say that I was three stories away from them.

"We have a notebook for you, R!" Daphne whisper-yelled, sliding off her bike and waving up at me.

Rin had dismounted and set the kickstand. "Daph! Sorry about that, R, don't let us disturb you. Actually, you might want to get inside, her aim is pretty good but there's always a chance of maiming. Nice to meet you!" Without waiting for me to respond, she turned to the little trailer attached to her bike, and then I couldn't see what she was doing.

I took her advice and stepped just inside the room, keeping the door open a crack so I could still hear them.

They made a lot of noise. M had said she was going to meet them out there at dawn, but she wasn't on her balcony yet. Daphne apparently got tired of Rin not letting her help with whatever she was doing at the trailer, so she turned to face the building and walked backwards into the quiet street, hands hefting some small object. She walked forwards again, assessing, then pulled out a small slingshot and shot at the balcony, the pebble hitting M's doors with a soft crack.

"Did you bring rocks specifically for this, or did you just happen to have them in your pocket?"

"I never leave the house without at least one way to cause mischief."

"Might as well do it again," Rin said, crossing her arms as she stared at the dark doors. "Running out of time. I don't want *her* to get caught, either."

Daphne nodded and slung another pebble, hitting her target again. This time, light flooded the balcony, the door rumbled open smoothly, and M stepped to the railing, waving at her friends.

My stomach flipped. Of course I remembered what she looks like, I spent the better part of a day on a plane with her. But I hadn't seen her since we started flirting, and I got goosepimples. She wore a voluminous powder-blue robe that covered everything from her neck to wrists to ankles—yes, I see why she described her style as Victorian Widow. Hair was a wild mane of dark blond tangles. She must have still been asleep when Daphne knocked on her window.

"Hi! Hi!" She called down. "How are we doing this?"

Both Rin and Daphne jumped up and down, waving back, squeeing, whispering too loudly.

"I definitely told you dawn," Rin said. Daphne reached to take something out of the trailer.

"I've been stuck in this room for nine days. Time has no meaning anymore."

"Okay, stand back," Daphne said, turning back to M and raising a bow and arrow.

Let me repeat that: a BOW and ARROW.

"Whoa, whoa!" M said, raising her hands in a placating gesture.

"Go back in and close the door," Rin said. M must have a lot of experience with these two, because she did as she was told without any argument.

I braced myself for the inevitable shatter of glass. But as soon as the door slid shut, Daphne let loose the arrow with a twang, followed by a dense thud. "Excellent shot," Rin said. M opened the door and looked at the arrow sticking to the glass, and the thin rope that trailed off it and over the balcony.

"Suction cup arrow," M said. "I'm impressed."

"Be impressed later. Pull up the rope." Rin pantomimed reeling in a length of rope. M did, until a thicker rope appeared, tied to the first one. "Tie that to the railing," Rin said, watching her friend. Daphne struggled to carry over a cloth tote bag, stuffed to bursting and tied to the other end of the thick rope.

"Ready!" She said, setting it on the sidewalk close to the building. "Now pull it up and you're welcome!"

M made a sound of surprised appreciation and started hauling it up. "Jesus Christ," she said, grunting. "What's in here, dumbbells?"

"Your list was long and we figured we'd only get one chance at this." Rin glanced up and down the street, but nobody was coming to stop them.

It was slow going. I wished I could jump out there and help her. Between the two of us, it would have taken no time at all. As she worked to get the bag up, Rin kept watch, and Daphne danced in the street.

It was getting lighter out, and I could see them more clearly. Rin is nearly a head taller than Daphne, and her quilted jacket couldn't hide her athletic frame. I know you hear "athletic frame" and picture a slim runner, but I mean maybe a body builder or a boxer. This woman looks like a powerhouse. If this were an RPG campaign, Rin is the tank. Daphne is some kind of impish mystic or trickster—pale dress and jumper with neon running shoes, slingshot and bow, delighting in the game. I want to say M would be the paladin. She has likened herself to a "grizzled mastermind" and can't walk away if she sees something wrong.

M had pulled the heavy bag almost to the bottom of her balcony when the shouting started. As she paused, startled at the sound, Rin and Daphne lurched into motion, scrambling onto their bikes as three men in beige uniforms ran down the sidewalk towards them, yelling at them to stop.

I can only assume that what happened next was part of the plan, in an effort to give M more time to finish lifting her stash and slink back into her room undetected. The women below got onto their bikes quickly, but instead of making their getaway, they pedaled slowly so the security chaps could catch up with them. When they were on the verge of being caught, they looped back and forth, making the men chase them in circles.

Daphne howled and laughed, dodging several near-hits from a guard, while Rin concentrated on maneuvering her bike and trailer. Round and round they went, like some 70's slapstick routine. One of the guards even tripped and rolled onto his arse.

Yet unseen by security, M had finally gotten the bag up over the railing. She stumbled as she pulled it towards her, spilling several items out onto the balcony. "Shit," M said, shoving everything back into the heavy tote and lugging it into her room. She came back out a moment later, untied the rope, un-suctioned the arrow, and brought those inside too.

"Vanessa, only two more days!" Rin called. "Two more days until you're free!"

"Wooo!" Daphne shouted in response. "Come to us, your Betty and Fran, Vanessa!"

At which point, the men started looking at the building, trying to find a Vanessa. I laughed, thinking they had gotten away with all of it, when I saw the green shawl still tied to the railing. I sucked in a quick breath. What could I do? I ran to the door between our rooms and banged on it, shouting, "The shawl! Bring in the shawl!" I heard a faint "Fuck," and ran back to the glass door just in time to see M crouch down, pull the garment off the railing in one motion, and dive back into her room.

The women outside cackled like villains, biked a few more circles around security—who were beginning to give up anyway—and rode off into the sunrise, victorious.

This is exactly the kind of trouble you and I are so fond of getting into. As much as the thought of joining you on the set of *Broke* gives me pre-post-traumatic-stress anxiety, the thought of spending any time with M and her friends gives me the kind of anticipatory joy I experience on stage just before the curtain opens. Let's do whatever we must to befriend them.

—Raph

***

Text Message
between Matalina, Corinne, and Daphne
8:40 a.m.

Matalina:

Did you two get away without trouble?

Daphne:

Of course, Vanessa.

Corinne:

It was a close thing, but we made it. Don't think we were followed.

Matalina:

I'm so glad, omg, what were you thinking?! I mean, holy shit, thank you, for everything, it means so much to me, but also it was just so much fun to be a part of a wild plan with you two again. I missed this!

Daphne:

Let's stay in NZ longer for more adventures together!

Corinne:

With the inevitable travel ban, you'll have to. Lucky you.

Matalina:

I can change my plane ticket right now. Do you have any places for us, Rin?

Corinne:

The place we're staying near the wedding is available for the foreseeable future. But I have others if that won't work for you.

Matalina:

You think a month more?

Corinne:

I'm telling you, you won't be able to leave anyway, so, sure. Change your flight to stay another month. You'll call them in a few weeks to extend it again anyway.

Matalina:

You seem pretty sure about that.

Corinne:

Tourism industry. We smell the weather turning before anyone else.

Matalina:

Right, how is nipple doing, anyway?

Corinne:

I thought we outgrew these childish taunts.

Daphne:

Have you met us?

Corinne:

North Island Pinnacle Leisure is panicking, thank you.

Daphne:

nipple.

Corinne:

NIPL. Focus, Daph, what were we going to tell Mattie?

Daphne:

Oh, right! We think we know who R is.

Matalina:

WHAT

Daphne:

He was on his balcony when we pulled up. We talked to him.

Corinne:

More like we yelled at him to get inside before Daph accidentally impaled him. Also, I stand corrected. He does cut a nice figure.

Matalina:

Is he famous?

Corinne:

Yes.

Matalina:

Do I know who he is?

Daphne:

yes

Matalina:

Ok tell me. I'm ready.

Corinne:

Raphael Callan.

Matalina:

lmao ok

Daphne:

no, it's true. Raphael Callan.

Matalina:

R isn't Raphael Callan.

...

Oh shit R is Raphael Callan.

...

Daphne:

i think we broke her

Corinne:

Mattie, how are you doing, dear?

Matalina:

It all fits, with everything he's told me. Oh shit. I'm a little overwhelmed.

Corinne:

Well, good news, he's probs going to tell you himself today, since he knows we saw him. So this gives you some time to figure out how you're going to respond. And you're going to respond like a person and not a starstruck dummy, right?

Matalina:

Rin, I promise I'm going to try my absolute best. But holy shit.

Daphne:

holy shit.

Corinne:

Holy shit indeed.

***

Dear M,

I saw the entire thing. What absolutely bold, mad, generous, brilliant friends you have. I won't lie—I'm jealous. What necessities and amusements were worth such a dangerous endeavour?

Also, why were they calling out for Vanessa? Have you given me a false letter by which to call you, M, to further disguise your identity?

Speaking of. Your friends definitely saw me, which means there's a chance they recognized me, which means now's the time I confess. Though I gave you a true letter by which to call me, I've been careful not to reveal things about me that are public knowledge. This has nothing to do with you, or how we've come to know each other through our letters, but rather, a necessary precaution for me for a number of reasons.

Bollocks, I'll just say it: I'm Raphael Callan. I know it's narcissistic of me—again—to assume you've heard of me, so if you haven't, the internet will tell you a lot about me. And if you have, well, I hope you can understand why I wasn't forthcoming with that information, and can forgive me for being so secretive.

It's up to you whether our correspondence continues. I would like it to. But if this is too weird for you, or if you feel uncomfortable for any reason, I completely understand.

Yours,

Raph

***

Hello Raphael Callan,

It's nice to meet you.

I can't pretend I'm not familiar with your name or your work, but I will say it makes sense. You're here for an artistic project, they want you to read that terrible book (I'm more sorry than you know that you got roped into that adaptation, and if you're looking for any bold, mad, brilliant plans to get out of it, have I got a trio of masterminds for you). Knowing what HEA is because you've been the leading man in a handful of romances. People thinking they're entitled to your body and time because of your profession. Luke is Luke Maston, I'm assuming.

I didn't know precisely who you were, but I got the feeling you were well known and trying to protect your privacy. I totally get that. I said before that you're entitled to feel safe in your workspace, free from harassment, but that holds true for every space you're in.

If you've been honest with me in your letters, besides choosing not to include details that could potentially expose yourself to harm from a super-fan, then I don't see why we can't continue writing to each other. I've gotten to know someone through those letters, someone I really like, and I hope I'm the kind of person that someone like him would also like to get to know better.

That sentence was so clumsy. I am actually a writer, I swear.

There is a care package for you on your balcony. Notebook, romance novel, popcorn. I kept the other two notebooks, foods and tea, scented candles and diffusers (which I immediately put to use, the cleaning products the hotel gave us can only do so much in a sealed room), sexy reading material, a vibrator, batteries, and notes from Rin and Daph. All very, very much appreciated, and worth the risk. Though it was bold of them to assume I didn't bring my own vibrator.

Vanessa is my code name. Betty is Daphne, and Fran is Rin. They shouted that I only had two days left in quarantine to further muddle our captors' suspicions about who's breaking protocol. This may have been the first time we did this specific thing, but it's not the first time we've done something *like* it. We even have a name for ourselves: the Honest Mischief Alliance. We're nowhere near a professional skill level, but we're pretty good. Well, we're okay. We've never been caught. Except Daphne that one time. Or two times. Possibly three.

Below are my handles on social media. It's unfair that I could easily find and peruse your photos and posts, but you can't look through mine, so here we are, on more even ground. You'll also find info about me if you Google my name. Maybe not as much information as I may have passively learned about you through the years, but, it's a start, and I don't have any control over it, so again, more equal footing.

I do hope you keep writing to me.

Yours,

Matalina Redgrave

(Mattie or Mats, to my friends)

***

MATS!

If you're reading this, dear sister, we have succeeded in our grand scheme to get you snacks, smells, and sexual goodies! Your letters to R have inspired us (to write you letters but also to include condoms in your goody bag, YOU'RE WELCOME).

Enjoy your time in paradise, sharing letters with some hot, mysterious guy who's obviously into you. Let me tell you, it's a good thing Rin got us this house to stay in, because I've been to the hotel where the rest of the Redgraves are (same place as the wedding, it's like one big event property), and I would not be able to deal with being a floor or two away from their drama at any given moment.

As soon as I got there, they wanted to do a "family portrait," and I was like, "Uh, no? Because the whole family isn't here?" And they could NOT REMEMBER who was missing. Granted, there are six of us siblings, five spouses or soon-to-be, and a smattering of children, not to mention grandparents, aunts, uncles, cousins, etc etc. Finally Topher, of all people, was like, "Oh wait, do you mean Matalina?" Flames, Mats. Flames...on the side of my face...

They asked where Cinnamon was, while suspiciously eyeing Rin. !! Like this Kiwi hasn't been our best friend practically since we were born. I doubt that's what prompted the wedding invitation, though. Did you know Rin has bus stop ads now? Picture and everything. Plenty of local clout to warrant an invite, and mother probably recognized the name, even if she couldn't remember exactly how she knew it.

Ok, enough talk. Good luck with R! Text me!

—Daphne

***

Kia ora, Mattie!

The Honest Mischief Alliance rides again! We have to get into situations more often, because this was such a dag. Even if it fails, which, if you're reading this, it has not. I think Daphne is the only one of us who has been able to easily balance adulthood with mischief. A bow and arrow, Mattie. You'd never guess she's an ace accountant. I want to be just like her when I grow up.

We took some liberties with the bag contents. Figured you'd appreciate a vibrator (batteries included), after all these hot letters with R. Condoms are from Daphne and the best idea of the lot. We believe in you.

I've been thinking about what Daph said, about you inviting R to the wedding, and I think it's a great idea. Yes, yes, you don't know him, he has things to do, I know all the excuses you're making already. But what if he says yes? At the very least, you'd have a bit of a buffer, and it will piss off your relatives, and you'll show up with someone hot. Why not do something that improves your mood instead of just wallowing in the toxic shallows of your relatives with only me and Daphne holding you afloat? Don't be a muppet. Ask him.

Love,

Rin

***

Auckland Grand Eastview Hotel

Dear valued guests,

In these uncertain times, it is more important than ever that we take our commitment to your health, safety, and enjoyment very seriously. While many of you did not have a choice of where to spend your 14-day isolation upon arriving in Auckland, we still consider you as important as any guest during our normal operations.

We know how difficult it is to be quarantined for two weeks, and we want to extend to you our heartfelt gratitude that you're doing your part to keep yourself, your family, your friends, and the people of Aotearoa New Zealand safe.

Our aim is to make this process not only tolerable, but enjoyable. We hired world-renown chef Samira Griffin to create a menu for your included three daily meals and snacks, to bring the tastes of this international city to your door. The basket of cleaning supplies provided to each guest includes local and handmade products from top New Zealand vendors, and it's our hope that you enjoy them enough to take them home with you. We're also proud to offer access to several streaming services for free: turn your in-room television to channel 0 to see what's available.

In return, we ask you to continue to follow our isolation protocols to the letter. If you are unsure of something, channel 1 is exclusively broadcasting a video guide on these protocols, in several languages. If you still have questions, dial the front desk, and we will connect you to the appropriate department.

We must stress that you avoid all personal contact with anyone not staying in your room, and you must avoid giving, receiving, or otherwise exchanging any items with anyone not staying in your room. Without a clearer idea of how the virus is transmitted, all outside items are suspect. Items can only enter or leave your room through our nurses and other approved personnel. Failure to comply can result in FINES or ARREST, as it potentially endangers the public.

In compliance with the New Zealand Ministry of Health—Manatū Hauora, any guests who break protocol will be referred to them for disciplinary action, including but not limited to prosecution.

Our number one priority is your health and safety, so please join us in maintaining the highest standards of caution. We're grateful and honored that you've chosen to travel to Aotearoa, and we can't wait to let you explore it in just a few short days.

Ngā mihi nui,

The Staff of the Auckland Grand Eastview Hotel

***

Dear Mattie,

I absolutely want to continue our correspondence. You're the most interesting person I've met in a long time, and I'm not saying that just because we're trapped here together. There's always a chance that someone you meet in a textual setting could be lying, exaggerating, catfishing. But we've seen each other in person, and your letters feel genuine. And I've only been secretive about, well, my name. There's no way you can know that everything else I've written has been sincere, but it has.

Thank you for being so understanding, truly. And for getting our letters back on track.

I love that you three have "code names." Tell me more about some of the adventures you've had in this Honest Mischief Alliance. I'm especially interested in the one time or two times or three times Daphne got caught.

It was a close thing, and I'm glad you weren't caught this time—though if the official letter we got from the hotel threatening FINES or ARREST is any indication, they know someone broke protocol, but not who. Better make sure all these letters are kept in a safe place so they don't incriminate you.

I'm also glad you weren't caught not only because I now have enough paper to write you one hundred letters—thank you for that, too—but because I was rooting for you. I watched with rapt attention and even saw what fell out when you stumbled with that impossibly heavy bag. I'm a little surprised that you voluntarily disclosed those contents to me in your last letter. Is that part of the compulsive speaking your mind/being honest that gets you in trouble with your relatives? If so, I look forward to more of it.

Now that you're restocked, do you happen to have an extra diffuser or candle you would be willing to share? I can shower multiple times a day, clean the entire room with everything they've seen fit to supply me with, and somehow it's still not fresh. I'm seriously considering keeping the door open, despite the threat of those large crickets, if only to air this place out.

I looked at your social media a bit. Haven't searched your name, though I plan to do that later. All it's done is made me eager to spend time with you.

Relatedly, I would like to cordially invite you to the Ceremonial Tossing of *That Scarlet, Beating Heart* this evening at 6 o'clock PM. We can meet on our balconies, where I will say a few words about how terrible the first half was, open the floor for anyone else's comments about it, then throw it into the street with the enthusiasm and desperation of a soldier getting rid of a live grenade. It would bring me such joy to share this with you.

Yours,

Raph

***

Dear Raph,

I'm in. I'll bring you a candle.

—Mattie

Day 10
Monday, March 30, 2020

Email

From: Luke Maston, getoffmylawn@tepidemail.com

To: Raphael Callan, raffinityraccoon@wormwood.gb.ww.co

Subject: our new friends, and set drama

8:15 a.m.

I'm going to suggest you for the *Broke* rewrites, bro. Your tale was riveting. Have you invited Mattie and her friends to hang out with us yet? Are either of the sneaky cyclists single? Tell me more about the boxer-looking one.

Payton is panicking. Good for us, but, like a dying animal, likely to lash out in his desperate attempt to survive. They're only able to hire people who aren't quite qualified, because the people who *are* qualified recognize that the salary is far too low and they're not enamoured enough of Payton to work for less. And Payton et al are hammering out new safety protocols on top of everything else, so it's all a right mess.

Lena and Cassidy want to know when they get to see Uncle Raphael and what manner of gifts you're bringing them. I told them they'll only get gifts if they behave for their Grams, which they're obviously incapable of—I've never doubted they're mine—so you're off the hook on that front. I've missed them since I got here. It doesn't matter that they're just a few kilometres away. Knowing I can't see them until after my own quarantine after this terrible production is over is its own kind of torture. I know people tell you, "You can't understand until you have children of your own," like child-free adults are somehow incapable of love, or sacrifice, or simply missing someone. But you know how it feels.

Were you able to see M face to face? More than a diving blur of blue robe as she narrowly escaped detection from your captors? It's miserable here, and your antics give me much needed levity. And I'm not kidding, I'm going to suggest to Payton that you do the rewrites. Get your typing fingers ready, you have a lot of work to do.

Luke

***

Email
From: Raphael Callan, raffinityraccoon@wormwood.gb.ww.co
To: Luke Maston, getoffmylawn@tepidemail.com
Subject: RE: our new friends, and set drama
8:55 a.m.

Nobody could rewrite that script into anything resembling an interesting, coherent story. And why would I, a biracial Englishman, want to adapt a racist manifesto? For that matter, why on earth does Payton want me for his disgruntled supremacist role model? I seriously need to talk to him. For now, though, I'm glad I'm not there. I'm still hoping everything will fall apart before I report for duty.

There are so few things that New Zealand will let anyone bring into the country, but maybe I can find something for the girls here in the city before I leave to meet you out there. Why punish them for being as creatively chaotic as their father? And I do know exactly how you feel, since I, too, have yearned to be reunited with missed loved ones.

The boxer, huh? I thought Daph would be more your speed, but she's married, and a lesbian, so if you're looking for a best friend to snicker with at the back of class, she would be perfect. I don't know Rin's story, but I'll ask Mattie.

Right, so, that's her name. Matalina Redgrave. I told her who I was. She suspected that I was a well-known person trying to protect my privacy and she understands. She told me how to find her online so I could have access to her she couldn't control, like she does for me. We exchanged a few more letters, but we only saw each other face to face last night, when I led a Tossing Of That Terrible Book into the street.

She laughs like she's not holding anything back, and given her propensity for honesty and straightforwardness, I believe her. When I stepped on the balcony for the book-throwing, she was sitting at her table, bare feet propped on the chair opposite her, writing in a notebook. Perhaps even writing me my next letter. I'm certain her outfit was actually worn by a Golden Girl at some point: blue plaid shirt-dress, collared and button-down, with a dark blue cardigan over it, large glasses—more modern than the 80's-style ones from the show—with a glasses chain in gold and pearl.

And as I stepped out, she glanced up, locked eyes with me, and smiled.

Seeing her smile is one thing. Having her smile at me is another. But knowing I'm the reason for it? I couldn't help grinning like an idiot, then nearly tripped into my own chair and forgot what words were. She said "Hey," and "Nice to finally meet you face to face." And I must have said something in response, because she laughed, but I couldn't stop looking at her. I was probably mimicking her voice, and if that's the case, she was very gracious about it.

After a while, I stood, the still-wet book in my hands, spoke a few words about how shitty it is, and invited her to join in. She shook her head and said, "It doesn't deserve any more of our precious time. Get rid of it." And I threw it into the street.

We stayed out there for a bit, talking about little things. I could have stayed out there with her for hours, but after a while, she seemed flustered—maybe she was as nervous as I was?—and went indoors. Haven't gotten a letter from her yet today, but it's still early, and yesterday was a long day.

If I didn't have decades of experience being a curmudgeon who doesn't believe in love, I might start to worry that I was developing a crush. But since it isn't difficult and grueling and dramatic, I'm not sure I would recognize it if I were.

-Raph

***

Hi Raphael,

Sorry I was weird last night. After six-ish days of just letters between us, I don't think I was prepared for you to be, like, a real-life actual person with a body. Obviously I know you are, but you've existed solely in my mind for most of the time we've known each other and I didn't think to shift my perspective.

Also it was more awkward than I expected that I'm familiar with a lot of your work (yet another way you existed in my mind and not IRL) and then you're sitting like ten feet away from me. The only way I can think to fix this is to see you more often, despite the weather's unwelcome fluctuations. Maybe a lunch date today on our balconies? Let me know.

You said you were going to wait to text me, and I'm not sure what exactly you're waiting for, but I stand by my decision to give you my number.

Obviously I will continue to hand-write letters to you.

Between the thrill of another adventure with Daph and Rin, and Rin's uncanny sixth sense, I've decided to extend my stay here. In the country, I mean, not here in this hotel room. I missed my friends and our antics, and Rin says NZ is going to shut its borders soon and I'll be trapped here anyway, so might as well.

She has her own company that leases vacation homes across North Island, specializing in high-end properties. Of course, that means that when I come to visit, Rin makes sure we stay nestled in the lap of luxury. She got us a place near the wedding location, so we don't have to stay at the hotel with the guests. We'll be there another month at least.

What does your next month look like? You said Luke is already on site at the production, how's it going? Hopefully suffering a curse worthy of such a terrible story. Where are you staying while filming? I can keep a secret.

That book made a very satisfying plop when it hit the street. When I looked outside earlier, I saw that it had been run over, flattened pulp against the pavement, unrecognizable, as it should be.

Not sure I want to get into even more stuff about my relatives, but if you've looked me up online, it's possible you have questions, so I'll preemptively answer one. My brother's wedding is in New Zealand because my father is a Kiwi, and my mother is from the US. I was raised between the two countries: school year in the States, vacation on North Island. An unconventional upbringing.

You may be asking yourself how I got into this situation, staying in a quarantine hotel for non-nationals, with you. Since my mother is American, and I was born in California, I would have to petition for my New Zealand citizenship, aaaand I never got around to it. The rest of them have dual citizenship, even Daph. But, stubborn as I am, I wanted to distance myself from everything my father represents. And it pisses them off to no end, so, I'm happy with my decision. Especially because it's delayed having to see them by two weeks. No regerts.

The problem with using larger paper to write letters is that I want to fill the space, and then we end up with excruciatingly long missives.

So, lunch date? What do you say?

—Mattie

***

Hi Mattie,

Let's do lunch. I'm partial to those sweet potato fries, and the fish and chips—"fush and chups," as they say here—and the meat pies, though now that I'm listing everything, I don't think I've disliked any meals they've brought us.

Thank you for the candle, any little bit helps against the tide of an unaired room. Perhaps I should say the low tide of an unaired room.

Our meeting wasn't too weird. I was also nervous, for the same reason. Well, not the "familiar with your work" one. I think we did really well for ourselves. May I suggest that we act like we're already friends—since we already are—and then it won't be awkward? Lunch together is going to be fun and chill.

Luke wants to know when we can all hang out. And, specifically, he wants to know more about Rin. I swear, all I've told him is that your friends are, as you said, maniacs, and I recounted their successful ploy to get you notebooks and candles. Tell me she wouldn't be interested and I'll let him down gently. Or, if I were to find her as one of our mutuals online, I could direct him there, if she weren't averse to it.

Luke says the production is going about as well as one would expect from a last-minute, half-cocked idea that requires the calling in of favors from around the globe on the cusp of what is most likely a devastating pandemic. So: smashing! If everything holds together by the time I get there—and, again, let us all pray that it doesn't—I'll be staying at the Billingstead Hotel, an upscale place a few kilometres away from set. I'll be there until filming wraps.

It's a very small production. I would compare it to when Joss Whedon took a bunch of friends and cameras to some villa and filmed *Much Ado About Nothing*. Very loose. Lots of shortcuts. If I recall, there are two investors besides Payton, who is the director and showrunner, and we should have a team of people for each department. It's just not really...I was going to say "not really the type of larger project I'm used to" but perhaps what I mean is "not entirely above-board." Shutting it down will affect a small number of people, but I worry for their loss of income. He's paying us a pittance because he framed it as a favor, and I'll be fine without it, but other people won't be.

If the production is somehow scrapped or postponed, Luke has invited me to stay with him and his kids indefinitely. He doesn't live very far from the Billingstead.

So that's my next month sorted. I will get time off to see you, if you'd like. I would like. And if it's cancelled, I'll have a lot more time to see you. Then Luke will get his wish and the five of us can go on adventures together.

See you soon,

Raphael

***

Email

From: Mattie Redgrave, bloodymattie@prismbridge.com

To: Daphne Redgrave, daphno@spiritmissives.net; Rin Butcher, c.butcher@nipl.co.nz

Subject: Too long to text

1:38 p.m.

Yes, he's Raphael Callan. I tried to be so cool and I only failed a little. But we talked and it's all good now. We finally saw each other last night when he got rid of *That Scarlet, Beating Heart* by chucking it over the balcony and into the street. It was a whole ceremony. He cordially invited me and everything.

He is...super handsome. Like, "I can't function if I look at him" handsome. "Punch in the gut when I remember him" handsome. I obviously went and read everything I could about him online, which seems like a waste of time because he's literally next door and we're in constant communication and I could ask him anything I want to know and he would answer me. But I didn't want to seem too eager. I didn't realize his dad is Middle Eastern. I knew he was biracial, but I never cared enough to look into it further (I feel good about that, like, at least I haven't been a creepy fan to this guy). It explains why he doesn't look like he bundles up against the cold during the half of the year he's not bundled up against the rain. His dark eyes, his thick, black hair that looks so silky to touch...

Anyway, after he threw the book, after we'd already been talking and laughing and had seen each other, that's when my body decided it was going to be nervous, and I had to make a hasty getaway back into my room. I apologized but he didn't seem to have noticed. He said he was nervous too. !!

We had lunch together today, on our separate balconies. It was pretty chill. He asked me what my flaws are (he told me some of his when I asked earlier), and I couldn't come up with enough. I said he'd have to ask you two.

Relatedly, he's been telling Luke Maston about me, and you, and our adventures, and now Luke wants to hang out with us??!

So it looks like we'll be hanging out with Raphael and Luke over the next month or so. I would give you three guesses as to where they're staying while filming here, but you would both get it in one: the Billingstead. Here you two have been telling me to invite him to the wedding, and he's staying at the same hotel anyway. Poor him.

Thanks again for the goodies and the notes. I'll be texting.

Love you both,

Mattie

***

Raphael,

You were right, lunch was fun and chill.

Lmao at Luke Maston being interested in the amorphous, second-hand description of Rin. Truth be told, she's amazing, but neither of you know that yet. I don't want to speak for her but she's maybe potentially interested in getting to know someone who's an adult and not an asshole. She's kind of no-nonsense, despite all the nonsense we get into. It's hard to embarrass her. I would call her dependable and she would hate it, because it could make more work for her, but she's not a superhero and definitely needs support too. She needs solid people around her. For as long as I've known her, she's been trying to figure out gender stuff. I wouldn't normally out her like this, but if Luke is only interested in 100% cisgender women, don't point him in her direction. If his sexuality is more flexible, you can send him to her socials. Corinne Butcher.

Also, I regret to inform you, you'll be staying in the same hotel as my relatives and will be there for the wedding. Welcome to hell.

—Mattie

***

Mattie,

Luke is a decent man, a good friend, and an engaged and loving father. It was hard for him after his wife left—an amicable parting, by the way. Even the internet knows that. But sharing custody, a whole new schedule, trying to find a path forward that looks different from everything he expected—it's been a lot. And he's done really well, in my opinion. I also wouldn't usually out my friends, but Luke's affinities would include someone testing the gender waters. He hates to be tied to a label, though, so he wouldn't say he's bisexual, like I am. More like he'd date whoever he was attracted to, which could possibly be anybody, and leave the esoteric definitions of sexuality out of it completely.

I would love to see him find happiness with someone like Rin.

How is it possible you and I are already playing matchmaker to our friends, when we should be matching ourselves?

I will be there for the wedding, because now I'm planning to crash it. See these assholes first hand. Support you in the face of it all. Couldn't have arranged it better myself.

Yours,

Raphael

***

Email

From: Daphne Redgrave, daphno@spiritmissives.net

To: Mattie Redgrave, bloodymattie@prismbridge.com

Subject: BRACE YOURSELF, sorry

3:22 p.m.

To start, one of the bridesmaids is sick and can't get into the country, so you've been promoted to a bridesmaid? cringe emoji. They did it reluctantly! To ensure absolutely nobody is happy! The dress is here, they'll fit you when you arrive.

But. There's worse news. I told them you were too old to be a bridesmaid, and they said it's fine because you're the same age as the groomsman you're paired with.

Mats, I had no idea they even invited him, but it's Mike Spencer. I told them no. Kyle wouldn't listen to me when I listed the many, many reasons he shouldn't be invited, let alone in the wedding party. I complained to mom next, and she waved me off. Finally I went to dad, who told me I had nothing to worry about. Oh?? Our number one bully throughout childhood? Who grew up to be the face of one of NorCal's most organized white supremacist movements? THAT GUY?? I didn't know he and Kyle even knew each other, but apparently they met at some rally after college and they've been bffs ever since.

There is no way anyone will feel safe at this wedding. Donna The Wedding Planner gave me a copy of the seating chart and I spent the last few hours tracking down whoever I could online. Lots of people from his group will be there. The mood is going to be GRIM for us.

I know you said this wedding is the one last thing you have to do before cutting off all ties with these monsters for good, but I know how you are. If you come here, you're going to say things, and I worry that they're going to hurt you. Won't matter if you're Kyle's sister. What a fucking shit show.

Daphne

***

Email

From: Mattie Redgrave, bloodymattie@prismbridge.com

To: Daphne Redgrave, daphno@spiritmissives.net

Subject: RE: BRACE YOURSELF, sorry

3:48 p.m.

I don't really know how to react to this. I can't say I'm surprised, because this is definitely something they would do. But this feels so personal. Vindictive. I'll text mom, and Kyle, see if I can do anything about it. I need time to think.

***

Text Message

between Matalina and Marjorie/mother

4:19 p.m.

Marjorie:

Update on the wedding. You're a bridesmaid now. The seamstress will tailor a dress for you. Are you sure you can't get here any sooner?

Matalina:

I can't get there any sooner without breaking the law and going to jail and missing the whole thing completely, but also, I'm not going to be a bridesmaid. I've met Celeste once and Kyle and I are basically estranged. It's almost inappropriate for me to attend at all.

Marjorie:

Don't be so dramatic. The whole family is working to make sure the wedding is perfect. You have to think about someone besides yourself sometimes. Your brother says you're a bridesmaid, so you are. The dress is already paid for, if that's what you're worried about.

Matalina:

I'm not worried about money. I don't want to be in the wedding, the bride and groom don't really want me to be in the wedding, so the solution is for me to not be in the wedding. And Daphne said I'm paired with Mike Spencer. Do you remember that guy at all? Why would they even invite someone who caused me so much torment? It feels like a personal attack.

Marjorie:

This isn't about you, Matalina.

Matalina:

So you're saying you expect me to show up at this event where I'm not welcome, fill a role I don't want to, wear an outfit I didn't choose, and interact with a guy who spent our entire childhoods *physically hurting me* because your son wants symmetry for his wedding photos? That's more important to you than your daughter's safety and well-being?

Marjorie:

My job was to tell you that you're in the party now and that there's a dress here for you and you need to get here as soon as you can. If you have any opinions or complaints, take it up with Kyle. But he's very busy and doesn't deserve your interrupting him with trivial things like this when he has an entire wedding to coordinate.

Matalina:

He has a wedding planner. He's spending his days and nights getting drunk and being an ass, same as always. But sure, I'll text him. And if he doesn't want to take my very real concerns seriously, I'll just not come at all.

Marjorie:

Manipulating your brother because you dislike one of his friends? That's low, Matalina. It's never been a secret how ungrateful you are toward this family, but for some reason I expected better of you. It's very hurtful. I don't know why you act this way when we go out of our way to make you feel like a part of the family.

Matalina:

I'm going to text Kyle. Consider your duty to inform me of being a bridesmaid fulfilled.

Marjorie:

OK. See you soon honey.

***

Text Message
    between Matalina and Kyle Redgrave
    5:00 p.m.

Matalina:

The only way I can be a bridesmaid is if Mike Spencer isn't a groomsman.

Kyle:

Well luckily you have no authority to make those kinds of broad ultimatums since it's my fucking wedding

Matalina:

That guy caused me and Daphne physical and emotional pain throughout our entire childhood. You should be protecting us from him, not giving him a place of honor and making us interact with him.

Kyle:

once again making it all about you

Matalina:

Why would you want me to be in a situation where I don't feel safe?

Kyle:

Mike is my friend and it's not my fault if you misunderstood something he said, and it's definitely not on me to sort out whatever fucked up lies are making you imagine that he's a danger to you

Matalina:

and what about all the other extremists you've invited?

Kyle:

You think anything other than your beliefs are "extreme," so figure it out yourself

Matalina:

You're setting me in a nest of vipers and telling me they're kittens.

Kyle:

Save the drama for your books, Matalina. You won't ruin my wedding. This is exactly why I didn't want to invite you but I, unlike you, actually give a fuck about this family, so I sucked it up. If you can't descend from that pedestal you've put yourself on to be among us lowlifes for a few hours, don't come. Prove to everyone once and for all what a selfish, entitled brat you are, to protest your own brother's wedding because you misjudged another guest.

Fucking typical.

Day 11
Tuesday, March 31, 2020

Hey Mattie,

I know you don't owe me anything, not a letter or note, or your time or energy, but I hope that the lack of correspondence from you isn't a response to something stupid I said in my last letter or on the balcony. I've gotten used to a steady stream of communication, which of course doesn't mean you're obligated to continue it, but if it's because I put my foot in my mouth, let me apologize. I can't say I was joking when I said we should be matchmakers for ourselves first, but I've grown to like you very much and wanted to hint at my interest instead of being vulnerable and stating it outright, like I imagine you would do.

And I won't crash your brother's wedding if you don't want me to. It's hard for me to say that and mean it, when knowing what little I do of how they treat you has me primed to fight. If I were to go, I might commit assault, so, best not to tempt fate.

Or, if it's that I suggested Luke and Rin should get to know each other, and I overstepped, please tell me. You're right, I don't know her, and you and I are talking about them secondhand, so it's not really fair to either of them.

Care to start reading *The Magpie Lord* together today? Perhaps outside? The rain is supposed to clear later, maybe if it gets drier and warmer after lunch?

Hope I haven't messed things up already,

Raphael

***

Raphael,

You haven't messed anything up, I promise. I think Luke and Rin would get along well, and I think you and I do, too.

As for crashing the wedding and throwing punches, that's actually tangential to my current dilemma. Something came up and I'm having a hard time deciding what I can or should do. My options swing from one extreme to the other and back again, it all goes round in circles. I'm so tangled up in everything, I don't even know how to think my way out. Been trying since the problem arose yesterday afternoon, and I'm still waffling.

Let's meet for lunch again, or after lunch. I'd love to start rereading *Magpie Lord*, but if the choice is between that and just talking to you, I think I'd prefer the human interaction. That isn't usually the case, by the way. There's a reason I expected my quarantine to be the best of the time I'd spend in New Zealand, and that was before I met you. Solitude, quiet, no people.

I'd say that you're making me like people, but I suspect that I just like you.

See you outside,
Mattie

***

Mattie,

Tell me the problem. If nothing else, I can be a sounding board. I don't have anything else to do. Should I text you? Here's my number.

—Raph

***

Raphael—

No, no, don't text, I'll write it out. It'll give my brain more time, and my angry hands can do less damage throwing a pen and notebook than my phone. I'll try to be quick, but it might take a while, to formulate the prose at least. I'll try to get it to you before lunch.

Isolation has not made me so stupid that I forget I could ask you to meet me outside right this minute, and I could tell you everything in person. But it's an emotional thing, and I tend to cry when I get upset even the smallest bit, and I don't want to cry in front of you right now.

Thanks for listening. I'll try to write quickly.

Mattie

***

Email

From: Raphael Callan, raffinityraccoon@wormwood.gb.ww.co
To: Luke Maston, getoffmylawn@tepidemail.com
Subject: Mattie, and Rin
10:25 a.m.

This is going to sound like a weird question, but have you noticed a large family of rich assholes staying at the Billingstead with you? That's Mattie's family. She's here for her brother's wedding, and that's where they're staying and where the ceremony will be. I would love to get some inside information about them before I get there. Do a little recon. I'm beginning to suspect that Mattie downplayed how awful they are; it sounds like they were unduly hard on her as a child—which continues as she's an adult, unfortunately—and I'd like to hear your take on them.

As Mattie tells it, Rin appears to be single and "potentially interested in getting to know someone who's an adult and not an asshole." It sounds like she would enjoy mischief but not bullshit. Lends and needs support in equal measure, as a true partner would. She works for—or owns?—a company that leases posh vacation homes. The three of them are staying at one such place near the hotel so the sisters don't have to be within shouting distance of their relatives for anything but the most necessary of events.

It sounds like Daphne and Rin have already been to the hotel a few times and plan to be there more, leading up to the wedding, so it's entirely possible you will, or have already, seen both of them. Let me know if you do. Links to Rin's social media below. Corinne Butcher. I've already friended her and Daph, and of course Mattie, on my private accounts, so you can look through their posts as you like.

Raph

***

Email
From: Luke Maston, getoffmylawn@tepidemail.com
To: Raphael Callan, raffinityraccoon@wormwood.gb.ww.co
Subject: RE: Mattie, and Rin
11:01 a.m.
Well holy shit, the Redgrave-Tamsyn wedding is Mattie's brother's wedding. Mate, from what you've told me about her, what a nice person she is, level-headed and genuine, how in the absolute fuck did she come from this family of entitled wankers, and why

in the absolute fuck has she decided to ruin her life by attending what will surely be a hard-won disaster? Are they blackmailing her? Did she kill a man?

There seems to be hundreds of them, and they've taken over the entire hotel, which would normally be difficult to do in a place that also boasts of being an event centre and should be accustomed to many hundreds if not thousands of guests. But I'm assuming with the pandemmy and restricted travel, lots of people canceled their bookings. Freeing up the staff and the unfortunate smattering of non-wedding guests to witness the buffoonery of this multigenerational circus of viciousness and vacuity.

I watched an adult woman pour a bottle of lavender bath oil into the indoor pool because the smell of the chlorine "gave her a headache." I saw a child sucker-punch a maid in front of his father, who pulled her aside and gave her money and said "boys, so rambunctious," before patting her ass and pushing her away. Every night is a bachelor party, where the drunkards conclude their evening (morning) by pissing into the lobby's potted plants and singing Creed at the top of their lungs. Every afternoon is a bachelorette party, row after row of women who all look the same, insisting on sitting by the outdoor pool, braziers and torches at full blast so they can wear their tiny togs out in the chill.

It almost makes me want to spend more time on set. Almost.

If I had known it was Mattie's family, I would have told you about them sooner. I just thought, "bad luck for us on multiple fronts," and focused on sabotaging the work. Now I'll split my focus to include sabotaging the wedding.

Based on the pictures they've posted, I don't think I've seen Rin or Daphne at the hotel yet. Tell Mattie to tell you when they'll be there, and I'll meet them. Or actually, give her my email and number, so she can tell me directly. You're basically a couple, so it's time to introduce her to your black sheep brother Luke.

—your black sheep brother, Luke

***

Raphael,

This letter is going to seem so short for the amount of time it took to write.

Growing up, I was always told I was too sensitive. I feel a lot of emotions, and nobody liked that I felt emotions. And since it singled me out among my siblings and peers, *I* also didn't like that I felt emotions. Any mean thing that anyone said or did to me was tolerated, and sometimes encouraged, in order to "help me build a thicker skin." It took me a long time to realize that they were wrong to do it. And now, I like being soft. But when you pair this with my need to call out people's bullshit or voice the problems that everyone else is ignoring, what I end up with is me calling attention to myself in a situation that is potentially harmful for me, shaking and crying, and nobody takes me seriously. I still stand up for what's right because that's important, but I have to be okay with crying while I do it, because that means that I care. Nobody has ever stood up for me if Daphne and Rin aren't there to do it.

Fast forward to now: my biggest bully, an all-around abusive person, is a groomsman at my brother Kyle's wedding. I didn't know this earlier because the less I know about the wedding, the better. Daphne emailed me yesterday saying a bridesmaid isn't able to get into NZ, and Kyle and Celeste (his fiancé) "promoted" me to the position so the groomsmen/bridesmaid numbers match. Daph advocated against it on my behalf and discovered the guy I'd be paired with is, you guessed it, that same bully.

His name is Mike Spencer, and after all his practice torturing me (and others) throughout school, he has moved on to doing it professionally as part of a hate group in Northern California. Other members of this group are also attending (thank you, Daph's detective work), which means that more people than just me will be put in a very likely unsafe situation.

My first thought was to not go to the wedding at all. Protect myself. But. He would still be there, and other people would still have to deal with his bullshit. And maybe those other people aren't as strong as I am, and they'd be hurt. My second thought was to tank the wedding. Go, and make a scene about it during the ceremony. Or maybe show up for rehearsal and confront everyone then? Write a letter? Protest it some other way?

I texted my mother and Kyle, who is definitely gaslighting me. He says I'm misinterpreting what Mike has said or done, and it's unfair of me. I know he's wrong but I still end up doubting myself, like, maybe it wasn't as bad as I remember. Maybe I *have* been misinterpreting his intentions.

Their friendship doesn't even make sense. We whakapapa Māori on our father's side. Maybe Kyle didn't forget, but hates that part of himself.

Anyway. Look him up, you'll find plenty of info to form your own opinion. But I'm stuck on what to do next. What's best for everyone. We can talk about it outside, if you want, if you have questions. Or maybe you can distract me from it for a while. I have a few days before I need to figure it out.

—Mattie

***

Mattie,

I looked up that guy and I want to assure you that it IS as bad as you remember, they ARE gaslighting you, and you absolutely cannot go to that wedding. Give me Daph's number. Rin's too, it will take all of us to come up with a plan. I'll be seeing you outside in a few minutes but I wanted to let you know immediately that you can trust your memory, and you've got people to support you and get you through this.

—Raph

***

Text Message
between Raphael, Luke, Daphne, and Corinne
1:02 p.m.

Raphael:
So Mattie can't go to this wedding, right?

Daphne:
Uh, new phone who dis? Oh there's Rin. And yes, I agree.

Raphael:
Raphael. Sorry, she gave me your numbers, and this is important.

Daphne:
HI RAPHAEL

Corinne:
Who's this other number?

Raphael:
My friend Luke, he's staying at the Billingstead and wants to help.

Luke:

well hello ladies, I heard about your bike escapades. bikescapades.

Corinne:

oh god

Daphne:

hello Luke and welcome to the best group text of your life.

Luke:

A bold claim.

Daphne:

group TEXT, darling, not group SEXT

Luke:

ah, my mistake, how do I opt out then?

Raphael:

Luke. Focus.

Luke:

which number is Corinne and which is Daphne?

Corinne:

It's just Rin, actually.

Luke:

nice to meet you, Rin.

Corinne:

Hello, stranger.

Luke:

Fair enough.

Daphne:

ffs Rin

Corinne:

Daph

Raphael:

LUKE

Luke:

Raphael. Now that we got that out of the way

Daphne:

Operation Save Mattie

Raphael:

So we're all on the same page. The answer is she can't attend, right?

Corinne:

That's obvious to everyone but her, but, yes.

Daphne:

There's no way to prevent her from going. Believe me, I've tried my whole life. The best we can do is make what she DOES do as safe as possible.

Luke:

So kidnapping won't work?

Daphne:

I mean, how attached are you to your fleshy bits?

Luke:

uh. very.

Daphne:

then no, kidnapping won't work.

Raphael:

Is there a way to convince her this is the right decision?

Corinne:

For Mats, the right decision is the one that serves justice, or, barring that, does the least harm. She'll put herself in more danger to protect the most people. She's going to find a way to get there and "say shit," as she says. And that's going to be bad, with this crowd.

Raphael:

If her relatives haven't believed her about any of this before, they won't believe her even if she stands up in front of everybody and calls this guy out on his bullshit. And he won't be swayed by someone he never respected anyway. So it sounds like all that will happen is she'll expose herself to harm and it won't change anything.

Corinne:

Yeah. That's usually how it goes.

Luke:

So what can we do?

Raphael:

I think we have to apply the same level of sabotage here as in Project Shut Down Broke.

Luke:

AHHH

Daphne:

WHAT IS THAT? I AM EXCITED TOO

Corinne:

OK, I like that word "sabotage," that's something I can get behind.

Luke:

Raph and I have been scammed into making the worst movie of all time, so we're workshopping how to get out of it.

Corinne:

You're talking about That Scarlet Beating Heart, aren't you?

Daphne:

Oh nooooo, that book made Mattie so angry.

Luke:

For good reason. We agreed to it before knowing what it was and here we are. Our ideas include faking our deaths and actually getting Covid.

Corinne:

What I'm hearing is that neither of you are allowed to brainstorm anymore. Leave it to us professionals.

Daphne:

First of all Raph you need to be Mats' date.

Raphael:

Done.

Corinne:

Uhhhh, no. That's not going to work, Daphne.

Daphne:

(whispers: WE HAD A PLAN, RIN!)

Corinne:

Tell me honestly that your relatives will be more starstruck than racist.

Daphne:

you know I wish I fucking could.

Luke:

Well I'll attend too, as one of your dates, so they see me and Raph at the same time and focus on our celebrity.

Raphael:

That works for me.

Corinne:

Pretty sure I just said neither of you should brainstorm.

Luke:

Yes ma'am. Sorry ma'am.

Daphne:

Oh I like this one. Rin, bring him as your date.

Corinne:

I am no longer taking suggestions. I am finding solutions to the problem at hand. I'll text if I need an opinion. Raph, if Mats says anything to you that might be relevant, let us know.

Raphael:

I will. And thanks, all of you. I know it's odd, I've only known Mattie a week.

Corinne:

You like her. It was inevitable.

Daphne:

You're good for each other.

Luke:

Oh he definitely wants to be her boyfriend.

Raphael:

LUKE for fuck's sake

Daphne:

GOOD, because she's definitely got the hots for him too

Corinne:

I'd normally say not to talk behind her back but Daph is right, so, get to wooing!

Raphael:

lol I plan to.

***

Email

From: Mattie Redgrave, bloodymattie@prismbridge.com

To: Daphne Redgrave, daphno@spiritmissives.net; Rin Butcher, c.butcher@nipl.co.nz

Subject: no progress

1:59 p.m.

Well things have become muddy since last talking to either of you. Raphael and I had lunch together on our balconies, and I gave him your numbers. He's going to "coordinate a multi-frontal attack" on the wedding/bridesmaid/Mike Spencer situation. But it felt like he was just saying lines and doesn't actually know what he's doing, so, maybe help him out a bit? Not that we know what we're doing either. God, we're a bunch of clowns trying our best, aren't we?

I have to get some work done this afternoon. It'll be good for me to be able to focus on something besides the wedding. I don't have any more insight into what I should do, but talking to Raphael made me feel better anyway.

-Mats

***

Email

From: Rin Butcher, c.butcher@nipl.co.nz

To: Daphne Redgrave, daphno@spiritmissives.net; Mattie Redgrave, bloodymattie@prismbridge.com

Subject: RE: no progress

4:22 p.m.

For clowns trying our best, we're pretty fucking good at it.

No ideas from me yet, but I'm letting it brew. What I do have an idea about is a potential date for you and Raph. I'll have to track down some equipment, but, ask him if he wants to go on another date with you tomorrow night. 21:00, on your balconies. It's a surprise. Daph, I'll need your help. Fran and Betty ride again.

***

Raphael,

You started our correspondence today saying that I don't owe you anything, "not a letter or note, or your time or energy," so I'd like to point out that the same applies to you. I'm grateful for your compassion and insight and time this afternoon. Sure, we've gotten to know each other pretty well this past week, but it means a lot that you would sit down with me and listen to my problems. We might not have solved anything, but I still felt better afterward.

Loved our classic New Zealand lunch: fish and chips, hokey pokey ice cream. Honestly some of the best cuisine these islands have to offer. You said your previous time here was enough to direct me to well-known tourist attractions, but I wonder if you've ever had food from a gas station here? I don't know what it's like in the UK; in the US, it's ubiquitously suspect. But New Zealand gas station food is surprisingly good. Like, "go out of your way to stop for their food" good. However you're getting to the Billingstead from here, make a detour and get an espresso beverage and a meat pie. I can picture you cringing, but I swear it's true.

Would you care to have another date night, tomorrow night? I can't tell you what it is. It'll be a surprise and probably legal. LOL, this letter isn't even legal. Okay forget all that except date, tomorrow, 9 p.m.

You have Rin and Daphne's numbers, but you haven't given me Luke's. Oh, is it the celebrity thing? Gotcha. It just seems like, if you're going behind my back to plot with my friends, then I should have the opportunity to do the same.

I have to do some work this afternoon, so, don't be alarmed if I don't respond right away. If there's an emergency, just knock on the door, or text me. "If there's an emergency," what does that even mean, what kind of...sorry, my brain is still in recovery mode. Signing off now before I lose it for real.

Yours,

Mattie

***

Dear Mattie,

I'm going to make time for you whether you ask me to or not, and a good portion of that time will be devoted to listening to you.

So while I appreciate your appreciation, it's not necessary for you to express it. I think I would like being your teammate, working on problems together. But here you are, upset, and I'm upset on your behalf, and I don't know how to help. I did text your friends, so you have four of us working on it.

Part of me thinks the solution is obviously violence—I know it's not, I'm just so angry at the people who hurt you—but mostly all I want to do is tuck you into my arms, kiss your forehead, and make you feel safe enough to rest for a while. Emotional distress leads to physical distress, and if I can't alleviate one, I have to try the other. But know this: I'm not going to let anyone hurt you. Your friends don't think it's a good idea for me to attend this shit show of an event with you, but I disagree. If you have to be there, I have to be by your side, Mattie. You're not going to face it alone.

It seems so soon for me to feel this way about you, but I said I'd be honest, and that's it there.

I don't have a good segue from serious to lighthearted, so this will have to do.

I've never had New Zealand service station food, and based on what we have in England, I'm reluctant to try it. The American kind, I've had, and I understand it. You lot like things cheap and convenient, and that means compromising on quality. Not a complaint. In fact, I respect it. You know what you're getting and can't be disappointed. I don't know what our excuse is. But it's difficult to believe the food in NZ would be that much better than I would find at an Esso along the A5. That being said, I trust you. I'm a little wary, but I'll try it.

Luke's number and email are below. We're both already following all three of you across the internet, too, on our private accounts. It shouldn't attract attention, but if your notifications explode for some reason, you have my apologies.

Date tomorrow night, absolutely. And you don't know whether it's in line with our isolation protocol? Have you not decided what we're doing on our date? You have a lot of things on your mind—if you'd like me to plan something instead, I can do that. Care to meet on our separate balconies tomorrow for lunch? And we can decide what to do on our date then?

I can't foresee any emergencies for the rest of the evening, so I'll leave you to your work. Not to sound matronly, but, try to get to sleep early if you can. And drink some water. Text me if you need me.

Yours,

Raphael

Day 12
Wednesday, April 1, 2020

Email

From: Luke Maston, getoffmylawn@tepidemail.com

To: Raphael Callan, raffinityraccoon@wormwood.gb.ww.co

Subject: foreboding

9:45 a.m.

These people are insufferable. Am I talking about work or the Redgraves? Yes. Yes, both. Besides Payton, everyone on set is really trying their best. Tensions are high. I've tried telling him there's no shame in tabling the whole thing. The empty positions, the fear of catching the mysterious illness. In fact, he would be considered a brave leader for it. But no. He said the conflict builds character and just like the book, we must persevere, especially when the entire world is against us. "The harder it is, the more worthy we become," or whatever bullshit. Honestly, it's my fault, I should have at least asked questions before agreeing to work on it. Sorry I dropped the ball, mate.

Speaking of trouble, I met Rin and Daphne in person last night. Coordinated it ourselves. Daph had to attend some family thing here and Rin wouldn't let her go alone, so I graced them with my presence. I know you're not religious, mate, so who do I thank for you meeting Mattie?

Can't wait for the production to stall. The five of us are going to have a smashing time.

There is one more thing. It's more of a suspicion, a feeling, a foreboding. Payton is keeping something from me. Besides what we've come to expect due to the nature of this production. I don't know what it is, but it feels like The Shire before the Nazgûl arrive. I'll be cautious. I would tell you to be cautious too, it feels like you're a part of it, but you're not even here. I guess, be cautious where you are. Will keep you updated.

—Luke

***

Email

From: Raphael Callan, raffinityraccoon@wormwood.gb.ww.co

To: Luke Maston, getoffmylawn@tepidemail.com

Subject: RE: foreboding

10:35 a.m.

Get a list of the cast and crew so we can advocate for them to work on our next projects. We're trying to save all our asses from this film, but obviously some people might need the paycheck, so we have to make sure to get them the opportunity to do that as soon as possible. You and I need to be getting in the way of bad behaviour, not causing more harm.

"The harder it is, the more worthy we become." What utter shit. There's the case for overcoming adversity, and then there's this fucking quote, which in context belongs in some MRA manifesto. We fucked up on this one, Luke. We might have to pull a Mattie. Get to set, tell everyone it's harmful bullshit we refuse to be a part of, then walk away and deal with the consequences.

She's made me brave. Possibly stupidly brave.

I'll try to talk to him in person first. I'm wound tight, between this, and Mattie's bully at the wedding, and the coronavirus, I'm just over all of it.

I knew you would like Rin and Daph. Tell me more about hanging out with them, I need some good news over here.

So there's a shadow on set. Not surprising. Considering all the shortcuts Payton is taking on everything, he's bound to have done something unsavory to ensure the continuation of his pet project. I know they're busy, but maybe ask Daph and Rin for their opinions? They seem insightful, and, unlike me, they're physically there. I'll see you in two days.

Watch your back, bro.

Raph

***

Text Message
  between Matalina, Corinne, and Daphne
  10:45 a.m.

Corinne:

> Got what I needed. Your date tonight is a go.

Matalina:

> Excellent! What will we be doing?

Corinne:

> You'll be on your balconies for 21:00 and you'll figure out the rest when you get there.

Matalina:

> That sounds like a lot of work.

Corinne:

Ungrateful child.

Matalina:

LOL you know I'll love it, and I love you, and I'm so lucky you're my friend. I don't know how I would have gotten through this quarantine without you.

Daphne:

We had to save your sanity. And your budding love with Raphael.

Corinne:

Speaking of, thanks for writing to him, because it led to me and Daph meeting Luke Maston, so, cheers, mate.

Matalina:

Wait, you met him? Like in person?

Corinne:

Fuck yeah. You gave Raph our numbers, and he gave them to Luke, and Luke did what Luke does I guess, which is whatever he wants, and he wanted to meet us. So we went to a pub.

Matalina:

Oh man. I'm jealous.

Corinne:

You should def be jealous. Luke is even more handsome in person, the lanky bulk with the nerdy glasses just WORKS, and I was able to act like a normal person instead of what my body wanted to do, which was scream and pass out.

Matalina:

Aw Rin, I'm so proud of you. What are his fans called? Are you a Mastondon now? lol

Corinne:

Oh yes. I think he might even have been…flirting? With me?

Daphne:

Of course he was. And I like him too. He's just a really cool dude.

Matalina:

Not surprised there was flirting. Raph might have said something about how Luke wanted to meet you after hearing about the goody bag hijinks, based on Raph's description of you absconding into the night lol

Corinne:

Well, whatever you did, thank you. Oh, you'll need to bring your phone or laptop out on your date. I'll have a website you have to log into.

Matalina:

Curiouser and curiouser.

Daphne:

I don't even know the details! I just show up!

Matalina:

We know, Daph.

Corinne:

When I give you details, you show up with a bow and arrows. We don't need that level of prep tonight.

Daphne:

(mumbling: we always need bow and arrows)

Matalina:

You can't stop her, you know.

Corinne:

I know.

Daphne:

And you wouldn't want to if you could.

***

Raphael,

I keep thinking about the letter where you said, "hope is utterly necessary for me." I don't think I knew, really, what you meant at the time. As a kind of nebulous concept, sure. In the context of our confinement, yes. But as a core tenet to be carried and considered and acted upon regularly, not so much.

Here I am, holding another letter from you, a different one than the one about hope, and I think I understand what you mean. You said you want to stand by my side when I face my problems, and you want to hold me, and make me safe. I met you only twelve days ago, didn't see your face until three days ago, have spent less than a day in your physical company, and only know you from a series of letters we've written each other in isolation.

Here I am, holding onto a hope that is absolute madness. It is madness to have it, and madness again to divulge it.

But you somehow know my nature better than I do, when you said you imagined I would be straightforward and vulnerable and state my interest if I had feelings for you. On a totally objective level, I know that a week, under these conditions, shouldn't be long enough to fall for someone, let alone gather the courage to say it.

On a totally subjective level, I know that it doesn't take any time, and these conditions are unprecedented, and I'm at the point where I'm willing to risk rejection and embarrassment because it would be easy to avoid you forever if that happened, and absolutely nobody would judge me for developing an attraction to Raphael Callan. Even you couldn't judge me for that, you who told me so early on that you were charming and handsome, as though you were preparing me for my inevitable crush.

So. I'm falling for you, Raphael.

I could say so much more, but I'm going to stop there, in case I need to make a retreat. This is why I waited until after lunch to give this to you. Don't spare my feelings. You said you want to hold me, and I want that too. You want to kiss me, and I want that too. If I've misread it, I'm sure it's my fault, just, set me right.

I wondered if what I'm feeling is just the compression of isolation that's forced us together, a scarcity of available partners. But I wasn't looking for anything when I met you, and I've been isolated before. So I'm inclined to believe that my feelings are real and not forced.

I'm sure this isn't the kind of letter you thought you'd get from me today. Allow me to move on to another topic that should cause less embarrassment on my part. Here, I'll practice my own segue from serious to lighthearted.

Speaking of meeting new people, it looks like Daphne and Rin met up with Luke last night. (OK that was a terrible transition, but let's keep going like it was fine.)

If they're going to be required to spend time with my relatives, I'm glad that they're able to experience the palate-cleanse that is Luke. They had a good time. It sounds like they went to a bar. God, I want to go to a bar. It would be a room that isn't this one, and I could choose what to eat and drink, and see and touch people. It would be overwhelming and I would love every minute.

Must give you credit for suggesting getting to bed early. I felt like an old woman, but I did it and felt better for it. I already dress and act like one so I guess criminally early bed time would be the next step toward my final form.

No updates from any relatives regarding the situation there. If they talked about it at their gathering last night, Daphne didn't mention it to me. Which means no change.

I'm starting to think maybe you should be my date to the wedding. Wait, let me keep practicing this directness thing:

Raphael, I would be honored if you would be my date for my brother's wedding in four days. It will be the most uncomfortable, inappropriate, embarrassing, dramatic, and possibly violent event you'll ever attend, but I can promise you unceasing leers of both the unwanted sexual variety as well as the casually (and openly!) racist kind. Come for the gaudy display of wealth by tasteless trust fund babies, stay for the staggering lack of self-awareness among socialites whose greatest tragedy is that someone has a bigger yacht than they do.

At the very least, the experience will give you an otherwise unattainable view into the lives of people who will defend *That Scarlet, Beating Heart* until their dying breath.

If I have no choice but to face them, at least I have a choice to face them with someone by my side.

This letter was a lot. If you need time to process it, or decide it's too much and don't want to deal with me anymore, I totally get it. You've already agreed to a date tonight, just let me know if you want to cancel.

I hope you won't cancel.

Yours,

Mattie

***

Text Message
  between Raphael and Luke
  3:15 p.m.

Raphael:

I hate to even type these words because I don't want to know, but I have to ask because my manager just emailed me about it. What's Edie saying now? We're getting back together? Seriously?

Luke:

This was why I asked if there's anything she could do that you'd want me to tell you about.

Raphael:

Well, tell me about it now, I already know something is happening if JC is asking how to publicly respond to her.

Luke:

An interview with her was uploaded yesterday and they asked her about her love life (like ffs just leave us alone unless we bring it up first), and she said you two were getting back together.

Raphael:

Was that it? She's said that before.

Luke:

I only watched a minute of it, but if your manager thinks there's more, you should watch the video yourself. I'm not sure if being a good friend means hanging on to her every word in case she slanders you, or ignoring her completely.

Raphael:

No worries Luke, I appreciate however you try to help. I'm going to hate myself for doing this, but, send me the link to that video.

Luke:

Will do. I don't want to leave you in a funk, so tell me how Mattie's doing.

Raphael:

She sent me a letter.

Luke:

No way, a letter? I'm shocked.

Raphael:

She said she has feelings for me.

Luke:

Aha, way to go, bro.

Raphael:

It's a beautiful letter, and I hoped she felt that way, I'm just trying to respond as vulnerably and honestly.

Luke:

"I feel the same way, let's make out"

Raphael:

Basically. But now this Edie thing has me worried.

Luke:

Eh, Edie has nothing to do with you and Mattie, and nothing she does can come between you.

Raphael:

> I've dealt with stalkers before, and Edie's no different. It's just a headache.

Luke:

> Understandable. I'll send you that link. Sorry you have to watch it.

Raphael:

> Appreciate it. Cheers, mate.

***

Dear Mattie,

I want to say so many things first, but it's impossible, only one thing can be first, and everything else will have to settle for after. Everything I want to say has already been said before, by many people, in more florid and beautiful ways, so I'll follow your lead and be clear, and direct, and vulnerable.

I'm falling for you, too.

Date night tonight is still on, because my crush on you grows with every letter you send me.

Nothing can stop me from being your date to your brother's wedding, because I want to be by your side when you fight an injustice, or confront an abuser, or defend yourself from bullies.

I also want to be by your side when you fall asleep at 5 p.m. wearing a high-necked dress, scratchy cardigan, and orthopaedic shoes.

Please don't avoid me. Do the opposite of that.

In two days, we'll be out of here, and a few days after that, you start a month-long holiday to celebrate your newfound freedom from any and every familial obligation, and I'll make time to see you as often as you like.

You're right, this seems like a lot, now that I've written it all down. It isn't, though, is it? Just two people who like each other, developing a growing fondness. And I think we should cultivate it.

I'm going to do away with segues entirely. They're too difficult. I blame isolation.

Luke told me he spent some time with Daphne and Rin. I'm not picky at this point, I'll take any not-hotel-room location where I could physically touch my friends. Up to this point in my life, I haven't been a fan of much physical affection from anyone who I didn't hold dear, but I think the lack of human contact is affecting me psychologically now.

And speaking of things that affect me psychologically (finally a decent segue), I did want to tell you something. A problem I've been having, that you might have seen in your online searches of me.

Earlier this year, I was dating someone, Edie Everette, and we broke up a little over a month ago. It wasn't serious—at least, I didn't think it was serious—but she's been vocal about how hurt she was by the breakup. It doesn't make sense to me. We didn't really get along. I mean, we tried, and it didn't work, and when things don't work, you assess whether it's worth it to try to fix things, or you bow out, to give each other a chance to find something better.

It's sometimes difficult to date outside the industry because it takes up so much time and is such a different world than reality. Not having to explain work is a relief. But what I first admired in her as assertiveness, I began to recognize as entitlement. What I mistook for confidence became condescension. She treated some people badly, but charmed whoever she had use for.

It was clear from the start that I wasn't what she was looking for. But instead of acknowledging that, she acted like I was, ignoring me when I said something she didn't agree with or "correcting" me if we were around other people. It felt like she was in love with the idea of me, and the reality of me was just a bother. Two months in, she said she was looking for someone to be her husband and give her babies, which, no. I'm not that guy. She said I would change my mind.

I wish I knew why I stayed with her so long. I was unhappy, but I was more unhappy with myself. I might have thought I deserved to be treated that way. That isn't something I believe anymore, for the record. I'm skipping over *a lot* of things that happened between us. Eventually, I ended it. Since then, she's been telling people we're just taking a break, that I broke her heart but she forgives me and wants me back. She's completely lost the plot.

In fact, I decided earlier today to ask my team to consider her a stalker. I guess there's a new video of her telling people we're back together—which, I want to be clear, is not true. I have no idea why she can't move on. Her behavior is absolutely inappropriate.

I wanted to tell you about this because I don't want you to stumble across a recent interview where she says we're a couple and think I've been lying to you. Totally understandable if you want to confirm, with whomever you think you can trust. I'm giving you total access, you have but to say the word.

I also wanted to tell you because it's one of the two things making my life difficult right now. Trying to get out of this film project and dealing with Edie's stalker bullshit. I want to help with the biggest problems you're facing, and I think you want to do the same. So, here are the issues taking up most of my mind.

They don't eclipse your bully situation, though. Yours is an immediate and potentially volatile and physically dangerous crisis, whereas I've blocked my ex from my life and across social media, and I have Luke's laid-back chaos fighting with Payton's own ineptitude for the prestige of shutting down production.

Now this letter is a lot more than a lot.

Balconies, 9 p.m. I'll be there.

Yours,

Raphael

***

Raphael,

So. Looks like we're on the same page.

insert meme of dog grinning at dad joke

As you can see, I totally know what I'm doing. We tell each other our romantic feelings, and I respond with a pun. Just a preview of the delightful neurodivergence you'll be experiencing with me on a regular basis.

You know, I *like* like you, but it's also pretty clear that you'd be a great friend to me. And look, I'm comfortable enough making a silly joke after a lot of emotions and trust and sharing. This is a good sign.

Edie sounds like a nightmare, and I am so sorry it's happening to you. Celebrities have never really interested me, so rumors or reports of your love life have sailed under my radar, and I had no idea you even dated her. But obviously if someone is harming you, I want to know about it. Instead of plunging into the poisonous waters of what I might find online, I asked Daph if she heard anything about it. She tries to keep up with celebrity gossip and reality shows for small talk in her office, and she gave me what I imagine is a very condensed version of how Edie is the worst person who ever lived and you're clearly meant to be with me.

That second part seems accurate, but I'm biased.

I'm also angry on your behalf. Why wouldn't she just find some-one else who she actually likes instead of trying to change you? How can anyone treat you like that? Like you've said before, in one of your first letters, if a man treated a woman the way she treated you, everyone would recognize it as abuse.

How can I get in her way? This seems like something I should be texting Luke about, the way you're texting my friends about my bully situation.

Maybe burn this letter. For legal purposes.

We keep saying how we want to get out of here, into movement and freedom and sunlight and the life that's waiting for us outside these rooms, but do you think if we stayed here and refused to leave, our problems would solve themselves? The wedding would go on without me, I would avoid Mike Spencer, your project would be delayed or they'd recast your character, and without any response from you, maybe Edie would, I don't know, get bored and disappear?

Maybe we can slip out of here quietly. Throw our phones into the ocean. Rin can hide us any number of places in New Zealand, and if we had to leave the country, Daph could easily secrete us away in San Francisco. You want to go back to England instead? Let's go.

This week has taught me that anything's possible. These sce-narios might be absolute fantasy, but if I have to confront reality, I'm glad to meet it with you by my side.

It isn't too cold out, so I'll be outside right after dinner, in case you want to spend some time together before our date starts. Also, Rin set this up and I have no idea what it is. I just know the time and place, and she said to bring our phones or laptops out with us because we need to log onto a website. Thankfully, she didn't fill

Daph in on the details, so it shouldn't include a bow and arrows, but with Daph, it's never a guarantee.

See you soon,

Mattie

***

Email

From: Raphael Callan, raffinityraccoon@wormwood.gb.ww.co

To: Luke Maston, getoffmylawn@tepidemail.com

Subject: Amelie

11:38 p.m.

I don't know if Daphne and Rin clued you in on what they had planned tonight, but they set up a—shouldn't be surprising at this point—rather clever movie night for me and Mattie. Glad the rain stayed away long enough for them to pull it off.

Trouble rode in on their two bikes again, no trailer this time, no bow and arrows in sight, a little before nine. Mattie and I had been outside for a bit. We went out there after dinner, first time we saw each other after professing our affection for each other. No, I didn't take your advice of "I feel the same way, let's make out." I'd like to think I responded in kind, honestly and poetically, though of course that's for her to decide. The poetic part, at least.

She was sitting in her usual chair, typing on her phone, wrapped in a blanket when I got out there, and when she saw me, her face lit up. She came over to the railing closest to mine and leaned over it, so I mimicked her. Tried to reach out to her, she laughed and tried the same, but we were still separated by about a meter.

"Two days," she said.

"Two days," I repeated.

"What'll happen then?" She asked.

"I have a few ideas."

She smiled and turned away. Pretty sure she was blushing. Neither of us had turned on our outside lights, and the dusk had snuck up faster than previously, night expanding in increments as we ride each day towards the solstice.

We talked about you, our friends, what the next few weeks might look like. I'm close to convincing her to definitively decline her brother's bridesmaid request, skip all events leading up to the wedding, go to the ceremony as a guest—with me by her side—and leave immediately after, no dinner or dancing. Her sense of obligation will be fulfilled, she'll have minimum contact with everyone, and if Mike Fucking Spencer wants to try to start something, I'll knock his teeth out.

It took some effort to get to the point of "just the wedding," and I don't think we can get a better scenario out of her. If this is the plan, will you crash it and sit on the other side of her? So she'll always have one or the other of us to look out for her. Daph and Rin are fierce and capable, but guys like Spencer will never see women as a threat, so it's up to you and me to, uh, I want to say bookend her, but that sounds suspiciously like a sex term and I'm not suggesting that at all.

I asked her opinion about the *Broke* situation. It sounds like she and her friends regularly make plans to disrupt what needs disrupting. I told her how we're worried about the crew working in these conditions, but we also don't want them to lose the paycheck. Just another snag in this tangled web. She said she would ponder it and let me know if she has any ideas.

Anyway, we watched Daphne and Rin bike down the street and stop about ten metres before they came parallel to Mattie's door. She flashed her phone at them twice—some kind of code from their Mischief Alliance—and they waved up at us. They were much quieter than they were the other morning.

Finally, against the tall, white wall across the street, a line of text appeared near the ground, directing us to a website for sound. Mattie glanced at me and shrugged, put in her ear buds, and typed into her laptop. I did the same. A few minutes later, a picture popped up above the text on the wall, and the sound from the website kicked in, and I realized they were projecting the movie *Amelie* against the white concrete like a movie-in-the-park situation.

Mattie's friends really, really love her.

They parked farther down the road so, if caught, they weren't directly underneath our rooms. They kept the website name up under the screen and several other people came out on their balconies to watch. Bribing people who might otherwise snitch. At one point, Mattie looked over the railing and laughed, and texted me: "They're sharing a giant bucket of popcorn." Sure enough, Daphne and Rin sat astride their bikes, side by side, passing the popcorn back and forth, ready to ride off if trouble found them, projectors secure in their baskets.

Nobody came to chase them off, and as they packed up for the night, we heard several people whisper thank-yous to them before heading back into their rooms. Before we went back inside, they stopped beneath us and whispered, "Love you, Vanessa. Bye, Elliot."

So I have an HMA alias now. I've truly been accepted into their pride.

I hate to ruin such a nice evening, but I saw that you sent me a link to that video, so I might as well watch it before turning in for the night.

I'll put in a good word, see if we can't get you a spy name, too.

—Raph

***

Text Message
between Raphael and Luke
11:58 p.m.

Luke:

Bad news, Raph. The foreboding has become a boding. We've got two problems here. You are definitely going to have to pull a Mattie and ghost this entire production.

First, I found Payton at the hotel bar with the Redgrave guys. Guess he's been hanging out with them a lot. He introduced me to his new hero, Mike Spencer.

But wait! There's more! The original actress for your character's wife is stuck in L.A., and Payton somehow got Edie into the country to replace her.

mate?

Raphael:

Of course this all happened at once. Edie's interview? She's saying we're getting back together.

Because she's pregnant.

Because I'm the father.

Luke:

shit.

Raphael:

Yeah. Shit.

Day 13
Thursday, April 2, 2020

Text Message
  between Matalina, Corinne, and Daphne
  9:30 a.m.

Matalina:

Last night was magical. You are wizards.

Corinne:

You're welcome. How did it go with Raph? You two looked like you'd been out there for a while before we showed up.

Matalina:

I sent him a letter telling him I'm falling for him. He sent one back saying he feels the same way.

Daphne:

OMG!!!

Corinne:

MATTIE

Matalina:

He said it way better than I did, I rambled on and on, and he was so patient and direct. And then the first thing I say to him is a pun.

Daphne:

LMAO

Corinne:

Oh Mattie, that's one of the reasons he loves you.

Matalina:

Want to be clear: he did not say love.

Daphne:

not YET

Corinne:

So, really, no puns or metaphors, tell us.

Matalina:

He's. I mean. I

Daphne:

is this the texting version of blushing or is she having a stroke

Matalina:

He's everything I was afraid to want because I thought I'd never have it.

Daphne:

uwu

Corinne:

Damn. And now you have it?

Matalina:

Kind of? Almost? Still in this room until OH MY GOD we get our final tests today! If we're negative, we get to leave tomorrow morning, holy crap, it snuck up on me! I CAN TOUCH HIM TOMORROW

Daphne:

I LOVE THIS

Matalina:

There's still a whole day ahead of me, how am I supposed to get anything done?

Corinne:

You won't. Distract yourself until the swab.

Daphne:

Then jump over to his balcony when you're negative.

Corinne:

Do not do that.

Matalina:

Not gonna do that. I'm horny, but not that desperate. I can wait one more day. Probably.

Also, vibrator.

Daphne:

Never forget. And try not to be sick so it'll be negative.

Matalina:

A good reminder.

Daphne:

Here to help.

Matalina:

ONE MORE DAY!

Daphne:

one more day!

Corinne:

One more day!

***

Email

From: Luke Maston, getoffmylawn@tepidemail.com

To: Raphael Callan, raffinityraccoon@wormwood.gb.ww.co

Subject: this fucking, fucking film

9:45 a.m.

Jesus fuck mate, I just watched the video. I can't believe—I mean, I CAN believe, because I believed you at the time that she was manipulative—but this level of commitment to try to get you back whatever the cost is mind-boggling. What does she think you're going to do? You're going to get back together, and oops, she's not really pregnant, or oops, she is and it's someone else's, and, what? What then?

Oh. She thinks you just need more time to fall in love with her, so when you find out she's lying, you'll be ready to forgive her. Meanwhile, there will be months and months of guaranteed harassment from her.

This is making me sick. She's gotta be dealing with a lot of personal issues to get to this point. I don't pity her, and I'm not making excuses, but I think it's time to bring in some professional help.

Confronted Payton this morning. I wanted to say something about Edie, and had to say something about Spencer, so it all came out. Told him he was a douchebag for calling in our favors on a propagandist film for douchebags, like we wouldn't find out, and that bringing in Edie was a betrayal of trust and friendship and he should be ashamed of himself. He didn't have any coherent response. I threatened to walk.

He said he'd give me the day to cool off, but Edie's coming in tomorrow and so are you, so we all have to be there to try to get this thing going. He said he's sending a car for you in the morning so you won't have to worry about getting to the Billingstead. Wants you to text his PA tonight with what time you're getting out—his number's below. I'm back at the hotel for the few golden hours between the Redgrave bros passing out and the Redgrave women taking over the public spaces. Might text Daph and Rin, see what they're up to. Maybe they can recommend something to burn up this energy.

If you have any better ideas, direct me.

—Luke

***

Email

From: Raphael Callan, raffinityraccoon@wormwood.gb.ww.co

To: Luke Maston, getoffmylawn@tepidemail.com

Subject: RE: this fucking, fucking film

10:20 a.m.

You're echoing everything that's running through my mind, and I can't tell if it helps to have someone who recognizes this situation for what it is, or if it's just amplifying my anxiety and ire.

First of all: Payton. I'm glad you didn't start a fistfight, but I don't trust your willpower, so definitely find something to do outside and do not return to the set today. Take Rin and Daphne with you so they can run interference in case you see Payton on the way.

Don't do anything else until I talk to him in person. He needs to tell me to my face why he brought Edie on. I'm so goddamned disappointed in him. I want to let him make his case before I commit to quitting. I can't imagine a good reason for his actions, but that doesn't mean there isn't one.

And if I don't like what he says, I'm gone.

Oh yeah, getting lawyers involved. Don't know if that's the "professional help" you were talking about, but that's what I have. I'm about to email JC with instructions. I looked it up, and paternity can be tested a few months after conception, so at least she won't be going on for months playing the victim while every aspect of my life suffers. So my lawyers tell her to stop slandering me, we get a restraining order, demand proof as soon as possible. I hate to think it but it's likely she won't accept the results and will continue harassing me until...well, when would she stop? And meanwhile, if I show even the slightest bit of anger, *I'm* the one who'll face backlash for it.

What a fucking mess.

Thanks for your support, bro, it means a lot to me. I'll see you tomorrow and we'll figure out at least the Payton part.

—Raph

***

Dear Mattie,

It feels like a late start, almost lunch time, and I'm just writing you the first letter of the day. I've spent all morning trying to clean up this Edie mess, and—it's a little worse than I initially thought. You have no reason to do as I ask, but please don't watch that new interview with her. What she says isn't true, and I just need some time to sort it out.

I can't believe we dated for four months and I thought I could trust her. A few letters ago, I told you I'd blocked her from my life as effectively as possible, but I want to send her an email or call her to yell at her, which is not a good idea. I have people taking care of it, but I don't know how long it will take. Any distraction would be welcome.

Over on set, Luke finally blew up at Payton, who told him to take the day off. He's going to try to get outside with Daph and Rin so he's not simmering in his own emotions. Heaven help Payton when Luke and I walk in tomorrow, refreshed and ready to argue.

I can't wait for our tests today. I need some good news, this has been one of the worst days I've had in a while.

Movie night was fantastic. Your friends really love you, to go through all this trouble. They could have just texted or called you a couple times during quarantine. Instead, they track down equipment, buy you a bag full of popcorn and porn, and risk FINES or ARREST because they can't stand to see you suffer and can't wait to be in your presence again. If your letters hadn't made it clear to me that you were something special, Mattie Redgrave, their loyalty would have made it undeniable.

Also, can I just say how adorable it was that you had tissues in your sleeve, ready to go, like an actual old lady? Absolutely endearing. If I hadn't seen your face in daylight multiple times, I might suspect you were actually an old woman. And if you are, you should know, it doesn't change how I feel about you.

How are you getting out of here tomorrow? I'm guessing your friends are picking you up and taking you to the house they rented, with one necessary detour for your flat white and meat pie. Have I got it right?

Lunch outside today? It's colder than yesterday. Maybe a coat-and-blanket situation. If lunch arrives before you get a response to me, text me.

See you soon,

Raphael

***

Text Message
between Matalina and Donna
11:55 a.m.

Donna:

> Hi Mattie, this is Donna, wedding planner for Kyle and Celeste. Your mother asked me to contact you about fitting you for the bridesmaid dress. Do you know what time you'll be at the Billingstead tomorrow?

Matalina:

> Uh, hi Donna, I'm surprised my mother didn't inform you that I'm not going to be a bridesmaid. So you can check that off your list.

Donna:

> Oh. Well, I know you want your brother's special day to run as smoothly as possible, and with the restrictions on getting into New Zealand, they're down a bridesmaid. We're really lucky she had a role that can be so easily filled by one of Kyle's sisters.

> Why don't we make a plan to meet, and you can try on the dress in case you change your mind later. According to your mother, your schedule for tomorrow includes the Girls Party at 3:00 and family dinner at 7:00. I have time at 2:00 and again at 5:30, which works best for you?

Matalina:

Look, Donna, I know you're just doing your job, but I'm not going to be a bridesmaid. And even if I were, I first have to test negative for the virus tonight, and get checked out of the hotel tomorrow, and I don't know what time that would be because they won't tell me that until my test results are in. And I wasn't going to attend those functions tomorrow anyway.

Donna:

That's great, so you have the whole day free. I'll write you in for 2:00 p.m. Others who have had to quarantine say check-out is in the morning, so you should be able to make an early afternoon fitting. Great! So I'll meet you in the Ruby Room in the Billingstead main building, that's in the basement, tomorrow at 2 p.m.

Matalina:

You can write me in, but that's no guarantee I'll be there.

Donna:

I believe in you. See you then!

***

Dear Raphael,

Blankets were the right call, thank you for suggesting them. Glad I already dress in layers.

I want to repeat that I won't watch that video, because it obviously bothers you a lot, and if I can do anything to lessen your worry, I will. It's tempting to want to contact and talk reason with your ex, but I get the impression that she won't listen to reason. Any contact initiated by you will only reinforce her belief that you're going to reconcile.

I may not know exactly what's going on, and if you were anyone else, I wouldn't be so quick to believe and defend you, but I have no excuse. I like you and want to believe and defend you.

It was only a matter of time before Luke blew up at Payton. That job will crush you to powder. I told you so in one of the first letters I wrote, before I even knew what it was. All I needed to know was that your boss worshipped *That Scarlet, Beating Heart* and expected you to emulate it. From what you've told me about Luke, it's unsurprising he would take a stand. I'm glad that he stood up for himself and for you.

Are there other options besides walking away? I don't want to tell you to abandon your job, but that's probably what I would do. I don't know the nuances of filmmaking or what that would mean for you, but I want you to be safe. Ha, I say that, then invite you to my terrible family's wedding, where you have even less of a chance of holding your own. At least on set you have, like, OSHA or something? Rights? A contract? At the wedding, you'll be at the mercy of hundreds of bloodthirsty narcissists who expect to be treated like kings.

Movie time last night was phenomenal. I'm always so impressed with Rin and Daph. To think of something so great, and execute it flawlessly? I'm proud of them. Yes, they really love me, and I really love them too. I can't believe they picked *Amelie*. They know it makes me cry every time.

Yes, yes, laugh it up, tissues in my sleeve, but Daphne warned me to bring some, and I didn't want to bring out the box because the tissues would get cold. This way, they were warm against my skin and didn't irritate my nose or eyes. You know, old ladies have very good reasons for everything they do, even if young, able-bodied men can't discern why. I always think of the Winchester house, do you know it?

Basically, the "mystery" of the house is no mystery at all, but a patriarchal, ableist view of a woman with health issues that loved architecture and had a fortune and a lifetime to spend indulging her affinities. "Why are these stairs so narrow?" Asks the able-bodied man. "Clearly she is trying to confuse the ghosts that haunt her, what a silly witch." Actually, bro, she suffered from vertigo, and narrow stairs made it less likely she would fall, but go off.

And so on. It's absolutely fascinating. I hope you look into it.

But yes, I've always been an old woman, for my entire life, in spirit. Of course, in standard time measurement, I'm a Pisces, and according to the internet, three years younger than you. Or were you hoping for a Harold and Maude situation? I can't blame you. Maude was hot.

I'm looking forward to getting out of this room, but I'm not looking forward to seeing my relatives. I think the wedding planner just hoodwinked me into a bridesmaid dress fitting for tomorrow at 2 p.m. Maybe with Daph, we can defeat her in person.

Rin is picking me up tomorrow, with Daph in tow (in a car, not on bikes, I assume) (I shouldn't assume). We'd better stop for meat pies and flat whites. What about you? Do you need a ride to the Billingstead? It's just a few minutes down the road from the cottage, I'm sure Rin would be happy to drop you off. Let me know.

Fingers crossed our tests are negative tonight. I also need something to go right.

Later,

Mattie

***

Text Message
  between Matalina, Corinne, and Daphne
  3:00 p.m.

Daphne:

> you asked about Raphael's relationship with Edie. There's a new interview with her. We've already talked to the boys and they confirm she's lying. But that doesn't mean you have to see it.

Matalina:

> Raphael told me there was a video out there and asked me not to watch it, and now I'm starting to freak out because I'm worried it's something really bad.

> Serial killers' neighbors describe them as quiet and nice, wouldn't expect him to kill anybody. Rapists' friends are always shocked, there's no way he would ever, the girl must be lying. But they do, these men do, and everyone is fooled, so how do we know he didn't do whatever she says he did?

Corinne:

> Do you want us to tell you what she's saying?

Matalina:

> If she's saying that he abused her, then yes. I don't want him to be that guy, but if he is, I need to know so I can block him and avoid him and try to forget this whole thing ever happened.

Corinne:

> That's not it. Unless you count breaking her heart when they split.

Matalina:

> Ok. So now I'm more confused. In your opinions, can I trust him?

Corinne:

I want to say yes. Luke says he knows for a fact that she's lying, but won't tell us how. Says it's personal and he can't break Raph's trust in him.

Daphne:

I believe the boys. Among all the gossip I've absorbed, Raph's coworkers appreciate his professionalism, he treats people kindly, never heard any rumors about bad behavior.

When he dated Edie, in their pictures together, he looks miserable, always leaning away from her. So the brevity of their relationship wasn't surprising. He didn't look angry with her. Exasperated, like it was an obligation and not something he chose.

Corinne:

Maybe his publicist or agent or whatever put him up to it. I don't remember hearing about him dating very frequently.

Daphne:

He just seemed like a private person, is the impression I got.

Matalina:

And then he dated Edie, and broke up, and she's turned it into the opposite of private.

Daphne:

She's been saying for a while that they're just taking a break, but he hasn't issued ANY public statement about it since the break-up.

Matalina:

He doesn't want anything to do with her, but he said he has people taking care of it now.

Corinne:

Luke said he's kept her as a friend on different sites so he can monitor what she says about Raph. She's been DMing him, trying to get to Raph through him.

Daphne:

gross.

Matalina:

Yeah. He's said before that he's had incidents where he was harassed or even assaulted, but no one takes that seriously because he's a man and "should like the attention."

Daphne:

GROSS!

Corinne:

What the fuck?

Matalina:

He also didn't give any specifics, but I got the impression that Edie manipulated him.

Daphne:

Now that I 100% believe. Lots of women she worked with have said that about her.

Matalina:

I don't want to dismiss another woman's claims. I'm not a part of that industry and I know it's a big problem.

Corinne:

I don't think that's the case here, Mats.

Daphne:

> You're concerned about that because you're a decent person and know that that happens a lot, but Rin's right.

Matalina:

> All right. Yeah. I feel like I'm taking a leap of faith here.

> Going to take a shower before "evening," so I'm all clean when they come to take my snot away for science.

Daphne:

> Good luck!

Corinne:

> Text us when you know the results.

Matalina:

> I will. Thanks for looking out for me. Love you both.

***

Dear Mattie,

Just got swabbed. I'm glad they did it before dinner, so I can get the taste of it out of my brain. I think it's probably too chilly to eat outside, so I'll wait to have a celebration meal with you until breakfast. I am vibrating with excitement about getting out of here. I know the problems of real life are waiting for me on the outside, but for now, the idea of leaving this room forever is giving me a kind of high.

If I get out first, I'll wait on the sidewalk for you, so we can properly meet before going our—not separate ways, since they're in the same direction, but, before being separated for a few hours.

You'll be at the hotel at 2 p.m., apparently, hoodwinked or no, so I know where to find you then. Will you give me your schedule for the next few days?

I hope to confront Payton tomorrow afternoon. Well, "confront." I'm just looking for an explanation. He's been good to us in the past, and a part of me still wants him to have a real reason for everything he's done. Though I'm afraid that if he does, I won't quit.

Luke and I call it The Mattie Solution. We want to channel that courage to walk away from this soul-crushing project and take responsibility for all the dominoes that fall because of it. We've seen a wrong, and we want to do what's right.

So you don't have to encourage me to abandon my job. I'm way ahead of you.

I'd heard of the Winchester house and the mad woman who was cursed to have it under constant construction to keep haunting souls at bay. I thought it was an urban legend, but what you said makes much more sense. Affinity and accessibility, filtered through the lens of patriarchy.

I wouldn't say Maude was hot? I'm attracted to a lot of different kinds of people, but she doesn't do it for me. Did she keep tissues in her sleeves? Did she wear more layers than a historical romance heroine? These are the important questions.

Payton is sending a car for me tomorrow. As much as I want to spend more time with you, I have to shift into confrontation-mode before I get to the hotel so I'm prepared for what I have to do. If I spend the car ride enjoying your company, it'll affect my mood in a positive way, and I must be broody and irritated to face him. Part of the "don't like emotional confrontation, but am fine with physical confrontation." I have to psych myself up for it.

And if that means I get a private car in the process, so be it.

When you give me your schedule, be sure to tell me when and where you need me, and what you'd like me to wear. I have a suit but not a tuxedo. It might be impossible to get one on such short notice, and with more and more businesses closing because of the virus. Maybe that wedding planner has an extra tux too. Snoop around and see what you can find.

Yours,
Raphael

***

Text Message
between Matalina and Marjorie/mother
4:45 p.m.

Marjorie:

> Why did you tell Donna you aren't a bridesmaid? You made me look like an insane person.

Matalina:

> Because I told you I wasn't going to be a bridesmaid, so why would you lie to someone that I was?

Marjorie:

> We already had this conversation, Matalina.

Matalina:

> You're right, we did, it was the conversation where I told you that I wasn't going to be a bridesmaid.

Marjorie:

And I told you that you are. It's your brother's wedding. If we're lucky, he only gets one. And if your participation is required, it is literally the least you can do to put on a dress at no cost to you and spend a few hours pretending to care about this family. So just do it.

Matalina:

And when has Kyle ever done even the "least" he could do for me? I would say the least he could do is not invite the guy who made my school years a total nightmare. Or the least he could do is, barring that, NOT try to force me to interact with said guy.

Marjorie:

Everybody has to do things they don't like sometimes, Matalina. It's part of being a woman. You just smile through it and get it done. It's an absolute mystery why you're being so difficult about this. Nobody is asking for anything from you besides being here. We said we would pay for your room and airfare, all you have to do is show up, but apparently that's too difficult for you.

Matalina:

Once again, this isn't about money. I'm happy with my job and what I make, which I know is inconceivable to you because I don't have five homes and a mega-yacht, but it's true. This is about respect. Why would I spend time with people who don't respect me and never have? I'll attend the wedding, as I said I would, as a guest, and nothing more.

Marjorie:

What's it going to take, then? Do you want a car? An apartment? An apartment complex? I should have known you would do this, hold out for a better deal, see how much you can get out of your parents before doing the simplest thing they ask of you.

Matalina:

You're not even listening to me.

Marjorie:

A hundred grand. My final offer. You're going to stop whining, keep quiet, paste a smile on your face, and show up to every event this weekend. Daphne says you're bringing a date. He will also smile. If you make a fuss, the deal is off, and you will no longer be a part of this family. Don't bother responding to me unless it's an apology.

***

Text Message between
Matalina and Raphael
5:17 p.m.

Matalina:

Don't mean to bother you, Raph. I know dinner should be here soon.

Raphael:

You never bother me.

Matalina:

You say that now.

Raphael:

I'll say it later, too. Again and again.

Matalina:

Ug, that makes me sound tedious.

Raphael:

Never tedious. What's on your mind?

Matalina:

Just got into an argument with my mother.

Raphael:

Do you want a distraction, or do you want to talk about it?

Matalina:

Maybe advice? I'm starting to wonder if things are really as bad as I made them out to be.

Raphael:

Well, you have friends who care about you and want to protect you, and they're saying don't go. It's not worth it. They're saying it IS as bad as you think it is. And now, your mother texts you, and you're full of doubt again. She's manipulating you. And that is something I do know about.

Matalina:

I feel the way I feel about things, and I make decisions based on that, but then the people I'm supposed to trust tell me I'm remembering things wrong, or my feelings are wrong, and, yeah, I doubt myself again. Like, my mother, of all people, I should be able to trust her.

Raphael:

Before meeting you, I would agree that mothers should be trusted, because family. But you're right. Family isn't blood. It's heart. It's the people setting you up for success and bringing you vibrators when you're stuck in isolation for two weeks, risking fines and arrest. The ones who call you on your bullshit, but also help you get through it. Family doesn't manipulate you or treat you like shit, those are the traits of your enemies. Who do you believe more, your mother or Daphne and Rin?

Matalina:

We both know the answer to that.

Raphael:

And if you texted one of them with this dilemma, what would they say?

Matalina:

That my memories and feelings aren't wrong. That I need to trust my gut. That I can't trust my relatives to do the right thing by me.

Raphael:

Do you want to text them now, to bolster your resolve?

Matalina:

You've done a pretty good job of it.

Raphael:

Thanks. I try. So what are you going to do? You want to do all the events and dinners, cool, tell me where to be. You want to do just the wedding ceremony? Also good. You want to skip the whole damn thing, wedding included? I have some ideas of what we can do instead.

Matalina:

I would love to hear your ideas. I would also love to make a decision and stick to it without doubting myself every moment until this weekend is over. But I don't think that will happen. All this new stress makes me feel so disconnected, from my body, especially. It's weird, I almost feel like I'm dissolving. I have to wrap up tight to contain myself.

Raphael:

It would be an honor and a pleasure to wrap you up tight.

Matalina:

With luck, we'll be released from this prison tomorrow, and then we can entertain all your good ideas. You said earlier that today has been a terrible day for you, and now I join you in that sentiment.

Raphael:

It wasn't all bad. I got to have lunch with you.

Matalina:

That part was good, it's true.

Raphael:

And we get our results at some point tonight. But you're right, overall it wasn't a great day. Hopefully tonight will be better.

Matalina:

Thanks for being the voice of reason. I have to get some paperwork emailed in the next half hour, so, I'm going to disappear for a bit. Let me know when your test results are back.

Raphael:

You too. I'll pass you a note.

*****

Auckland Grand Eastview Hotel

Dear MATALINA REDGRAVE,

Congratulations, your final test result for the Covid-19 coronavirus is NEGATIVE.

Your check-out time is 11:00 a.m. Be ready 10 minutes before your check-out time.

THERE IS NO CHANGE IN PROCEDURE until you check out tomorrow morning. Temperature checks are still required, as is door protocol and distance guidelines on the balconies.

At the time noted above, you will be collected from your room by a nurse and escorted to the lobby, and you MUST PROPERLY WEAR THE MASK PROVIDED TO YOU until you leave the building. Make sure you bring all of your belongings with you. You are invited to keep the basket of cleaning supplies we provided you with when you arrived. Anything left in the room will be quarantined and/or sanitized, and we cannot guarantee we'll be able to return it to you.

Upon check-out, you will receive documentation from the New Zealand Ministry of Health, Manatū Hauora, that you have completed the 14-day quarantine for incoming non-native travelers and are CLEARED FOR TRAVEL within the country.

Thank you again for your participation in this 14-day quarantine. We appreciate you taking the time to ensure the health and safety of yourself, your loved ones, and the people of Aotearoa, and we hope you enjoyed your stay.

Please accept this coupon code for 20% off your rate when you book a room at the Auckland Grand Eastview Hotel. This code expires one year after your check-out date tomorrow.

Ngā mihi nui,

The Staff of the Auckland Grand Eastview Hotel

***

Text Message between
Matalina, Corinne, and Daphne
7:32 p.m.

Matalina:
NEGATIVE!

Daphne:
by Odin's beard!

Corinne:
Excellent! We will get to hug you tomorrow!

Matalina:
I'm so happy, I'm crying.

Corinne:
aww, Mattie. Do you know what time you check out?

Matalina:
It says 11 a.m.

Corinne:
We'll be there. Meet you outside the front doors.

Matalina:
Are you picking me up in a car or on bikes?

Daphne:
oooo Rin-Rin, we should!

Corinne:

CAR. She has luggage, Daph. Can't carry luggage on a bicycle.

Daphne:

not with that attitude

Matalina:

I have to tell Raphael

Daphne:

go, girl!

Corinne:

Yeah, don't let us keep you. See you at 11!

***

Auckland Grand Eastview Hotel

Dear RAPHAEL CALLAN,

Congratulations, your final test result for the Covid-19 coronavirus is NEGATIVE.

Your check-out time is 11:15 a.m. Be ready 10 minutes before your check-out time.

THERE IS NO CHANGE IN PROCEDURE until you check out tomorrow morning. Temperature checks are still required, as is door protocol and distance guidelines on the balconies.

At the time noted above, you will be collected from your room by a nurse and escorted to the lobby, and you MUST PROPERLY WEAR THE MASK PROVIDED TO YOU until you leave the building. Make sure you bring all of your belongings with you. You are invited to keep the basket of cleaning supplies we provided you with when you arrived. Anything left in the room will be quarantined and/or sanitized, and we cannot guarantee we'll be able to return it to you.

Upon check-out, you will receive documentation from the New Zealand Ministry of Health, Manatū Hauora, that you have completed the 14-day quarantine for incoming non-native travelers and are CLEARED FOR TRAVEL within the country.

Thank you again for your participation in this 14-day quarantine. We appreciate you taking the time to ensure the health and safety of yourself, your loved ones, and the people of Aotearoa, and we hope you enjoyed your stay.

Please accept this coupon code for 20% off your rate when you book a room at the Auckland Grand Eastview Hotel. This code expires one year after your check-out date tomorrow.

Ngā mihi nui,

The Staff of the Auckland Grand Eastview Hotel

***

Text Message
   between Raphael and Luke
   7:40 p.m.

Raphael:

Test is negative. I'll be there tomorrow. Can you tell the PA my check-out time is 11:15 a.m.? I don't have the energy to deal with them.

Luke:

Great news, bro. I'll text them. And I'll be waiting for you at the Billingstead, so text when you get there.

Raphael:

Thanks. Gotta go tell Mattie.

Luke:

wink wink gotcha

***

Raphael,
  Negative!!

***

M—
  Negative.
  —R

PART TWO

Thursday, April 2, 2020
Evening

Mattie held the scrap of paper in her hands, the one word neatly printed in Raphael's compact handwriting. Negative. She smoothed the word with her thumb and forefinger, the paper identical to the one she had slipped under their doors moments before. In fact, she hadn't even straightened up from leaning over to deliver it when Raphael's response slid over. He must have been standing, still, on the other side, holding the "negative" she had sent him in her own embarrassingly messy script.

Her stomach did a little flip. Raphael was just two locks away, and they were both cleared to leave isolation. A week ago, he said that he stopped himself from opening the sliding door to his balcony before he was allowed to, because he had to hope that he would be able to do it legally later in the day. *This is different*, she told herself, reaching for the deadbolt. *This is the moment we've been hoping for.*

She paused, fingers brushing the cold lock. Recklessness was an old friend, though not a good one, and never when it came to her relationships. This week had changed her. Maybe it was the isolation, maybe the uncertainty and frightening novelty of the spreading illness, maybe the freedom waiting for her on the other side of her brother's wedding or the terror of needing to confront her most dangerous bully.

Most likely, it was all these things that convinced her to turn her back on the caution that had kept her heartbreak-free but alone.

She had fallen in love with Raphael Callan. It had taken, if she were honest with herself, a few minutes at most. It had taken a little longer to let herself be vulnerable and believe he might feel something similar for her. And they had never even touched.

An injustice she was ready to amend.

***

Raphael stood before the closed door, reading Mattie's one-word note. Neither of them had caught the virus. They were cleared to leave isolation. Sure, according to the letter from the hotel, safety protocols were supposed to be followed through tomorrow morning. But what was supposed to change between now and then? How could either of them actually be at risk if they opened the doors between their rooms and spent some time less than two meters apart?

He sighed and ran a hand through his hair. It had been a shitty day, capping a shitty week. He didn't want to think about how much worse it would have been if he hadn't met Mattie, if she hadn't indulged his archaic idea to exchange hand-written letters, if she hadn't been the brilliant, funny, understanding woman she was. Something about her made him want to open up, display who he really was.

They were so close. She was probably still just on the other side of her door. This week hadn't been good to her, either. They had done everything right, and if they continued to do so, they wouldn't see each other until they left the hotel late the next morning, and they wouldn't be alone together until who knew when? He started to talk himself out of it, the idea rapidly taking shape in his head. But it was no use. He was going to be bold.

Still holding the note from Mattie, Raphael unlocked his door and swung it open.

***

When Mattie opened her door, Raphael had already opened his and was standing there, about to knock. Three feet away. The closest he'd ever been. He looked at her in surprise, then relaxed into his easy smile, the one that made him famous, the one that dazzled and charmed. And it was genuine, reaching eyes that were so dark they were nearly black, flecks of amber and gold ringing his pupils.

Her stomach did that flip again, the butterflies making their way farther south.

Raphael took a step forward and was inside her room. Two feet away now. The new closest he'd ever been. So close, she could see the smallest wrinkles in his long-sleeved, navy-blue shirt, collar of the black tee beneath it peeking out; she could almost read the rivets on his jeans, the weave of his dark socks. A paper fluttered from his hand and she recognized the note she had slid to him moments before. He took another step.

"Mattie Redgrave," he said, looking her over, his voice smooth and deep. She still couldn't say what specific accent it was, besides a general English to her American ears, but he spoke with a precision that matched his handwriting. His eyes found hers again and his smile deepened. She reached up to push her glasses back up her nose, forgetting she'd put in contacts earlier, and hit herself in the face instead. She tried turning the motion into smoothing her hair back, but the laughter in Raphael's eyes told her he wasn't fooled. Not knowing what to do with her hands, she crossed them over her stomach.

"Mattie Redgrave, I think you've taken this layers-of-clothing thing too far."

"I—" She glanced down. She had forgotten what she'd put on and didn't have the focus to try to count every piece now. "I wanted the fresh air, but it was cold, so I—"

"You decided to wear every piece of clothing you brought."

Mattie raised an eyebrow. "I didn't know you'd be visiting, and I didn't know it would bother you."

"On the contrary. I'm intrigued." He took another step forward. Less than a foot away.

"It's nice to finally meet you face to face," she said. Her gut was still jumpy and sensitive to his voice, his proximity, his heat, but she was becoming more comfortable being in his physical presence.

"I think we should kiss," Raphael said, staring at her lips. She glanced at his—full and slightly parted, in a sea of dark stubble she wanted scratching against her. As she took a breath to answer, he brought his hands up to her face, cupping her cheek on one side, his palm soft and cool. He moved a stray strand of hair away from her eyes and cradled the back of her head, thumb stroking her ear. Mattie was so overwhelmed by the feeling of their first touch, her eyes closed involuntarily so she could concentrate on the sensation.

"Um," she said. "I—words."

Raphael chuckled. "You only need one. Either one. I'll respect your decision."

"Is this not still illegal?" She teased.

"No." He leaned in a little more, close enough that Mattie could smell him, coffee and cedar and incense. "It's the second most mildly forbidden thing we can do."

She tilted her head in invitation and raised herself up on her toes as he closed the distance between them and softly brushed his lips against hers.

"Still need that word," he murmured.

"Yes," she said.

Raphael pressed their lips together, holding Mattie in place as they kissed. It was slow, and deep, and she indulged in the feel of his mouth and hands against her. She tried to let in every sensation, their sliding lips, his soft breath a sigh, scent of soap from his cheek, the press of each finger pad from the thumb on her cheekbone to the rest across the back of her head, all of it competing with each other and with every excited thought bursting through her consciousness.

"I'm doing something wrong," he whispered, pulling away. "You aren't touching me."

Mattie blinked her eyes open, some of the turmoil within her dissipating. She repeated to herself what he said. It took a moment to remember her arms were still crossed over her stomach.

A gentleman, she thought. *I can be a gentleman, too.* "You haven't given me permission." She should have said something before they even started kissing, but, there was a lot going on. Raphael tilted back and looked into her eyes. "You told me how other people don't respect your boundaries," Mattie continued. "And I want you to know I don't feel entitled to your body. I respect your autonomy, and you're safe with me. So I was waiting for you to ask."

He gave a huff of a laugh and rested his forehead against hers, hands still holding her face. "What a thing to say," he murmured. "You can touch me. I wish you would. I think I need it. To know I'm still here."

Anticipation jolted through Mattie. *He wishes I would touch him. I've wanted to, and he wants me to, how did I get so lucky?* "How?" She asked, the thrill of his permission flustering her. "I mean, how do you want me to touch you?"

"Any way you want." He swayed them slowly, and the movement comforted her. "If I don't like it, I'll say, and I know you'll stop. I expect you to tell me the same, if you don't like something, and I'll stop. Is that okay?"

Mattie nodded and reached for him, one hand on his waist, the other against his chest. She pulled him closer, and Raphael inhaled against her. "You smell like a gardener come inside to bake," he said. "Green and fresh, tilled earth or leaves after it rains. Then coconut and cardamom."

"I assure you I've done neither gardening nor baking any time recently."

"So you just naturally smell like tending to what you love?"

She squeezed him tight in answer, and he responded in kind.

They stood like that, swaying, gazing into each others' eyes, fingers tracing lazy paths across fabric and skin and hair. It was new, to be touched, to be held, to hold someone. Thirteen days without it hadn't seemed like enough time to crave it, but in reality, it had been much longer. Mattie thought Raphael might have been feeling similarly, though where she had foregone touch because she needed to feel safe first, based on how he described his last relationship, Raphael needed to feel respected.

"This still all right?" He murmured.

Mattie laughed and sniffled. "It's kind of emotional. I'm feeling a lot, and I don't know if it's appropriate."

"It is," he said, squeezing her a little. "I told you I wanted to hold you to me. Do you want to stand like this until you sort it out?" She shook her head against him.

"Yes, but I'm not sure that's going to happen, no matter how long we stand here."

"Then, as I said, I do have some ideas about what we can do." Raphael ducked his head down to kiss the side of her neck, beneath her jaw.

"I like your ideas," she said, closing her eyes again at his touch.

He smiled and pressed his lips against her ear. He took her robe's collar between his fingers, following its edge around her shoulder. Powder-blue with ruffles, covering nearly every inch of her, falling open like a duster. Beneath it was a high-necked black blouse. And a sweater.

"Mattie, honestly," he said, pulling back to look at her clothing. "How many layers are you actually wearing, because I think I count three tops so far, and somehow, if you told me there were more, it wouldn't surprise me." Mattie tugged at his shirts.

"Well, how many are you wearing?"

"Two. Just two. The proper amount."

"I am also wearing the proper amount," she answered. "Which, for me, as I've told you, means Victorian widow."

A blush crept into her cheeks as she thought about how much she'd like him to undress her. Their eyes met again, and she saw a hint of mischief this time.

"Cheeky," he growled. "If I remember correctly, you also wrote that each layer is a mystery."

"Yes?" She drawled. He grasped her collar on the other side and smoothed down both sides with his palms.

"That you're a walking secret."

"I did write that."

"So," he said, kissing one cheek, then the other. "I think that you should let me solve those mysteries. Reveal that secret."

The butterflies in her stomach became something more substantial, a flustered beast, trying to rock her hips toward him. She licked her lips. "How do you propose to solve it?"

He slipped his hands beneath the shoulders of her robe, between its soft material and the next ridiculous piece of clothing below it.

"For each item I remove, you tell me a secret."

"That hardly seems fair," she protested, blush deepening. "If I'm supposed to do the same for you, that means you only need to tell me, like, three secrets, while I tell you—"

"A dozen?" He finished, smiling. "I wasn't planning to reciprocate, anyway."

Mattie barked a laugh. "Oho, I see how it is."

"I've already told you a few," he said. "And I don't tie secrets to my clothes. That's a Mattie thing."

She sighed, feigning exasperation, and held him tighter. "I guess it wouldn't hurt to shed a few layers, since the balcony door is closed and it's getting much warmer in here."

That was all the permission he needed. He slid the robe off her shoulders. She let go of his waist and brought her arms to her sides to help him. When he leaned over to free the last of it, he brought his lips to hers again and gathered the silk against her hands, pinning them to her back as she opened her mouth for his tongue.

If their first kiss embodied the slow romance that she had always wanted with a partner, this kiss was the desperate, unleashed desire of a lover gone away too long. She pushed her body into his, letting the last of her nervousness slip away so her desire could expand. It filled her stomach and skin, it filled her head, it filled the room and time and she was nothing but desire and infinity.

A little noise escaped her mouth when he pulled away and she had to return to the earth. Mattie cursed at herself for wearing so many fucking pieces of clothing. Too much fabric between their bodies.

Raphael's gaze was dark, his mouth open as he stared at her lips.

"I have another proposal," he said, his voice husky.

"Tell me."

His breath hitched and he closed his eyes in almost a wince. *Oh, I know the feeling*, Mattie thought, thrilled that she could spark desire in him the way he did with her. Raphael swallowed before opening his eyes again.

"Whenever removing an item of clothing reveals skin, I kiss it."

"I am wearing too many fucking pieces of clothing," Mattie whispered angrily. Raphael nudged her nose with his own.

"I thought you were wearing the proper amount."

"Not for this. Not today," she growled. He laughed. She attempted a laugh, but it was half-hearted, steeped in frustration.

"Let me?" He asked. She exhaled slowly.

"Yes, absolutely. But hurry."

"No." He kissed her mouth again, running his tongue over her lips before removing the robe from against her hands. Free to touch him again, Mattie slid her palms across his chest and held the back of his head, running her fingers through his thick, silky hair. *Softer than I even imagined*, she thought. Raphael held her by the waist and shook the robe in his other hand.

"Robe off," he said, tossing it toward the desk chair. "You owe me one secret."

This was going to take forever. Mattie sighed and leaned against his chest.

"Okay." It couldn't be something too salacious. And this wasn't the time to get into all her troublemaking with her fellow spies. "Rin was my first kiss. Actually, we got married."

Raphael raised an eyebrow. "What?"

"I told her I liked her bracelet, and she made me one, and then we kissed, and then we got married. We were six years old. Believe it or not, it didn't last. After about three hours, we realized we were better as friends and got divorced."

"I'm shocked," Raphael said, giving her a half-smile. She shrugged.

"We've been best friends ever since. And as a bonus, to this day, my mother blames us for 'awakening' Daphne's sapphic desires with our homosexual wedding. Daphne, at the time, was four. To be clear."

"If anyone has the power to turn women gay, it would be you."

"That is an unacceptable insult to the lesbian community."

Raphael inclined his head in agreement. "I meant no offence. I only meant to comment on how anyone would find you irresistible."

"Irresistible, hmm?" The most beautiful man she'd ever seen, and he was calling her irresistible? Raph bit his lip and nodded. "Does that mean we'll be taking off these clothes a little faster, then?"

"Absolutely not."

It wasn't like Mattie didn't have the ability to be patient. He'd just gotten her riled up, and she riled herself up, with expectation and longing, until she felt tight enough to snap. For over a week, this thing she wanted—this person, these feelings, this experience—occupied so much of her time (which she'd had in abundance) that it had begun to haunt her. Now he was here, they both felt it, it was happening, and she didn't want to rush through it, not really. Despite fantasizing about it all week, she now felt overwhelmed.

She had closed her eyes and stood very still. Any other lover would have said something by now, trying to fill the quiet she needed to orient herself. As she wondered how long he would give her to emotionally regroup, a hopeful voice within her whispered, *all the time I need*. A few moments later, Mattie opened her eyes and looked at him.

"I'm ready," she said. Raphael smiled and smoothed the hair behind her ear.

"Whatever you want to do, or not do."

"This. I like you, and I like this. It feels like a physical version of writing letters to each other, if that makes any sense. I'm not sure it does."

He held her a little tighter. "And slow is acceptable?"

She shrugged. "You're not going anywhere, and you're choosing this, so there's no reason for me to be afraid that this opportunity will disappear."

Sunset had come and gone, and the darkness in the room was held at bay by the small desk lamp, radiating just enough light that Raphael could see the resolve, the passion, and the desire in Mattie's eyes. Hopefully he didn't also see the ever-present worry that she wasn't good enough. He bent to kiss her, soft lips yielding beneath his own, meeting him in a languid dance that sent shivers to the farthest places in her body.

Mattie slid her hands over his shoulders, down his chest, to his waist, where she found the hem of his shirts and pushed both up a few inches.

"This next?" She asked. He shook his head, their noses bumping.

"One more of yours, I think, or I'll be naked before we get to your socks." He reached for the top button of her black cardigan. "There's at least one blouse beneath this."

She gave him an enigmatic smile but didn't answer. As he unbuttoned her, Mattie caressed the sides of his waist beneath his shirts, then lowered her hands reluctantly so he could push the cardigan off her shoulders. He kissed her lips again as he freed it from her hands, and threw it in the same direction as the robe.

"That's another secret," he said, eyeing the sheer blouse that somehow still covered everything the other two pieces of clothing did.

"Right," Mattie said, a nervous titter escaping her lips. "I'm trying to think of things to tell you, but the whole you-taking-off-my-clothes thing makes it difficult to concentrate."

"All part of the plan." He gently swayed their bodies. "It doesn't have to be a serious secret."

Mattie nodded thoughtfully. "I have a stupid long-term stress that you'll learn soon enough if we end up, um, maintaining our friendship after this weekend."

"'Maintaining our friendship,' she says. As if I weren't standing here making out with her and removing her clothes in the most frustrating and romantic way possible."

She laughed. "You know what I mean. I don't want to assume."

"I think you should assume."

Mattie's stomach twitched with the thrill of her desires coming true. "Is that your secret?"

"What, that I adore you? If you think that's a secret, I've done a shit job of communicating. Go on, then. What's this long-term stress?"

Mattie blushed. "Well, now I want to talk about how you adore me."

"Later," he said. "We have time. Jumper secret first."

Yes, get the secrets over with quickly so you can lick from his jaw to his belly button. Her blush had reached its vibrant limit, though her body kept sending out pulses of heat. "You told me you weren't good at budgeting because you were raised in a family that was well off. I have the same problem. I'm getting by, but it's stressful. My parents ask if I need money, and I say no because I don't want to give them the satisfaction of knowing I need them."

Raphael kissed her forehead. "That must be incredibly frustrating. But of course you're sticking to your principles. I wouldn't expect anything less." Mattie nodded and tugged on the bottom of his shirts. Why was she giving him more than one-word answers when they could both be naked by now?

Mattie caught his eye and gave him a mischievous grin, grabbed the hems of both his shirts, and pulled them over his head in one motion. They caught at his elbows and he doubled over with laughter.

"Mattie, for the love of—that's both my shirts."

"Yes," she said, helping him shimmy out of the sleeves and tossing them into the growing pile of clothes. "I have been patient, but I need to feel your skin. I need your bare chest and arms and stomach. I need to touch you, and kiss you."

He sighed and buried his hands in her hair. She let her eyes wander over him, from the stubble on his jaw, to the soft hollow of his throat, across his shoulder and down his chest to his stomach, all so close. Then she let her fingers follow the same trail. His skin was smooth, its tawniness looking even darker beneath her pale fingers. She outlined his clavicle, the slight definition of muscles across his torso, then leaned over and pressed her lips against the middle of his chest.

He sucked in a breath and ran a hand down her back, pressing her to him as she left a trail of kisses over his heart. Feeling where her shirt tucked into her pants, he grabbed a handful of her flimsy blouse and pulled it out, recruiting his other hand to free the rest of it.

"Buttons," Mattie breathed.

Raphael paused. "Don't you want a secret? Or two? That was two shirts." Mattie shook her head. "You don't care about my secrets at all, do you? You just want to get my clothes off as quickly as possible."

"You caught me," she said. "Also, you said you didn't tie secrets to your clothes. That's a Mattie thing."

"So I did," he murmured, starting with the bottom button. "Wait. Is this even a shirt? I can see right through it. Do you have even more shirts on beneath this?"

"Wouldn't you like to know." She kissed him again. They kissed as he unfastened each button, her hands trailing over his slender fingers, his forearms, up his biceps and shoulders, to rest again in his dark hair until he got to the top button, when she brought her hands back the way she came and let him remove the sheer material.

"For the purposes of actual clothing, this isn't a shirt," he decided, gently throwing it with the others and glancing at the opaque, long-sleeved black blouse she had worn beneath it. Still covering the same amount of skin as everything else he'd already taken off her. "But for our purposes tonight, it counts as a secret."

Mattie bit her lip. It was getting easier to think of things to share with him. "I'm scared of this virus."

It would have been impossible not to think about it since arriving, or, really, since deciding it was enough of a risk that they bought masks to wear on the plane. The entire point of their letter exchange was to distract from the reality of what brought them there and what awaited them once they left.

"I'm worried about what's going to happen next," she said.

He wasn't a scientist or a psychic, so Raphael had as many answers as Mattie did. He rubbed her arms—comforting each other was the best they could do.

"We'll do whatever we can to protect ourselves," he said. "You stay cooped up in that cottage with Rin and Daph, and I'll meet you there as soon as I can untangle myself from this project. We'll isolate again, but at least we can be together this time. Other than that?" He shrugged. "Follow the science." Mattie nodded against him.

"It scares me too," he added. "But I think we're in one of the best places we can be. New Zealand is taking it seriously. If we had been in England or the US, it might have been different."

"And we wouldn't have had the opportunity to become pen pals."

"Pen pals," Raphael mumbled dismissively. At the small of her back, he bunched a handful of her shirt in his grasp and tugged. Mattie squeaked and jumped away from him.

"It doesn't work like that!" She said, reaching behind her.

He held both hands in the air. "I'm sorry, I did the same thing with the last shirt, and that was fine?"

"It's attached," Mattie said, adjusting herself. Raphael's brows creased in confusion.

"Attached to what?"

"Well, itself. It'll have to be, um, pants next. Or socks." Mattie might dress like a prude, but she at least knew how a bodysuit worked.

He nodded slowly and reached for her hips, still frowning at her shirt. "You'll see in a minute what I mean," she assured him. His lips twitched in a smile.

He let his fingers slip just beneath the waist of her pants and meet at the buttons in front. "At least we'll finally expose some skin."

Mattie couldn't help a bubble of laughter. "Oh, that's cute that you think so."

His eyes shot up at her. "Matalina Redgrave." He tugged on the front of her pants. "Matalina Redgrave, are you telling me you're wearing pants beneath your pants? Of all the—" He grabbed her around the waist and lifted her up, muttering under his breath as he deposited her on the bed.

"You're just going to have to find out," she said, smiling up at him. At least she was sitting on the bed now. Progress.

He growled and shook his head, pushing her to lie back while he hastily undid the buttons, grabbed the cuffs, and slid the pants off. He let them fall to the floor between them.

"Tights," he said, rubbing his chin in disbelief. The shirt made more sense now, as it looked more like a leotard. Tugging on it would have wedged it up between her legs. "Give me a secret. Quickly."

"Oh now you want to hurry," she teased, sitting up. "Yes, tights and pants, I was cold." Her demeanor changed slightly as she decided what to reveal, so she said it quickly before she could change her mind.

"I still want my relatives to be my family. That's why it's been so difficult to decide what to do about the bridesmaid thing. Why I can stand up for what's right and walk away from any other situation, but this one..." She trailed off.

Raphael kneeled before her, placing his hands on her knees, and kissed her cheek. Before she could say anything else, he reached down and pulled off one of her socks.

"And?" He asked, tossing it on the pile of their clothes.

Mattie swallowed, not meeting his eyes. "And I'm afraid that, even once I decide to totally cut them off, I will eventually bend to them again. Especially if they're kind. I'm afraid I'll forget my resolve. I'll forget that I deserve better than the best they're able to treat me."

He waited in case she wanted to say more, then kissed her other cheek, took off her other sock, threw it to its mate, and waited.

She sighed. "And the fact that I want abusive people to think well of me is one of the things I hate about myself."

Raphael rubbed the tops of her thighs and leaned in to kiss her on the lips this time. "I think you're entirely too hard on yourself," he whispered. "You deserve better. Better than how they've treated you, and better than how you're treating yourself. I want to drag you into the sunlight and kiss you beneath the sky until that annoying feeling of inadequacy disappears. But I can't wait all those hours until sunrise."

When his hands paused over her knees, she grasped his wrists to hold him there, a solid support for when her emotions threatened to sweep her away. *I want that too*, she thought, but couldn't say, as though naming that feeling of not being good enough had summoned it.

"Your socks, next, I think," she murmured.

"Not my jeans?"

"Not before socks. Otherwise, you'll be in underwear and socks, and that bothers me."

He ducked his head in a halfhearted attempt to hide his laugh. "That's fair," he said, shifting back to sit on the floor and bring his feet between him and Mattie. She released his wrists and reached down, pulling off a sock in each hand.

"Let me tell you something now," he said, eyes following one sock, then the other, flying in a gentle arc to land beside the other clothes. "So you don't feel like the only one sharing. Is that okay?"

Mattie's gut flooded with warmth, her heart opening a little more. She cupped Raphael's cheeks and brought him in for another slow kiss. "I want to hear anything you want to tell me." She sighed dramatically. "However long that might take."

"I'll try to keep it brief." He paused, as though assembling his thoughts into something coherent—a practice Mattie was very familiar with.

"If I could give up fame without giving up my career, I would do it in a heartbeat. I love acting, but having to play the part of myself-as-celebrity every moment of every day is exhausting. Running to New Zealand for a secret, low-budget production where I can hide for a few months is a needed reprieve, but hardly a resolution."

Mattie gave him space to say more if he wanted, but when he didn't continue, she said, "I know something about that, you know. Not fame, obviously, but the weariness that compounds when you have to always wear a mask. You realize it isn't working and make changes slowly, or you let it reach a breaking point and let it break. I have experience, if not expertise, if there's anything I can do to help."

Raphael looked at her as though he had just figured something out. He reached up to run his thumb over her lower lip, staring at the place he caressed. "Maybe you know exactly how I feel. But for right now..." He slithered to standing and put a hand against Mattie's chest, pushing her back onto the bed as he drew up one leg, then the other, to straddle her. Her breath caught, and he grabbed beneath her armpits and dragged her farther up onto the bed.

"Now," he started, knees against her hips. He ran his hands down her arms, over the soft fabric of her long-sleeved shirt, then plucked at its high collar around her neck. "Why am I afraid you're going to break into a tap dance at any moment?"

She laughed. "It's not a leotard, it's a bodysuit."

"With tights," he added. "But sure, bodysuit, aptly named because it is still covering your entire body. I have removed twenty pieces of your clothing and have uncovered *no* skin whatsoever, you mummified schoolmarm, you impertinent cocoon, you burrowing winter mammal, you—you cocktease."

Mattie's jaw dropped. "I beg your pardon!"

"Well, you can't have it. How do I get this off?" He slid his hands behind her, looking for a zipper or buttons on the back, and rolled her to the side to see for himself when he couldn't find any. He held up one of her arms and then the other, looking for the secret to peeling it off of her.

"Snaps!" She said, breathless from laughing. "There are snaps!"

"What? Where?"

"In the crotch, where they always are."

He looked up, searching her eyes for a hint that she was teasing him. Finding none, his smile took on a mischievous tilt.

"Oh, really?" He purred. Shifting back to sit on his heels—and her legs—his gaze wandered down to the last place he thought to look. "Did you want to? Or did you want me to...?"

"You can," she said, still smiling. She brought a hand down to his knee. "I trust you."

Without waiting for more, Raphael slipped his hands beneath the bodysuit to grasp her hips, and leaned over to kiss her stomach through the fabric. Mattie gave a little sigh and ran her fingers through his hair. He stayed against her another moment, like he was collecting himself, before sitting up and lifting the edge of the garment away from her body and following it down between her legs, where he kept it pulled away from her. He shifted one of his legs between hers, giving him the space to move without touching her, and she looked at him expectantly.

"Not yet," he said, voice husky and eyes dark. He flicked open the two snaps—easily, once he knew where to find them—and pushed the freed fabric up over her waist. The tights beneath still covered much of her stomach, so he adjusted his legs again to straddle her and pulled the bodysuit up and off as quickly as she had stripped him of his shirts. The tight collar stuck over her head, but the stretchiness of the material won out and popped off, static electricity sending strands of her hair in every direction.

Before she could smooth it out, Raphael threw the shirt to the floor and returned to her lips, pressing against her almost hard enough to bruise. His hands explored her skin, finally visible, finally touchable, and Mattie's stomach and lips and chest vibrated where he rested unobstructed against her. She moaned beneath him and snaked one hand into his hair, grasping, the other clutching against his back to hold him to her.

She hoped he would keep his promise to kiss every part of her as he uncovered it in his slow and methodical undressing. He kissed across her face, her neck, across her collarbone and over the strap of the black bra that would follow the rest of her clothing soon enough. He kissed down the softness of her inner arm to her wrist and palm, then mirrored his path down the other side of her.

Mattie's breath came faster, and Raphael looked up at her, mouth against her fingertips. She watched him, heavy-lidded, and nodded when he caught her gaze. He shifted again and started over at her lips, this time trailing straight down her neck, between her collarbones and down her chest. Only a thin strip of skin showed between the top of her black tights and the bottom of her bra, but it was so soft, and the heat of her body had kindled her scent, and he trailed his lips along this band of skin, his enthusiasm a testament of how he reveled in the feel of her.

"I—" Mattie said, breathless. "I've never been called a cocktease before."

Raphael paused in his devotion and glanced up.

"That counts as a secret," she told him.

He kissed her stomach one more time then shifted to meet her lips again. "Now you have," he said. "But I'll allow it." She laughed against his kiss and wiggled beneath his hips, finally in a position to feel how hard he'd become.

"Jeans?" She asked.

"Jeans," he agreed, scrambling up off the bed and removing them himself. Mattie glanced to see what he had on beneath his pants—she'd never understood how some women can just tell what a guy is wearing for underwear—and bit her lip at his dark blue boxer-briefs, his erection straining the expensive-looking material. "Tights?" He asked, kicking his pants away. Mattie nodded and reached for them, but Raphael stopped her.

"Ah, no," he said. "That's my job."

"But you just—"

He interrupted her with another kiss and removed her hands from the tights, replacing them with his own. He pulled them down a few inches and planted kisses across the newly exposed skin of her stomach until he reached the top of her dark underwear. Adjusting his grasp on the tights, so he wasn't holding an edge of the underwear too, Raphael peeled them off her legs. They caught at her ankles, and he knelt on the floor to untangle them.

As he grasped one of her heels, he leaned over and kissed her knee, running his other hand from her ankle to the back of her thigh, and she jumped. He smiled against her skin, kissed farther down her shin, slipped the tights off past her toes, and kissed the top of her foot. He repeated the process on her other leg, dropping the freed tights onto his pile of jeans.

Climbing back onto the bed, he kissed the tops of her thighs, just under her belly button, and ran his tongue between her breasts, back up to her lips. He let his hands wander and linger over her breasts, palming where her nipples made faint outlines against the smooth material. Mattie let out a little whimper, wrapping her arms around him tight, not wanting to let him go. He splayed out against her, arms circled around her—one hand in her hair, the other at her back—one leg between hers, and the hard length of his desire between them both.

"That's the last secret," he whispered. "So I want to request what it is."

"I'm wearing two more things," she said, disappointed she could still do math under these conditions.

"Knickers and bra don't count. Unless you want to tell me you have on another bra under this one? A thong beneath these briefs?"

Mattie shook her head.

"So," Raphael continued. "Maybe you were cold." He traced her lips with his forefinger. "But I suspect there's something more to it than that. Why so many layers, Mattie Redgrave?"

She stilled beneath him. A part of her mind told her this was too personal, all of it: she didn't need to share her secrets and fears with someone just because she wanted to sleep with him. But another part of her hoped he was sincere, that he wanted to share her burdens instead of watching her struggle with them alone.

If she told him she didn't want to answer, that she wanted to just get on with making out, or more, or whatever else he wanted to do, she knew he would agree. He wouldn't hold it against her. But he had found a way to get her to open up that didn't feel so awkward she was paralyzed, and there were more rewards for doing so than the physical ones she most anticipated.

She blew out a breath, the caress of Raphael's hands steadying her. "Are you ready?"

"I'm ready," he said. "I'm here. I've got you."

Just hearing that almost brought her to tears.

Mattie cleared her throat. "Society is not kind to people who don't fit into specific beauty standards. I know you run into this in your profession. You might have a director saying you need to bulk up or lose weight to fit the aesthetic of a role. But I encounter that in *every* aspect of just living my life. It is literally built into every facet of our society. I can be out walking, and people shout things at me, and anyone who witnesses it thinks it's acceptable because I'm not thin. It's such a casual thing to them. And that's after a childhood of being bullied ..." She trailed off.

Raphael's gaze hardened. "Fucking Spencer," he said.

"Yeah, Fucking Spencer," she agreed. "But also: the entire world."

"Well, fuck them too," he said. Mattie laughed without humor.

"Sure, I just have to live in it."

"There is nothing to ridicule you about," he said.

"Of course there is. I'm more comfortable in layers because my body is flawed."

It was Raphael's turn to laugh, though his sounded genuine. "It is absolutely not."

Mattie shook her head. "You're, you—you're just horny."

"Yes," he said. "And this body of yours, that you find so much fault with, is really doing it for me." He rocked them from side to side playfully.

"No, I mean, I'm soft. I'm—"

"You're the woman I've been falling for—and still am, by the way—without having seen you like this before. How could I, when you wear an entire wardrobe at once? But I've seen enough to guess at your shape, because my eyes work, and now I'm here, and we're very close to being naked, and you are stunning, and I want you. Believe me when I say I wouldn't be here if that wasn't the case."

Mattie wanted to believe him. Perhaps sensing that she was still upset, Raphael nuzzled his forehead against her temple, kissed her cheek, and wrapped himself around her protectively.

"My aim was to make this fun," he said, voice muffled in her hair. "I'm sorry I demanded you bare your secrets as well as your skin. I just want all of you. I've wanted all of you in a way I haven't felt..."

Mattie shook her head against him.

"It's not that bad," she said with a sigh. "Like I said, I just get emotional. The smallest thing could get me crying, and that doesn't mean I'm upset. It's just how I process things. It's just part of who I am."

He breathed her in, the scent of Mattie, the one that no one would be able to smell unless they got through all those layers. It was the secret for him alone that she kept against her skin. He held her tighter as he pressed his open mouth against her shoulder and grazed his teeth against her skin.

"Oh." Mattie pulled him closer. He made his way back to her lips and they were kissing again, a tangle of mouths and tongues and teeth and breaths. Her hands found their way down to his boxer-briefs and she played with the elastic band, not able to reach any farther. He shifted his hips to rub his cock against her leg, while his hand at her back found the clasps of her bra. Mattie wondered if he'd be able to undo it one-handed, but he pinched the line of hooks and eyes using his entire hand, massaged at it once, and they all fell open like a wonderful miracle.

Instead of quickly disentangling it from her, he moved slowly—their entire encounter had been slow, but their skin was touching now and they were kissing and there needed to be more time between baring emotional secrets and finding pleasure in each other. He slid his hand and forearm against her spine, his fingers wide to feel as much of her skin as possible, the muscles beneath, no clothing in his way. She sighed against him, and he kissed down her neck and shoulder again, this time pulling the bra strap aside so he could get to the skin beneath.

Raphael ran his tongue along the swell of her breasts still covered, though loosely, from the barely-attached bra, and brought both hands up to cup them, rubbing her nipples over the material with his thumbs. Mattie moaned and writhed beneath him.

"Off," she breathed. "Bra. Off." Raphael smiled and bit her lightly, then did as she demanded, tossing the bra over the side of the bed. Holding one breast firmly, he leaned over the other, watching Mattie's face as he kept his tongue flat and slowly licked her nipple. She twitched beneath him and grunted. He did it again, and again, before covering it with his mouth, sucking, swirling his tongue.

Her hands were everywhere, trying to grasp him, rocking her hips up against him, and he repeated his ministrations on the other side.

"God, Raphael," she said. "I have condoms."

He paused and pulled himself up to be face-to-face with her.

"And you want to use them?" He asked.

She nodded. "If we're going to—if you're going to be inside me, then yes."

He smiled and nipped at her nose. "That's what I meant. Do you want me inside you?"

"Absolutely," she said breathlessly, and pointed to the night-stand. "They're there."

Just out of reach. Raphael started to climb over her to get them. "Don't move," he said.

"Not going anywhere."

"Did you bring these in the hopes of meeting a dashing gentle-man such as myself?" He examined the box, frowning at it.

"They were included in the Great Tote Bag Adventure of Day 9. I didn't request them but I guess my friends know me better than I do. Are—are they ok?"

Maybe he doesn't like the brand, Mattie thought, noting his hesitation.

With a smile and a quick breath of a laugh, Raphael resumed his position straddling her, opened the box, and put it within reach. His arousal had waned, but seeing Mattie topless and enthusiastic seemed to bring him right back. "They're perfect. Remind me to thank them later." He smiled down at her, and her heart fluttered at how ridiculously handsome he was.

Taking advantage of their position, Mattie sat up and teased the elastic band at his hips before sliding her hands inside and around to his lower back. She hooked her thumbs over the top and pulled them down over his backside, the front still covering his erection, which poked into her stomach. He ran his hands through her hair and rocked into her, letting a groan escape his lips.

"One more secret," Mattie whispered, kissing his chest, testing how it felt to dig her fingers into his ass cheeks. His cock twitched against her and he exhaled sharply into her hair.

"Anything," he said. "Anything you want to know."

"One of mine. I want you to touch me."

"That's not a secret, love."

"I want to touch you. I want you, I just—I want all of you." There was desperation in her voice, and it matched Raphael's. He leaned down and covered her mouth with his own, at the same time lowering her down to lie on the bed. It was a hard and slow kiss that he ended by outlining her lips with his tongue and softly biting her lower lip.

"Stay put," he said. He jumped off the bed just long enough to take off his boxers. He bowed over her from where he stood, kissed her stomach, grasped her underwear, and finally, finally removed the last piece of her clothing.

Mattie looked at him, watched his face with all its focus on her. Raphael's eyes wandered over her. He reached down and grabbed the base of his cock, caressed the length to the slick tip, and pumped it twice. His breathing changed, heavy and needy. Kneeling between her legs, he pushed them farther apart to kiss her inner thigh. She shuddered and made a little noise, encouraging him. He licked, slowly, from her thigh to her vulva, where he planted a kiss just next to her slit.

"Can I touch you?" He asked, voice gravelly and low.

"Yes, god, please."

He kissed right in the middle of her, his tongue darting out inside her, before moving farther up to her clitoris. Mattie writhed against him, watching him between her legs, his tongue dancing and sliding against her, his fingers caressing her before one of them slid inside.

She was close already. She shuddered and closed her eyes, the pleasure building up and up, and remembered that the man whose mouth was against her, whose tongue and hand were working to bring her to orgasm, was Raphael fucking Callan. She glanced down at him again, and he caught her eye and moaned, the vibrations heightening the sensation, and she was lost.

She pushed against him, crying out, as her pleasure crested and pulsed through her body in wave after wave of hot, devastating languor. It took a moment, after calming down, when her breath was still broken, to realize that Raphael had considerately slowed to a stop and was watching her face intently, lips pressed against her thigh.

"Fuck," she said, pressing the back of her wrist against her forehead like the overwhelmed Victorian widow she emulated. Raphael laughed, low and roguishly, and kissed up her leg and across her stomach.

Mattie ran her fingers through his hair and grasped handfuls of it at the back of his head. "How do you want me?"

They locked eyes. Raphael might have been wondering if she were sincere, but Mattie made sure he saw her genuine desire.

"Any way you'll have me."

"In—inside," she stammered. "Inside me."

"Are you sure?"

"Yes. Please." She moved her hips against him again, and he grinned. He reached for one of the condoms and sat back on his heels to open it. While his hands were busy, Mattie reached up and stroked his cock. Raphael groaned, closed his eyes and paused. He braced against the bed, looking like he was appreciating the feel of her hand around him. He let her get a few strokes in, but when she sped up, he grabbed her wrist.

"Stop, stop," he said. She let go immediately. "Unless you want me to come like this instead."

"However you want," she said.

"Do you still want me inside you?" He asked. Mattie nodded.

He let go of her wrist and finished unwrapping the condom. As he started unrolling it over his tip, Mattie reached out.

"Can I?"

He nodded. She used both hands to roll it down his length, and stroked him again before lying back, biting her lip.

Raphael growled at her playfully and positioned himself over her so his condom-clad stand was against her lower belly. He snaked one hand into her hair and kissed her on the lips while his other hand grasped at her breast, pinching her nipple, and she moaned against him. He slid his hand from her breast, down her side, and between her legs, where he teased her with his fingers. Her breathing sped up and she clutched at him.

He shifted back until his cock rubbed against her slit, and she jumped.

"Are you ready?" He asked.

"Yes, Raphael—"

He pushed inside her, slowly, and she gasped. He was perfect, hard and eager, and she whimpered. He wrapped his arms around her, holding her close. "Mattie," he breathed. His body, his breath, his words, all felt like a gift. He pulled out a little, then started thrusting, slowly at first, then faster, like he couldn't help himself.

Mattie's mind didn't wander. It couldn't. She had felt earlier that day that her body was detaching from her consciousness, that she was breaking apart in all the problems life flooded her with. But Raphael's physical presence had gathered her together again, and the rhythm of him inside her pinned her to the moment and herself and she felt whole again and strong.

"Fuck, god, Raphael—"

"Mattie," he whispered, speeding up. "Mattie, I can't last—"

"Come," she demanded. "Please. Come inside me."

His whole body shuddered as he came, thrusting against her hard, crushing her in his grip as he groaned and spent, his cock pulsing again and again inside her. He clutched her against him, spasming as though aftershocks of pleasure rippled through him. Mattie caressed his back and shoulders, kissed his hair and ear and temple.

"That was..." Mattie trailed off, her fingers making lazy circles against his skin.

"Yes."

A moment passed, and she sighed as he pulled out of her.

"Stay here," he told her, heading to the bathroom.

She couldn't help the smile that crept across her face. Few times in her life had an outcome met her expectations, but this was the first time it ever exceeded them, and she marveled at it. This man had written to her, courted her. And she wanted him. She had wanted Raphael from the beginning, and except for the one time at the height of her passion that she remembered he was gut-punch handsome celebrity Raphael Callan, the man she had just shared everything with was exactly the man he presented himself as in his letters.

The faucet shut off, and Mattie rolled onto her side, propped up on one elbow, to watch Raphael walk back into the room.

"How does your bathroom smell like a spa?"

"Oil diffuser," she murmured. He hopped onto the bed and curled himself around her, pulling her close so his chest and stomach pressed against her back. He buried his nose in her hair then kissed her cheek. Time got soft again, comfortable and warm, both of them still enveloped in the sense of wonder and joy and intimacy, until the reality awaiting them outside began its irrepressible seeping back into their thoughts.

"Do you think," Mattie asked, "if they found out we broke protocol, they would sentence us to another ten-day isolation? Or
would we be fined?" It would solve the problem of the wedding,
at least.

"Both," Raphael answered. "And they would put us on separate
floors. You were thinking they'd put us next door again, and we
could have an extended holiday, just the two of us, but no doubt
they'd punish us instead." He sat up. "And you and I have to get
out of here to slay some demons."

Mattie rolled away from him and curled into a ball. "Ug, I don't
wanna." He tugged on her arm.

"Mattie," he said, cajoling. "If you do another round here, you
won't find closure with your relatives. And I'll have to face the
fallout of confronting Payton and—alone."

Mattie gave him her best overdramatic sigh. "Fine," she said,
feigning exasperation, but not by much.

In the other room, Raphael's phone chirped.

"You can get that," Mattie said. "I won't keep you."

"Well that's the problem," he said, rolling on top of her and
growling into her neck. "I want you to keep me." Mattie shrieked
and laughed.

"Fine, fine," she said. "I'll keep you, but you're allowed to answer
your phone."

With a final growl, he jumped up and walked to his room,
picking up and putting on his boxers on the way. Mattie rose, too,
and put on her robe, the first thing he had taken off her. She sorted
their clothes onto the bed as Raphael leaned against the doorway
between their rooms.

"No, it's all right, mate, I'm just in the middle of something now.
I appreciate it. I'll call you back in ten minutes." He ended the call
and gathered his clothes. "My room is so cold, I'm considering

inviting the weta inside to keep me warm. That is, unless I can sleep in here with you?" His smile turned mischievous.

"I would like that," Mattie said, crossing her arms over her stomach. "This day has utterly exhausted me, though, so if you don't mind, I'm going to get into bed now. My alarm is for nine. When do you check out?"

"Quarter after eleven."

"I'm at eleven. Two hours is probably enough to shower and finish packing."

"Yes, but is it enough for shower and packing and sex?"

Mattie blushed. It was absurd to blush, she thought, the man had just been between her legs. Her blush deepened.

"Or not," he said. "If you're embarrassed, or—"

"No!" She winced. She hadn't meant to yell. "I'm not embarrassed, I'm—this is still new, and we're getting a feel for it, so, maybe we can decide tomorrow?"

"Sounds perfect. I do have to return this call tonight, it can't wait. You're sure I can come to bed when you've already fallen asleep?"

"Yeah, of course. Just make sure to shut your balcony door. And, um, in case you don't know, don't, I mean, no sexual stuff while I'm sleeping. If I can't consent, then—"

"God, no," he said, aghast. "I wouldn't, I promise." He leaned in to kiss her, his armful of clothes between them. "I'll join you soon."

Mattie reached for his arm as he turned away. "Hey," she said, biting her lip. "I like this."

Raphael's smile spread like the dawn, genuine and brilliant. Like he knew exactly what she meant.

"I do, too," he said.

PART THREE

Friday, April 3, 2020
Morning

Muffled and otherworldly, an electronic chirping wound its way through the dim fog of Mattie's sleep. There had been no nightmares, no sharp sounds or anxieties to wake her once she had drifted off, relaxed from sex and comfortable in her body. The bed was warm, the sheets against her silky, and she was just aware enough of the physical world to know that Raphael's bare chest rested against her back, his arm around her stomach. Thirteen days was plenty of time to convince her that alarm clocks were for suckers, and she tried to burrow further into her subconscious to escape the shrill reminder that she had to re-enter the world and *do* things today.

But the noise grew louder as her sleep dissipated, and whatever had been restored by deep, uninterrupted slumber was effectively broken by the insistent ring tone.

Mattie flung out an arm in the direction of her phone, tapping its surface indiscriminately while trying to rub the blurriness from her eyes. Raphael stirred next to her, inhaling loudly as he stretched, and she heard a tinny voice by the nightstand.

"Mats? Hello? Are you okay?"

She sat up on an elbow and picked up the phone, her cocoon of comfort falling away.

"Hi. What? Rin?" She tried unsuccessfully to stifle a yawn. "Sorry, I wasn't looking, I must have called you by mistake."

"What?" Rin said. "I called you. We're on our way. Do you need us to bring you anything? Should we make any stops?"

Mattie squinted at the phone and reached for her glasses. "Why are you leaving so early?"

"Uh, it's already ten. We left on time. Oh shit, did I wake you up? Didn't you set an alarm? Oh my god, did you stay up late sexting with Raphael?" Mattie snorted. The man in question leaned over to kiss her shoulder, got out of bed, and went into his room.

"Wait, it's ten?" She tore back the covers and stood up. "Shit, I set my alarm for nine. Or could have sworn I did. Fuck."

"Oops. Well, I'll let you go. Text if you need me, love you, see you soon...no, Daph, she forgot to set her alarm—"

Forty-five minutes might be enough time to finish packing. Not enough time for a shower, especially if she wanted her soap and shampoo bars to dry before storing them. Most likely, she would be paralyzed with panic for ten minutes, forego the shower, stow everything sloppily, and the rest of the day would pick up more and more little irritants like a snowball of shittiness until it smothered her at the family dinner tonight.

She jumped when a hand rested on her shoulder.

"Sorry," Raphael drawled, giving her a squeeze. "Didn't mean to startle you."

"Yeah," she said, putting down the phone and turning to face him. He had changed into jeans and a dark tee and looked ready to step out into the world again. Some people worked hard to get that just-woken-up aesthetic, but Mattie was pretty sure his bed-head was charmingly real. If only her snarled hair, pillow-creased face, and eye crusties were as endearing. "Overslept. I have less than an hour to get ready now."

"Hmm. So. Not enough time for sex?" He wrinkled his nose, and she laughed.

"I'm so sorry." She snaked her arms around his waist and lifted her head for a kiss. "I would very much like to. Being rushed like this, it's going to affect my entire day already."

"I understand," he said, smoothing her hair behind her ear. He brought his other hand up and framed her face, fingers tangled in her hair, thumbs caressing her cheeks. "I won't be sure what my day looks like until I get to the hotel. Text me. We'll find time to see each other." Mattie nodded and he kissed her again, slow and sweet.

"I don't want to take up all of your packing time," he murmured.

"Worth it," she mumbled, and he laughed as he stepped away, retreating to his room to finish his own chores before checking out. Mattie rolled her head to stretch her neck and went to track down her luggage.

The day was going to last forever and throw her a thousand things that wanted to break her. But she'd be steadied by the physical bolstering of her two best friends—her stalwart partners in crime—and the emotional support of a man who would remain one text and ten minutes away from her at any given moment. Taking a deep and stabilizing breath, she focused on the tasks before her, knowing that for all its havoc and gloom, the day would also include love and humor. Her friends would see to that. And that was the best she could hope for.

***

Mattie closed her eyes, removed her mask, and stepped into the late morning sun. It warmed her face, despite the cool breeze that tugged at her hair and teased her memory with the scents of ocean, diesel, and curry. Traffic was light, though she could hear honking in the distance, tired brakes squeaking in the stop-and-go of the busy road. The street below her balcony had been quiet, and although she generally preferred quietude to commotion, she had to admit that she missed watching—and maybe even participating in—the bustle of city life. One more thing that fourteen days in isolation had changed in her.

She opened her eyes and looked around, blinking. There were a number of people on the sidewalk, though no one was going into or out of the hotel behind her. They staggered the check-out times of people being released, and new guests were bussed in some time in the afternoon. Still, she stepped to the side, away from the doors, her considerate nature going strong even after isolation.

Maybe she hadn't changed that much, then.

Lost in thought, she was unprepared when someone grabbed her into a bear hug from the side. Daphne laughed, a sound both maniacal and tinkling.

"Mattie!" She shouted, too close to be so loud, but Mattie couldn't be mad about it. She yelped and hugged her back, and Rin ducked around Daphne to come in for a group hug.

"Welcome back, Mats," Rin said, kissing her forehead. She was almost a head taller than Mattie, so they fit together well. "There. Your first physical contact with another human in fourteen days."

"Oh!" Daphne grabbed Mattie's face and planted a quick kiss on her cheek. "Me, too. My poor Mattie, all alone for so long."

"Uh," Mattie said. "Well. Actually." She cleared her throat.

"No," Rin said, eyes widening. "Matalina Redgrave. You didn't. You and Raph?"

Mattie pursed her lips and ducked her head.

"What?" Daphne frowned, eyes darting between the two of them. "Wait, what? WHAT?" She let out a long shriek and jumped up and down, still clutching her sister. "Why didn't you tell us?"

"I was busy, obviously."

"Okay, okay, keep it down, Daph," Rin said, glancing around the sidewalk from beneath her wide tortoiseshell glasses. She ushered them closer to the side of the building, pulling Mattie's suitcase behind them. She wore a black beanie over her mid-length auburn hair, a cropped maroon puffy coat, thick black leggings that looked like they were for jogging, and black boots. "If they see us together, they might recognize us from the other night, so, let's tone it down a smidge in the name of stealth but holy hell Mattie did you have sex with Raphael Callan?"

"Yes, and it was amazing, and I'll tell you all about it on the ride to the hotel, but we need to change the subject because his check-out time was only fifteen minutes after mine, so you're about to meet him in just a few minutes. And while it would be very on-brand for you, I don't want 'sex with Raphael Callan' to be first words he hears you say."

Rin made a face and nodded. "Fair enough."

"Is he your person? Is he your Cinnamon?" Daphne gazed at her with sapphire-blue moon-eyes. Of course she didn't wear a hat. Her short, platinum-blond hair framed her narrow face perfectly, somehow always falling right into place despite all of Daph's chaos. The coat was new, white and fluffy, and oversized. Mattie imagined it was made from the hides of skinned teddy bears. It was open just enough to see the Peter Pan collar of her mint green shirt or dress, matching tights visible for the few inches between the bottom of the coat and the top of her neon orange running shoes.

"He might well be," Mattie said softly. Daph's eyes glimmered with happy tears, and Rin playfully hit her shoulder.

"Good on you," she said. "If you get a stable romantic partner out of this, I guess having to deal with the wedding will have been worth it."

Mattie and Daph both gave her a look. "You forget how bad it is already," Daphne admonished her.

"Maybe she's right," Mattie said. "Anyway, he should be out in a minute, you can meet him, then we can get going. He's got a car coming to pick him up and he said he needs the alone time to psyche himself up to confront his director."

"Hmm," Rin mused, glancing around. "Who told the paparazzi?"

"Oh, is that who they are? I wondered." Daphne sighed.

"What?" Mattie asked. Rin described a couple of the people close by, and Mattie tried not to stare at them.

"The director sent the car," she said. "He must have leaked Raphael's location to them for some kind of publicity thing. He's going to be unhappy about it. I should text him."

Rin angled herself to block Mattie's view of them.

"He'll be unhappy, but he has plenty of practice dealing with them," Rin said. "You, on the other hand, might have a problem."

Before Mattie could respond, the crowd converged on the hotel doors in a flurry of motion and camera flashes, and Raphael walked out, one arm holding his dark coat, the other pulling his rolling luggage. Either he knew about the photographers waiting for him or was used to being in this situation, because he graciously nodded and held up his coat-draped arm in greeting as he scanned the crowd for Mattie. People shouted his name and told him to take off his mask.

"We should go," Daphne said, tugging Mattie's arm.

"Yup," Rin said, taking Mattie's other arm and grabbing her luggage.

"But—"

"Text him once you're safe in the car," Rin growled. She was in Mama Bear mode, and she and Daph all but dragged Mattie down the sidewalk. Mattie glanced back, hoping to catch Raphael's eye. His gaze met hers, darted to Rin and Daphne, then locked on her again, and he gave her a slight bow. She inclined her head—the best she could do looking over her shoulder while her friends forced her feet in the opposite direction.

"Is it true that Edie Everett—"

"MEAT PIES!" Daphne screamed, drowning out the rest of the photographer's question. "Let's stop and get meat pies on the way. And some coffee. Mattie, you must be tired, and don't think I forgot you texting us that you would escape for decent coffee so CONSIDER THIS YOUR PRISON BREAK FOR COFFEE! Ha-hahah!"

"Jesus, Daphne, are you on drugs?" Mattie pulled up the tote bag that had slid down to her elbow, and the women turned onto a side street. "Also, you can let go of me. I'm not about to run back into that."

"No, no, she's right," Rin said, releasing her grip on Mattie's arm. "It's practically lunch time, and you need your coffee." She took her phone out of her pocket and a few moments later, an engine roared to life halfway down the block. Mattie squinted to look for the car, and recognized the two bicycles on a roof rack.

"Ooo, new car?"

Rin smiled. "Business is good. Or at least it was, before—" She gestured at nothing. "We're getting a lot of cancellations due to Covid restrictions."

"That sucks," Mattie said. Rin had taken over her parents' business the previous year, when her father died. Her mother had passed the year before that, and Mattie knew that Rin had been struggling with all of it, emotionally of course, but as a business owner, too. "How...what are you going to...is there any...?"

"Exactly." Rin agreed with a sigh. "There aren't any answers at this point. Going to have to improvise a bit. Maybe everything will be shut down and I won't have a choice but to take an actual holiday for the next month."

"I love when you dream big," Daphne said. Rin snorted.

"Well," Mattie said, as they came alongside the car. "No matter what, we're here for you, Corinne, so if you need any help, look no further."

Rin grimaced, and Daphne's head shot up. "Rin, didn't you tell her?"

"When would I have told her?"

"Text! Email! Phone call!"

Mattie glanced between them. "What's happening?"

"No big deal." Rin sighed, reaching past them to open the trunk. "I'm just going by Rin now. No Corinne."

She stowed the luggage while Mattie stood on the sidewalk, staring into the middle distance. Daph crossed her arms in front of her chest and raised an eyebrow at Rin.

"And your pronouns?" Mattie asked, figuring it out.

Daphne let out a yelp. "I told you, you had nothing to worry about!" Rin tsked and shut the trunk.

"If you want to use they/them, it'll give me a chance to try it out. But if you forget, she/her is also fine." They shuffled around the car and opened the passenger door, but neither Redgrave moved to get in. They sighed. "What?"

Mattie stepped forward and hugged them. "I just love you," she mumbled into Rin's shoulder. "You know this isn't really surprising, right?"

"I should hope not," they grumbled. "Though I'd forgive you. It took me this long, and I've known me longer than you've known me."

"Have you, though?" Daphne asked playfully. Mattie released her friend just in time to see Rin's eyeroll.

"Into the car, one of you. Both of you. Some of us have to get back to work."

With an air kiss, Daphne took the passenger's seat, leaving the back seats for Mattie to lie down and take a nap. Mattie didn't argue. Her sister was sensitive about getting motion sickness so easily, and she didn't mind letting Daphne sit in the front.

"Can we take a detour around the front of the hotel?" Mattie asked once she had buckled in. "Make sure Raphael gets away all right."

Traffic was a little heavier when they turned onto the main road, due to a black car double parked at the hotel entrance. A man in a suit and black driving cap was loading Raphael's suitcase into the trunk.

"Oh good, his car is here," Mattie murmured.

"Mattie," Daphne said, voice low. "Hand me my slingshot."

"Ah, fuck," Rin said, hitting the steering wheel with their palm.

"What? Why?"

"Give it to me, quickly."

Rin growled. "No, Daph, we're not going to do that because there are cameras. It will be filmed, and you will be arrested and put in jail."

Daphne reached into her coat pocket and shuffled a handful of what sounded like pebbles. "My aim isn't as good bare-handed, but I'm willing to take that chance."

"What am I missing? I can't see—" Mattie broke off as they came up beside the hired car. On the sidewalk, the photographers

ringed Raphael in a half-circle, his arms crossed and mask still on
as a lithe, blonde white woman dressed all in white leaned against
him, face tilted up to his.

Daphne fought with the window, her movements exaggerated,
but Rin had turned on the child locks so she couldn't open it. Rin
didn't slow as they passed, and there was no way for Raphael to
know Mattie was in that car, but he glanced up and directly at her
anyway. Mattie couldn't recognize the look in his eyes. A moment
later, they were out of sight.

"What the shit," Mattie muttered.

"That," Daphne said, finally sitting back in her seat, "was Edie
Everett."

***

Raphael saw the photographers from the front desk. He recognized them easily: he'd had nearly a lifetime to learn how. Unless
they waited outside every quarantine hotel every morning for
several hours, hoping for a break, someone must have talked. A lot
of people knew where he was, but a much smaller number would
have sold him out.

As the clerk at the desk printed out his quarantine certificate,
Raph sent Luke a text about the paparazzi. His response was
quick: "fucking Payton." He slid the certificate into the messenger
bag stacked on top of his luggage, adjusted his mask, and thanked
the clerk. Maybe Mattie was right. The alarm never went off, they
overslept, had to rush to get ready, and now the day was just going
to snowball disaster after disaster.

But no matter how the day ended up going, nothing would
eclipse his memory of the night before.

Giving Mattie that first letter was one of the bolder things he had done in his life, and even so, he hadn't had any expectations. Nobody could have predicted he would meet someone he could connect with for the first time in a decade. But if he had known someone like Mattie existed, he would have spent that decade trying to find her. Now that he knew, he wondered how he never thought someone like her might exist.

His only regret was that he hadn't told Mattie that Edie had been hired on the project at the last minute. With everything she had to deal with this weekend—between the wedding and her relatives and her bully—it didn't seem fair to add another worry to her anxious mind. At least, not until it couldn't be avoided any longer.

It wasn't an ideal plan. It wasn't even a good plan. And a part of him knew it was a coward's plan, with a large margin of error.

But between the two of them, they had enough problems to face, and only a few short hours left to ignore all of it. For now, Edie remained a later problem.

The more immediate threat was the possibility of being accosted by photographers when he left the hotel. It would have been an inconvenience either way, but Mattie had said she would wait for him outside so he could meet Daphne and Rin in person. Crossing the lobby, he paused and considered waiting inside for his car. Would it be worse to leave Mattie hanging and just dive into the hired car when it pulled up without acknowledging her, or go outside and try to talk to her while being harassed?

Isolation had made him a little desperate, and Mattie made him more desperate, so he took a deep breath and walked outside.

And knew immediately that he had made the wrong decision.

The photographers pressed in. He waved and nodded, looking for Mattie beyond the cameras. Someone shouted for him to take off his mask, they wanted to see his face, and he decided to leave it on as punishment for them ruining his release from quarantine. Another said Edie's name, and he panicked. They would definitely ask him about the pregnancy, and if Mattie were still there...

No, there she was, being dragged away by Daphne and Rin. He didn't know how to communicate to her that leaving was the best idea, so he ducked his head into a bow. She gave him a half-smile and nodded before turning to face the direction in which her friends pulled her.

"Is it true that Edie Everett—"

"MEAT PIES!" He heard one of the girls scream, before prattling on nonstop and loudly, and he was grateful for their intervention. He'd explained the Edie problem in their group text, and by the sound of it, they hadn't told Mattie, but were trying to protect her.

"It's so kind of you to join me in celebrating my release from quarantine," Raphael joked, pretending to be at ease. "I even got a graduation certificate." A few of the photographers laughed, but more shouted questions about him and Edie. He ignored them and continued talking about his time at the hotel. He made it clear that whatever inconvenience he experienced by needing to isolate for fourteen days was a small price to pay to assist the global effort to slow the spread of the virus. Making the virus the bad guy was a much better idea than making Edie the bad guy, even if all he wanted to do was scream that she was lying. His manager would be so proud.

After what felt like forever, a sleek black car pulled to a stop in the street. A short white man in a black suit and cap got out of the driver's seat and jogged over to Raphael.

"Mr Callan?" The driver asked, dabbing sweat from his brow with a handkerchief. "I'm assuming. Because, uh, well, these folks" He gestured to the paparazzi.

"That's me," Raphael said, pulling his suitcase forward for the chauffeur to take it. As he reached for it, a knocking sounded against the car's tinted back window. The man pursed his lips and closed his eyes.

"Excuse me, just one moment, sir."

God, it was probably Payton, come to make sure his leading man didn't get any ideas about escaping. Call the photographers, then show up to talk to him in person so he couldn't make a scene. That didn't sound like Payton, but based on the whole situation with this project, he obviously didn't know the man as well as he thought.

The chauffeur opened the back door and two white-clad legs appeared, followed by the rest of a tall woman who beamed at Raphael.

For a moment, he had no idea what was happening. He tried to place her in relation to the film, then his stomach dropped as he recognized her. In the span of a few seconds, his entire body went cold and his hands bunched into fists, which he tried to hide by crossing his arms in front of his chest.

"Hi, sweetie!" Edie sang, hopping over to him. The cameras around him clicked furiously. "I'm so glad you're out of that nasty hotel. You're more likely to have caught something from staying there than to have brought something in, am I right?" She laughed outrageously at her own joke, and Raphael pictured her as a braying donkey.

"What the fuck are you doing?" He asked through clenched teeth, hoping that between the mask over his face and the sound of the cameras and shuffling, only Edie would know what he said. She grasped his arm and smiled up at him.

"It must be fate," she said. The chauffeur grabbed Raphael's luggage to put in the trunk. "When Payton asked me to join the cast here, I knew I had to come. I mean, working with him is always a dream, but to work with my man, too?" She squeezed his arm and leaned closer, as though she were going to try to kiss him despite the mask.

Out of the corner of his eye, he saw movement in a car driving past, and looked up to see Mattie in a backseat, staring at him, brows furrowed in a look of confusion. Daphne, he guessed, was having some sort of fit in the passenger's seat, and then they were gone.

Shit. Shit, shit, shit. He didn't want to spend the next two hours in the backseat of a car with Edie. If he tried to walk away, get a taxi or rideshare, the paparazzi would follow and badger him. So would Edie. The trunk closed, and the driver opened the back door for them. Edie tugged on his arm once then ducked inside. Raphael closed the door behind her without getting in and bowed his head to the driver.

"I know it's probably against protocol," he said, stealthily removing a $100 bill from his wallet and handing it to the surprised man. "But I think you understand why I really, really need to sit in the front with you, and not in the back with her."

The man's face settled into a mien of understanding, and he nodded and took the money. They got into the car and buckled up.

"Uh," Edie said from the back. "What do you think you're doing?" Raphael ignored her and pulled out his phone to text Mattie. "Raph, what are you doing? You can't sit in the front, you have to sit back here with me." The driver checked his mirrors and pulled out into traffic.

"Hey, you!" She said, agitated. "Driver! He can't sit in the front!"

"I'm sorry, ma'am, but I'd rather he not be sick in my car. It's a long drive to the Billingstead, and the severity of his car sickness makes it a medical accessibility issue."

"He doesn't get car sick," she said.

"You wouldn't know," Raphael said bitterly, pausing his texting to remove his face mask. "So grateful I never had to go to hospital when we dated. You wouldn't even have been able to tell them what I'm allergic to."

Edie crossed her arms over her chest. "Well, I'm here to fix that. I've been trying to contact you for a month and you've just ignored me. It was selfish of you and it really hurt my feelings. I even tried to get Luke involved, but that man is a child. The only way I could be sure you'd talk to me today is if the press were there to act as chaperones."

He'd been trying not to listen to her, but her words sank in. "You told the paparazzi where I'd be," he said, closing his eyes.

"Payton sent the car to pick me up first," she said, avoiding his accusation. "He hoped you and I could talk about the film. He thinks you're going to bail, which, I guess that's what you do." Edie waited for the barb to land, but Raphael barely heard her.

Since she didn't get the response she wanted, she launched into a monologue, which both men ignored. Raphael knew anything he said would be used against him.

He texted Mats that Payton hired Edie on the film last minute and sent the car to pick her up first without telling Raph about it. He was not happy about it, so he was going to call Luke and hopefully talk to him all the way to the hotel. Mattie didn't respond right away. Finally, the ellipses appeared, and her reply was disappointingly short. "That sucks. Hope Luke can help."

Was she upset? He couldn't blame her. But he also couldn't handle trying to text her about it while Edie's voice grated at him from the backseat. He sighed, feeling the beginning of a migraine pulsing against his skull, and once again concluded Mattie was right about the day getting worse.

Luke accepted the video call, understood what was needed of him, and after exchanging a few heated words with Edie when he saw her in the background, spent the rest of their call telling Raphael the plots of the last few kid movies he took his daughters to see.

Almost two hours later, Raphael stepped into the lobby of the Billingstead Hotel and ended the call with Luke, who was on his way to run interference with Edie.

"Hey!" Edie hissed, pulling him to a stop. Raphael had thought he'd be able to get away from her while she struggled with her luggage, but she had left it at the door. "You're going to have to get over whatever it is you're mad at me for and talk to me like an adult."

"You're not pregnant, Edie." It took all his willpower to keep his voice level instead of shouting it across the atrium.

"Look. Raph. I know it must have been hard for you, being with me. I know I'm a lot, I'm intense. But I love you. And we have a chance to reconcile. I just want you to try, one more time, for me."

It wasn't lost on him that Edie didn't confirm or deny his claim that she'd been lying. If she had actually been pregnant, she wouldn't let him forget it. He took a breath and looked across the empty lobby. Nobody to watch, nobody to overhear and report to the tabloids. Nobody to impress or perform for. Just him and Edie, and the brief opportunity to actually talk without interference. What would Mattie do?

"Your intensity wasn't the problem," he said, looking her in the eye. He questioned whether honesty would get him anywhere with Edie, but at least he would know he tried. "You were in love with someone who only exists in your mind, and when I acted like myself instead of him, you had no interest in that version of me. I can't compete with him. I don't want to, and I shouldn't have to. We aren't what either of us want or need. It took me too long to see that, and I'm sorry."

Edie stared at him as he spoke, frowning. "I was never in love with a fictional version of you," she said. "I'm the only one who could tell that all of your interactions were a fiction. You're always hiding who you really are, and I could tell you were tired of it. Maybe you weren't ready, and I pushed you too hard, but that's because I love you and I want you to feel like you can be yourself around me."

"I *was*," Raph said, starting to get worked up again. "And you didn't like it, so you decided it wasn't the real me, but it is. And the lies you've spread to try to get me back are utterly unacceptable, especially if you expect a relationship that needs to be built on trust and respect. You and I are through, and there is no future where we get back together. Do you understand?"

Edie didn't respond right away, her gaze dropping between them, and then she nodded slowly. For a moment, Raphael thought he might have gotten through to her, but as her eyes flicked up to meet his, she smiled, tense shoulders relaxing.

"See?" She asked. "This is great. We're opening up a dialogue. And we can keep talking about it for as long as it takes. I asked Payton to get us adjoining rooms so it's easier to find each other when we're not on set."

Raphael closed his eyes. It was cold comfort, knowing he was right about how well she'd listen. She was as invested in her fiction of him as the fans that called themselves Pro-Raphaelites. He had tried. Mattie would be proud of him. But the best thing to do would be to go back to ignoring Edie completely. To start, he would switch rooms. That should be easy enough. Luke had said that the place was pretty empty.

As if summoned by the thought, Luke stepped into the lobby at that moment and shouted for Raphael. He was dressed casually in a pair of light-blue jeans and a purple-and-black striped tee, and Raph smiled and stepped away from Edie as he jogged over. Luke was a little taller than him and usually a little more narrow, but his muscles strained at his shirt thanks to his recent work on an action movie franchise. His sandy blond hair was just reaching that "90's teen heartthrob" length, and his boyish face looked even younger with his blocky glasses. Since they met, Luke had always looked like a comic book nerd, but now he looked like a jacked comic book nerd. He and Raphael met in a solid embrace, and Raph's stress began to subside.

"Brother," Luke said, hitting him on the back. "It's been too long."

Raphael pulled away first, grin on his face. "God, it's good to see you, Luke. Today has been absolute shit."

Luke glanced over at Edie. "I can imagine."

Raphael followed his gaze to make sure Edie was too far away to hear him and lowered his voice anyway. "Can you do me a favor and distract her for a few minutes? She somehow managed to get a room adjoining mine, and I have to change it. I don't want her following me and knowing where my new one is."

"Oh Edie!" Luke called, stepping away from Raphael. Edie eyed him suspiciously. "Look at you, in your chic outfit. It's too early in the season for skiing. Or is it a fashion statement? Either way, you *will* be ridiculed."

She scoffed. "As if anyone here knows anything about fashion."

"On the contrary, you'll love what they've done with the place. There's an enormous wedding here this weekend and all the women are very fashion-forward. And there's a lounging-by-the-pool party every day after lunch, where all the ladies line up in togs under the torches and pretend it isn't too chilly to be wearing nearly nothing. You've got some competition."

Edie rolled her eyes and turned to Raphael.

"Oh, was that your luggage I saw outside?" Luke asked, motioning behind him with a thumb as he started walking backwards. "Just sitting there, nobody watching it, where anybody could take it? What did you bring? Did you bring me any snacks?" Edie's eyes went wide and she followed him out, the two of them racing to be the first to her bags.

The clerk at the front desk switched his room to another wing of the building, and Raphael decided to upgrade to a full suite. After his time at the quarantine hotel, he wanted a bit more space, a bed in its own room, and a long soak in a big bathtub that he wouldn't have to clean himself. Before walking away, he glanced around to make sure Edie was still distracted—he could hear her yelling at Luke from the front doors.

As he entered his room and locked the door behind him, he breathed in the fresh scent of an upscale hotel suite and felt an embarrassing amount of relief. He set his bags down by the couch and walked to the enormous windows. Hills dense with trees hugged three sides of the dark and placid lake. He scanned the shores. Mattie hadn't told him exactly where their rented house was located, but if Rin's business was exclusively luxury properties, he would bet it had a view similar to the one from his room.

Lying to Mattie had been a mistake. They had been honest about other problems, other complications and things bothering them, and telling himself that he didn't want to add yet another challenge to the list was another lie. He should have known Edie would just show up, and if he had been thinking clearly, he might have figured it out early enough.

This was a conversation to have in person. While he was at it, he should tell Mattie exactly what Edie was claiming and exactly how it was a lie. He had finally found someone he really clicked with, and he didn't want his uncomfortable past with Edie to touch it. He texted Mattie his room number and that he'd left a key for her at the front desk. He asked her to text him when she was at the hotel, and she said she would.

He took a deep breath and turned toward the bathroom, pulling his shirts off over his head like Mattie had, and he smiled. The smell of her still clung to him, and he didn't want to wash it away. But he needed to shed the gritty confinement of his previous room and the almost tactile violation of Edie's ambush. As he passed the desk, he saw that the Billingstead had also thought to provide him with hotel stationery. Inspiration struck. The shower could wait until he wrote Mattie one more letter.

Friday, April 3, 2020
Afternoon

The entrance to the hotel property was almost a mile away from the main building. "This is it," Daph said, turning onto a wide driveway flanked by stone columns and a wrought-iron fence only five minutes from their rented cottage. The trees stood tall and dense, trunks blocking the view of the lake, canopy blocking the view of the sky. Storm clouds had rolled in, and what would usually be a pleasant, shady path beneath the branches became a dark metaphor for Mattie's descent into the mire of her relatives' malice.

"So close to our house," she murmured.

"The entrance, yes," Daphne said. "Main building is still a little ways off."

Smaller paved paths ran alongside the road—for jogging and biking, but also golf carts bringing guests to outbuildings, barns, fields, and courts. Mattie gasped when she saw an archery range.

"No, I haven't," Daph said preemptively. "If I did, they'd know where to find me. I've been driving up to Franklin to shoot, but they've been talking about closing for a few weeks because of Covid." She scrunched up her nose. "If they do, I'll come here, but I won't be happy about it."

They passed several buildings that looked like cottages—though Mattie would bet that they were as well-appointed as the "cottage" where she was staying. The car slowed to a stop and Mattie glanced around at the close trees, paved road continuing its winding way through the forest, and lack of main building.

"Uh, Daph?"

Daphne put the car in park and turned to her sister. "There's still time to change your mind. There's no point where you have to say, 'I'm too far in now, it wouldn't make sense to leave.' I'll be there to rescue you at every moment. But when you say that later, it will be because something hurt you. I want to give you one more opportunity to turn around before you get hurt at all."

Mattie grasped Daphne's hand, blinking away tears. If only the rest of her relatives loved her this much. To tell her she shouldn't do things that made her uncomfortable, instead of believing that money would make up for all the ways she would be upset. She hadn't argued with her mother, even though she wasn't accepting the bribe. She was tired of arguing and it was enough that she knew her own reasons for being there.

"I can't not try," Mattie said slowly. "Not for them, but for me."

"That's what I thought," Daphne said, squeezing her hand. "But I just want to make sure you're remembering that Spencer is now in the mix, too."

"Oh, I know," she answered. "But that requires a totally different approach that I don't want to think about yet if I don't have to."

"And Edie."

Mats waved her free hand in dismissal. "Not an influence on this weekend."

"Sure." Sarcastic Daphne wasn't subtle.

"No, seriously," Mattie emphasized. "I hate what she's doing to Raph, but I don't know her, so I'm free to despise her without conflicting emotions and can commit to supporting and defending Raphael." She shrugged. "Easy."

"Great, now apply that to our parents."

Mattie let go of Daph's hand with one last squeeze. "That's...less easy."

"Mmm," her sister said thoughtfully, putting the car back into drive. "Fine. But I had to try."

"You're a good sister like that."

"The best." Daph grinned, waggling her eyebrows in time with the revving of the engine.

Eventually, the road turned one final corner and the forest gave way to the palatial main building of the Billingstead. Mattie gawped. It looked like a golden castle from a fairy tale. Growing up, her parents had taken her and her siblings on many trips, staying at the best accommodations, visiting the most impressive feats of architecture, art, and history. But for some reason, she still expected anything chosen by her relatives to be tasteless.

Or maybe it had just been a while since she had indulged in actual luxury.

Daphne took the circular driveway faster than Mattie would have liked, stopping short in front of the main entrance. A valet opened Mattie's door for her, and she grasped his hand in her struggle to get out. Daphne didn't drive at home, but when she traveled, she liked to rent the lowest, loudest, fastest, most-likely-to-be-rented-by-a-douchebag car she could find. So she could drive like a douchebag and, when pulled over, dazzle her way out of a ticket—wasting the cop's time—but also to ensure the car wouldn't be available to rent by actual douchebags, making them angry. She considered it a win-win-win situation. Mattie didn't disagree, her awkward attempts to get out of the car notwithstanding.

She had packed her goody-bag tote with the different outfits she'd need over the course of the day, originally planning to check it at the front desk and change in the ladies' dressing room as needed. But Raphael had texted that she could use his room as she wished, so she had told Daphne to pack up her dresses, too.

Rin hadn't been invited to any of the day's events. Not a shock, since they had only been accompanying Daphne there at her request, and now she had Mattie to go with her. Rin wouldn't have been able to attend anything anyway. With the immediate future of New Zealand travel in a kind of limbo, they were dealing with more and more cancellations, rescheduling, and general and specific panic from their clients.

It was almost two o'clock, and as much as Mattie wanted to exert a little pettiness over Donna the Wedding Planner and her mother, she knew it would only come back to bite her in the ass. When she retrieved the key to Raphael's room from the front desk, the clerk also handed her an envelope that said "To M." She smiled and slid it into her tote while she texted Raph she was at the hotel but had to run to the dress fitting. He said he was about to leave for the set and he'd text her when he was back.

"Do we have time to meet Raph? Stow our stuff in his room?" Daphne swung her arm around Mattie's shoulders.

"No, we should try to be on time," she said, sighing. Daph led her through the lobby and down a hallway.

"You're still struggling with how to deal with this, aren't you?"

"It's harder now that I'm actually here," Mattie admitted, already feeling lost in the labyrinthine building despite her guide. "I know you'll support me no matter what I choose to do, but the problem is that I can't decide. And if I tell you one thing now, and you make plans for that, I'll feel like an asshole if I change my mind."

"On top of the feeling bad about everything in general," Daphne extrapolated. "So we'll take it one decision at a time. You want to be on time for the dress fitting."

"I'm not sure it's what I want, but it's what I'm going to do."

"That sounds good enough for me. And if you change your mind, at any time, we can do something else. Just like consent!" Daphne beamed.

"Just like," Mattie said, laughing.

***

Mattie, Daphne, the tailor, and the wedding planner were all on time, but Mattie's mother was clear that they shouldn't start the fitting until she arrived, and she was, as usual, late. Jenny—the tailor—had taken one look at Mattie, shook her head, muttered something under her breath, and went back to work on another dress, alongside two assistants. Donna spent her time wheedling people on the phone, manipulating them as deftly as she had Mattie.

The Ruby Room was one of the many mid-sized conference rooms at the hotel, its windowless basement location perfect for presentations requiring darkness or a lack of distractions or both. Wide, heavy sea-green curtains decorated the walls and didn't quite succeed in convincing anyone they weren't underground. For the Redgrave-Tamsyn wedding, dozens of dresses and tuxes hung on rolling clothing racks. The seamstress's work area took up an entire corner, next to a three-way mirror and a row of flimsy makeshift dressing rooms. While Mattie looked through the tuxes—remembering that Raph said he might need one—Daph found a small wine fridge with champagne and poured her sister a glass, keeping the bottle for herself.

"If you don't, you'll wish you had," she told Mattie.

At quarter past, Marjorie Redgrave floated into the room, laughing loudly as she said goodbye to whoever was on the phone. Donna snapped to attention and glanced around the room. "Mattie!" She hissed.

The girls had found a cushion among the clothing racks and were halfway through the bottle of champagne. They emerged from the rows of dresses as Donna brought over the garment bag.

"Oh, my," Marjorie said, her gaze looking Mattie over as her face fell into a frown. "Matalina, honey, it's so nice to see you." Instead of trying to recover her expression, she leaned in for air kisses, keeping her hands up by her shoulders.

Mattie was very familiar with that look. It was the look that Redgraves gave when confronted by the physical disappointment of her. And even though it communicated everything from "I thought you started that new exercise routine" to "I guess you didn't contact the private chef I found for you" to "still fat, I see," they somehow always found a way to say it aloud, too.

"Why did I think you'd lost weight?" And there it was.

"Mattie is hot," Daphne corrected, pulling the bottle of wine to her lips. Marjorie made another face and told Donna to get her a glass, too. The tailor unzipped the bag and brought out the bridesmaid dress.

"Jenny can work miracles, but I didn't realize we'd need such a big one," Marjorie said.

The tailor held out the dress, glancing between it and Mattie, and huffed. "I might as well try to make a new one from scratch."

"Oh, wasn't there another bridesmaid dress? An extra one?"

"It's the same size as this."

"But maybe if you can use the material from the second one, just sort of sew the two together...?"

Mattie's cheeks burned, far beyond the alcohol's effects. Her mouth had dried up the moment they began talking about her, like her body knew she wanted to defend herself and made it impossible. She hated this part. It wouldn't even cross her mind to hesitate if she saw someone else being bullied, but why was it so goddamn difficult to do the same thing when she was the one who needed help?

She closed her eyes and held her glass out to Daphne, who filled it, then took the glass and gave Mattie the bottle. What a good sister. What a terrible mother. What terrible women, to stand around and embarrass her for the least interesting thing about herself.

"We'll skip trying it on," Jenny said. "I'll take her measurements and work from that."

"If you need more material, I can get some flown in within an hour," Donna said.

"Can you get me a plus-size dress form? I doubt the ones I have will expand that far, I was told every woman in the wedding party was a normal size."

"Jesus Christ," Daphne sputtered, glaring at Jenny with naked disgust.

"Language," Marjorie chided.

In the day-to-day of her life, Mattie's size didn't bother her much, beyond what was structurally designed to bother her. But unlike the few inappropriate comments from strangers, the cruelty of her relatives tipped her confidence into a nose dive. She was already on the verge of tears, and she hadn't even found her voice yet. Right. Right, *this* was why she wanted to skip all these extra events.

"Or we can go with the simplest solution and she won't be a bridesmaid," Daphne said, crossing her arms.

"Oh, I don't think she wants that, do you, honey?" Marjorie's tone took on a cold edge. Mattie opened her eyes, finding her mother's leveled gaze. The money. She thought Mattie was there because of the money she offered, and putting up with their remarks was something Marjorie expected as part of the deal. But it wasn't anything she hadn't heard before. Even the humiliation of being treated this way in front of, and by, strangers wasn't new.

"I'd love to not be a bridesmaid," Mattie said with a shrug. "But it sounds like I need to step up and do it. A familial obligation." She pointedly turned to Daph. "One that I can look back on and know that I did everything I could."

Daphne frowned at her. Marjorie smiled and said, "Good girl. Contributing to your brother's wedding. I'm so proud of you."

"You." Jenny gestured aggressively to Mattie. "Into the dressing room, strip down to your bra and underwear. You're wearing the underthings you'll have on for the wedding? No? Of course you're not. Well, I'll do the best I can, but you're not giving me much to work with."

Confident that Mattie would behave, Marjorie excused herself, and Donna followed her out of the room. Jenny went to find her measuring tape. Daphne cornered Mattie in the dressing room and yanked the curtain shut behind them.

"What the fuck was that?"

"Mother being mother." Mattie set the champagne bottle on the floor and started unbuttoning her sweater with only slightly shaky hands.

"Not that part. The bullying. I was taking my cues from you, but you were acting...weird."

Mattie shrugged, combining the motion with removing the cardigan. "I've heard it all before. It bothers me, but, what good will yelling do?"

Daphne pursed her lips and searched Mattie's face. "Sometimes, yelling does wonders. Regardless, I want you to remember something." She reached out and put her hands on Mattie's shoulders, stopping her from taking off any more clothing. "Something very important. Very, very important."

"Oh god, Daph, what is it?"

"You are beautiful."

Mattie's eyes teared up. "Daph—"

"Do you know how I know this?"

"Because you're my sister?"

"And?"

"And...because you're smart?"

"And?"

"And...I don't know. Why else?"

Daphne leaned in so her lips were by Mattie's ear.

"Because," she whispered. "You had sex with Raphael Callan." Mattie burst out laughing, and Daphne joined her.

"Nobody can take that away from you," she said. "And look, you can't base your self-worth on what other people say, but if people saying you're worthless is going to affect you, you should let people telling you you're gorgeous affect you, too. If a guy even I can admit is ridiculously handsome thinks this—" she ran her hands down Mattie's arms. "—this heavenly body is sexy and desirable—which the best of us already believe, by the way—then it must be an objective scientific fact."

"You know what?" Mattie looked at herself in the mirror. "Fuck it. You're right."

"Damn straight."

Jenny pulled the curtain open, and the girls jumped. "You, out. You, why aren't you undressed? I don't have all day." The girls giggled.

"I'll be right here waiting for you," Daphne said, stepping out and settling on another cushion in front of the dressing rooms.

"Waiting for me, five feet away?"

"Always," she said, winking.

***

It was almost three o'clock when Mattie and Daphne left the increasingly claustrophobic room and the tailor's sharp commands issued with military precision. Mattie leaned against the wall by the door and took a deep breath as Daphne's fingers flew over her phone's screen.

"I'm not sure we have enough time to get to Raph's room, change, and be at the Girls Party thing on time," Daph said. "Would you rather be a little late, or just change in the dressing room by the pool?"

Mattie couldn't remember the last time she had had to do so many things that would emotionally pummel her in a single day. She knew the dress fitting was going to be bad no matter what, though the presence of her mother took it to new and unwelcome heights. Then the Girls Party—re-named in her head the Babes Retreat—which was just all the women gossiping and getting drunk while they sat by the outdoor pool. She didn't know what the difference was between the event this afternoon and what the women had been doing every other day, but she didn't care enough to ask.

And of course, the last event of the day would be the "family dinner." It would be interesting to see who was currently considered "family," a term that encompassed different individuals based on who was doing the inviting, who had fallen out of favor, and who had demonstrated sufficient fealty. Funny how her relatives regularly redefined who was family when it was convenient for them, but she wasn't allowed to do the same thing without being sensitive, overdramatic, or ungrateful.

Still, she needed to leave them behind knowing she did the best she could by them, even if they couldn't reciprocate that respect.

"Let's try to be on time," Mattie said, bringing out her phone and texting Raph that the fitting was great if she ever needed an origin story for her inevitable villainy.

"I was hoping you'd say that." Daph motioned with her head for Mattie to follow her. Mattie, realizing she wasn't going to be able to remember the layout in the few hours she'd be on site, let herself zone out while Daphne took the lead. They walked in the opposite direction they'd taken to the Ruby Room, up a narrow but bright set of stairs and several more hallways before passing through a long, many-windowed hall overlooking the outdoor pool area.

Her mind was still far away when they paused at the double doors to the patio, a tall, muscular man blocking their path. When Daph stopped instead of skirting around him, Mattie blinked and looked up into the face of Luke Maston.

"Mattie!" He cried, much louder than necessary, pulling her in for a bone-crushing hug. After a moment of getting over the surprise, she hugged him back. "I already feel like I've known you forever," he said, voice muffled by her hair.

"Oh my god," she said, giving him one last squeeze before pulling away. "I honestly forgot that I haven't met you yet. You already feel like a lifelong friend. I thought you'd be on set with Raph."

"I think you'll find me much improved in person. And I just left him, actually. He wanted a private conversation with Payton before deciding to bring in the big guns." He flexed a bicep between them, and Mats couldn't help laughing.

Luke shifted aside so two of Mattie's distant cousins could get out onto the pool deck, though they slowed down to ogle what was a totally incongruous scene to them. Mattie glanced out the doors and saw more cousins and aunts and other women she didn't know staring at them.

"Uh," she said. "All eyes on us."

Luke smiled and set a hand on her shoulder, drawing her close. "It was Daphne's idea. You know she's my new partner in crime? Raph's been too broody to be any fun, but this woman's mind is only a few turns ahead of mine, and she had enough forethought to bring grenades."

Daphne smirked and crossed her arms. Seeing Mattie's horror-stricken face, Luke quickly amended, "Figurative grenades."

"They're real enough," Daphne said.

"Well, they're still a metaphor, though," Luke said. Daph brought a pebble from her pocket and flicked it at his chest.

"Ow?" He said.

"How's that metaphor working out for you?"

Luke rolled his eyes. "Anyway. She said the fitting was a shit show, as expected, and if you continue to insist on participating in all of the optional events, we should at least fuck with these wankers whenever we can. They want to underestimate you, insult you, well, they'll have to do it knowing that Luke Maston will hate them forever for it."

This guy had never met her. Everything he knew about her was second-hand, much of it from someone who had only met her a few days ago. And yet, here he was, treating her like a cherished friend, in stark contrast to basically everyone else here for the wedding. Mattie ducked her head in case her tears decided to fall, not wanting to make him uncomfortable.

"I—thank you. That means a lot. I don't know how that will work," she admitted, "but if you two have confidence in it, who am I to judge?"

"Well, it will work until the actual wedding," Luke said. "Then you'll show up with Raph, and I'll show up with Rin, and everyone will think we lied or we're the sexiest polycule in existence."

"Oh, are you officially Rin's date?" Daphne asked. "Last they mentioned it, they were only considering it."

Luke nodded, a smile tugging his lips. "I gave a convincing presentation that included irrefutable facts such as 'My presence will detract from the bride and groom and they'll hate that,' and 'I will be one more person who knows how to be in a fight,' and 'You can boast having the hottest date.' And so on."

He squeezed Mattie's shoulder playfully, and she adjusted the tote bag on her other shoulder. "When will you know if Raph needs backup?" She asked.

"I'm going over there now, to be close by. I'd be distracting Edie if she hadn't had some kind of phone-in interview thing to do at the same time—ah," he cut off, grimacing.

"We found out she's here this morning," Daphne said, sighing. "We saw her at the car when Raphael got picked up."

"It's honestly over between them," he said, emphasizing his words with a sweep of his hand. "He wasn't hiding it from you to try to get away with anything. She's just a total douchebag and he doesn't want her to get anywhere near you."

Yet another thing that Mattie had pushed aside in her mind to make room for all the other insults and microaggressions she would experience today.

"We'll keep her away from you," he promised, reading worry in her expression. "And I'll keep her away from Raph. And I'll keep your relatives from treating you like total shit." He squinted into the distance. "I'm doing a lot of protecting today. I'm a protector."

Mattie laughed. "I appreciate it, Luke. And hey, if it works, you may even earn a place in the Honest Mischief Alliance." Luke beamed, and Mattie could see the resolve in his eyes.

A pair of voices approached, and two of Mattie's older cousins came alongside the doors and stopped, tittering like teenagers.

"Um, excuse us, but you're Luke, right? Luke Maston?"

Slipping his hand up around the back of Mattie's neck, he frowned and faced the girls.

"Do you mind?" He asked, letting irritation color his tone. "I haven't seen my—my friend Mattie in too long, and it's incredibly rude of you to interrupt us."

The women's eyes went wide. "Oh my gosh, we're so sorry, um—"

"Mats, you know these people?"

They leaned in and raised their eyebrows pleadingly.

"My cousins," she said.

"Are they cool?" Mattie couldn't interpret whatever they were trying to communicate to her with their pinched faces, but Luke cut in before she could answer, anyway. "Doesn't matter. I've got to get to set. You can tell me about your family later."

He leaned in and planted a kiss on her lips, and despite not crushing on him, a thrill ran through her. She supposed that was just a consequence of being kissed by beautiful people. When he pulled away, he nodded at Daphne.

"Daphne, always a pleasure," he said, rubbing the spot on his chest where she hit him with the pebble, before turning down the hallway and leaving them alone.

"Holy shit," one cousin said, staring after Luke's retreating form. "Did he really just kiss you? Do you know him?"

Daphne snorted and pulled Mattie through the doors past the cousins. "What does it look like?" She said, leading Mattie across the patio toward the changing rooms. "We're going to get changed, do excuse us."

It didn't take long to get into their swimsuits and robes. The day had remained overcast, though the storm itself hadn't arrived yet, and the lack of sun would only make it colder, blazing modern braziers be damned. When they emerged from the dressing room, a hush cascaded down the lines of lounge chairs before several of the women called for Mattie and Daph to sit by them. Daph waved thanks and plopped the two of them down into a pair of chairs set away from the others.

As they set up their spot, a waiter came to offer the bride's signature cocktail—something fruity and far too sweet and exactly what Mattie wanted. When asked if there was anything else he could get them, Mattie remembered the letter Raphael had left for her at the front desk.

"I know this is a weird request," she said. "But is there any way I could get a sheet of hotel stationery?"

***

"This could have been a play," Raphael murmured, rubbing at his stubble as he stared at the dirt-caked log cabin. He didn't want it to be a play any more than he wanted it to be a film, or a book, for that matter, but a mostly-single-location narrative heavy with dialogue and significant looks? That was a play. Or a film so ambitious that Payton saw it as an opportunity for him to find his way back to significance in the industry.

Raph checked his watch: almost three. Though Payton had said he wanted Raph, Luke, and Edie there today to start as soon as possible, nobody had followed through with call times, and the number of people on set and at the production's outbuildings was curiously light. Raphael was even more convinced that Payton's cry for "raw authenticity" was just an excuse to half-ass everything more than usual.

He lifted his eyes back to the grim cabin, steeling himself for the meeting. Mattie had texted just as he was leaving the hotel, and he wished she could have been there with him. She would have made a good replacement for his backbone when he went to talk to his director. Luke would join him, but not for another half hour. Before then, he was on his own.

As he walked through the cabin, every doorway doorless and every window a simple hole in the wall, it was impossible to know if the set was incomplete or if they were filming at an actual shack Payton had stumbled across in the woods. The rugs and furniture were well-worn and slightly grimy, and despite the cross-breeze, Raphael smelled faint mildew in every room. The size of the windows didn't let in much natural light anyway, but the day was cloudy and getting darker, and a gloom settled over the house. Payton's makeshift office was in a back room, and Raphael stopped in the doorway to watch him.

They hadn't seen each other in person for over a year, but as soon as Raph saw the scrunched shoulders, messy black hair, and hands that spoke for themselves like birds in flight, he knew that arguing with Payton was going to be difficult. It had been almost fifteen years since Payton had released *Crosshatch Fugue*, the debut film that had launched the director's career, attracted the attention of serious producers, and gained him a loyal cult following. Raphael loved it when it first came out. Edgy and violent, a meditation on the depths of human horror and exploitation, how the real horror was that some people refused to be desensitized to violence.

When he heard that Payton was casting for his second film, Raphael devoted all of his time to landing a part. Any part, he didn't care. He just wanted to be involved in whatever this genius would come up with next. But his persistence and willingness to do almost anything had impressed Payton, and he got the lead. It was the role that made his career. His talent was undeniable and he had the right look, but he also knew how much of the industry depended on straight-up dumb luck, good timing, and who you knew. And for him, Payton was all three. It was why Raph couldn't say no to him, even with all his initial misgivings about this new project.

Bringing his thoughts back to the present, Raph took a deliberate breath as he decided how to approach the situation. After the loneliness of the rest of the house, the bright room had an assuring lived-in feel to it. Payton sat at a flimsy wooden desk with his back to the door, while an assistant knelt by him, watching and nodding as the director sketched something on a piece of paper. Corkboards and whiteboards furnished the walls, filled with sticky notes and poorly printed reference pictures, affirmations, and penis doodles in dry erase marker. Never great at strategy or confrontation, Raphael decided to start out on the defensive.

"This place looks like shit," he said. Payton turned with a start, the anger on his face giving way to something like relief when he saw who had spoken.

"Raph!" He said, crossing the room to give him a hug. The assistant stood and hastily left the room through another door. "Am I glad to see you. Yeah, it looks great, huh? Straight out of the book." Raphael returned the embrace for a moment, remembering the familiarity of Payton before remembering wanting to set better boundaries with him.

"Payton," he sighed, using one hand to gently push him away. "What am I doing here?"

"Not wasting any time, huh?" Payton gave him his best crooked smile. The smudges of purple-blue skin below his eyes popped against his pale complexion, and his dark hair had gone too many days without washing. "I could say you're here to save my ass and make the easiest money of your life and to star in a film that will win all the awards. But you're annoyingly altruistic, so if that doesn't grab you, you're here to give voice to the silenced and assure them that their struggles are real and seen."

Raphael huffed and stepped farther into the room, scanning the scattered notes on the wall. Payton was committed, if sloppy. Maybe the best way to get him to reconsider everything wasn't to blow up at him, like Luke had, but to let him explain himself first, then counter with why he should shut it down.

"Honestly, Payton, I'm not feeling confident about any of this. Walk me through it. Why this story?"

Payton leaned against a windowsill as Raph wandered, and he could hear the smile in his answer. "See, you cut through to the heart of things, ask the right questions. You make decisions based on the reality of the situation and not on other people's feelings. This is how I knew you'd be the perfect Daine Hunt."

Raph's stomach twinged, nauseated that Payton—someone who had known him for over a decade—might see any parallels between him and the personification of bigotry.

"Is that why you went all in on this project? The main character?" he asked, taking his eyes off the inscrutable notes and drawings to look back at his friend.

Payton lit up, animated by the chance to share his obsession. "It's a story about a man without a story recognizing that he's meant to have one, and doing everything necessary to reclaim his life, his voice, his freedom. Even if—especially if—society says he's wrong to want it, and wrong to pursue it. And it's terrifying, and freeing, to realize the institutions you used to believe in, rely on, are actually trying to destroy you." He pushed off the windowsill and started pacing, a note of agitation in his voice. "Like Hollywood. Fuck, man, there was a time when people recognized I was trying to buck the status quo, but now, between this 'Me Too' thing and all these calls for 'diversity,' it's trendy to dump the white man, and harder and harder for me to get the message out there."

Raph's heart sank with every word. His disappointment was bitter, but he couldn't ignore it. He didn't want to lose someone who had done so much for him, at times a friend, a confidant, a mentor. Had Payton always been like this, but Raph was too wrapped up in his own pursuits to notice? When Mattie described her brother's wedding as her "one last job," he didn't understand why she would give any of them another chance to hurt her once she had already decided to walk away. But as he stood there with Payton, contemplating doing the same thing, her actions seemed less inexplicable, and he felt guilty for judging her.

Maybe he didn't have to argue about it. Maybe Raph could avoid that confrontation but still stop—or at least postpone—the project. "Things are certainly changing, it seems." As the words left his mouth, he was annoyed with himself that he wasn't taking a firmer stance. "But besides that, I'm concerned about this new virus. It's gotten everywhere now, and people are dying from it. Believe me, I've had fourteen days to do nothing but watch the news, and I don't know how we can keep the cast and crew safe."

Payton shook his head. "It's not real, Raph."

That brought him up short. He opened his mouth to respond, but didn't know what to say that wasn't "are you fucking joking."

Two weeks in quarantine for him, entire countries shut down, people dead and dying, and Payton just...turns the other way because it disrupts what he wants to do. Raphael didn't know how to reason with someone irrational.

"It's real enough for me, and I don't feel comfortable tempting fate. Neither does Luke." Where was his backup, anyway? "His daughter has asthma, you know. What if we delay it for a month? See what happens. Then we can introduce comprehensive protocols. You'll be able to fill all the empty positions—"

"No." Payton abruptly stopped his pacing on the other side of the room, rubbed his whole face with his hands, hard, and slapped his cheeks. "This is a film about perseverance in the face of adversity. Filming it in the midst of all these restrictions will mean more than doing it the easy way. Daine is all of us, and making this movie is *my* scarlet, beating heart. Succeeding when the entire universe is working against you, that's—that's the whole point."

His arms dropped to his sides, and he looked at Raph like he'd expected better from him. Which was rich, coming from Payton.

"Is the entire universe working against you," Raphael asked, "or did you just not do the work?"

"Come on, Raph. I worked my ass off."

"You sent me the script a week ago." He tried to keep his voice level, keep his cool despite growing hotter with agitation. "No table reading, no blocking, no planning. Zero support from Miramar, as far as I can tell, and it's becoming clear that your slapdash approach has less to do with wanting something 'raw and authentic' and more to do with the fact that everyone who might help you can recognize that it's garbage."

Payton laughed. "It's okay, Raph. I trust in my vision and I trust my instinct to bring the right people together to make it happen. It'll make sense. You just need some time."

"Payton," Raphael whined, putting his face in his hands. Maybe there was no way to get through to him. "If I make this film, my reputation will be irreparably damaged. I'm not comfortable legitimizing propaganda, and you shouldn't be, either. This character isn't a hero, he's an asshole. There is absolutely nothing in the script that makes him redeemable."

Payton clenched his teeth. "I agree the script isn't where I want it to be. Luke mentioned you were a good writer. If you wanted to try some rewrites yourself, I would consider them. But I don't want to alienate the audience that loved the book. Actually, it might help if you sat down with its fans. There's a group of them staying at the Billingstead. They have a really firm grasp on what it's all about."

Oh, Raph knew exactly who those fans were. "I suppose that includes Mike Spencer?"

"You've heard of him?" Surprise flickered across Payton's face. "Oh. Luke. He's got the wrong idea, I think."

"You know that New Zealand considers politics like his to be hate speech? And his actions terrorism?"

"Oh, come on."

"And," Raphael continued, "besides that, he spent his childhood bullying a good friend of mine. So no. I'm not going to sit down with him and his bros. I can't think of anyone whose opinion I value less."

"All right, so you don't like the guy," Payton said, his irritation finally finding its way into his words. "You don't agree with him or Daine Hunt. So what? You've been Hamlet. You've been Patrick Bateman. You've played plenty of complicated characters. And if you don't agree with them, well, we'd never know it, because that's what acting is."

Raph took a breath and tilted his head back, as if he could find the solution in the ceiling.

"This story," Payton continued, "has been a struggle from the beginning, between funding and writers and permits and just every fucking thing that could go wrong. And now this pandemic nonsense? Shit, I don't blame you for wanting to bail." He ran a hand through his hair and stared out one of the windows into the darkening woods.

"I know I'm asking a lot. But I'm gonna ask for even more. Because I know you have it in you, and struggle makes achievement even greater. This can be epic. And I want you in it."

Payton had always been a terrible actor, so to be this committed, he must have genuinely connected with the story, the character. Before, Raphael would never have described him as racist or sexist. He definitely pushed boundaries. Flirted with the taboo. Made plenty of people angry. But the quality of his work was a testament to his talent.

Maybe Raph was wrong about the book. Everything he felt about it, the script, the production, had formed during the last two weeks in isolation. It was possible he had been quick to judge, sitting in his own echo chamber. Maybe he needed to hear other people's thoughts before cementing his own. This was Payton. He'd done so much for him, Raph was reluctant to lose him.

"I can't promise you anything," Raph said, hating that he wasn't standing his ground, that it took so little for him to second-guess his convictions. "But if you'd genuinely like my help, I'll go over the script again, with an eye for improvements. If I still don't feel comfortable with it, we're going to have another conversation."

Payton turned around and sat on the empty windowsill. He didn't respond right away, staring at the scuffed floorboards between them. When he spoke, his voice was low and measured. "I always felt that our fates were entwined, Raph. Even though I'm a lone wolf. We'll bring each other to stardom, or to ruin, together."

A chill spread up Raph's spine, raising the hairs on the back of his neck. Did Payton have enough pull to blacklist him? Or did Raph's influence eclipse the director's? The idea of facing off with his career on the line made him very uneasy.

"Oh, also." Payton stood, and his sinister mood morphed into embarrassment. "I didn't know things were so bad with you and Edie. Luke told me you'd had a big falling out, but I didn't realize it was so serious. You know I don't pay attention to that shit."

"Yeah, I do know that."

"Just one more conflict daring you to scurry away from this." Payton laughed. "She's the only one who could get into the country in time. If she gives you any trouble, tell me, and I'll step in. It's my job to tame these wild actresses. For what it's worth, I thought you made a good couple."

"We didn't," Raphael said quickly. "And she's been harassing me since we split up. I'm in the middle of getting a restraining order."

"Oh shit, man." Payton crossed the room to him, putting a hand on his shoulder. "I had no idea. Okay. I can fix this for you. You're so good, you would have chemistry with an empty chair, so we can film a lot of the dialogue for you two separately. But at least you get to rape and murder her. That should be cathartic."

Nausea hit him fast, threatening to bring up his lunch. "No," Raph said, remembering the scene. "That—no. I'm not filming that."

"I mean, it's a key beat. It's gotta stay."

"I can't." He put out a hand to steady himself against the desk.

"Hey, I hear you, we'll figure it out," Payton said, giving him a tentative smile. "I could be your stand-in. I do love strangling beautiful blondes." He winked, and Raphael had a sinking feeling that it was meant to let him in on a secret, not assure him that he was kidding.

"Enough about that." Payton clapped him on the shoulder one more time before settling into the desk chair. "Grab that chair and sit with me. Tell me what's been going on in your life, besides dodging crazy Edie. Luke said you met a girl."

From Payton's perspective, their difference of opinion had been resolved—with his opinion coming out on top—and Raphael knew that he couldn't get any further with him until he regrouped and sorted out his own issues. He pulled up a chair, and the two caught up on their personal lives—as much as Raph felt comfortable sharing, at least—before turning to the script and trying to outline the changes they wanted to make.

***

After thirty minutes of evading questions about Luke and their possible relationship, Mattie decided that the best way to escape these vicious women would be to fake falling asleep.

The guests—Mattie's relatives, her brother's girl friends, and the bride's friends and relatives—had been instructed to wear the same outfit: two-piece bathing suit, lightweight lounge pants, lightweight robe, sun hat, high heels. It was getting cooler every day. A big thunderstorm threatened on the horizon. No sun in sight. But the bride was particular about her photos, so everyone wore the same summer style and smiled when the photographer took their group photo.

Daphne had the nerve to match. She always did, so it wasn't a surprise. Mattie just wished she occasionally had that skill, too. In a true show of her fashion sense, Daph's poolside outfit matched the one she wore to pick up Mattie from the quarantine hotel: mint bikini with little pink bows, loose pants with green, pink, and white brush strokes, a startlingly white robe, and neon orange heels.

Mattie's sole two-piece swimsuit was pink and sporty. She had found a pair of black poolside pants that were SPF 50 (not that she would need it beneath the cloud cover), and a lightweight black and white robe whose brushstroke pattern was similar enough to Daphne's pants that Mattie thought she might have accidentally bought something stylish. Her heels were matte-black peep toe, conservative in comparison to everyone else's strappy footwear and unsuitable for anything poolside, but the other pair she brought was for the wedding and even more inappropriate for anything casual, outdoor, or wet.

With the noise of conversation, Mattie couldn't take a nap or feign one, so she settled back as though she were actually sunbathing—in pants and robe, on a cloudy fall afternoon—and half-listened to the women's gossip until they came back around to Luke.

"I'm pretty sure I saw Raphael Callan earlier, too," Ola said. Mattie and Daphne's older sister had never had much interest in them, but a potential brush with celebrity would be one of the few things that would attract her. She and several cousins and other women they didn't know had relocated to sit near them and hear the gossip. Mattie blushed at Raph's name, her gut giving a little tweak of anxiety, knowing the kind of objectification that was coming next.

"He is so hot," someone said.

"I would cheat on my husband with him so fast."

"If Luke's really taken, I suppose I could settle for him."

"Have any of you even met him?" Mattie asked, turning around to frown at them over her sunglasses. There was no sun, but they all had to look the part.

"Why would I have to meet him?" Ola said. "Handsome, charming, good at his job. That's all I need to know. That's a lie, all I need is handsome." Some of the women giggled, nodded, hummed agreement.

"Heteros," Daphne muttered with an eyeroll.

"He deserves better than that," Mattie said. The vodka and Daphne's presence had helped her find her voice. "You don't know him. You're not entitled to his body, or his time or energy, just because you've seen his work. Your behavior is really gross."

Ola huffed and adjusted her robe. "I guess you would know, since you're a part of their world now."

"He definitely was about to say 'girlfriend,'" said one of the cousins who had interrupted Luke at the doorway. "I mean, he changed it to 'friend.' Do you not want your relationship coming out? Or, no, probably he doesn't, right?"

"What is that supposed to mean?" Mattie said. The woman blushed.

"I just mean that—that you're not famous, so, if you went public with it, you'd be flooded with all kinds of attention."

"I can't tell from their socials, but it looks like Matalina and Daphne both followed a couple of the same accounts recently." said the other cousin, staring at her phone.

"Suspicious," someone murmured.

"They didn't start dating in the last week," Daphne said with a snort. "Why would we wait until now to friend them?"

The women made thoughtful noises and resumed their theorizing.

Daphne leaned closer to Mattie. "I didn't think they were so tech-savvy," Daph whispered.

"I don't think it matters," Mattie replied at the same volume. "I was warned this might happen. I just thought it would be a bunch of strangers who think they're in love with him, sending me death threats and retweeting some of my saltier opinions in an effort to turn him against me. Being harried by relatives about it might be worse."

Ola leaned between their chairbacks and whispered, "Hey." Daphne and Mats jumped.

"Ola," Daphne said at a normal volume, rubbing her forehead.

"Sorry," Ola said more loudly. "I thought we were whispering. I just remembered when we went to Disney World and I met my own movie star crush. You were both still in elementary school. Well, I was in middle school, so I wasn't that much older, but do you remember that?"

"Oh my god," Mattie said, that day unfurling in her mind like a forgotten scroll. "JTT."

"JTT." Ola nodded.

"I'm drawing a blank," Daph said with a frown. "How old was I?"

"Seven," Mattie murmured. Because Mattie had been nine, and Ola had said she didn't want either of them coming because they hadn't hit "double digits" yet. She'd wanted the experience all to herself, but their parents had paid so much money, all the kids were forced to participate.

"It was some kind of marketing thing, obviously," Ola continued. "But Mom and Dad knew how much I liked him, and we were due to go to the parks that year anyway."

"It was a room inside a building, but it was set up like a tent, right?" Mattie asked, the memory filling her. "Reds and oranges and yellows. It smelled like air conditioning and hay in sunlight, and it was so cold."

"Oh!" Daph yelled, pointing at Ola. "And I kept saying that you were going to throw up on him!"

Mattie laughed. Ola had been furious. She was so worried that Daphne would say that in front of her crush, and Daphne was doing her best to be insufferable and succeeding like only seven-year-old-Daph could. Everything was coming back to Mattie, from the smells and sounds to the texture of the draped cloths, one sister's impish laughter and the other's high-pitched protests to their parents. At the time, Mats was withdrawn, struggling with her own crush, hoping that, even though it was supposed to be for her older sister (and the boy was probably a teenager at that point—way over "double digits"), maybe he would look past Ola and his eyes would find Mattie, quiet, in a mysterious and intriguing way, and he would fall in love with her instead.

That obviously didn't happen.

Present-day Daphne and Ola chuckled together, finding humor in a moment that had caused them so much stress so long ago.

"You know," Ola said, wiping away tears of laughter, "for years, I thought he had invited me there. I wrote him a letter every week for months and told all my friends that we were going out. When he never wrote back, I was heartbroken. I was a kid, I didn't understand—well, I didn't understand anything—but especially not fiction and movies and marketing. It's funny, I still think of him sometimes."

Emotion welled up, and Mattie swallowed and clenched her teeth to keep it from turning into tears.

This was why she had come, why she couldn't just walk away from everyone. There was too much history, and a childhood's worth of memories that only a handful of people would remember like she did. Would she have ever thought of that muggy Florida day again, without Ola's prompting? What other joyful and mundane and formative memories would remain forgotten forever, once she cut these people out of her life for good?

Were any of those memories worth the decades of disdain and manipulation that had buried them in the first place?

This back-and-forth was the reason Mattie hadn't been able to commit to cutting off her relatives until she was in her thirties. She wanted them to respect her as an adult, apologize for bullying her as a child, and participate in a relationship on equal footing. And all of them were unwilling, every chance she gave them.

So this was the last one. She would meet them halfway, with the wedding, being a bridesmaid, going to parties and dinners and brunches and anything else they would ask of her. If they wouldn't make the same effort to stand on common ground with her, they didn't deserve her, and she'd be gone. And she could feel confident that she, at least, had done everything she could. She had shown up.

Ola had drifted back to a conversation with their cousins, and Daphne was talking to the maid of honor. The braziers were doing a valiant job against the chill, but they couldn't do much about the wind that had picked up. It cleared Mattie's mind, and she spent several minutes letting it cool the more intense feelings to leave her in an almost calm state. The cocktails helped.

With the dropping temperature, staff members brought them heavier blankets and hot snacks and refreshed their cocktails several times. Mattie was full of cheese and alcohol and appreciated that these servers knew what would keep women warm.

Just like Raphael knew how to keep her warm.

She blushed, remembering the night before. That had been fantastic. She wanted an encore performance as soon as possible. He hadn't texted in a while, but she'd send him another message soon. Before that, though, she was going to read his letter and write one in return.

"Sorry, but I'm on deadline," she told the group, gathering her tote bag and drink. "If you don't mind, I'm going to try to finish these pages in a quiet corner."

The storm was close. It had been threatening for hours, taking its time like the persistent but ambling villain in a slasher movie. Inevitable, but no less scary. Mattie snorted. The metaphor was too obvious, but when had the universe ever graced her with subtlety?

It would be easy enough to run back indoors when the skies opened up. She settled into a lounge chair away from the others, adjusted her robe, brought out the envelope she'd received with Raph's room key, and started reading his letter.

Greetings, fellow prisoner,

Released from the tedium and confinement of what I now realize is a mid-grade hotel at best, the entirety of this beautiful country open to our desires, wind in our hair, sun on our face, dirt beneath our nails, free to embrace and kiss and run and run away—it is with the deepest condolences that I inform you: we were ushered through the doors of one prison directly into another.

The room itself is an improvement. I don't know if you'll read this before you make your way up here, but I upgraded to a suite. Bedroom behind its own door. Enormous bathtub that someone else will clean. View of a spectacular lake and surrounding hills and not a tired city street. And of course, I can leave the room whenever I choose.

It is missing something, though. It feels empty.

I miss you.

And though I hope I'll see you again soon, our release—as I said—has flung us into circumstances more dire than our previous isolation. You—facing an assembly of tormentors collected over the course of your life thus far. I—evading a project and a former confidant that both promise potential ruin. I'm beginning to think we can only make it through all of this together, Mattie.

I only found out yesterday that Edie had been brought onto the project. It was a hard thing to hear. She'd been bullying me from afar, but now she would be in my physical space, and I pretended it wasn't true. I didn't tell you because telling someone else about it would confirm that it was actually happening.

Eventually, I realized that keeping it from you was wrong. You had no reason to tell me about Mike Spencer, yet you did. Then I find myself in a similar situation and I don't confide in you.

It should have at least crossed my mind—once I knew she'd be working with us, and Payton was sending someone to pick me up—that she would maneuver her way into seeing me as soon as possible. But she stepped out of the car and it was a total surprise. I didn't even recognize her. And then, suddenly, I did, and I have never felt so sick in my life.

And with the photographers around, everything I did would be reported and scrutinized and criticized and repeated. Of course Edie is the one who told them where to be: she knew I couldn't get into an argument right there on the sidewalk. I considered stepping away, but there was nowhere to go. If I refused to get in the car, or called another car and took off without her, I would look like the bad guy. I should have been brave and just left her there, walked away, gotten a cab, or called you and asked you to come back and take me with you.

And then you drove by and saw us, saw her, and the look on your face—you hadn't put it together yet. I'd disappointed you. I couldn't have prevented Edie from pulling this stunt, but at the very least, I could have told you she would be around.

I bet Daphne knew what she was seeing. I watched her have a fit in the front seat.

I rode in the passenger seat beside the driver. Edie tried to harangue me from the back, but I got Luke on a video call and stayed on with him for the entire drive. That man—I owe him a lot. He distracted me but he can also serve as witness if Edie lies about what happened during that car ride. I hate to think in those terms, but that's the reality of where I am right now.

Edie being here bothers me. But I'm more concerned that I've upset you.

I'm leaving to see Payton soon. I have no idea what I'm going to say to him. When I'm writing to you, all my thoughts line up. But when I have to confront someone, in person, who's mistreating me? I can't remember any of my indisputable points.

In case my improvisation includes losing my temper and getting arrested, I want you to know that these past weeks have been the best of my life. I'm mostly kidding about getting arrested. Not kidding at all about your affect on me.

I hope you'll be waiting for me on the outside.

Yours,

Raph

Mattie reread the letter. When they drove by Raph and Edie, Mattie had wondered with the slightest twinge of jealousy who the woman was before she noticed how upset Raphael looked.

His whole body tense, leaning away from her as much as she was trying to lean in to him. He had looked...trapped. The image that came to mind was the photo that Daphne had described of them: Edie clingy, Raph bored and unhappy.

Not all of her objections to the situation were based in Raphael's wellbeing. She wanted him to be safe, protected. But between Edie's classic beauty and the emotional assault of the dress fitting, Mattie's self-confidence was circling the drain. It had been a while since she let people she didn't know make her feel worthless. The stress of the wedding, Spencer showing up, the virus, these new feelings for Raphael—her emotions were stirred up, and the years of practice she had masking them felt like the walls of a sandcastle in the face of a tsunami.

A splash at her feet brought her out of her reverie, and for a moment she thought she had conjured the wave her mind was using as a metaphor. A loud peal of thunder growled over the lake and mountains, echoing through the Billingstead, the only warning before cold rain hit them in a sudden downpour.

Across the deck, women shrieked. They all knew it was coming, but few of them had prepared a quick getaway. Typical of them to assume the weather would bow to their wishes. Mattie shoved the letter in her tote, thankful she hadn't spread out across the chair and side table, and ran with the other women into the hotel.

"This isn't the end!" Someone yelled, holding aloft her half-empty martini glass in victory. "Girls Party continues at the indoor pool, where there will be games!" The group let out a collective groan. "And more martinis!" She added, to a round of enthusiastic cheers.

Daphne appeared and slung a soaked arm over Mattie's shoulder. "Nobody would notice if you slipped away right now," she whispered too loudly. That fruity signature cocktail was deadly. Mattie shook her head.

"Nah, I'm good, actually. Just find me a quiet corner. I'm going to write Raphael a letter. Also, who would keep an eye on you if I left?"

"Mattie, nobody can keep their eyes *off* me. Have you even seen how cute my outfit is?"

Before she could answer, the martini woman called for everyone to follow her, and the crowd of them obeyed, drinking, singing, laughing. Mattie got caught up in the collective march. It wasn't so bad, now that they were all buzzed. The women stopped pretending so much, and stopped pretending interest in her. She stopped caring so much. It was almost fun.

Not quite. But almost.

***

By five o'clock, Raphael was back in his room. As soon as he left Payton's physical presence, he mentally kicked himself for being so easily influenced. He hadn't had much of a plan, but he had his convictions, and Payton just dodged them like a martial arts master sidestepping a blow.

He knew what the problem was. He wasn't weak or susceptible, but after decades of "yes, and"-ing absolutely everyone about absolutely everything, setting and keeping boundaries was a recent and unfamiliar skill that took practice. And he didn't want to say no to Payton.

Even if the director was actually an asshole—whose talent was in paying talented people to work for him so he could take credit for their genius—there was no denying that his decision to hire Raphael all those years ago had had a profound impact on the actor's life. If nothing else, Payton was responsible for that, and Raphael wasn't able to stop feeling grateful for it.

But that didn't mean he was entitled to treat Raph like shit.

He paused, realizing this was exactly what Mattie meant when she explained the difference between relatives and family. Payton had taken him under his wing, given him opportunities, guided him and celebrated his success. Before coming to New Zealand, he would absolutely have called him family. But by Mattie's definition, he wasn't. And he wasn't related, so he wouldn't be a relative. Former mentor? Former co-worker?

Mattie would know. He could see things more clearly when she was around. He pulled out his phone and texted that he was back in his room. The last text from her was just after her dress fitting, and he figured that as long as she and Daphne had stayed together, they probably didn't get in trouble. Oh they would have made plenty of trouble. But they wouldn't have been caught in it.

Her response was immediate: Leaving the pool, coming to his room. Needed a hot shower. Would he like an arancini or some kind of small mushroom thing stuffed with what appeared to be crab? He didn't.

A few minutes later, he opened his door for Mattie. He wasn't sure what he expected—well, he expected her to show up in a nineteenth-century bathing costume, draped in layers of floor-length skirts and housecoats—so seeing bare skin around her pink swimsuit top was almost as shocking to him as if they had actually been living in the nineteenth century.

"What," he said, pulling her inside the room, "are you wearing?" The door latched closed, and he reached behind her to throw the lock.

"Oh, you haven't seen this robe before," she said, setting down two tote bags. Her hair was damp and she smelled of chlorine.

"No, this skin. I'm seeing skin."

Mattie smiled and looked away. The sun was close to setting, so he couldn't tell if she was blushing. "Pool party," she said. "Do...you like it?"

Raphael reached up to trail a finger from her jaw, down her neck and chest, to the edge of the top. "Still too many layers," he said, voice low and breathy.

"Oh." She shrugged out of her robe and let it fall to the floor. "Better?"

Raph wrapped his arms around her, pulling her in for a hard, desperate kiss, and she met his passion with her own. She gently entwined her fingers in his hair and held him against her, as his hands explored all the exposed skin of her back and arms and stomach. He had thought about her all day, in every quiet moment, in the midst of arguments, in the spaces between every line he read. After over a week of near-constant communication, a handful of texts scattered throughout an entire day wasn't enough for him.

Beyond the chlorine, her scent rose from her, from the covered and warmed places that Raphael wanted to explore again and again.

"You taste like candy," he whispered. She laughed.

"Cocktails by the pool."

"Are you sober enough? For this?"

"Yes. I planned ahead." She kissed the tip of his nose.

"Good. I want to hear all about your day," he said, trailing kisses down her neck. "Later, though." Mattie grunted in response and slid her hands beneath his shirt, pulling it up over his head.

"I want to hear all about yours," she responded, kissing his chest, running her nails up his back. "Definitely later. Show me the bedroom." Raph's smile lit her up, and he led her across the living room.

"Oh, wait," she said, slipping free of his grip and diving toward her bag. "I planned ahead," she repeated. "Condoms."

The car pick-up situation was a fiasco for many reasons, but it bothered him even more because he had forgotten to stop at a service station on the way to the hotel like Mattie had recommended—not only for the food, but for condoms. Her deciding to include them in her daypack even though his ex was hanging all over him the last time she saw him gave him hope that Edie wasn't going to be a problem for them. And the fact that Mattie was thinking about sex with him when they were apart filled him with desire.

As Mattie retrieved the condoms, Raphael backed into the bedroom, stripping off the rest of his clothing as he went. When she turned back to him, she inhaled sharply, letting her eyes wander over his body. They rested on his cock, and as she watched, he grasped his jutting member and stroked himself.

"I want you naked before you step through this doorway," he told her.

She gave him a mischievous smile and tossed him the box of condoms. It only took five steps and four seconds for her to cross the room, peeling off her swimsuit top like a pro, getting her pants and bottoms off in one motion between steps.

Raphael barely had time to toss the box onto the nightstand before Mattie was in the room, not one piece of clothing on her. A stark contrast to the entire wardrobe she'd worn the night before. He wouldn't have changed anything about their first time together. It was slow, sweet, fun, and sexy—a genuine exploration of each other. It was the kind of connection he had always sought, but never found, and didn't have the words for.

But Mattie stripping naked in the blink of an eye because he had told her to—it flooded him with arousal, his whole body ready and wanting.

He didn't wait. He couldn't. They both reached for the other, grabbing arms and hair, their bodies as close as possible, their lips pressed together so hard it was almost painful, but still not close enough. Raphael's hands roamed over her soft back, her luscious backside, up to grab her breasts, his lips pulling away from hers just long enough to cover a nipple with his mouth and flick his tongue against her.

Mattie groaned and clutched him tighter, then wound her hand between them to find his cock. She stroked him gently, and Raphael had to pause, had to breathe, because he couldn't concentrate on anything else while her hand was on him. He closed his eyes and kissed her neck, her temple, tried to distance himself a little so the pleasure wasn't overwhelming. It was a fine line, taking himself out of the moment just enough that he wouldn't come before he wanted to, but not so much that he would lose all arousal.

Just as he got control of himself, Mattie slipped from him, and he opened his eyes. She knelt before him, reaching out to wrap her hand around him again as she looked up and their eyes met.

"Can I?" She asked. Raphael reached down to run his fingers through her hair. He nodded. He didn't have any words.

In the last of the day's fading light, he watched Mattie lean toward him and lick the bead of liquid off his dripping cock.

"Mattie," he whispered, one of two words he remembered. "Yes."

He wanted to watch, as she closed her lips around the head of his prick, her tongue massaging its sensitive underside, but his eyes closed anyway, sensation flowing through his body. Instead, he grasped her dark, golden hair—not holding her in place, or guiding her, just wanting to touch her, any part of her, as she touched him so intimately.

There was no doubt that she would make him come like that. She would have that affect on him no matter what they did together, so he wasn't in any rush to get there before her. He wanted to bring her to pleasure first.

He reached down and grabbed her upper arm. "Up," he demanded, pulling her to standing, his cock sliding reluctantly out of her mouth. He kissed her, lips slippery with saliva, his hands moving down to knead her ass cheeks.

Mattie made a noise against him. "Do you want me to do something different?" There was a note of worry in her voice.

"No, that was—" He huffed. "I want you to do that as often as you'd like. Right now, I want a chance to please you."

"I was pretty pleased with your cock in my mouth." As if on cue, it twitched between them, the thought of it making him harder.

"Well, I'll be pleased when my tongue is slipping between the folds of your pussy."

"Jesus," Mattie breathed.

"No, but close enough. On the bed. Hands and knees." As Mattie rushed to comply, Raphael turned on the bedside lamp. He didn't mind making love in the dark, but he wanted to see her, to watch her writhe and shudder, knowing he caused it. He detached one of the condoms from the strip and set it on the bed, within reach.

"We'll get to that in a bit," he said, coming up behind her to grab both her thighs and playfully bite one of her cheeks. She yelped and pushed back against him, and he took that as encouragement. He drew his tongue across one cheek, then the other, pausing to nip at her as he went. He drew in a breath and was rewarded with her aroma of warm cardamom and almond.

When he pressed his lips to the top of her crack, she stilled, and he slid his tongue down the length of her, down across all her folds, to stop against her clit. She shuddered, her breathing ragged, and he started eating her out in earnest.

Resting her forehead against the bed, she surrendered, and Raphael took care of her. For he didn't know how long, his world was simply Mattie, her pleasure, and his pleasure, and he was lost in it. At some point, she whimpered as the flat of his tongue made circles against her, and he was brought back to the moment.

"Raph," she said, grabbing for the condom. "Fuck me, please—"

He heard the crinkle of the wrapping and looked up. "You're sure?" He asked, reaching for it. "I can keep going."

Mattie raised her head and pushed the condom toward him forcefully. "Open it, put it on, and fuck me. Just like this." He didn't need to be told again. He put on the condom, carefully, as was his habit, and positioned himself behind her, one hand clasping her hip, the other rubbing the head of his prick against her. She moaned and pushed back.

"Yes, Raph, please!"

He slid into her slowly, using both hands to hold her hips steady as her breath hitched and she rocked back toward him. When he was inside her completely, he exhaled a ragged breath, pausing before withdrawing and doing it again. It only took them a moment to find a rhythm, and Mattie made little noises with each thrust. She snaked her hand between her legs and started rubbing herself, but Raphael slid his hand beneath hers to take over.

Mattie braced herself on all fours again, her breath more ragged as Raphael fucked her faster. He paused to reposition himself, more on top of her, one hand still between her legs, but the other wrapped around her chest, clutching her shoulder, pulling her against him as he pumped her harder. It was frantic, and hot, that possessive grabbing, thrusting, and before she could say anything, Mattie was already coming, her body stiff and shuddering as it pulsed through her again and again, her mouth frozen open but unable to make a sound.

"Oh!" She finally breathed, her jaw and limbs looser as the intense pleasure slowly ebbed.

"Fuck, Mattie," Raphael growled, before stiffening even more, holding her tight against him as his own orgasm hit. He groaned, low, and long, a yearning attained, his hands grabbing desperately at the woman who brought him there.

He wasn't lost anymore. He wasn't floating. He was finally inside his body, aware of every sensation in the most physical way. Mattie hadn't sent him to the stratosphere—she had found his pleasure in his own body, as much as he had found pleasure in hers.

They stayed there a moment, panting, sweat rolling down Raphael's face and onto the back of Mattie's neck. He kissed her hair, her neck and shoulder before pulling back and slowly out of her. She made a sound of disappointment as he left her, and he laughed.

"You okay?" He asked, as she slid onto her side.

"Yeah," she said breathlessly. "I'm just going to nap here for a while though."

"That good, huh?" He curled up behind her and caressed her arms, from her shoulders to her fingertips.

"Mmm."

Her face was peaceful, and he liked watching her in repose. Satisfied and comfortable. He trailed his hand across the hills and valleys of her side, hips, thighs.

"Talk to me," he said, playfully tapping her backside as he got out of bed and crossed to the bathroom.

"Oh yeah," she said. "There was going to be talking too. I forgot."

He laughed from the other room. "Have I fucked you senseless? That's something of an achievement for me."

Mattie huffed and sat up. "Basically," she muttered. Louder, she said, "Still have my senses. But with added languor."

"You wanted a shower?" Raph stepped back into the room and leaned against the door frame. Mattie looked at him and blushed all over again.

She got out of bed and walked to him, took him into her embrace, kissed his chest and neck.

"So handsome. Yes. Shower. But we can talk while we do that."

"We?" He raised an eyebrow. She gave him the most sultry look she could and led him back into the bathroom.

***

The shower was too brief to start anything, since Mattie did actually have to get clean before the family dinner. Daph would be there about six thirty to wash up and change—a dangerously short amount of time before they had to be downstairs by seven, Mattie thought. But that gave her and Raph about an hour to catch up.

From the oversized couch, Raph started the fireplace with a remote control—an amenity that would have been unimaginable in their previous hotel—as Mattie curled against him. They talked about what happened when they were apart, wishing they had been together.

"I knew that I would have trouble standing up to everyone in person," Mattie said. "Every time. I'm not sure I can explain it."

"I'm not sure you need to," Raph said. "I felt the same way when I saw Payton. There's history there. I would listen to him, so I feel he should listen to me, but when he doesn't, I second-guess myself. So when I want to confront him, I'm already doubting why."

Mattie nodded slowly. "That's exactly it. Did you get any kind of resolution?"

"Nothing I'm happy with. He said he would consider any notes or rewrites I want to make to the script."

"Which we both know is unsalvageable."

Raph shifted, reaching for his water glass. "The producers are coming in for a meeting tomorrow and Payton wants me to be there."

"He knows it's a failure and he's trying to reassure the investors that everything's fine by demonstrating your loyalty to it."

"Yeah," he sighed. "I came to the same conclusion."

Night wasn't far off, and Mattie liked finding comfort in the fire's dim glow and each other. The highs and lows of the day had given them emotional whiplash, and the next day promised to be no better, but they had a steadiness together.

Raphael cleared his throat. "There's something I wanted to tell you." Mattie raised her head and an eyebrow.

"Sounds serious."

"It is." He put his glass down and took a breath. "I'll try to say it quickly so you don't worry.

"I came here to be alone," he said.

Despite his warning, Mattie did feel a tendril of anxiety creeping up. "For the chance of a few days or weeks of not having to perform in my personal life. To be alone with who I really am, and maybe like who that is enough to bring him into my public life, too. But writing to you these past two weeks has allowed me to be open and honest about myself for the first time in years. You gave me the opportunity to get to know someone without artifice or manipulation, without expectation, and without my celebrity coloring your view of me. And you just...accepted me."

Raphael huffed a laugh and ran his hand through his hair. When he looked back at Mattie, she stared at him, her emotions flickering through worry, hope, yearning. Whatever reservations she still held over whether Raphael really wanted her disappeared. Besides the man stopping her mid-blowjob to bury his face between her legs (which would have convinced her on its own), the fact that he felt comfortable telling her such private truths was a testament to his sincerity.

She'd had many lovers, and before Raphael, she would have said she shared an intimacy with them. But this—their immediate connection with words, then the absolute necessity of touching each other the moment they were able to—was unlike anything she had experienced before. And she was ready to give herself up to it.

"Be mine," he whispered, reaching out to caress her cheek. "And mine alone. I couldn't have imagined wanting this two weeks ago, and now I don't want to imagine anything else. It seems fast, but it feels inevitable. It feels right."

Mattie reached up and took his hand from her face, lacing their fingers together. "It feels right," she agreed, bringing his hand to her lips and kissing it gently. "I want whatever parts of yourself you'll share with me, and I want to share all of myself with you. We already feel like a team." Raph nodded when she paused, and kissed her hand, to mirror her. "So, yeah. Let's just be together. Whatever that means for us."

He grinned, and Mattie watched the parade of emotions cross his face, until he frowned.

"Edie won't come between us," he said firmly. He was probably thinking of their future without the immediate problems of exes, bullies, and illness, before remembering that those problems were still ongoing. She hesitated.

"I promise, you don't have anything to worry about," he emphasized.

"I'm not concerned about her specifically."

"You frowned."

"I trust you, and I don't care about her, beyond the fact that she's hurting you." Mats adjusted her position on the couch so she could lean back against the cushions. "It's more like the *idea* of her is troubling."

"You have no reason to be jealous."

"No, not jealousy." Mattie sighed. "What I'm feeling is dumb and selfish."

"Jealousy is selfish."

They sat in silence as Mattie tried to put her thoughts into words. "You recognized that Edie wasn't good for you and broke off your relationship. But even though you defined your boundaries, she still won't leave you alone. That's like, the number one thing I'm afraid of with my relatives. How do I make sure they don't bother me anymore?"

Raph eyed her with amusement. "I only did what Mattie told me to do. Earlier today, I talked to Edie. I was honest and direct. I was clear about my boundaries and serious about enforcing them. Beyond protecting yourself by blocking your relatives wherever you can, that's the best you can do."

"I know," she said quietly. "How'd you get so smart?"

"I'm literally repeating your own advice back to you."

"Hmm. How'd I get so smart?" She snuggled up to him. "You know, I never wanted to have to rely on anybody for anything, but I think you're going to be the reason I survive this weekend."

He laughed, but there was a lot of truth behind what she said. "It would be my honor."

"It may be your doom."

"There are less worthy things to be damned for," he said. "But you have your wits and a crew of friends who care for and support you—including Luke, who will be crashing the wedding."

"Actually, he's officially Rin's date, so he'll just be attending, not crashing."

"Oh, not your date?" He teased. "When he made out with you in front of the entire guest list?"

"Oooooh, right, first of all, it was a peck—"

"I know Luke Maston and that man doesn't know how to kiss with anything less than his full passion," Raph said.

Mattie pulled away from Raphael so she could look into his eyes. "Oh my god. You've kissed Luke, too."

"Even if I had, I'm not the type of person to gossip about who's been my partner, and besides, it would have been a decade ago and not in the middle of courting someone else."

Plenty of Mattie's partners had been, like her, bisexual, but the women and enbies outnumbered the men by a lot. There was a stigma to being a bisexual man, a stigma as stupid and nonsensical as any other, and she could be sure Raphael had experienced at least some of that bigotry.

"I respect that." She glanced away and picked a piece of white fuzz off Raph's shirt. "But if you did want to gossip about any of your previous partners, I would listen without judgment."

He narrowed his eyes at her. "It sounds like you're trying to distract me from the fact that Luke kissed you."

"He did kiss me. But if, as you say, he only kisses at full-volume passion, then it's a good thing I met you first, because I found him to be disappointingly chaste."

Raphael huffed. "You're just saying that so I won't get jealous."

"Kiss him again to refresh your memory." Mattie shrugged. "Or kiss me and make me forget about him."

It wasn't much of a choice. Raphael brushed his hand along her jaw and cupped her face, turning her toward him. "Challenge accepted."

Friday, April 3, 2020
Evening

The Baroque Dining Room at the Billingstead Hotel welcomed its guests with the warmth of champagne-colored tapered candles, the lushness of blood-red velvet drapes, and the luxury of thick, squishy carpet in a color that reminded Mattie of a dark and bold wine. Every room at the hotel impressed, but the Baroque was their most sought-after intimate venue—it was the location of the enormous, red-and-tan greywacke stone fireplace they used in their logo, and easily the most beautiful room in the main building. A mahogany chair railing and lower paneling matched the dining table and its velvet-seated chairs, and paisley wallpaper splashed across the room in deep red and cream, accented in forest green and gold.

Three chandeliers scattered the firelight through their cascades of crystal, their bulbs dimmed to a soft glow that mirrored the candles in the gold sconces along the walls and candelabra on the table. When Mattie entered the room, she was struck speechless. She stood blocking the door, surprised by how the colors and light and warmth affected her. The table was set immaculately: cream-colored tablecloth, gold and cream utensils and plates with the Billingstead monogram. Low bowls of red hydrangeas and white Nerines ran along the center of the table between the candles. The smell of fireplace filled the room and filled Mattie with comfort, like coming home to a warm hearth after a day of playing in the snow.

She looked down at her shoes—the same black pumps from that afternoon—wondering how the carpet could possibly be so soft and spongy, and in a dining room, no less.

Someone subtly cleared their throat next to her, and she looked up to see a waiter had snuck up on her.

"Champagne, madame?" He asked, offering her the tray. She smiled and thanked him, taking a flute. "Please make yourself comfortable. Dinner will be served shortly."

"Oh, Matalina!"

The atmosphere of the room had calmed her, but true to form, the atmosphere of her relatives threatened to overpower it. She only had to go through the motions for a few minutes before Daphne entered, the last of the guests. Mattie had to roll her eyes when she saw what her sister wore.

She knew it was a status symbol that all her outfits for the day matched each other, but Mattie thought it was a little over the top: a strapless, mint green wiggle dress with a wide, pink belt; a large white, feathered fascinator; and neon orange slouch boots with stiletto heels. Mattie had opted for a 70's-style black silk maxi dress, with a high collar and billowing sleeves cinched at the cuffs. Raphael had sighed, missing the sight of her skin, but he perked up when she said it was only one layer. Well, two, if you counted the tights.

When they told her it was going to be a "family" dinner, it could have meant anything, but Mattie couldn't remember the last time it had meant their parents, all siblings, all spouses, and all grandchildren. The only one missing was Cinnamon—not from any slight by her parents or brother, but a deliberate choice that Daphne made to protect her wife. She may have had better luck navigating "family" events like this, but that didn't mean she was going to subject the love of her life to it.

In total, the twelve adults and twelve children filled every seat at the table. Mattie's place card put her in a chair with her back to the fireplace, which was colossal but thankfully far enough away that she wouldn't overheat. Daphne sat to her left, after switching with their 10-year-old niece. On her right was their broody 14-year-old nephew who seemed just as happy to be there as she was. He muttered a greeting when she sat down and turned his attention back to the video game he was trying to hide below the lip of the table.

Me too, kid.

The event didn't turn out as bad as she feared, thanks to soothing ambiance and phenomenal food. She had been hungry, wishing she had eaten more of the snacks at the pool, but it was worth it to be able to savor every bite of the ten courses they served for dinner. She was surprised to hear her relatives talking about *That Scarlet, Beating Heart*, though she should have expected it. Tuning them out, she let herself focus on the experience of the meal itself.

However tacky she had expected her relatives to be, the hotel had come through with a truly elegant and memorable dinner. After the first glass of champagne, the waiters offered the house whisky, specially crafted to complement the unique fireplace scent of the room, and she fell in love. And thought of Raphael.

Was this the kind of lifestyle he was accustomed to? Had he sat in a room like this, sparkling and gold, sipping bespoke spirits, eating local beet and cheese mezzaluna, snapper en papillote, New Zealand pavlova? Would he judge her for missing the trappings of luxury more than she missed her relatives? Think less of her for using them to experience material comforts?

"Mattie's adult love life isn't really an appropriate topic."

She hadn't thought she'd drunk enough to zone out, let down her guard. But she raised her head and looked around the table, and everyone was staring at her.

"Oh, the boys love the *Knuckletracker* movies, they'd be so excited to meet Wisdom Connor!" Mattie didn't understand any of the words Leda said, even though her sister-in-law's comment seemed to be directed at her.

"I don't know what any of those words mean," she said.

"They want you to talk about Luke," Daphne clarified, finishing the last of her whisky and motioning toward the waiter for a refill.

"We're just friends," Mattie said, blushing. She pushed the last few flakes of the snapper across her plate before a waiter picked it up.

"No, no, no," Ola said, gesturing with her wine glass. "We saw you two at the pool and he *kissed* you. He called you his *girl-friend*." She shifted her elbow to let the waiter place the eighth course dish in front of her.

"He said that?" Someone asked.

"He's kind of a prankster," Mattie explained, feeling every pair of eyes on her. "He'll be at the wedding, but as Rin's date."

Her mother frowned at her. "Daphne said you were bringing a date."

"Who's Rin?" whispered a male voice down the end of the table.

"I am bringing a date. My date is not Luke Maston."

"Well honey, who are you bringing? We'll have to update the seating chart. This is very last minute."

"I never said Luke was my date." The hot flush of frustration was seeping into her cheeks. She didn't want to talk about it at all, but especially not with each and every one of her relatives staring at her.

"Next she'll tell us her date is Raphael Callan," Hayden muttered, loud enough for everyone to hear. The adults snickered.

"My date is Raphael Callan," she said, deadpan. The room was suddenly quiet, the soft sound of plates placed on the table the loudest noise.

Then Hayden laughed, a surprised guffaw, loud and annoying and like a man underestimating a woman. The rest of them followed suit.

"You never used to have a sense of humor," he said, raising his glass to her.

"Still don't," Mattie replied. She looked down at the new dish in front of her, something with scallops, and her stomach churned. "Excuse me."

She pushed away from the table and made for the door, clenching her fists so no one would see her shaking. Maybe they'd think she was angry—which they would respect—instead of sensitive, which they considered a weakness.

The restroom was almost as lavish as the dining room. Heavy, dark wooden doors secured the stalls and the sink basins were made of hammered copper. Oversized gilt mirrors lined one wall of the anteroom, reflecting the champagne-colored couches and dark green and black wallpaper. Once Mattie had taken a few breaths, all the green made her feel like she was alone in a dark forest. She sat on a couch with a sigh, reached into a pocket, and took out Raphael's letter from the other day.

Eventually, she might stop carrying it with her. But she didn't see anything wrong with rereading it to remind herself that there was someone who would take her seriously. That she deserved to be taken seriously. *"I'm falling for you, too,"* he had written. He was just a text away now, but she liked seeing his handwriting. It was deliberate. His words were deliberate.

They'd be together. It felt odd, to be so comfortable in a relationship that was this new. To know so soon that was what they both wanted.

But Raphael had described it best. This felt right.

The door to the restroom opened and Daphne made a beeline for the couch, plopping herself next to Mattie with an oof.

"That good, huh?" Mattie asked, tucking the letter into a pocket and draping her arm around her sister.

"Time to bail?"

"Nah. I don't want to miss the pavlova."

Daph snorted. "Sure, the pavlova."

Mattie frowned. It was unlike Daph to get upset about dessert. "What?"

Daphne sat up. "You said you'd make an effort as long as it didn't get bad, but I keep watching you deal with shitty people, and you don't tell me you want to leave. So I have to wonder if there's something else going on. Is it guilt? Because it shouldn't be. Is it forgetfulness? Is it a stroke? Are you having a medical emergency? Did you kill a man? Oh my god, is it blackmail? Are you being blackmailed?"

"I'm not being blackmailed."

Daphne nodded, eyes wide. "Just what someone being blackmailed would say."

"Our mother offered me one hundred thousand dollars if I show up and play nice." There was no reason to tell anyone about the bribe, since she rejected it, even if she hadn't told their mother that in so many words. But at least Daph could laugh about it with her.

Her sister sucked a breath through her teeth. "Only a hundred grand? For them, that's insulting."

"I know," Mattie groaned, lowering her head into her hands. "It's like asking a child to behave during dinner and they'll get a twenty."

Daphne was quiet, and Mattie peeked at her from between fingers to look at her thoughtful face.

"You need money," Daph said softly. "You took that obvious bribe because you need money."

"Well, yeah. Wait. No," Mats said. "Yes, I need money, but no, I didn't take the bribe. Sorry, I thought that was obvious."

"One thing at a time." Daphne held up her hands. "You didn't take the bribe."

"Nope."

"Then why the hell have you put up with all of this?"

Mattie's reasons hadn't changed, but maybe there was more to it than she thought. "If you're seeing something I'm not, I must have developed a tolerance to it over the years. But I can't gauge it by your parameters. I had one job this weekend, and it was to survive the relatives. I don't even know where to start with Spencer, he wasn't even on my radar. So I'm focusing on our siblings and parents until he becomes an unavoidable problem. But I can do it," she added hastily, holding up a hand. "And if I hit my limit, I'm gone, I promise."

It was Daphne's turn to wrap her arm around Mattie's shoulders. "I know it's hard. This whole weekend is the perfect storm of emotional tornado for you. But if you need money, too? Cinnamon and I have more than we know what to do with, and we're happy to share. That's what happens when two trust fund babies grow up and get unrelated high-paying jobs and then marry one another and never have kids."

Mattie snorted, and sniffled. "I don't want to take advantage of you."

Daphne rolled her eyes. "As if you could. Come on," she said, standing. "They've moved on to arguing about Topher's newest business venture, which is definitely a multi-level marketing scheme. Again. We'll sneak in, drink more of that delightful whisky, eat several helpings of dessert, then fly out of here to meet our friends at the pub."

Mattie sighed. "I think I can handle that."

***

The unusual chill had lifted when the storm passed hours ago, and Raphael found himself on a hotel balcony again, the evening's coolness just sharp enough to keep him focused on his work.

But the fresh air and quiet night could only hone his attention, not solve his problem. Mattie had called the script "unsalvageable," and she was right. It wasn't the quality of the writing that he objected to, but the crux of the story itself: that certain individuals are entitled to happiness and safety at the expense of others and should be considered heroes when they achieve it. Payton pitching it as a story of an underdog was ludicrous. And legitimizing it would only embolden the people who had always thought they were entitled to whatever they wanted at the expense of everyone else.

Raphael sat back and crossed his arms, gazing across the dark lake to the distant pinpricks of lights along the shore. Luke would be knocking at his door soon, to pick him up for a late dinner with Rin at the pub Luke recommended. Raph hadn't been much of a friend lately, with everything that was going on, and he'd been neglecting Luke. But at least, if he wasn't mistaken, Luke had found a good companion in Rin.

He still had a few minutes before he had to leave, so he took out the new letter Mattie had written him. Billingstead stationery, just like the one he wrote. He started reading it and smiled.

Dear R,

Well, here we are again. Back to the beginning with hotel sta-tionery. Full-sized pages though. A definite upgrade.

You're right. We're trapped. We've traded one prison for another. Hopefully, this one will be more short-lived. Also, my accommo-dations this time are WAY better. You should see the cottage Rin got for us. I have an entire wing to myself, compliments of them both, who wanted to give us privacy for your frequent visits. I share their assumption that you will be visiting often. I even left room for your clothes in the closet and drawers. In the hope.

Pretty sure my bathtub will fit two. If you were interested.

It's not my fault this letter will probably be horny.

I can't wait to see you again.

I'm sure you and I will talk about everything that happened to us today, so I'll try not to get into too much of it here. With the exception of Edie, because I have to.

I saw that she was there to pick you up. I'm trying not to let it bother me, but, fuck it, it bothers me. It should. A selfish part of me is glad that you're worried about how it would affect me, because the same selfish part of me was definitely jealous. But mostly, I'm angry that she blindsided you like that. You deserve better.

I haven't seen her at the hotel yet. You mentioned that your meeting with Payton might result in a fist fight (which I'm hoping didn't happen, but I haven't gotten a text from you for a while, so who can say?), and I feel obliged to tell you that any meeting with me and Edie might result in the same. I could take her. Um, I want to make it clear in writing that you never asked me to hurt her. But I will defend the people I care about, unasked.

Okay girl, calm down, let's just wait and see what Raphael has to say before we go off decking people.

I'm spending all day at the hotel. I met my mother, Donna the Wedding Planner, and the seamstress for my bridesmaid dress fitting earlier and it was a holy nightmare. Daph was there, and so was alcohol, so it could have been worse.

Later tonight is the family dinner. The guest list is a mystery to me. You know, usually my relatives care more about how much money they spend on something than whether that thing is useful or beautiful or of good quality. Imagine my surprise when the Billingstead turns out to be all those things. I have no doubt the food will be the best part of dinner.

(I'm so hungry.)

(They're only giving us snacks here.)

I'm currently at the Babes Retreat. We've taken over one of the indoor pools and full disclosure: the signature cocktail they made for the bride is a deliciously sweet and fruity vodka thing and I had several. Just enough to take the edge off of being in a bathing suit around a bunch of shallow women. Who are all super hot for you and Luke.

Running into Luke after the dress fitting made me feel better. I feel like we've always been friends, though we've only said a handful of things to each other. We just fell into an easy banter. He feels safe.

Don't be jealous. You've got my heart.

And not to gossip, but I think he might have a thing for Rin.

Oh, the waiters are bringing out arancini. Snack time. I'll see you soon.

Love,

M

The fluttering in Raph's gut spread to his limbs, his fingertips as he touched the word.

Love.

Mattie hadn't used that word before; he would have remembered. He'd called her love as a term of endearment.

Heat grew in his body, down the same paths as the fluttering. Did he love her? Was that what he was trying to say, earlier, when he said it felt fast but right?

Being immediately open and trusting wasn't normal for him. But maybe all the stress of what needed to be done—walking away from Payton and his project despite the consequences of doing so; confronting Edie about harassing him; adapting to a growing pandemic; addressing his usual feelings of inadequacy—had forced him to evolve in order to deal with it all, in a matter of days.

He was still himself. If the only change was no longer accepting being forced into uncomfortable situations, it could only be for the better. If that somehow included trusting his gut when it came to happiness—embracing and running with it instead of second-guessing it—well, that was how he got Mattie.

They had taken a chance, trusting that the other would be honest. In a world where so many people present themselves as a version they've edited, cultivated, or completely fabricated, it was a relief—a new freedom—to simply be himself and not worry about impressing anyone. And she loved him for exactly who he was. How could he ever go back to hiding himself, now that he knew what it felt like when he was sincere?

Raph swallowed, his emotions threatening to overwhelm him. Mattie had done the same thing, trusting him with herself, and he loved her for exactly who she was, too.

His phone chirped, and he cleared his throat and wiped his eyes, hoping it was Mattie. But it was a text from Luke, telling him to meet them in the lobby to go to dinner.

Despite the ongoing challenges of the production and Edie, Raphael felt hopeful again. Mattie had made space for him in her closet, and he was absolutely going to share it with her.

***

The Pub was far enough away from the Billingstead that any non-locals—like Payton, Edie, and the Redgraves—wouldn't show up by accident, but still close enough to get to quickly when, say, two women full of pavlova and whisky needed to escape the crushing scrutiny of a room full of opinionated relatives.

Luke's favorite watering hole was fifteen minutes away from both the Billingstead and his house. It was hard for him, being so close to his daughters but unable to see them yet. Lena, his youngest, had asthma, and there was no way he was going to fuck around with potentially bringing a lung-attacking illness into his house. He knew he was taking a chance, being in a public space, but the science wasn't definitive yet and he planned to go into isolation before finally heading home.

His mother, a retired nurse, was even more careful than he was, and she would look after her granddaughters until Luke was done with *Broke*. They loved their Grams. He doubted the kids even missed him. Oh, they'd be excited when he returned. But they were also excited when they found a dead lizard in their sandbox.

And when they threw up. So they weren't the best objective observers.

If he couldn't introduce his new friends to his family, at least he could introduce them to his regular haunt. The Pub was a comfortable English-style tavern if the decorator had only been told about English taverns second-hand, but nobody went there for colonial authenticity. The bar had a good mix of old standards and new craft beers that they rotated regularly, and the food was better than passable.

Raphael felt right at home.

He'd visited Luke before, but there had never been time to come out here and just relax. He worried that meeting Rin would be awkward, setting him on edge when he was hoping for reprieve, but they got along as easily and as quickly as he had with Daph and Mattie. Rin must have felt the same way, because they asked him to use gender-neutral pronouns when discussing them. An easy way to show respect to a new friend.

The three of them were just finishing dinner when their booth vibrated with the thunder of a hundred motorcycles revving into the parking lot.

"Good lord," Raphael said, choking on his ale. "I thought you said this place was low key?"

"That would be Daphne," Rin said, dragging one of Luke's potato wedges through a caper-and-bacon aioli.

"Oh, did she drive a motorboat here?"

"McLaren 720S Spider," Luke said, pushing his basket closer to Rin.

"No shit. You think she'd let me take it out?"

"Sorry, bro," Luke said with a grin. "I already asked. No boys allowed."

Moments later, Daphne and Mattie entered the restaurant and made their way to the booth. Daphne pulled a chair over to sit at the head of the table, and Mattie slid onto the bench beside Raphael.

"Hey," Mattie said, leaning in for a kiss. He snaked an arm around her and pulled her against him.

"Hello. What is that delightful taste?" He asked, sniffing her mouth.

"The Billingstead Baroque Room's signature whisky. I've had too much alcohol today, but that stuff was worth it."

"Nice to see you again, Raph," Daphne said, leaning in to grab several of his kumara fries.

"You too," he replied. "Help yourself."

"How was dinner?" Rin asked.

"Best meal of my life," Mattie said. Daph nodded. "But you caused a lot of trouble, Luke."

"Me?" Luke asked, placing a hand over his chest. "That doesn't sound like me." Three of the people at the booth snorted. Rin got their server's attention and asked for water for the two newcomers while the sisters summarized the evening with their relatives.

"They were always going to goad me," Mattie said, once everyone was caught up. "At least this way, it was about a fictional relationship that they inferred from a kiss."

"A kiss? I didn't hear about that." Rin squinted.

"A friendly kiss, I swear," Luke said, lifting his hands in surrender.

"Kind of a disappointment." Mattie wrinkled her nose.

"Rude," Luke muttered.

Daphne knocked the salt shaker against the table like a gavel. "Okay people, down to business. We've got two days to figure out what Mattie is going to do regarding our relatives and Mike

Fucking Spencer. We've got a little more time than that to help Raphael with his Edie problem, which is now a part of the Scarlet, Beating Heart problem."

"*Broke*," Raph said. "They changed the title."

Rin rolled their eyes. "Of course they did."

Raphael gave the group a rundown of his meeting with Payton that afternoon. "I can't believe I went in there thinking I was going to upend the whole production and save everyone, and I left agreeing to help him instead. Some superhero."

"It takes practice," Mattie said. "When superheroes get their powers, they need to practice first. Just watch any of the dozen Batmans or Spider-Mans."

"Plus, you were alone," Daph added, gesturing at him with her water glass. "No practice, no preparation, no recon first, confronted him all by yourself. The only way it could have been worse is if Edie had been there, too."

"Which, speaking of," Raph interrupted. "Edie isn't a problem that needs a group effort, so you can leave her to me. Emotion and reason haven't worked, but maybe she'll listen to her lawyers when they say how bad this is for her." He shrugged and took another sip of beer. "There's nothing us mere mortals can do about it. I see the gears turning in your head, Rin, and I implore you to stop."

"Me?" They asked, hand to their chest in a parody of Luke. "That doesn't sound like me."

"I can get them to stop," Daphne mumbled into her water glass.

"I don't know if I can help," Mattie mused. "But committing violence might make me feel better. Toward Edie, not Rin. Never Rin."

"Thank you, darling," Rin raised their glass.

"No punching, no plotting, no going rogue. My plan is set and it will work. I just need patience. From all of you. Luke, you too."

"I didn't even say anything!"

"And that's the tell. Honestly, the four of you are perfect for each other. Consider Edie dealt with. Seriously. Doing otherwise will only complicate things more."

Grunts of reluctant acquiescence rumbled around the table.

"So the wedding," Daphne started. "In case any of you were wondering if our relatives knew how much of a hardship this would be for Mattie, our mother offered her one hundred thousand dollars to attend."

"What?" Rin shouted.

"Shit, bro, you need money? I'll give you money." Luke took his basket of potato wedges from Rin and pushed them toward Mattie. "You can have my chips, too."

"If anyone is going to give her money, it's me," Rin said defensively, pulling the basket back. "But if she wants chips, she can get her own."

"You should have told me," Raphael said quietly. "I wondered why you changed your mind about attending everything. I can help, you know."

"Excuse me," Daphne called. "I already told her I'd take care of her."

"I didn't accept it!" Mattie yelled over everyone. "All of you, I—" She took a deep breath and closed her eyes. After a moment, she laughed and looked around the table, a little teary. "Somehow, my support system has doubled in just a few short weeks, and it's enough for my softened heart to make the final transformation to complete mush. I appreciate all of you, and you have to stop saying such nice things, because I'm already too close to crying, so let's table the discussion of my unrelated financial issues until at least after the wedding, because that's not an immediate problem. I didn't take the bribe, and I'm not here for the money."

Raph gave her a squeeze. "So what's your plan? For this weekend. What do you actually want to do?"

"Well. Everything today was less terrible than I was expecting."

"Was everything less terrible than if you hadn't done them at all?" Raphael asked.

"You must not have seen Spencer," Rin said. Mattie cringed.

"You both make good points. But part of me still wishes it will work out. So as long as it's working out, I'm going with the flow instead of against it."

Raphael rubbed her shoulder. "Whatever you need, Mats. We're here to support you, so, just tell us what that looks like, and if it changes."

Mattie nodded. "I know, and thank you. For right now, I'll just play it by ear. Make decisions as they arise."

"And Spencer?" Daph asked, twirling the salt shaker on the table.

"Avoid him, I guess." Mattie shrugged. "Try to always be with someone, so he can't get me alone. His actions are somehow both unexpected and completely predictable."

"You can't avoid him if you go to the wedding," Rin pointed out. "Certainly not if you're a bridesmaid."

"I don't like this at all," Raphael muttered, shifting in his seat beside Mattie.

She reached out to take his free hand. "Me neither. But, like with making decisions about my relatives and then having to adjust them when I actually see those people, I won't know what I'm capable of doing unless—until—I see Spencer in person. As long as I have a lot of contingency plans, I'll be able to do something. I just don't know what, yet."

The table was quiet for a moment. Raphael guessed that each of them was wondering what else they could do to help Mattie get through the weekend. Someone had put ABBA on the jukebox, and the rest of the pub sang along.

Rin cleared their throat. "As far as the film goes, a solution may be forthcoming. The government has been ordering new restrictions to try to stay ahead of the virus. Mattie and Raph got caught up in the travel quarantine, and Luke will be in self-quarantine before he gets back to his kids. There have been rumors about initiating a country-wide lockdown of sorts, a kind of shelter-in-place to slow the spread."

"Do you know what that would look like?" Mattie asked.

"Shutdown of all but essential services, grocery stores, service stations, hospitals, the like. Restrict the number of people who can gather in a group. From two to six weeks. If my sources are correct, this will probably start within the next week or so. Filming will at least be delayed, which could give you two the opportunity you need to bow out with a legitimate excuse."

"Not wanting to participate in a propaganda film is a legitimate excuse," Raphael said.

"True, but this'll give you a legal excuse, too." Rin tapped the side of their glass. "If you can be like Mats and stick it out a little while longer—a week, tops—then that problem will be solved."

"Then Raphael can come stay with Mattie, and Luke can get back to his kids," Daphne said.

"It won't happen in time to affect the wedding, though." Rin grimaced. "It's not like I can call up the government and ask them to bump up the launch date."

"I think," Raphael said slowly, "I want to quit before the lockdown."

The others glanced at each other but didn't say anything. Raph took a deep breath.

"I don't want to avoid this project based on a technicality. I want to be able to say I stood up for my principles and, when I realized the harm it would cause, I made the choice to walk away. Payton set up a meeting with the other investors tomorrow morning. I want to hear what they have to say. If they're in agreement with Payton, then I'll quit. If they're not, I'll still quit, but at least there's a chance I won't be a complete pariah."

Mattie squeezed his hand. "I have never been more attracted to you."

"Me either," said Luke. "Also, if you jump, I jump. Text me the moment you're out, and I'll go in for my turn."

"You don't need to follow my lead if it means risking your ability to get work," Raph said, considering for the first time what being blacklisted would mean for his best friend.

"Naw, mate. We're all in it together. Sink or swim." Luke raised his glass and Raph clinked it with his own.

"Sink or swim," Raph agreed.

***

With their immediate problems as solved as they were going to get, the table moved on to other topics: the virus, Daphne's outfit, Luke's kids, the stupid film and the stupid book it was based on, how Rin's company would handle the lockdown. Mattie tried to pay attention, but her tired mind wandered.

When they had met, Raphael thought the film was nothing more than a headache, and Mattie was dead set on avoiding and dropping her relatives as soon as possible. Now, Raph was quitting, even though doing so might put his career in jeopardy, while Mattie dithered about and made excuses for why she had to put off cutting these toxic people out of her life. Whatever pride she might have felt at influencing his decision was squashed by the fact that she was definitely compromising her own principles by waffling back and forth.

Her friends were right, though. The moment she actually saw Spencer—because no matter what happened, it was inevitable that she would run into him at some point—her fight or flight response would kick in. Running away would save her for a while, and the people sitting at this table with her would say she did the right thing to protect herself. "Fight" didn't feel like an option, either. What was one punch, or even one good beat-down, compared to the years he spent terrorizing her? No, violence wouldn't make her feel better. She needed something more impactful. Something that would take his power away and give it back to the people he would victimize.

By the time everyone left The Pub—Daphne and Rin to the cottage; Luke, Raphael, and Mattie to the Billingstead—Mattie was wishing she could be more like Raphael, who was ready to stand up for his principles in a way that he said channeled Mattie, and her head spun with the reversal, the long day, the emotional rollercoaster, the alcohol.

They fell asleep quickly, too tired to do anything but find sanctuary in each other, the grasp of the day slipping from them as they slid into tomorrow through a sweet and welcome unconsciousness.

Saturday, April 4, 2020
Morning

For the second morning in a row, Mattie awoke to a ringtone instead of the alarm she forgot to set. It took her a moment to burrow out from the warm and copious blankets, remembering slowly what bed she was in and who was supposed to be there with her. But when she surfaced, Raphael's side of the bed was made, the man nowhere in sight, and her phone was about to vibrate off the nightstand.

"I'm awake," she croaked into the speaker.

"The only people who start a conversation with 'I'm awake' are the people who are not, in fact, awake." Daphne sounded too chipper for the early hour of...nine o'clock. Mattie had gotten almost ten hours of sleep. Why did she feel like she could have slept another ten?

"I'm boycotting being forced to wake up. Morning alarms are violence against women."

"Look at Mattie, taking a stand."

"I spent the last fourteen days sleeping until my body decided it was time to get up. Mornings are patriarchal fabrications designed to control us."

"Yes, yes, you're very clever. I'm about to leave the cottage. Did you want me to bring you what you'll need for today, or do you want to come back here so you can pack for yourself?"

Mattie swiped to her calendar. "What is it today? Mani/pedi this morning? Brunch? Rehearsal and dinner."

"That's it, as far as I know."

Parts of the outfits she brought the day before could be worn again, and she did some quick calculations to figure out what additional clothes she needed her sister to bring her. They switched to video, and Mattie walked her through the closet and dresser so she wouldn't miss anything. When Daph was on her way, Mattie scrolled through her text messages.

Rin:

You're probs both still sleeping, but let me know if we need anything for the house in the event that we'll have to shelter in place there for the next month or so.

Daphne:

alcohol

Rin:

There are three cases of wine in the basement and a full bar.

Daphne:

I said what I said.

Rin:

So you've decided to spend the lockdown developing an alcohol problem.

Daphne:

tampons. chocolate. bread.

Rin:

Daph are you maybe PMSing?

Daphne:

Ooo, oops, right, good call. You solved the mystery but we still need those things

more wood for the fireplace. first aid kit. eggs milk bread chocolate wait

Rin:

Overstock the kitchen, got it. I'm working in Auckland all day so just text with anything else you think of. Mattie, I patiently await your response.

After a few minutes of consideration, Mattie replied, "Toilet paper, coffee, I think Daphne undersold the importance of chocolate. This is not a comprehensive list. Will text with more later." If Raphael was going to be staying with her, she should ask what he thought they might need. She didn't have any new texts from him, but when she got up, she found a note on—of course—hotel stationery.

My Dearest Mattie,

Left early to talk with some of the crew. Took Luke with me. Will grab breakfast on the way. Meeting with the producers is at 10, not sure how long it will take. I'll text you.

I was going to wake you up but I couldn't find you beneath all those blankets. Then your little snores told me you were still fast asleep, and how could I ruin that?

Good luck today, whatever you choose to do. Don't take any shit from anybody. Text if you need me. I'll see you soon.

Love,

Raphael

The word stood out from the rest, and Mattie grinned like an idiot. They hadn't had time to talk about it, but apparently Mattie using "love" to sign her letter to him yesterday hadn't gone unnoticed.

Oh, she loved him. And she was going to tell him in person. But sometimes people got weird about it—especially if they thought it was too soon to feel it.

Personally, she didn't believe that emotions followed many, if any, rules, and trying to corral them into arbitrary fixed spaces—like how humans measured time—guaranteed frustration. Combine that with her habit of being truthful about what she felt, and she boasted a predictable history of scaring off friends and lovers.

So her most recent letter to him was an opportunity to test the water. See if the L-word made him run. And look. He used it in return. A very good sign.

She texted him her itinerary for the day and asked what supplies he might need to get through the inevitable lockdown.

He hadn't responded by the time Daphne showed up with a flat white from the in-hotel café in each hand. Mattie was disproportionately grateful, but with less than thirty minutes to wake up, put on clothes and mascara, and meet the women of the wedding party at the spa downstairs, the coffee was a significant factor in her success. After changing into her long-sleeved blue plaid dress and matching bike shorts, Mattie let her sister lead her to the spa.

If there was one benefit to having an event in the morning, it was that the usually talkative and snippy women didn't have the cumulative disappointments of a day to make them even cattier. That and, Mattie thought, their meds were probably just kicking in. Nobody asked her about Luke this time. Even her mother failed to needle her, sighing as she slumped into the massage chair like an overwhelmed starlet, the wave to her daughters more a weak gesture of dismissal than a greeting.

Raphael texted her a little before ten.

Raphael:

> About to go into the meeting. Wish you were here, but Luke is a good substitute in this case. I imagine your hands are occupied anyway.

Matalina:

> Worse. Feet first, and they're in the bath. I'd still come if you need me.

Raphael:

> Not necessary, but thanks. How awful is it?

Matalina:

> Surprisingly not. I think it's too early for them all to be in a sour mood yet. I dislike the color they picked for us but that's the worst so far.

Raphael:

> Oh the humanity.

Matalina:

> You have no idea. Any thoughts on lockdown supplies?

Raphael:

> I haven't thought about it. Condoms.

Matalina:

> For someone who hasn't thought about it, you answered that pretty quickly.

Raphael:

> Condoms, toilet paper, alcohol.

Matalina:

I'll let Rin know. Any preference?

Raphael:

I'm happy with the ones we have if you are.

Matalina:

Oh yes. I'd much rather be with you making sure we're both happy with them than whatever it is I'm doing here.

Raphael:

God yes. Let's meet in my room

Change of plans. Rather, no change of plans. Going in to meeting now. However it goes, thank you for inspiring me to expect more from my job and the people I work with. I'll do you proud.

Matalina:

I'm already proud. I'm there with you in spirit.

She was about to add "I love you," but she knew she had to say it in person first. Closing a letter with "love" was different enough that it didn't break that guideline. She sent the Rin and Daph group text "condoms," resulting in massive teasing from Rin by text, and Daphne hooted aloud at her from two spots over, gyrating in her massage chair until their mother frowned at her to stop. It was the most raucous part of the morning.

If her family's discussion of *That Scarlet, Beating Heart* had surprised her the night before, their early morning casual exchange regarding local politics and pandemic response was even more shocking. Celeste's friends at least seemed to be keeping up with the latest news about the government's suggestions, restrictions, edicts, and potential next steps. One woman had read that the government was going to pay people to stay home to slow the virus spread. Most of the Americans laughed.

Mattie's coffee-filled, yet-unnourished, tired brain, trying its best to ignore the stressful situations Mattie kept putting it in, obnoxiously clanked together several puzzle pieces, but she wouldn't be able to fit them together at the spa. She closed her eyes and let the vague, nagging ideas roll around while she focused on the foot bath, the scrub, the polish, then the different and strange sensations of her manicure.

By the time Mattie's nails shone with the same opalescence as the rest of the bridesmaids', they'd all moved on to their next spa service. The morning had gone so well, she was almost disappointed that they hadn't invited her to join them. Then she remembered herself and shuddered. This was how easy it was to be lulled into compliance: as long as nobody openly mocked her, she considered it a good day.

Her phone chirped, and she expected another text from Rin, but it was Wedding Planner Donna. Jenny needed her in the Ruby Room for another fitting, ASAP.

Brunch wasn't until 11:30, so she had a little bit of time to take care of it. She replied that she was on her way.

"Jenny needs me for a fitting," Mattie told Daph.

"You still want to do that? Do you need me to come? I have a mini facial and neck massage now."

"Nah, I can handle it. I can handle anything with these newly gorgeous nails."

"Make good choices. See you at brunch?"

"I'll be there."

Daph kissed her cheek distractedly and left her for the more secluded part of the spa. It was too much to hope that the fitting wouldn't be as awful as the day before, but she felt good. Confident. And if she got upset, maybe she wouldn't cry. Very optimistic of her.

***

Raphael and Luke got lost twice looking for the outbuilding where Payton was holding his meeting. Luke had rung Raph early with the idea of talking to the crew to see how everyone felt about the film's subject matter and working conditions. Luke did most of the talking. Raphael might have had more charm, but people were more likely to respond to Luke's laid back, working-man appeal.

Most of the crew hinted at concern about both script and environment, a few of them going so far to say that they definitely did not feel safe, but with a production this small, they didn't have many options for recourse, and they needed the money. If Payton were going to listen to anyone, it would be his top-billed actors, so they would have to present everyone's concerns as their own.

Since the crew was put up in a nearby motel, and not the shrine to hoarded generational wealth and billionaires newly minted at the expense of the poor, nobody could tell them how to get to the Wakefield Outpost on the Billingstead campus. Raphael looked up a map on the hotel website, and the two of them went off in search of the building.

Eventually, they had to admit that either Raphael didn't know how to read a map, the sun was too bright for him to properly see his screen, or the stylized drawing of what they called a map was more of a suggestion to keep out the riff-raff, since hotel guests would be escorted around in enclosed golf carts and UTVs.

After they retraced their steps back to the main building, the front desk got them a ride. While Luke and the driver talked about the vehicle's specs, Raph tried to memorize their winding path. If they quit in a huff and stormed out, he didn't want to be waiting for a ride back. Didn't want to give Payton an opportunity to track him down and pressure him again.

The Wakefield Outpost was an oversized cabin with a second-floor conference room that overlooked the lake. The ground floor had a large sitting area, a billiards table, foosball, a greywacke stone fireplace, a good-sized kitchen with a wet bar and espresso machine, and several discreet but well-appointed restrooms.

It also came with its own concierge, who took the coats from Raphael and Luke and offered to get them a coffee or something from the bar. Raphael saw his chance to finally try a flat white. Luke asked for a beer. The concierge directed them up the stairs, where the rest of the party was already gathered, and promised to follow with their drinks momentarily.

It all felt incredibly hypocritical, given that the film they were there to discuss was supposedly about the merits of being a down-trodden, dirt-poor hick.

The curved glass staircase opened onto the conference room that took up the entire second floor. Payton and two other white men sat at one end of a long, black oval table. Seeing Raphael, Payton cut off their conversation and rose to greet him.

"Raphael, man, good to see you. Luke." Payton leaned into bro-style side-hugs and back pats for each of them. "I don't know if you've met, but this is Mason Schiller—if you haven't been in one of the films he's produced, you've still seen about a hundred of them. And this is Clive Chansley. New to the game but enthusiastic, and a good friend. He's got a clear vision for *Broke* and I trust him with my life. More than that. With my creative vision." He beamed at the younger-looking guy with the blonde, buzzed-sides-floppy-top haircut currently popular in certain circles of Millennial white men. Raphael had no doubt exactly what Chansley's vision was.

In the world of independent films, Schiller was a legend. He had a nose for what would work, and despite being discerning, he still ended up backing an impressive number of films every year. And even if one of his projects didn't make a lot of money, plenty of them went on to become cult favorites years later. He was a heavy hitter, and proof that Payton still had pull.

Making Raphael doubt, again, that the story was as offensive as he thought, and fear, again, that quitting would lead to a drop in available work for him, thanks to Payton's vindictive influence.

The men all shook hands, and Payton gestured for them to sit. The concierge entered and served them their drinks, asked if they needed anything else, and left quietly at their polite refusals.

"Thanks for coming," Payton said. "I think getting together like this is a good opportunity to review some of the setbacks we've had and assure you all that continuing work on this project is not only possible, but imperative. I—"

"How is the novel coronavirus affecting production, and how are you ensuring the safety of the cast and crew?" Schiller got straight to the point. Raphael couldn't help his look of surprise, and tried to cover it by taking a sip of his coffee.

"All the necessary people are on site," Chansley said, leaning back in the chair and crossing his ankle over his knee. Raph noted that all three investors were American and wondered if any of them saw the irony in trying to make a film about American exceptionalism and bigotry in New Zealand. "Really, all we need is a handful of actors and two iPhones, so everyone else is just gravy."

"We've overcome every snag we've hit," Payton added. "It's an encouraging parallel to the story."

"And as for safety?"

Payton ran his thumbnail across the pads of his fingers, a small movement, but Raphael had spent enough time with him to recognize the tell that he was nervous.

"Everyone has followed the guidelines that New Zealand is enforcing," he said.

Raph glanced up at Luke, who was giving him an equally unconvinced look.

"But a number of positions are still unfilled," Schiller said. "If you're not able to fill them due to unexpected restrictions, the smartest thing to do would be to wait until those restrictions are lifted. If you're happy with 'a handful of actors and two iPhones,' what the hell do you need my money for?"

"Come on, Mason, you know the cost of business," Payton laughed. "We're saying that a film like this *could* be made on a shoestring budget, not that we want to, or plan to. And I think we've made a good investment here, I mean, Raphael Callan and Luke Maston." He gestured to the men like he was presenting a prize. "And Edie Everett, too."

"Edie? I thought you cast Olivia Dagne?"

"She couldn't get into the country."

"You should have told me," Schiller said. "I would have recommended Edie earlier, she's good friends with my daughter. They went out for her birthday in L.A. last weekend."

Raphael zoned out when they started talking about Edie. It wasn't making him as nauseated as usual, but he was still uncomfortable.

"The point is," Chansley said, his clipped tone bringing Raphael's attention back. "That despite several setbacks, we have a solid team here, the money is being spent wisely, and if this story of perseverance is made under trying conditions, it will lend a flavor of authenticity we wouldn't otherwise get. We have what we need, we just need to get it started. If we had started filming two weeks ago, we could have been almost finished by now."

"So what's the holdup?" Schiller asked.

"The story is shit," Raphael said, taking a sip of his coffee as everyone's heads turned to him. Making them wait was a power move. A lot of this role was Mattie, but he bolstered it with the same confidence and power mirrored in the two producers.

"We talked about this, Raph." Payton obviously didn't want him to bring it up in front of the others. "The script needs a little work, but that's not a deal-breaker."

"Oh, the script is a mess," Raphael agreed. "But I'm not talking about that. I'm saying the story itself, *That Scarlet, Beating Heart*, is pure shit. And if you have a script that faithfully adapts it, that is also shit. And if you create a film from that, then the movie is shit."

Chansley snorted. "Well, it's a good thing you're not the one making decisions here. You were hired to act, so stick to acting."

"*That Scarlet, Beating Heart* was a bestseller," Schiller said, turning to Raph. "I've made my fair share of adaptations, and best-sellers are always a good bet."

"If the sales are representative of a broad cross-section of readers, sure," Luke chimed in. Raphael was glad they had talked with Mattie about the book the night before. "But this book is a bestseller that has to be marked with an asterisk. Well, not an asterisk, a dagger-cross-looking symbol. While it technically has the sales numbers to qualify as a bestseller, almost all of the sales were bulk purchases. Not individual sales, and not even a dozen copies for book clubs here and there. I'm talking about thousands of books at once, purchased, in this case, by a number of organizations in the States and Europe that are considered terrorist organizations under Australian and New Zealand law."

"What utter bullshit," Chansley said.

Luke shrugged. "Look it up yourself, I'm not your research assistant. It's all online."

"Also, it was on the bestseller list for three weeks before dropping off," Raphael added. "The total sales for it so far is less than 100,000 units. And most of the books in the bulk purchases never made it into anyone's hands."

"Plenty of books were underappreciated in their time," Payton said, irritation in his voice.

"*Moby Dick. Brave New World.*" Chansley stared at Raphael, as if daring him to contradict him. "Hell, *Lord of the Rings* was almost universally panned when it was published in the fifties."

"You think this movie is the next *Lord of the Rings*?" Raphael drawled, unable to hide his amusement.

"I'm saying the potential is there, if we're brave enough to speak the truth that this book illuminates."

The two of them glared at each other, assessing. There were really only two choices. Payton wasn't going to abandon this project under any circumstances. Not when any obstacle that arose was considered a test of his worthiness of completing it. It was a challenge, and he would tackle it with the same foolhardy and misplaced determination as the character he idolized, Daine. He wouldn't listen when Raph told him it was racist garbage at best and propaganda at worst. He simply reclassified Raphael from an asset to another obstacle. Something he had to manipulate into submission, not someone he had to respect.

And Raphael deserved respect.

From his boss, from his director, from a man who called him family. He deserved to be treated better. Payton knew about

Raphael's self-doubts. He knew about his disordered eating and, arguably, contributed to it when they worked together. He knew that Edie dismissed and belittled him, even if he said he didn't know how bad it was. He knew that Raph had experienced plenty of racism for having a Middle Eastern father and a white mother, so asking and expecting him to play a character who thought he and his father should be exterminated, in a narrative that did everything to support that theory without criticism, was breathtakingly cruel.

Terror iced through his gut, but so did a growing thread of excitement.

He set down his coffee carefully, surprised his hand wasn't shaking. Bracing against the table, he stood up, brushed his shirt smooth, and turned to Payton.

"I quit," he said simply.

The other men were quiet for a moment, before Payton gave a bark of laughter.

"Raphael, you're the star here. I chose you."

"Why?"

Payton snorted. "Why what? You're my friend, you're good, you're one of *People*'s sexiest men alive, you're going to get butts in seats."

"You hired a biracial actor to play a white supremacist."

"You don't look it, and you've got an English accent."

Raphael heard, distantly, Luke's hissing intake of breath.

"I've already detailed my concerns." His steady voice was a testament to his acting skills. "And I won't repeat myself. If you won't acknowledge them, there's nothing more to be done. It is unsafe for me to continue working on this production." Raphael stepped around his chair and pushed it in, looking for his coat before he remembered that the butler had taken it downstairs.

"I'm out too," Luke said, standing and finishing the last of his beer in several rushed gulps. "I can't have my daughters thinking I actually believe in this rubbish."

Payton stood, laughing nervously, as though the actors were joking. "Luke, Raphael, come on. You've made your point. We can stay here as long as we need to find a solution."

"I'm no longer a part of this production, Payton." Raphael turned his back to the men and started toward the staircase. "So there's nothing to discuss."

"Hey!" Payton shouted. Raphael stopped walking but didn't turn around. "Are you serious? After everything I've done for you. This movie is gonna win you an Oscar, and you're just gonna walk away? How can you justify that? How can you do this to me?"

He didn't owe him an explanation. He'd already given plenty of reasons. Payton didn't listen to any of them, so it was unlikely he'd listen now. Raphael thought of how Mattie would phrase it. Succinctly. Powerful. No room for misinterpretation.

He glanced over his shoulder at Payton. "I no longer participate in my own oppression."

Payton's jaw dropped, and he closed it again, searching for something to say.

Raphael didn't wait for him to find the words. They'd only be lies, anyway.

Luke caught up to him and the two descended the stairs together, Luke's arm draped over Raphael, squeezing his upper arm.

"Proud of you, bro," he whispered. Raph just nodded, unsure what his voice would sound like if he tried to reply. They retrieved their coats and left the cabin, passing two parked golf carts as they started down the path. Cloud cover hid the morning sun, and the drop in temperature was noticeable.

"You know the way back?" Luke asked.

"Not really," Raphael admitted.

"Well, it wouldn't be first time we got lost. Today." He paused. "So. What are we going to do now?"

"I'm going to convince Mattie to skip literally everything she has planned for the next two days, move into the cottage with her, and spend the entire lockdown memorizing every inch of her skin and every note of her voice."

Luke nodded. "Okay, cool, bro. Yeah. I meant, like, for work. But that sounds like a good plan too."

Raphael laughed and let out a loud shout to dispel his excess energy. "Fuck, mate. Think we'll ever work in this town again?"

"As actors? Oh, not remotely. How do you feel about opening a charming B&B together and settling down to that hashtag slow life?"

"Not great, to be honest."

"Then the theater is your best bet, bro."

The two walked in silence for a bit. The exhilaration was wearing off, and Raphael wondered if he would start shaking from the lack of adrenaline. He hadn't thought of it before, but sticking to theater work would probably also cool the frenzy he had come to New Zealand to escape. "I should call JC, tell him what happened," he said. "Let him figure out how to keep me off the production without making too much of a mess of my career."

"That's mighty optimistic of you."

The rumble of a motor grew louder behind them, and they locked eyes.

"Payton coming to run us down?" Luke suggested.

"Best get off the path, just to be safe."

As the golf cart slowed to a stop beside them, Mason Schiller took his hands off the wheel long enough to light his cigar.

"Are you boys independently wealthy or just very, very stupid?" He cocked his head to look at them.

"Both," Raphael admitted.

"Very, very, stupid," Luke said. "So I just follow his lead."

Schiller chuckled. "You followed him right into unemployment."

Raphael stood up straighter. "I'd rather be unemployed than complicit in a film that glorifies selfishness and violence against marginalized people."

"Yeah," Luke agreed. "What he said."

"All right, all right," Schiller said, making placating gestures with his cigar. "Look, I asked for this meeting with Payton because something felt off about the whole thing. I usually follow my gut, but I ignored it this time because Payton called in a favor." He grunted and gazed into the distance. "Anyway. I pulled out too. For all those altruistic reasons you did, but also, it felt scammy, you know? I hate getting scammed. I hate it when people think they can scam me."

He smoked in silence for a beat. Luke and Raph looked at each other, and Luke shrugged.

"You made the right decision," Schiller said. "Hop in. We'll go back to the hotel—if we can find our way through this god-awful maze—find a meeting room that isn't out in the fucking wop-wops, talk about what's next for you, what kind of productions I have coming up, where you might fit in. Unless you'd prefer the consequences of Payton's ugly campaign to blacklist the both of you?"

The boys shared a look and didn't bother hiding their smiles.

"Thank you," Raphael said, jogging around to get in the passenger seat as Luke slid into the back.

"Call me Mason. And tell me everything wrong with the production, all the reasons why you quit. I know it wasn't just one. I need to know what to look for in case some shit like this happens again."

As they drove to the hotel, Raphael didn't hold back. He was willing to risk his career, and being honest with Mason couldn't make him less unemployable. Well, it could, but he wanted to believe that the man's intentions were, as he said, altruistic. He had to have hope.

***

The layout of the hotel was going to be a mystery to Mattie forever, so she asked the front desk if someone could escort her to the Ruby Room. They deposited her at the room a few minutes later with a smile that she could only return half-heartedly, and she braced herself for another passive-aggressive fitting. She took a deep breath and opened the door, announcing herself as she entered.

Nobody was there. The corner worktable's LED lamps were just bright enough to outline the rows of clothing racks and dressing cubicles, but the room was mostly dark. Mattie found the empty, dreary feel of it comforting. She stood for a moment, wondering what to do next. If she left, Jenny and Donna would return sooner rather than later and blame her for missing the fitting. Better to wait a few minutes and see if they showed up.

She flopped onto a fluffy cushion, brought out her phone, and texted Raphael to let him know she was out of the spa and had a few minutes if he wanted to talk. He called a moment later.

"How was your meeting?" Mattie asked in greeting. "Are you all right?"

"Yeah, it went better than I thought. I quit. I actually quit." He sounded a little winded.

"Ah, Raphael, that's so great! I'm so proud of you!" She hoped he could hear her smile through the phone.

"It's a long story," he continued. "But right now, Luke and I are meeting with one of the producers, who also backed out."

"I don't want to interrupt. That sounds important."

"No, no, he went to get us a meeting room here at the hotel, so I have a few minutes to talk. How was your morning?"

"Not as bad as I was expecting. In fact, while I was there, I got an idea."

"Dangerous, that." He was definitely smirking.

"No kidding." When Mattie had heard his voice, the solution her mind hadn't been able to piece together finally clicked into place. "At the spa, people were talking about how the rumored lockdown is expected to include a kind of financial compensation, like, an incentive to stay home. So people don't have the excuse of going to work."

"Seems like the smart thing to do."

"Right? I don't know how true it is. Rin didn't say, and I haven't been keeping up with all of that, what with—" She gestured broadly, then realized Raphael couldn't see her. "You know, All the Things."

"Yes, I'm familiar with All the Things."

"It got me thinking. When the country goes into some kind of shelter-in-place and the production stops, Payton doesn't seem like the kind of guy who will pay the crew who isn't currently working on his precious, paused film."

Raphael snorted. "He's reluctant to pay them even when they are."

"Well," Mattie drawled, "either way, they won't be getting a paycheck from the film for a while, so why not make that widely known among the crew and let them decide if quitting a week or so before the production is halted by the government is an acceptable trade for not working on said production at all? Then, hopefully, the government bribe to stay home will kick in. Or maybe there's some kind of fund that can help them with that week between, or the weeks after, if I'm mistaken about the federal funding thing."

There was silence on the other end of the line.

"Or is that a dumb idea?" She asked. "You already thought of that, didn't you?" She sighed.

"No, Mattie, that's a really good idea. I was just considering where the money would come from, but I'm literally about to meet with a producer, so I'll bring it up with him. Not sure how he'll feel about giving people money for nothing, though. He's still a businessman."

Mattie shrugged. "So, pay them for something. I bet everyone has a smart phone. Ask them to film themselves during lockdown. Take the videos and, I don't know, make a documentary about what everyone did during the beginning of the pandemic."

After a beat, Raphael muttered something.

"Didn't catch that."

"'A handful of actors and two iPhones,'" he said. "Mattie, you're brilliant, do you know that?"

"Well. Yeah."

Raphael laughed. "Of course you do. Thank you, Mats. I'll text when I'm done so we can meet up."

"Before you go," she said quickly, "I'm sitting here in the seam-stress's room, in a forest of dresses and tuxes, and I feel like causing trouble. If we end up attending the wedding tomorrow, you'll need a tux. Give me your measurements and I'll see if I can find one."

"You're going to steal a tuxedo for me? Won't they recognize it when I show up in it?"

"Nah," she said, rising and walking to one of the racks. "I'll switch out the accessories. There's a bunch of leftover fabric lying around."

He gave her his measurements, they wished each other luck, and said goodbye.

Mattie felt it was her duty to reward Jenny's embarrassing fatphobia with the consequence of missing an entire damn tuxedo. She had been tongue-tied and demoralized yesterday when she could have spoken up (a common occurrence when trying to defend herself and not someone else), but she felt good enough to dispense some petty vengeance today.

She couldn't find a tux in his size, but found one smaller and one larger. She shrugged and took them both off the rack. At a pile of discarded fabric, she salvaged sage-green scraps from the bridesmaid dresses, as well as a navy-blue square that was close enough to the dress she originally planned to wear. She stuffed them into her bag. Good to have options.

It would have been unwise to wander around the hotel carrying stolen tuxedos, and they wouldn't fit in her tote. She checked several gray garment bags hanging at one end of a rack. They were all occupied, so she unzipped the first one and took out the, frankly, ugly sequined dress that was inside. She guessed it was a mother-of-the-bride or -groom dress. Autumn colors, so there was a good chance it was her mother's. She smiled and hung the dress back on the rack, sans garment bag.

A glance at her phone told her she'd been waiting ten minutes. That was more than enough time to wait for someone who said they needed to meet ASAP. With the tuxes concealed, she strode to the exit with every intention of dropping off the stolen goods in Raphael's room before going to brunch.

As she approached the door, the handle rattled and turned, and Mattie froze in panic. What could she tell Jenny or Donna about why she was walking out with a garment bag? Even if she said something like someone had told her to get it, or it was her own that she had brought, or evaded answering the question completely, they would remember her when they discovered the missing suits.

Before they could enter, she threw the bag beneath the narrow, high table against the wall by the door. Hopefully they wouldn't look, and she could try to discreetly pick it up on her way out. As the door swung slowly in, someone knocked against it, and a male voice called out, "Hello? You wanted to see me?"

All the breath left Mattie's lungs. Her legs refused to move. She felt her adrenaline ramp up, a numbness spreading through her body, and remembered reading that the "fight or flight" instinct was actually "fight, flight, freeze, or fawn."

Should have listened to them, she thought, her brain flickering to the memories of Daphne and Rin smashing through her cavalier attitude by reminding her she only thought this weekend wasn't so bad because she hadn't seen Mike Spencer yet.

She could have dived between the clothes racks. Run to and hidden in one of the makeshift changing room cubes. Slinked behind the door and popped out unnoticed as he walked farther into the room. Her feet would let her do none of these things.

So when Mike Spencer walked into the dressing room, the first thing he saw was Mattie, alone and exposed, surprised and upset. His favorite kind of prey.

He let the door swing shut behind him. Average height, dark brown hair meticulously shaped in the same shaved-sides style he'd always had, slightly lighter beard and moustache trimmed close to his face, khaki shorts and a light blue polo shirt—Spencer could have passed as a regular guy. It was the flatness in his copper eyes and the uncanny-valley quality of his perfectly straight, white teeth and practiced smile that gave him away as a danger. Mattie imagined that dogs could sniff him out immediately.

"Hello?" He called out again, eyes locked on Mattie. "Jenny? Donna? One of those assistants? Are you here?" Even though she knew she was alone, Mattie hoped someone would answer.

"Matalina Redgrave," he murmured, drawing out her name as he stressed every other syllable. "Don't tell me you're all by yourself in here?" He slid his hands into his pockets and took a step closer, giving her a once-over with his gaze. "Did you arrange this for me? To meet, alone, in secret, after...how long? Didn't want to risk the embarrassment of me turning you down in front of other people?" He snickered. "Yeah, I get that."

"Mike. Fucking. Spencer." Her voice sounded far away and not her own. When she found out she would have to deal with him this weekend, she had foolishly thought that she might even be able to confront him. Tell him she knew that what he did to her was wrong. Get some closure. She'd practiced it in her head, trying out different scenarios, possible reactions. She liked to think that he would be swayed by her powerful speech, apologize, promise to change his ways.

She had forgotten that he just didn't fucking care. But now, in his presence? With condescension and cruelty oozing out of him and filling the room like a noxious gas? Oh yeah. She remembered.

"Out of my way," she said, trying to go around him to the door. She couldn't feel her legs very well, but they moved anyway, and she had to trust her muscle memory.

"Ah, ah," Spencer chided, stepping in her way. "I can't let this opportunity pass me by. At the very least, I have to thank you. You know, I always thought I was invincible." His smile was all teeth, and his glittering eyes bored into her. "But it wasn't until I knew I could get away with doing whatever I wanted to you that I realized I was right. I am untouchable."

He took a step back, never losing his smile. A chill flowed down Mattie's spine as her mind jumped to monsters with needle teeth and charming but dead-eyed serial killers. "And now look at me. You helped me become the man I am today."

Mattie tried to get around him on the other side, and he moved in front of her again.

"Nope," he said. "You don't get a pass just because we know each other. You're responsible for a lot of upset. Kyle told me you texted him. Ah, okay, you know what I'm talking about. No, don't step away from me, this is important."

Kyle told him? It was bad enough that Kyle had befriended him, invited him, disregarded her concerns, and gaslighted her, but why the hell would he *tell* Spencer about it? Mattie kept backing up, hoping he would follow her and she would get the chance to dart around him with enough time to open the door before he stopped her.

"Now, my boy Kyle," he said, following her farther into the room and away from the exit. "This is his wedding. That doesn't mean anything to you, because nobody will ever want to marry you, but it's a big deal for him. And here you are, texting him, throwing a tantrum because of me." His smile widened. "Fuck, Mattie. It's almost as though you don't like me."

How long until someone walked in? Could anyone hear her if she screamed? The soundproofing was probably a selling point. She wanted to tell him exactly what she thought of him. She wanted to tell him to fuck off, then walk out of the room unhurt and never walk alone through this hotel again. She wanted to be brave enough to embarrass him and not fear whatever disproportionate violence he would use against her in retaliation.

But danger warnings were pinging up, one after another, and she remembered that what her relatives had called "necessary bullying" had, in reality, made her scared for her life. They'd told her so often for so long that she was making a big deal out of nothing that she had convinced herself to write it off as her usual neurodivergent overreaction. But the danger had been real, and the vindication she felt knowing her intuition had been right all those times was close enough to relief that she was able to respond coherently.

"And yet, here I am," she said.

He frowned, probably not expecting such a measured reaction from her. "It isn't very nice to burden a man with your hysterical accusations. But maybe you're not nice. I think maybe you're not a very nice girl at all, Mattie."

She tried taking a deep breath, but fear had knotted itself in her belly and there wasn't any extra room for trivial things like her expanding lungs. Everything she ever imagined she could say or do to stop him crossed her mind like a flip book, each possibility igniting and disappearing the moment she thought it. Her body just wasn't functioning, wasn't listening to her, which would have been more of a problem if she could think clearly. But panic had taken over and chaos always followed.

"I—I—you don't know what kind of person I am at all." She willed her feet to try to get around Spencer one more time, but they shuffled her back instead.

Coward. I'm a coward. Every part of me.

Stepping closer, he overcompensated for the space she'd put between them so his face was only a few inches away from hers, that fake smile wider than ever. His hot breath stank of acidity, of drinking too much and throwing up the next morning, and Mattie thought if he touched her, if he brushed against her at all, she would scream or faint or implode.

"Oh, Mattie. I'm the *only* one who knows you."

Spencer lifted his hand, too slowly to want to hit her, and reached toward her, like a lover about to caress her cheek with the back of his fingers. Mattie's panic surged and she wished for anything and everything that could stop him.

Just before his touch landed, voices carried into the room from the hallway, the doorknob clicked, and Donna and Jenny entered the room laughing. Spencer turned toward the noise, putting distance between him and Mattie.

"Oh good, you're here!" Donna said, barely glancing at them as she turned on the overhead lights. As they moved around one side of Spencer, Mattie moved around the other, as though his attention was what had pinned her in place. The women didn't notice as Mattie dashed past them, grabbed the garment bag of tuxes, and ran out the open door.

***

By the time Mattie's brain caught up to her feet, she had no idea where she was. She could see that she was in a hallway without windows, its few doors unmarked, but none of it looked familiar.

It would be folly to assume she was still in the same building—she didn't remember using a staircase or going outside, but that didn't mean anything. A woman's muffled voice drifted from one of the rooms, and Mattie didn't know if it would be better to go toward it or away.

Anxiety gripped her, but at least it had downgraded from full-out fear, past blind panic, to a type of high nervousness that she termed the "alert chihuahua." Spencer hadn't followed her, as far as she could tell, and if he could guess where she might have led herself in this palatial building, he deserved to find her.

Clutching the rolled-up garment bag to her chest, Mattie glanced around and pulled out her phone. She tried calling Daphne, but her sister didn't pick up. She texted her "SOS" and waited. Must be at her facial.

Rounding a corner, she saw a glass door at the end of the hall. Beyond was a stone path and the forest, and she hurried toward the promise of freedom. She pushed and held the door open as she took a deep breath of the cool air and glanced around. The paths wound into the woods, and the little slate signs indicating where they led didn't mean anything to her. She had no idea what a "The Pitch" was, or a "Dens," and she hadn't memorized where the golf course was.

Fuck it. She let the door close and followed along the wall of the main building, which eventually brought her to the pool area from the day before. From there, she found the indoor pool, and with it, an attendant who gave her directions to the lobby.

She didn't remember having to walk through the solarium the evening before, but it was a pleasant room that smelled of wet earth and plants. All that green instead of expensive art and custom wallpaper let her breathe a little deeper, muscles relaxing just a little, heart rate working toward something less frantic than a frightened rabbit. Mattie silently gave the Billingstead props for providing at least one room where she could forget for a split second that she was caught in the middle of several shitstorms.

"Matalina Redgrave?"

The woman's voice, coming from behind her, sounded familiar, but anyone who would use her full name with a question mark at the end wasn't anybody she felt she had an obligation to answer. Besides, everyone she cared about had her number. They could text. Mattie walked a little faster.

"Are you Matalina Redgrave?"

Mattie didn't like the sound of that at all. That was the tone of someone whose next sentence would be "you've been served," as they put court papers in her hands. Or "Don Corleone has a message for you," right before they whacked her.

A few more steps brought her into the vast lobby and into view of several staff members at the front desk and several more guests at the tables in front of the café. As she tried to place whether the faces belonged to any wedding guests, the footsteps behind her sped up and a woman slid in front of her, stopping her in her tracks.

"Whew," the stranger said, smiling. "I wasn't expecting you to be able to walk so fast."

The blonde woman dripped wealth, in that subtle way rich people do when they've always had access to everything that makes life easier. Teeth, hair, skin, posture, jewelry, clothes. She looked like if Daphne were a little taller, a little curvier, and a raging fucking asshole.

"Oh shit," Mattie said.

"I'll assume that means you're Matalina," Edie said. "And that I need no introduction." She pushed a strand of hair out of her face with the back of a finger and took a deep breath.

"I have something to say to you," the actress said.

As though Raphael's ex could say anything worth hearing. As though Mattie had any obligation to entertain her. As though she hadn't had enough of everyone's shit today. Mattie stepped around her, and Edie glided back in front of her to stop her from leaving.

Oh okay. She wanted to get serious. Mattie might have had a problem standing up for herself, but she damn well would throw down for people she loved. Also, like she told Raphael, she was pretty sure she could take her. And with all her lingering fear and anger from getting cornered by Spencer, she was ready to tap into that excess energy. She drew her own deep breath and looked up into Edie's face.

"You're not the first person to try to block my way today," Mattie said, her voice low and measured. "I assure you it didn't work out how they thought it would, either."

Edie snorted and crossed her arms. "Like I care. Stay away from Raphael. He's mine, and you don't want me for an enemy."

Mattie waited a beat, to see if she had anything else to say, then burst out laughing, an uncontrollable reaction closer to sobs than a polite titter. She set her bags on the floor so she could lean over her knees for balance, when every glance at Edie brought on a new round.

"You—" she started. "You—" She devolved into giggles.

"What the fuck is wrong with you?" Edie's disgust warped her features.

"What are you, in middle school?" Mattie finally got out. "'He's mine,'" she whined, mocking her.

It was a ridiculous reaction. To be fair, it was a ridiculous situation. It was either laugh or cry or fight. She had promised Raphael "no punching, no plotting, no going rogue," so fighting was out.

No way she was going to cower and cry and back down from the person harassing her boyfriend. So: laughing.

"Are you practicing lines or something?" Mattie continued, wiping her eyes. "You sound like every villain in every bad movie. And honestly, I don't have the time for this drama."

Edie fumed. Laughter must have been the correct choice, if it made Edie angrier and Mattie a few degrees more relaxed. After the very real physical danger of Mike Spencer, this confrontation almost felt easy. Mattie stood up straight and stretched her back, groaning when she felt a stippling of satisfying cracks.

"Raphael decides things for himself." Mattie stretched her arms to one side, then the other. She sighed and put her hands on her hips in a Peter Pan pose. "I have no control over it and you definitely fucking don't. You've convinced yourself you're the center of the universe, and you selfishly make it everyone else's problem."

Edie recovered from her obvious shock and tsked at Mattie like a teacher scolding a student.

"Selfish? I'm trying to keep my family together. You're the homewrecker."

"That requires a home to be wrecked. He broke up with you over a month ago."

"It was an argument. All couples argue. He needed some space to think things through, not find a side piece."

Mattie ignored the judgmental once-over Edie gave her. Her family had been looking at her that way all her life, so she had plenty of practice. "Why are you so attached to a guy who obviously doesn't want anything to do with you?" She had meant to be meaner, but the question came out sincere, and Mattie was surprised that she actually wanted an answer.

"You know why," Edie said, shaking her head. "I imagine I want him back for all the reasons you want him, too. Everyone wants him. He's a prince. He's charming, but personal. Real. He and I started something and didn't get a chance to see it through, and we both know he's the kind of man who doesn't abandon people he loves."

Yeah, all of that was true. Mattie softened a little, understanding. It only lasted a moment before she remembered how this wonderful guy was trying, desperately, to get away from this person, that she hurt him and continued to hurt him, and Mattie's resolve returned with a snap. "He dumped you, Edie." Mattie wrinkled up one side of her nose as she said it.

"He wouldn't dump a pregnant woman. He's a better man than that. You could be a good person too, all you have to do is let him go back to the mother of his child."

Mattie's mind reached back for a response, but her grasp found nothing, all her senses misfiring from what Edie just said. As her mind started its slow tilt into confusion, she said, "That's between you and him." Proud she was able to dig up an appropriate canned response, she reached for one more. "But you aren't entitled to his body, his time, or his happiness, under any circumstances. I will make sure of it."

Good on you, she thought. *You've said your piece, now walk away and get to the room before your legs give out from underneath you, and you can process what the actual fuck she just said.*

Mats picked up her bags, unable to feel the material in her hands, and Edie let her walk away. As Mattie turned down the hallway with the elevators, Edie called out, "I'm getting him back. We can do this the easy way or the hard way."

"Looks like it's gonna be the hard way, Edie," Mattie called over her shoulder just before ducking into an open elevator car and frantically pushing the Door Close button. When Edie didn't follow her, Mattie pressed the button for the floor below Raph's room, intending to take the stairs up the one flight in case Edie was trying to track down where his new room was. She was running on auto, but she'd be able to give everything that happened her full attention once she was safely locked inside their room.

Edie was pregnant.

Jesus Christ.

***

Edie's anger made ripples in the lobby, and the staff who witnessed it smartly kept their heads down. They'd seen their share of rich-person fits and had a good idea of when to intervene and when it would play out on its own.

After watching Mattie disappear down the hallway, Edie stood there, wondering why that didn't go the way she wanted it to. She'd have to regroup and try a different approach later.

As she turned around, she nearly ran into Luke, who was standing uncomfortably close and eating a candy bar.

"Fuck!" Edie barked, regaining her balance and taking a step back. "Don't you have somewhere to be?" She whined.

Luke stared at her and took another bite of the candy bar, chewing slowly, his other hand in his pocket. "Righ hee," he said around a mouthful of chocolate and peanuts.

"Go harass someone else," she said, stepping around him. He moved into her path.

"Edie, Edie, Edie," he said, waving his candy bar. "You got sloppy."

"Excuse me?"

"No, I don't think I will," he mused. "When did you say you got into New Zealand?"

"You want my itinerary, Luke? Fuck you."

"Yeah, yeah. That's what I thought. Because I'm pretty sure you took a private plane from Los Angeles and arrived in Auckland yesterday morning. Payton sent the private car to pick you up from the airport then pick up Raph on the way back here. You're American. So." He took another bite. "When did you haf time to quarantine for fourteeh dayf in the two hourf between landing and fowing up at the Billingftead?"

Edie smoothed out her sleeves and shook her head. "Oh, Luke," she sighed. "This isn't something that someone like you would ever understand, but if you get rich enough, rules become suggestions."

Luke nodded sagely. "You've never been to New Zealand before, have you?"

She scoffed and crossed her arms.

"Also what I thought," he said. "So here's the thing. We take the safety of our citizens very seriously. Well, at least, from outside threats. There's actually a lot of internal problems. That's beside the point. The point is, it doesn't matter how rich you are. You try to sneak into the country to avoid a quarantine, that's pretty serious. According to the Ministry of Health, they could fine you—which I'm sure you'd have no problem paying—or arrest you, which is probably less than ideal for you. But that would be in addition to sending you immediately to quarantine for two weeks."

"I won't be doing any of that."

"No, I don't imagine you will. Not because you can weasel out of it, but because I'll keep your secret. And in return, you're going to leave Raphael alone. He and I quit the production, so you won't be seeing him on set, but you're also going to avoid him in this hotel. He's got a wedding date tomorrow and he deserves to attend without your interference. You'll also issue a statement saying that he isn't the father—"

"Ha!" Edie laughed.

"—because your choices are to either stop this rumor immediately and save face, or keep at it until the truth comes out and buries you. And if you do continue harassing him, I'm going to rat you out so quickly, you won't even have time to pack before they force you into quarantine at a two-star hotel with one bathroom sink and no paleo option.

"*And*," he stressed. "By the time you're released two weeks later, you won't be able to track Raphael down again." He shrugged and finished off the candy bar, crumpling the wrapper into a ball. "Or you can juft be a goddamn fucking adult and leaf him alone."

Edie was eerily still, her ire unmistakable and unavoidable. "Do your daughters know you blackmail women like this? Do they know their father is a misogynist? I could go to the press right now and tell them that you threatened me. Even if your divorce was amicable, everyone would wonder what really happened with your wife, if you're going around threatening women like this."

Luke's smile didn't reach his eyes. "I guess we'll see what happens, then."

Certain of her safety, Edie stormed off. Luke swung by the café to pick up coffees and sandwiches, then made his way back to the meeting with Raph and Mason. Raph had said no going rogue, so he'd leave out the part about his conversation with Edie. But he deserved to know that she was harassing Mattie, and Mattie was standing up for Raph in a way that warmed Luke's heart. After all, he might be right. Rin and the Redgrave sisters might be the best thing that ever happened to them.

***

Mattie didn't know how long she'd been sitting on the couch in Raphael's suite. She didn't remember getting there from the elevator, opening the door, setting down her bags, or sinking into the soft cushions. The phone in her hand buzzed, and she had the feeling it had been doing that for a while. Daphne.

"SOS?" Daph asked frantically, when Mattie accepted the call. "What SOS? Where are you? What happened?"

"I'm safe." Her voice sounded more like herself. "Spencer."

Daphne waited for more information, but Mattie didn't elaborate. "Did he hurt you? I just saw him leave to go golfing with a bunch of other motherfuckers. Tell me what happened. Do I need to murder him?"

"He probably needs to be murdered. Not by us, though. We have better things to do."

"I don't," Daphne muttered.

"I can't go to the wedding."

"I know. Meet me in the lobby and I'll drive you back to the cottage."

"Kyle told Spencer that I texted about him."

"The fuck? Why would—Jesus, Kyle. Guess it's time to dump them all. I'll meet you in the lobby in ten minutes. I have to collect all my stuff. I'm not coming back here, either."

"No," Mattie said, shaking her head. "I mean, I don't want to cause any rifts between you and everyone—"

"Oh, shut up."

"—but also, I have to go to brunch."

Silence stretched between them. "Mats, if you need food, we can go out somewhere once we leave, or I can make you a sandwich at the house."

"I do need to eat. It's been...a morning. But I need to make a scene. I need to tell them I can't attend my brother's wedding because of Spencer, and tell them all how awful he is. There might be someone who doesn't know and is vulnerable, and then they can decide how to avoid him and protect themselves. And I'll also have confirmation that our relatives would choose my bully over their own daughter, and I can walk away without any regrets."

Daphne let out a breath. "You know you don't *have* to do any of that."

"I have to expose him, Daph. He's had a hold on me for too long, and I thought being quiet would make it go away. If I don't bring his abuse into the light, he'll thrive in the dark. And I have to try to stand up for myself one last time."

She knew better than to argue, especially when Mattie got like this.

"Okay," she said. "I'll save you a seat. Our mother seems to be looking for you."

"I honestly don't care. See you in a few."

Mattie walked into the main dining room ten minutes later. She hadn't bothered to text Raphael—he would let her know when he was out of his meeting, and until then, she would keep what Edie had told her and all the emotions it brought up locked in a corner of her mind. Her current focus had to be standing up to her relatives and making it clear how awful and dangerous Mike Spencer was.

Raphael would have liked to be there when she confronted them. But it had to be done as soon as possible, and she didn't want to interrupt his own efforts to protect people from a bully.

Daphne had saved her a seat at a table in the middle of the room. First, she needed food. And she wanted to take a few minutes to appreciate the quality and luxury of her last meal at the Billingstead. She wouldn't be returning, and since Raphael quit, he would most likely cancel the rest of his booking to stay with her instead. Her stomach vibrated with nerves, but it was more likely she would pass out if she didn't eat than vomit if she did.

Mimosa for strength. Coffee for alertness. Kumara beignets, mascarpone and smoked salmon crepe, lobster tagliatelle in a butternut squash sauce. Chocolate hazelnut torte with gold-dipped strawberries because holy crap.

A good number of wedding guests had shown up for brunch, including all of Mattie's relatives. Kyle and Celeste sat with most of the bridesmaids, and Kyle was noticeably upset that he had to miss golfing with his groomsmen. Throughout the meal, several people had stood up to give impromptu toasts, so Mattie's speech wouldn't seem out of place until she actually started talking.

Daphne recognized the look in her eye. "Is it time?" Mattie nodded and slid her chair away from the table.

An insistent clinking from one side of the room stopped her.

"Oh, for fuck's sake," Daphne whispered, as Mattie sat back down. "Making a speech isn't required. It's an optional brunch the day before the wedding. Narcissists, all of them."

Their brother Topher and his wife, Leda, stood at a table across the room from the bride and groom. Celeste smiled neutrally at them, while Kyle gave his brother a look that said, "make it quick."

"I'll make this quick," Topher said. "I'd never want to upstage my brother and his beautiful fiancé on their wedding day, so allow us to steal these next fifteen minutes the day before." He and Leda glanced at each other and smiled.

"We're pregnant!" They said in unison.

Gasps echoed through the room, and people shouted their congratulations over the growing applause. Marjorie, Ola, and their other sister-in-law, Cece, rushed over to Leda with another half dozen of their cousins and aunts. Kyle and Celeste exchanged a look, then reluctantly followed to offer best wishes in person.

"Is it still such a big deal if it's your fourth kid?" Mattie asked. "Fourth, right? Or is it fifth?"

"Fourth, pretty sure." Daphne sat back and sipped the champagne that the waiters were bringing out. Mattie declined hers. The mimosa had been plenty, and she wanted to keep her head relatively clear.

"It feels like a competition at this point." Mattie drummed her fingers against the table. "Do they expect you to have kids?"

Daphne rolled her eyes. "They don't expect me or you to give them grandchildren. For different reasons. Actually, for the same reason, when it comes down to it: they've given up hoping that either of us will find happiness with a man."

A month ago, that would have bothered Mattie. Now, she didn't care.

"I don't want it to seem like I'm taking the first opportunity to weasel my way out of confronting them," Mattie said. "But I think the time for me to say something has passed."

Their phones buzzed at the same time and they looked at Rin's latest text. "State of Emergency announcement coming. Just found out. Effective immediately. Brace yourselves."

Mattie and Daphne looked at each other. *OK but did you get condoms for Mattie?* Daphne texted.

"Daph, for real?" Mattie whined.

"We knew it was coming. The alcohol is stocked. I'm just trying to look out for you, now."

Rin answered: *Got everything. You're lucky for my priorities. Will be back at the cabin in about an hour.*

Daphne downed the last of her champagne. "I've gotta call Cinnamon. Your confrontation is postponed, right? I don't want to leave you alone if you suddenly get motivated."

"Call your wife," Mattie told her.

As Daphne stood and crossed the room, more gasps erupted from a table near the door, followed quickly by whispers, louder talking, and a lot of people standing up. The group gathered around Topher finally noticed the commotion rippling through the rest of the dining room.

Mattie watched with a kind of satisfied detachment as one of her older cousins leaned in to the group and said in a stage whisper, "The government issued an immediate country-wide lockdown. They aren't allowing parties of more than ten people to gather."

"What? What does that mean for the wedding?"

"Surely they can't expect us to just call it off the day before. They have to make exceptions."

"The wedding planner will clear it up. Donna? Where's Donna?"

"The hotel would have told us if this was an issue."

Questions and exclamations of disbelief surrounded Mattie. The whole room swayed, everyone wanting to be somewhere else, wanting clarity and certainty. Mattie's father had moved to the quietest corner and was arguing with someone on the phone. Kyle stormed off deeper into the hotel, leaving his bride-to-be weeping in the arms of her bridesmaids while several men helped her half-collapsed mother into the nearest chair.

It looked like a Renaissance painting. Mattie snapped a photo to show Raphael later, then left to change into outdoor clothes.

Going for a walk would help her focus. It also didn't hurt that she was leaving her relatives behind in absolute chaos.

It was the little things like this that brought her joy.

Saturday, April 4, 2020
Afternoon

It would be funny how well things were turning out for Raphael if the road to get there hadn't been so fraught. Mason saw potential in Raphael's—well, Mattie's—idea for a lockdown documentary about film cast and crew put out of work by the pandemic. He'd seen the signs and guessed there would be some kind of government order coming soon. There were still details to iron out, but Schiller was a seasoned professional and was already calling in favors.

They'd reviewed the crew list, which, thanks to Payton's ineptitude, was incorrect and incomplete, so Luke had been sent out to try to update it. He would also spread the word about the new project and gauge interest in it. The three of them had considered staying at the Billingstead, but with everyone scattered or about to be, it would be easier to stay connected electronically rather than physically. Luke was absolutely glowing, knowing that he could start his personal quarantine as soon as possible so he could get back to his daughters.

And if Raphael didn't need to be at the Billingstead, that meant he could stay with Mattie as early as now. Or, if she still planned to attend the wedding, he would keep the room for convenience and check out the day after that.

He pulled out his phone to text her as he walked through the halls of the hotel. They hadn't spoken since she was about to steal him a tuxedo, and she hadn't texted him since. As he started typing her a message, one appeared from Luke.

Luke:

New Zealand in lockdown. Looks immediate. Only groups less than ten people allowed. I wish I was there to see them all freaking out. Payton AND the Redgraves. Sweet justice.

Raphael:

Shit, mate. Good news for Mattie. She won't have a choice to go to a wedding that's canceled.

Luke:

lmao. Bro. You think they're going to cancel it? They spent all that money, ceremony is tomorrow. They're gonna go through with it.

Raphael:

I want to say nobody's that stupid, but. At least she'll have another excuse for not showing up. I'll text her now.

Luke:

uhhhhh also I forgot to tell you when I got lunch, I saw Edie trying to harass Mattie. Mats was doing an amazing job of defending you and putting Edie in her place. But I'm pretty sure she told her she's pregnant.

Raphael:

I should have said something earlier. Shit.

Luke:

fwiw Edie seemed upset afterwards and that can only mean good things.

Raphael:

Let's hope. Text you later.

Luke:

Good luck, bro.

Texting Mattie suddenly seemed inadequate. Raphael had known he was tempting fate each time he put off telling Mattie about the nature of Edie's slander. A part of him had hoped it wouldn't matter. That, since it was an obvious lie, he and Mattie would shrug it off and it wouldn't affect what they had. But he still avoided it. And after everything Mattie had told him, her secrets and fears, it was the wrong move. It gnawed at him until he was only nerves.

Hopefully she'd be willing to listen. Hopefully she would understand. Hopefully his bad decision wouldn't be the thing that broke them before they got a real chance to be together.

As he continued down the corridors, the sound of voices that had begun as a murmur became an indistinguishable chorus. When he eventually stepped into the lobby, he stepped into chaos.

The room was filled with people, easily fifty or more, guests having heated conversations with hotel staff singly and in groups. A number of people were yelling. A few were crying. More were on their phones, with airlines or other hotels, trying to make alternate plans. They were all violating the restriction on indoor gatherings in their quest to get around having to comply with the restriction on indoor gatherings.

He saw Daphne near the café, speaking with two other women, and made his way over to her.

"Daph," he said. She turned and smiled.

"Welcome to pandemonium," she said. "How are you finding it? I'm in my element."

"I'm sure you are," he said. He felt the other women's eyes go wide as they looked at him. "Have you seen Mattie?"

"Not since brunch," Daphne said, shaking her head. "Is she not responding?"

"I haven't texted her. I guess Edie cornered her and it sounds like she told her—" he glanced at the women. "About that thing. I wanted to see her in person."

"Well, shit."

"Yeah. I fucked up."

Daphne sighed. "She must know it's a lie, with the four of us saying so. But between that and running into Spencer, she must be—"

"What? She saw him? When? Is she okay?"

"Sometime between the spa and brunch. She sent me an SOS, but by the time I responded, she was safe. She said she's fine. But it upset her enough that she decided not to go to the wedding tomorrow."

"Good," Raph said, glancing around. "Good that she's not going, not good that she was upset."

"Hey, if that's what it took—and that's usually what it takes—and as long as she wasn't hurt in the process, I'll take it."

"She must have run into them one after the other," Raph said, grimacing. If she decided to skip the wedding right after running into Spencer, it must have been bad. And then to immediately get confronted by Edie and told that she was pregnant with Raphael's child...

"I'll text her now," he said. "I'll check the room too. See if she's there."

Daphne nodded. "I offered to bring her back to the cottage, but she wanted to go to brunch. Stand up and tell everyone they weren't her family, they treated her badly, and that Spencer was a violent liability."

"She told them that?"

"No." Daphne snorted. "Our other brother and sister-in-law announced that they're pregnant, and two minutes later, we started getting notifications about the State of Emergency. She didn't get a chance."

So basically, everything had gone wrong all at once. And Mattie was somewhere processing all of it, without him, without her sister or her best friend, without Luke, even. Raphael nodded and clapped Daphne on the shoulder.

"I'll find her."

"Text me when you do," she said.

Raphael texted Mattie on the way to his room, which was empty. He tried to think of where she could be. Not with her relatives. She hadn't gone back to the cottage. At least, Daphne hadn't driven her back. He was starting to panic when his phone chirped.

Matalina:

> Out for a walk. Needed the fresh air to focus. And the forest.

Raphael:

> Where are you?

Matalina:

> Wish I could tell you. A path in the woods? Sun is behind the clouds.

Raphael:

> Are you lost?

Matalina:

I'm not sure where I am. If you leave out the door closest to the lake and farthest from the lobby, there's a sign for a hiking trail along the water. I took that.

Raphael:

I'm coming to you. Do you need me to bring you anything? A warm jacket? Umbrella? A snack? Mike Spencer's head on a platter?

Matalina:

Let's not go dirtying plates when there are plenty of good pikes available.

Raphael:

I'll find you.

Matalina:

You'd better.

***

By the time Raphael saw Mattie walking toward him down the hiking trail twenty minutes later, the sky had darkened from an almost cheerful light gray to a moody pewter. Though no thunder yet telegraphed an oncoming storm, the temperature had dropped, and the smell of rain blew in off the lake. Raphael wished he had picked up an umbrella, but he hadn't wanted to waste any more time on his way to Mattie.

He didn't know what to expect. Her texts had been as playful as they'd always been, if a little more abrupt. If she was angry with him, she would have said so or not replied at all. She must be trying to work through all the emotions and memories that got stirred up that morning. And trying to hide how much it hurt her.

As they got closer, he saw her half-smile, and she started to jog to him. He returned the smile and matched her pace, until they met and Mattie threw her arms around him, burying her face in his chest. He wrapped her up in a tight embrace and felt her shoulders shudder, heard her sob against him.

"Oh, Mattie," he murmured, kissing the top of her head. He held her close and let her cry, the first echoes of thunder reaching them from across the water. "I'm here. You're safe."

Mattie lifted her head with a wet sniffle. "I—I've had kind of a rough day."

"I heard," Raphael said. "Thought you could take on the world's two biggest assholes. Ambitious."

"Foolish," Mattie corrected.

"Not your fault." He adjusted his grip on her so he could wipe away her tears with his thumbs. "Tell me everything."

She stared at him, biting the inside of her lip, before glancing out past the strip of beeches and evergreens toward the lake.

"I'm glad you quit," she said. "That's one less thing to worry about. It makes me happy."

"And now I can devote all my time to you."

"A welcome consequence," she agreed, her lips flickering into almost a smile. "Though not the main reason."

"Don't underestimate your influence," he said. Mattie laughed and met his eyes again.

"I have no idea what's going to happen with the wedding. And Spencer is still roaming around, and I don't want to think about either of those things yet. For now, I want a hot shower. Then a nap."

Raphael nodded. She would tell him, in time, but her physical needs had to come first. "Room, then." She released her grip on him, and he reached for her hand as they started walking toward the hotel together.

Part of him had always been wary of trusting people. He could play along even when he was uncomfortable because that was what rewarded him with the opportunities he wanted. Even so, he resented having to share himself when he didn't want to. Mattie somehow understood this, when no one else did, and he knew she wouldn't ask him about Edie.

Raphael had told her that it wasn't true before she knew what it was, and that was enough for her. She wouldn't bring it up in an argument months or years down the line, and it was that respect for him that made him want to tell her everything.

"I want to explain. The Edie thing."

"You don't owe me an explanation, Raph," Mattie shook her head. "You only met me, uh, two days ago, and we've only been communicating..." She counted on her fingers. "I don't know, less than two weeks."

"Then why does it feel like I've always known you? Why do I want to share myself with you in ways I've never wanted to, with anyone, before? How do you already make me feel at home in my own skin?"

Mattie squeezed his hand. "I suspect it's my weird brain."

"I'm serious." He squeezed back. "I want to tell you about Edie. I know she approached you at the hotel."

She inhaled with a hiss. "First, I want to say that despite wanting to deck her, I remembered you asked me not to, so I didn't. I should get points for that. And second—"

"I'm not reprimanding you," he said. "Forgive me interrupting, but you have nothing to explain or answer for. I should have told you about it as soon as I knew I wanted a more intimate relationship with you. It was selfish of me to try to keep you in the dark, and to ask your friends to help. I'm so sorry I didn't respect you enough to tell you."

"But you don't owe me, you have no obligation..." Mattie trailed off, sounding genuinely confused. Raphael stopped walking and pulled her toward him. He reached his free hand up to push a rogue strand of hair out of her eyes.

"But I do owe you, and I do have an obligation, and I accept both, because that's what I do when I love someone."

Thunder answered him, closer now, as Mattie opened her mouth to say something, and closed it again. *It's too soon*, he told himself. *And after all the drama she's had to deal with today...*

"Mattie, I love you," he said, talking over his own doubts. "I've never met anyone like you. Your love is boundless and deep. You're brilliant and loyal to the point where you flew thirteen hours to quarantine for fourteen days to give a bunch of shitty people one last chance to love you back. So, okay, mostly brilliant and just a bit daft."

"You're really killing it here, Raph," Mattie whispered with a smile, her eyes full of mischief and tears. He smiled back and tugged on her.

"You are an adamant protector of your loved ones, but truly awful at protecting yourself, so it's a good thing you inspire such strong friendships. The world isn't fair, but you try to keep everyone from becoming complacent, in the hopes that it can be more fair. You make me believe that I deserve respect, and tenderness, and safety, and if it weren't for you, I wouldn't have had the courage to walk away from a job that, as you've said, would grind me to powder." He laced his fingers behind her back and pulled her close, her arms snaking around him.

"All that," he murmured. "And so beautiful." Mattie lifted her parted lips, and Raphael met them in a slow kiss. The wind picked up then, cool with the scent of ozone and petrichor, tousling Mattie's hair, and the first drops of the arriving rain announced themselves by sliding down their exposed necks, cheeks, hands, leaving chilly tracks across warm skin.

"I love you," Mattie said, pulling away just enough to speak. Her arms tightened around him, and he hugged her back. "I was going to tell you earlier. People sometimes get weird about it, like it's too soon."

"But it feels so right," Raphael said, grinning like a wolf.

Mats glanced at the thin canopy of branches above them. "I also have a bunch of words to tell you why I love you. They're here somewhere."

"I believe you," he said, laughing. "You'll find them soon enough."

"Speaking of words." She hesitated. "You really don't have to tell me anything about Edie. Honestly. I'm afraid I'm going to be jealous, whatever you say, and I'm not sure I want another emotion right now."

Sporadic, soft pattering through the trees became a wave of sound as the rain came down in sudden sheets, the canopy offering little protection for them on the dirt path. They wouldn't have been able to avoid getting soaked, but for all its abundance, it was gentle, and didn't drown out their voices. Raph took Mattie's hand again and led her back down the path.

"It isn't really about her," he said. "It's about me, and it's something you should know. It's something that someone who loves me should know."

Mattie cocked her head, and rain ran into her ear. She swallowed and shook her head. "Then I should know. Because I love you. Sneaky."

"Exactly."

He frowned, trying to remember how to tell his story. He was silent so long, Mattie must have thought he had changed his mind. But it had been a while since he'd told anyone, and never a romantic partner, and he had to take a moment to arrange the words before he spoke.

"All I ever wanted was to be an actor," he began. "I can't remember my earliest birthdays or other milestones, but I can remember my lines from plays my cousins put on at family gatherings since I was little. They likened me to my Uncle Paul, who was a professional actor, and who pulled me aside at 16 and told me the only downside to acting was accidentally getting women pregnant, which—"

"Excuse me," Mattie interrupted, stressing each syllable. "But what the fucking Christ does acting have to do with getting women pregnant? Was he in porn?"

"No, he was just a raging misogynist and an all-around terrible person, but I didn't know that, because I was a teenager and he was doing what I wanted to do."

"Accidentally impregnating women, apparently?"

"Absolutely not," Raphael said firmly. "That's my point. What he said, it got in my head. I wanted to act, and if I was good at it, and good-looking, more people seeing me meant more people who wanted to sleep with me, and if I wasn't careful, someone could pop up later claiming I was the father of their child, and I would have to step up with time and money and I didn't want to do any of that."

He paused to collect his thoughts. His trainers squished with each step, even though the rain had pulled back into a light drizzle. Mattie's squished beside him, and the sound calmed him.

"That was a shitty thing for him to say," Mattie said. "But you know you don't *have* to sleep with everyone, right? Or anyone?"

"I figured that out. But I was already struggling with my sexual identity, and he also said that he would hope I was gay but that has its own problems, especially in this profession, and now I had to worry about irreparable fallout of dating literally anyone."

"God, this Edie thing, then..."

Raphael grimaced. "Yes, this is basically one of my worst nightmares."

Mattie glared at the path ahead of them. "I should have hit her."

Watching her seethe beside him, he was struck by the fact that, from the beginning, her anger about the whole mess stemmed from the fact that Raphael was being hurt. Not that an ex was staking claim to her new boyfriend, not that Raph hid something from her, not that their relationship could be in peril. It was that she cared for Raphael, full stop. Someone was hurting him and she didn't want him to hurt. It was as simple as that.

He realized with a sudden clarity that he had to keep her. He wanted her to feel as worthy and loved as she made him feel. A fierceness bloomed in him, and he felt the urge to stalk Mike Spencer down and beat him to a bloody pulp in front of everyone and dare all of them to say one more awful thing about Mattie.

The desire for violence waned, though the desire to protect her didn't.

"Better you didn't," he said. "I don't want you to have to deal with her at all. But it means a lot that you want to stand up for me."

"Of course," she said. Like it was the most natural thing in the world.

"Do you want me to beat up Spencer?"

Mattie thought about it. "No. But only because I like your hands. I don't want to ruin them. His ugly face isn't worth it. But thank you. Please, continue, teenage you, sexual identity, now worried about impregnating, do go on."

"You're sort of extraordinary, you know."

"So you've said. Story please." She gave his hand she liked so much a squeeze and ran her thumb over his knuckle.

"So. I thought I would always have to choose between my career and children—the same way women worry about it—and the more I considered it, the more I realized that I didn't want children at all. Every time I revisited that thought, the more sure about it I became. Whenever I pictured the life I wanted, it was free of children. When I tried to imagine them in my life, it felt wrong. I had plenty of people who loved me, who I loved, and I never felt lacking. So when I was twenty, I got a vasectomy."

He looked over at Mattie, who still had a considering look on her face. She glanced up at him. "That seems logical," she said. "Did you—oh! You literally can't have gotten Edie pregnant."

"Once again skipping ahead in the story, but, yes, correct."

"Sorry. You keep pausing."

He paused again. "I need time to formulate how to say all this, since I've only ever told my doctors and Luke."

Mattie pulled him to a stop. "You've never told any of your partners about it?"

Raphael sighed. "Now we get into the adult, real-world consequences of how fucked up I became because my uncle had me believe every woman wanted to trap me into being a father."

"Yikes," she muttered, tugging his hand as she started walking again.

"Yeah. When I've been in a relationship where I could conceivably be a father—"

"I see what you did there."

Raphael smirked. "—and it's gotten serious enough for me to tell my partner that I don't want children, the response from all of them has been, 'oh, you'll change your mind.'"

Mattie squeezed his hand in a crushing grip, but didn't interrupt him.

"Once they say that, I can't help but wonder if they'll take it upon themselves to change my mind for me. They don't want to use condoms, but I insist, because I'm paranoid. Then I wonder if they tampered with the condoms somehow. They can tell something's wrong, the relationship becomes strained, and it all ends badly.

"They were so dismissive of me, I couldn't get it out of my head that they were emotionally manipulating me into fatherhood, disregarding my own choices. I learned to be wary of every romantic partner. No relationship can survive that lack of trust."

He went over what he just said, what it must have sounded like to Mattie. He could see the hotel at the end of the path, outside lights lit up against the cloud-darkened afternoon, the rain nearly stopped.

"Raphael," Mattie said.

"I don't want kids, Mattie." He rushed to get the last of his speech out. "Even if it's not too soon to love you, or to tell you I love you, it's definitely too soon to think about kids. But I wanted you to know this now, in case it's a dealbreaker. Before I embarrass myself. Before I'm in too deep to prevent a broken heart."

Mattie stepped in front of him. She reached to take his other hand in hers, straightened her posture, and looked him in the eyes.

"Raphael Callan. There is nothing embarrassing, or selfish, or shameful about protecting the parts of your life that bring you the most joy. No matter how deep, or fulfilling, or trusting a relationship is, you are not required to sacrifice any part of you for the other person. I am so sorry that nobody ever told you that before, or if they did, that their actions betrayed what they really thought." She swallowed loudly and huffed a little laugh.

"I can't promise that I'll always be the best person for you, or that I won't sometimes be inscrutable or withdrawn, or that I have any answers that make sense, or that I'll ever wear less than six layers of clothing. But I can promise that I will always respect your autonomy. I'll never try to tell you your mind. And I will always want you to find happiness, even if it's not with me.

"Wanting a child-free life isn't a dealbreaker, Raph. I've never wanted kids either, so I understand. And I want to be a part of constructing the life of your dreams, if you think there's room for me in it."

He grasped her hands harder, wanting to speak, knowing that, if he opened his mouth, the first sound out of it would be a sob, regardless of what he planned to say. So he shut his eyes and nodded and tears slipped out anyway, and he clutched Mattie to himself in an embrace that she returned, and they stood there holding each other as the rain stopped, soaked and teary and grateful.

When Raphael could speak, he said, "I think the room for you in my life is actually a Mattie-shaped hole. I didn't know what was missing until I met you."

"You've gotta stop saying such nice things or I'm going to fall in love with you."

Raphael laughed against her wet hair. "Let's go dry off," he said. "Get warm. Get the rest of the gang together. Make a decision about what to do next so we can leave all our bullies behind us and enjoy the next few weeks with as little drama as possible."

"Oh, the drama has got to go," Mattie agreed, turning to the hotel. "But I am going to miss the food."

Raph slid an arm over her shoulder. "I'll get you food. I'll take care of you."

She looked up at him and smiled. "I know."

***

The last rays of the setting sun reflected off clouds slung low in the east, and the brightness from the wrong direction made the late hour feel separated from time. The light bathed Raphael's room in a rosy glow that dissipated when their friends arrived and they turned on the lights.

Clean, warm, and dry, Mattie shifted to the edge of the couch as Daphne and Rin placed platters of food on the low table between them. The five of them wouldn't fit at the dining table, so Raphael brought plates and silverware from the kitchen area so they could eat in the living room.

"Sushi and salami," Mattie said. "That sounds like a mistake of a meal but a really good children's book."

"Hey, if we're abandoning the Billingstead, I am damn well going to have their sushi before I go." Daphne plucked a pair of chopsticks out of her bag. "They hired Manu Ono and I won't miss that man's artistry for a third time."

"A client sent the charcuterie board as a thank-you for helping them navigate the changing restrictions," Rin explained. "Obviously I'm going to share it, I can't eat it all myself."

"Not with that attitude," Daphne said. Rin snorted.

"And Luke's on his way," Raph said.

"What he texted was, 'Found the holy grail of feel-good foods, I'm about to be everyone's favourite person,'" Rin recited from their phone.

"Hopefully he's bringing alcohol," Mattie said, eyeing the salmon and avocado roll and prawn nigiri.

"Aha!" Daphne reached into her tote bag and revealed a bottle of peach sake. Mattie and Rin made appropriate ooo-ing sounds.

As Raph turned back to the kitchen, a clanking sounded at the door, like someone rolling a piece of metal across it. He checked the peephole, shook his head, and opened the door.

"Bro," Luke said, greeting Raphael with a nod because his arms were full of bottles of rum and packets of something wrapped in wax paper.

"Bro," Raph replied, gesturing him inside. "What on earth have you nicked?"

Luke set the bottles on the kitchen counter and emptied his pockets of more packets. "There's supposed to be a rum-and-chocolate tasting tonight, which will attract all the people we least want to see. They were setting up as I passed by, and I liberated a bottle of each rum and as many chocolate bars as I could. So we'd have the goodies without having to see the baddies." He stepped back and waved his hand toward the counter.

"Well, I'm in love," Daphne said.

"Me too," Rin added.

"I saw him first," Raph chimed in, swiping one of the fancy chocolate bars.

Luke grinned like he'd just won at friendship. "And lest you think I've gone and half-assed it, the pairings are listed on their website, so we don't have to combine everything indiscriminately. However questionably I acquired them doesn't reflect a lack of sophistication."

Raphael organized the bottles and bars according to their pairings while the others made themselves plates and poured the sake. Luke perched on the couch next to Rin, who rolled meat-and-cheese tubes for him, and Daphne handed out the rest of the chopsticks.

Mattie wanted it to never end. Sure, she was in a country she had complicated feelings about, for an event she would rather not attend, where she had to socialize with people who neither knew her nor really cared about her—all of which she willingly agreed to—and of course she got the surprise bonuses of having to face her childhood bully, navigate around the emergence of a new and dangerous virus, and deal with her lover's ex-girlfriend.

But as she sat in the hotel room listening to her sister retell the story of how she missed her favorite chef's pop-up restaurant in San Francisco, watching Rin and Luke flirt without saying a word to each other, knowing Raphael was going to bring her a tumbler of rum and a chocolate bar, she thought it might also be worth it.

"*Broke* is officially over. For us, anyway." Luke popped an olive into his mouth. "It should be over for everyone, with the new restrictions, but that won't stop them."

"'Every obstacle is a chance to achieve higher greatness in the face of even more opposition.'" Raphael mimicked the director. "I'm sure Payton sees it as a challenge to be conquered instead of a reasonable request to keep people safe."

"And the not-a-douchebag producer went for your documentary idea?" Rin asked.

"It was Mattie's idea, actually." Raphael smiled at his girlfriend as he set the rum and chocolate on the table in front of her as reverent as an offering, then perched on the couch arm next to her. "A lot of people wanted to quit the production but couldn't take the pay cut. You helped them leave a bad situation. Not only that, but we think it could be something special, not just a stopgap solution. I've never done a documentary. I'm excited about it."

"That's one down," Daphne said, chopsticks darting to take a grape from the charcuterie plate. "What's next?"

"Edie's taken care of," Luke said. The four of them stared at him, waiting for an explanation that never came.

"What did you do?" Raph asked, his voice flat.

Luke glanced up and realized everyone was looking at him. "Oh. Nothing."

"Luke."

"Nothing! I swear. I mean, nearly everyone here has told her to leave you alone. Between that and whatever your professional team's cooking up, I consider her taken care of, is all. They're still getting a restraining order, right?"

"Yes, I called JC earlier. He seems to have the situation well in hand." Raphael rubbed his forehead. "Rin, Daphne. Luke and Mattie know this. I had a vasectomy years ago and that's how I know I'm not the father."

Rin barked a laugh. "Pay up, Daph," they said, holding their hand out, palm up.

"I'm a cisgender lesbian! Married to another cisgender lesbian! I have the privilege of *not* constantly thinking up ways to not get pregnant."

"I was right, that's a hundred dollars."

"You bet that he had a vasectomy?" Luke asked, eyebrows near his hairline.

"You were one hundred percent sure she was lying. Daph bet they never had sex. But if that were the case, you'd just say that. So he had to know for sure he couldn't impregnate anyone. Hence." They waved toward Raph's crotch. "No offence."

He shrugged.

"You didn't have to tell them," Mattie said, squeezing his hand. "I mean, you only told me this afternoon, and I know it was difficult for you."

"Telling you made it easier to tell them. Besides, you told me not to be ashamed of it. I took that to heart."

"Ashamed?" Daphne asked. "No way. Good for you, taking charge of your future like that. That society considers it selfish is just a result of the effective marketing of an oppressive state. Also, a dozen niblings is already enough."

"Soon to be a baker's dozen," Mattie added.

"So that brings us to the last two things we need to deal with," Rin said. "And then we can all retreat to the cottage and take a much-needed hermitage for a few weeks."

"A hermitage is a hermit's residence, not a vacation." Daphne corrected.

"I'm using it like 'pilgrimage.' It's a pilgrimage to a secluded place of rest."

"Before the hermitage, there are two things *I* need to deal with," Mattie stressed.

"*We*," Rin and Daph said in unison, and Luke and Raphael nodded in agreement.

Mattie had been thinking about it all day. If she were honest with herself, she had been trying to find a way out of going to the wedding *as* she was RSVPing that she would be there.

"Either way, I'm not going to the wedding," she told them.

"Can we get that in writing?" Luke asked.

"How do you already know her so well?" Rin said, in awe.

"So that's one problem solved," Mattie continued, ignoring them.

Daphne paused, chopsticks halfway to her lips. "Not both? Which one does that solve? They're not cancelling the wedding.

I heard dozens of ridiculous excuses for why they should go forward with it."

Mattie frowned. "It solved the not-wanting-to-go-to-the-wedding problem. Are they still having the rehearsal tonight, then?"

Her friends shared a look before Rin asked, with rightful wariness, "Why do you want to know about the rehearsal, Mattie?"

"If they're not canceling the wedding, there could still be guests who don't know that Spencer is a danger to them."

When it looked like Mattie wasn't going to elaborate, Raphael slid an arm over her shoulders and gently said, "None of those people are your responsibility."

"It's all our responsibility," Rin said, staring at their plate, their arms crossed. "That's what makes us good allies."

"Most of the guests can pass," Daphne added. "The Redgraves are good at that. But that doesn't mean the people who are passing would feel comfortable with Spencer's views."

"He won't be able to help himself. He'll test the waters, see what he can get away with." Mattie sighed. "At least if everyone knows ahead of time, they can make informed decisions whether to stay or leave or prepare to confront him."

"Is there a way to do this remotely? Slip letters under everyone's doors?" Raphael nudged her. "Or is there an email list?" They all looked at Daphne.

"Not that I know of," she said. "But I wasn't involved in the planning process."

"The worst that will happen is what he's already done," Mattie said. "So what am I really giving up besides the silence that never kept me safe, anyway? But if I don't say something, the worst that will happen is he continues to harm people. This way, I can cut off his supply of potential victims here. I can do it, so I have to try. For my own conscience.

"And I want my relatives to have to decide on the spot whether they're going to believe and support their daughter and sister or her bully. I want to see it in person, in real time, and I want everyone else there to see it too. Because I know they won't pick me. I still—" She wiped the tears out of her eyes with the back of her hand. "I still have the smallest hope that they'll choose me. I can't help it. But I know they won't, and I want them to feel ashamed. I want them to remember."

Daphne nodded. Luke said, "Remind me never to cross you. Any of you."

"You would never," Rin told him, and he smiled. They turned back to Mattie and leaned forward. "I support all of this. But the ceremony isn't the best place to do it. You should do it—"

"During the rehearsal," Mattie, Daph, and Rin said in unison. They all grinned at each other.

Daphne sighed and said, "Fuck if I'm not going to support my sis in her time of need. From what I've heard, plenty of guests will be crashing it."

"Oh, we're coming with you," Rin said.

"And my axe," Luke said, in perfect imitation.

"There's no way in hell I'm letting you walk into this without me," Raph added.

Mattie blushed and bit her lip. She really had the best friends in the world. "Just be there. In the room. Just...witness. And if things get violent..." She turned her hands out and wrinkled one side of her nose. Luke perked up.

"Violent?"

"*If*," she stressed.

"But. My axe?"

"If," she repeated. "Don't instigate. Don't assume. Don't react. Violence will only be appropriate if my life is in immediate danger and I can't run away. Your job is to witness."

With their plan in place and just over an hour until the rehearsal was set to start, the five of them settled into easy conversation. Mattie was grateful for the distraction. If they spent any more time talking about her, even if it was nice (especially if it was nice), she wouldn't be able to get in the headspace she needed to confront everyone. Even so, their love for her buoyed her. She squeezed Raph's hand again and let herself hope for a less dramatic tomorrow.

Saturday, April 4, 2020
Evening

Daphne guided them through back hallways unused by anyone but the staff, who—if it weren't for her air of purpose—would have asked if they were lost. Mattie had no idea how Daph was able to navigate what to her seemed a vast maze, but she was grateful that her sister could slip them through the enormous building in a way that avoided everyone else.

They'd decided to wear their wedding outfits to the rehearsal, since this was their last chance to dress up for the foreseeable future. Daphne skipped her bridesmaid dress in favor of a silver one with lace sleeves and a balloon skirt, and the material shushed as she led the team onward. Luke and Rin trailed behind, him in a fancy black suit that reminded everyone he was actually a movie star, and Rin wearing a butterfly-sleeved maroon jumpsuit, tattoos just peeking out of the V-shaped neckline, their long hair pulled back into a slick bun.

In the middle, Raphael wore a suit similar to Luke's but with a thin black tie and a pocket square that Mattie made from the scrap material she stole from the seamstress earlier that day. Her navy blue dress was a bit of a departure from her usual style. For one thing, it was only one layer. For another, the hem fell mid-thigh, showing off her legs (as much as they could be shown off through sheer black stockings). Its high collar and long sleeves would have felt right at home with the rest of her wardrobe, but the fit was snug, and the flowered jacquard material less forgiving.

Mattie had wanted something slightly uncomfortable, to remind her not to let her guard down, but something she knew she looked fantastic in.

Nailed it.

Daphne stopped the group next to a set of double doors that led outside to a covered walkway. Fairy lights dotted the inside of the arched roof, and the path curved past where they could see.

"Decision time," Daph said with a clap of her hands. "Past these doors is the outdoor corridor to the chapel. There's also an elevator around the corner that we can take to an underground hallway that also goes to the chapel. I haven't run both, so I don't know which is quicker, if that matters. Outside is dark and chilly, but we're more likely to run into other guests underground."

"Where are we and how did we get here?" Mattie asked, in awe.

"In life, or in the hotel?" Rin asked.

"I know we want to show up a little late," Daphne continued, "but if we wait any longer, they'll have started already. With this much exposed skin, I need the not-cold route."

"With this hair, I need the not-windy route," Rin said.

"I need the cold," Mattie said. "And to not bump into anyone on the way there."

"I'm with you," Raphael said. "We'll see you three on the other side, then."

"The messy bun I did for you is only supposed to flirt with being messy, not actually be a mess," Rin told Mattie as they walked backward with the others. "Don't enter the chapel until I can give you a final once-over and fix anything that might float out of place."

Mattie nodded solemnly and watched her friends disappear around the corner. Raphael shifted into her view and leaned against the door.

"Ready?" He asked, offering his hand. She took it, and they stepped outside.

Without the wind from earlier, the walk was almost pleasant. It felt warmer than that afternoon, not only because they were on the other side of the hotel, protected from the lake's stiff breeze by the building and forests, but because the rain had moved on and taken its chill with it.

The chapel was yet another outbuilding on the Billingstead campus, technically close enough to walk to, set in the forest and higher on the hill, so its wide windows overlooked the castle-like main building and the lake. The underground path served as an option to avoid walking in adverse weather, its elevators available for anyone who couldn't use the stairs on the romantic, winding outdoor path.

Mattie and Raphael walked in silence, hand in hand, and when they entered a gazebo after the first set of stairs, halfway to the chapel, Mattie pulled him aside and drew him into a kiss.

Raphael smiled against her lips, slipping one hand around her waist and the other to the back of her neck. After their walk in the rain, they hadn't had any time for just the two of them. And after dinner with their friends, Daphne had stayed with them to change, while Rin went with Luke to change in his room. Rin said they didn't want to crowd them, but they weren't fooling anybody. Mattie was glad that Rin had found someone they wanted to be alone with. After all, she had found someone, too.

Mattie pulled away first and rested her forehead against Raph's. "Just in case," she said. "If things go wrong, if I feel overwhelmed, I can remember being here with you, and it'll steady me."

"You don't need an excuse to kiss me," he said with a smile. "You look fantastic, by the way. I'm loving this dress on you."

"You look fantastic," she echoed. "You look like...love at first sight."

Raphael kissed her again, letting his hands wander to her shoulders, down her arms, until he could take her hands and press them against his chest.

"I know this will be emotional for you, and I don't want to say anything to add to your turmoil."

"Oh no. Why do I sense a 'but'?" Mattie eyed him, forehead creased in worry.

"But," he said, laughing. "Simply meeting you gave me the courage to leave a bad situation. And when I had doubts, I told myself, 'do whatever will make Mattie proud of you,' and I did. So before we go in there, and you gather your courage to leave your bad situation, and try to help vulnerable people in the process, I want you to know I'm proud of you."

"Yeah," Mattie said, nodding, blinking away tears. "Yeah, you're making me cry."

"You can cry," he said. "And if you cry in the chapel, I know it's because you care. About other people, and about how you need to be treated. I'll be right there, and if they try to dismiss what you're saying because you're crying, I'll jump in. Don't reconsider because you're emotional."

"I never do," she said, making a low noise that sounded almost like a laugh. "That's where I get my reputation from. Can you tell me something nice about me that doesn't have anything to do with what I'm about to do? I think it'll help me focus. I'd like to hear about how I'm better than Edie."

Raphael grunted. "That'll take too long, you're better than her in every way. Are you sure you're not avoiding seeing your relatives?"

"I'm not, I swear."

He considered for a moment, looking out toward the shadowy lake. "You've eclipsed her. I can't remember anything about her that would even compare to you."

"So...I'm like the sun. And Edie is like...a tea light."

"No," he said, shaking his head. "More like, if you're the sun, Edie is ashes. The forgotten remains of an immature desire long extinguished, in a hearth so cold its only good use is for petty revenge. But she isn't worth the effort of revenge. Ashes are worthless. And utterly incomparable to the sun."

Mattie stared at him, his lips soft and parted, his eyes dark beneath the meager fairy lights. She didn't know what she'd done to deserve him. But she was ready to get her mission over with so she could spend the next month exploring in private what she and Raphael could mean to each other.

The night opened to her, and her life ahead of her, and she leaned into it and kissed him again.

"Okay Byron, let's get this thing over with, so I can sleep for a full day then be isolated with you for a month."

"Good thing we've had two weeks to practice," he said with a wink.

***

Mattie would have called it a church. Or a cathedral. "Chapel" made her think of the tiny, quiet places where people in a small town could marry, or the ones in Las Vegas that were just big enough for the bride, groom, their few witnesses, and the Elvis-impersonator chaplain.

But the Kendall Chapel was an enormous, dreary tribute to the never-ending battle of exerting human control over nature. All imposing angles, the building squat against the hill, the land before it cleared of trees that might otherwise disrupt the view from the expansive windows. To achieve the drabness of its uniform gunmetal gray, the builders must have spent days picking through otherwise adequate greywacke to find enough matching stones to cover the exterior of the structure.

It was the ugliest building Mattie had ever seen.

After the relative poshness of the rest of the Billingstead campus, she was surprised she had such a visceral reaction to it, until she remembered the usual clientele. This aesthetic must be what rich people wanted.

As they approached the oversized, oak double doors, Mattie looked back toward the hotel, with its skillfully lit colonnades and pediments meant to reaffirm to every guest that they were royalty, its staff that couldn't say no to even the most outrageous of demands, its apparent willingness to ignore or facilitate breaking laws if it meant securing more revenue. And the people who would want that were the exact people she meant to cut out of her life.

A warmth spread through her, the antithesis of every time her stomach dropped in fear. A confirmation. A vindication. A confidence that she was about to do exactly what needed to be done. Whatever the consequences, she will have done it. And before she even stepped inside, she was proud of herself, too.

Raphael held the door open patiently, watching her look out into the night. She approached the wall and ran her hand over the stones, their roughness catching her skin like sandpaper. She rubbed her thumb and fingers together and turned to him.

"I'm ready," she said. He gestured for her to go first, and she stepped into a red-carpeted foyer dimly lit by a row of chandeliers. Their friends were waiting in front of the elevator. Raphael shut the door behind him. The entrance to the main hall was another set of open oak doors halfway down the inner wall, and golden light and voices spilled into the anteroom as they regrouped out of view. Rin gave Mattie a cursory appraisal before nodding their approval.

Daphne walked into the sanctuary first, followed by Rin and Luke. Mattie and Raph entered last. The cavernous space felt too small to Mattie, who expected the two dozen members of the wedding party and maybe a handful of other guests. But she couldn't count how many people sat in the pews, talking and laughing, waiting for the rehearsal to begin. Eighty? A hundred?

Her footsteps didn't falter, but her focus shrank, the loudest voices becoming muted and distorted. She willed herself not to throw up or pass out.

"They probably expect the wedding to be cancelled tomorrow," Raphael murmured, close to her ear. She nodded, but he must have noticed her hesitation. "This is good. More people to warn, more people to witness—"

Mattie hadn't realized he had broken off until he gripped her hand a little too tight. She glanced up at him and followed his hard gaze to a pew near the front, where Mike Spencer was laughing with her brothers. He looked so relaxed, like he fit in perfectly, and the cold thread of fear that snaked through her veins was smothered by a new ire.

She had gone to the chapel to force her relatives to choose between her and her bully, but they'd chosen him a long time ago. They had rejected her sensitivity in favor of his indifference, her empathy for his cruelty. Her constant questioning in exchange for his easy acceptance and reinforcement of the status quo. Her pain for his pleasure.

None of them deserved her. She didn't owe them anything. But her friends had found aisle seats to her left and gave her fierce looks of encouragement, and Raphael pumped her hand once, his fingers sliding from hers as he sat down in a pew to her right.

Besides the minister and Kyle and Celeste on the dais, Mattie was the only one standing. With her hearing ebbing and flowing with her emotions, she thought the sudden drop in volume meant she had lost it altogether, until she heard an echoing cough.

"Matalina," her mother loudly whispered from three pews away. "Sit down." She pointed emphatically at an empty space in front of Raphael. Mattie felt tears gather in her eyes and swallowed, but didn't sit.

"Matalina," she said again, snapping her fingers for attention and pointing at the seat. Mattie shook her head. Beside her mother, Mattie's father stood up and turned to her.

"Matalina." Henry Redgrave's booming voice brooked no argument. "Sit."

The minister cleared his throat. "If everyone would like to take a seat, I'll give a quick run-through of what the rehearsal will look like, then we can get started."

When Mattie didn't move, he frowned, concern creasing his forehead. "Miss?" He asked.

"Sit down, Matalina!" Kyle ordered.

They wouldn't choose her, but she still had a job to do. If it meant even one person was able to avoid Spencer's malice, it would be worth it. She'd practiced what she would say all evening, her friends and her boyfriend were an arm's length away in case she needed backup, and was as ready as she'd ever be. *Just do it quickly, then get out.*

"That man," Mattie said, projecting her voice and pointing a shaking finger. "Mike Spencer. Is the co-founder and president of California's most vile hate group. He's a proud white nationalist with ties to several domestic terrorist groups under FBI investigation. He spent his childhood emotionally and physically abusing me. And I will not attend or participate in a wedding where he's been honored as a groomsman."

Pockets of whispers bloomed across the chapel, but Mattie's relatives were more vocal.

"For fuck's sake, Mattie," Hayden mumbled, his voice carrying. The minister winced.

"So leave!" Kyle yelled from the altar. "Nobody wanted you here. We all knew you would pull some shit like this."

"Kyle, language," Marjorie sighed, rubbing her forehead.

"Nobody wanted your sister here, but everyone's cool with the violent misogynist?" Mattie's voice cut through the din. "Just so we're clear. White supremacist? Welcome. Anyone rightfully upset about the white supremacist? They can just fuck right off. I got that right?"

"Kyle?" Celeste asked, face twisted into a frown.

"I'll take care of it, babe," he told her. "I fucking knew she would be a problem." He turned back to Matalina. "Why do you do this? Why do you have to say shit?"

"Because not saying shit has only emboldened him and people like him," Mattie said, finding strength the longer she spoke her truth. "And not saying shit hasn't kept me safe, so why not be loud and fuck up his plans to harm more people?"

Spencer had been glaring daggers at her since she spoke up, but she felt only the slightest bit of fear. It was drowned out by the fury coursing through her body. She couldn't believe she had put up with everyone's bullshit for so long. She could feel herself shaking and knew that any of her relatives that noticed would think it was from terror or embarrassment. That the tears flowing down her cheeks were a sign of weakness.

But her friends knew both were a sign of her bravery. And Raphael had said that if they try to use her tears as a reason to dismiss what she was saying, he would jump in.

Mats took a shaky breath and said, "My silence has only ever served him. That ends now."

Mike Spencer glared at Mattie as he stood up and shuffled past the other people in his pew. When he got to the aisle, Raphael rose and stood beside her. She broke eye contact with Spencer long enough to glance at Raphael, note his clenched jaw, tight shoulders, intensity and anger rolling off him in waves.

"Finally," Luke muttered as he sidled up to her other side, unbuttoning his jacket and casually slipping his hands in his pockets. His stance could easily be mistaken as ambivalent. His jackal-like grin and piercing eyes could not.

True to his cowardice, Spencer glanced between the men with a look of worry and thought better of getting any closer.

"Matalina Redgrave," her mother said, not wanting to speak loudly but also not wanting to get any closer, with the strange men flanking Mattie. "We had a deal. You couldn't make an effort to put up with this family for one more day? I'm not giving you another chance. You're deliberately trying to ruin your brother's big day, and you're not going to see a cent, do you hear me? You will get nothing."

"Wait, what?" Ola asked. "Were you paying her to be here? Are you serious?"

"Wow," Kyle said. "You've got to be fucking kidding."

"I never accepted her money. And I don't care what you think," Mattie said, and she almost believed it. "I came here to expose Spencer for what he is. If you don't want to take my word for it, look it up yourselves. But now everyone knows, and none of you can pretend not to know. If you choose him over me now, never call me your daughter or sister again."

"Matalina Redgrave." Her father didn't yell. Henry Redgrave never had to. Though he hadn't said anything since she began speaking, his face was crimson with wrath or embarrassment or both. He came around the pew and down the aisle, gently pushing past Spencer as he made his way to Mattie. Neither of the men next to her so much as twitched, their steady support bringing new tears to her eyes.

As Mattie's father approached, she saw a flurry of silver and in a moment, Daphne stood before her, blocking him from getting any closer. Whatever he saw on Daph's face made him pause, disappointment flickering in his eyes.

"This is my fault," he said in a low voice, turning to Mattie. "I indulged you too much, as a child. I didn't do enough to dismiss whatever fantasies warped your sense of reality, and you've grown up to believe you're the rightful center of the universe. You were a selfish child, and you're a selfish adult. And it's my greatest failing that I can't say I raised you better than this, than to sabotage your own brother's wedding. You've always had to make a scene. Always had to be so dramatic. Always—"

"Dramatic?" Raphael spat. "If any of you had the decency to listen to her concerns the first time, she wouldn't have to try increasingly desperate methods to get her voice heard. Though I do agree with you, this is your fault." The chapel fell utterly silent. Henry's face was frozen somewhere between shock and outrage.

"You're all at fault," Raphael said, projecting his voice and glaring at her father, her mother, and each of her siblings in turn. "She's said before that she's grateful you never had an effeminate son, because you would have beaten the softness out of him. Instead, you've spent your life trying to manipulate the softness out of her. When she tells you your actions harm her, you laugh at her and double down. You blame her for being a victim, and defend the people who harm her."

He put an arm across Mattie's shoulders and leaned into her, closing the short distance between them. "You are not her family. You are cowards, bullies, and liars. It's not surprising you support the men who treat her as horrifically as you do.

"I'm her family now. We're her family," he amended, nodding to Luke and Rin and Daphne. "And if anyone—*anyone*—" he stared at Spencer as if enough concentration could incinerate him. "Tries to harm her, in any way, an unkind word, a threat, a raised hand, it would be our pleasure to demonstrate how a real family protects its own."

Nobody said a word. Not a whisper of gossip, not a curse or mutter. Anger radiated from Mattie's parents. Most of her siblings and their spouses glowered at her, though Ola looked thoughtful, and Celeste was checking something on her phone. Raphael squeezed her shoulder, and she felt Rin place a hand just under his. Luke leaned in and subtly hip-checked her. Daphne still stood before her, between her and their father, as tall as she could make herself, arms crossed over her stomach.

"Are you done here?" Raphael murmured, turning to her.

"I'm done here," Mattie said, loudly, the phrase ringing with finality. Rin turned and started down the aisle toward the double doors, and Mattie and Raphael followed. Behind them, Luke sauntered backward, sizing up Spencer in a once-over that had its intended effect, as Mattie's bully avoided eye contact and shuffled to put more of her relatives between them.

"I'm leaving too," Daphne said. "Mattie's worth more than all of you combined."

"Daphne," her father said, shaking his head.

"Nope. You made your choice. You chose wrong."

As Daph caught up with Luke, he turned and offered his arm. She took it, and they followed their friends out of the sanctuary as a chaos of voices rose up behind them.

***

The night hadn't changed—they'd been indoors ten minutes, not enough time for the world to turn, the moon to rise, the stars to shift—yet everything felt completely different. Rin had led them out the doors and onto the covered path, correctly assuming that nobody wanted to wait for the elevator while the inevitable fallout happened in the other room. When the doors shut behind Daphne and Luke, Rin wheeled on Mattie and threw their arms around her, stopping everyone on the path.

"I'm so proud of you!" They said, sniffling. Mattie sniffled in return and felt another pair of arms wrap around her.

"I'm so proud of you," Daphne said, her breath hitching.

"I'm so proud of *you*," Rin told Daphne.

"No, I'm proud of you," Mattie said, and the three of them argued about who was proud of whom and tried to stop crying.

Rin stepped back and held Mattie at arms' length. "Are you free now? Finally?" When Mattie nodded, Rin bounced on their toes and shouted, "Mattie!" Daphne laughed maniacally then howled into the night.

"I'm both wired and drained," Mattie said, sighing. "And we shouldn't stop here."

Luke gave her a side hug and a kiss on the forehead as he passed her to join Daphne and Rin in their dance down the stone-paved walkway. She felt Raphael put an arm around her, and she turned to him and pulled him into a passionate kiss. It felt like a lifetime had passed since she'd last kissed him, on these same stones. She'd felt both outside herself and acutely aware of her body as she stood in the middle of the room full of people, and she wanted Raphael to remind her of her physical presence in the world. Her fingers brushed spots of wet on his cheeks, and she wiped them away.

"Don't cry," she whispered. "I love you." Raphael laughed.

"I love you, too," he said. "I'm emotional because I'm so proud of you."

"That seems to be the consensus around here."

"Mmm," he agreed. "It's all right that I said something? I was seeing red, but you asked us not to fight, so I had to speak up. Those were the only options."

"You were perfect. You...you listened to me. Not just about the not fighting, but you heard me and believed me when I told you how I'd been treated, and that's—you're the first person to believe me without seeing it firsthand."

He rested his forehead against hers. "I'll always believe you, Mattie."

She swallowed back a sob. "Me too."

"Cottage?" Daphne shouted, pointing at Rin. "Cottage? Cottage?" She looked at Luke, then Mattie.

"I won't make it," Mattie told her, taking Raph's hand and following them back to the hotel. "I love you all, but the space left behind by adrenaline is filling with exhaustion. I'll stay here with Raph tonight. Sleep for three days straight. Then we'll check out and move back into the cottage. What do you think?" She directed the question to Raphael.

"Sounds perfect." He beamed at her.

Rin cleared their throat. "Actually, uh, I was going to stay, too. Luke, um. He. Anyway, I'm staying here tonight."

"Oooooooo," Daphne teased. "You're spending the night together?"

Rin gave her an eye-roll, but Luke snaked his arm around their waist. "Don't tell us you're surprised, oh all-knowing Daphne?"

"Pah!" She replied. "Only that it took so long."

"We met, like, four days ago, Daph," Rin said with a sigh.

"So long!" She whined. "I just want everybody to be happy and kiss, and all of you—all of you!—could have been happy and kissing even sooner if you'd all just listened to me!"

"It's true," Mattie said with a shrug. "She told me I needed to hook up with Raphael on our fourth day of quarantine."

"To be fair, we eventually did break protocol to hook up."

"Very true."

"Well," Daphne announced. "Since my wife is safe in San Francisco, I'm going to indulge in my big romance, too. I'll get myself a room here for the night and enjoy in the most sensual manner possible a ridiculously delicious second dinner and their dreamy breakfast spread. Take myself on a nice little date."

Mattie didn't hear Rin's response, everyone's laughter muffled as she retreated into herself: her usual reaction when she was overcome with emotions but in a safe enough situation to withdraw a bit. Raphael saw the look in her eye, and instead of pulling her back into the present, he let her get comfortable in her own mind. He knew that, this time, she was trying to process the immense love that they felt for her, and he would never rob her of that privilege. Instead, he walked beside her, knowing she'd return to him, and he would be waiting.

***

Hours later, when the rowdier wedding guests would usually be mid-antics, drunk and destructive and who-knew-where across the Billingstead's thousands of acres of forest, lake, fields, and outbuildings, Rin Butcher made their quiet way down an unrowdy hallway lined with guest rooms.

They stopped in front of a door and ran their fingers through their hair, trying to make themself look as unassuming as possible. An impossible feat, really, with their arm muscles as big as they were. They were so used to seeing similarly sculpted bodies at the boxing gym that they hadn't realized it made them stand out. Not until they were among these rich, soft muppets. But he'd only seen them with their hair up, so having it loose could distract him enough for them to get inside before he dismissed them out of hand.

Checking the room number again, they knocked a quick pattern, took a deep breath, and adjusted their glasses. No sound of approaching footsteps or moving furniture, but Rin kept their gaze on the door, willing their shoulders to at least seem relaxed, even if the adrenaline of unavoidable confrontation was evident in their every tightened muscle.

A flicker of light at the peephole, a pause. Rin attempted a flirty grin but was sure it came out more like a grimace. The deadbolt unlocked with a thud, so when Mike Spencer turned the handle and opened the door a crack, there was nothing stopping Rin from shoving it wide open and pushing the vile man back into the room so hard he fell on his ass with a surprised yelp.

"What the fuck?" He scrambled to get back on his feet as Rin threw both locks and turned to him. When he finally stood up, he found himself inches away from Rin, who was eye-level and clearly unafraid of him.

"'The fuck' is that you're finished bullying the Redgrave sisters."

Spencer snorted and glanced around wildly, obviously wanting to take a step back, but not wanting to show weakness, either.

"I don't need to bully anybody, let alone those pathetic women. I have better things to do."

"No, see," Rin poked a finger against his chest and leaned in closer. "I don't believe you do. Because they embarrassed you tonight. They ripped off your sheep costume so everyone could see you for the predator you are. You can't fool anyone else now. Well. Anyone who doesn't want to be fooled."

Scared or not, Spencer stood his ground. "So what? What do you want, an apology? I don't fucking think so."

"Stay away from the Redgraves. Not just the sisters. All of them."

He chuckled, eyebrows raised in surprise. "What an utterly insane thing to say. Are you quite well, dear? Has all that feminism broken your brain?"

"You're going to get someone killed."

"Yeah, but at least it'll be someone useless, like Mattie Redgrave. So weak, all she can do to defend herself is just stand up and cry about it—"

He cut off with a strangled noise as Rin's flawless jab dropped him back onto the floor. He raised his hands to his face and mumbled something Rin couldn't understand. They shuffled so they were squatting next to his head, out of reach if he wanted to kick them.

"I want you to remember that I gave you a choice," Rin said quietly. "And that this is what you chose."

Spencer answered with an indiscernible moan that was somewhere between a sob and a grunt of frustration and pain. "This is why you people have to be put down." His voice was thick, and Rin wondered if they had broken his nose. "Always needing to resort to violence."

Rin stood and walked past him to the door. "We don't *need* to resort to violence," they said as they freed the locks. "But for you, Mike, it was my pleasure."

Leaving him curled up in pain on the floor, Rin made their way back through the hotel, and they couldn't help the satisfied smile that crept up.

Sometimes, punching a monster was necessary. Not to stop him, or frighten him, or teach him a lesson, but to remind the heroes that the bad guys weren't untouchable. Hitting him didn't solve anything except their nagging desire to hit him, but that was fine. They had a better plan for actually dealing with his presence, and they would barely have to lift a finger to do it.

And for one night, at least, the world felt a little more fair.

Sunday, April 5, 2020
Morning

For the third morning in a row, an alarm that Mattie didn't remember setting pierced through the gray veil of sound sleep and annoyed her into wakefulness.

"Violence," she rasped, curving her back against Raphael's chest and pulling his arms tighter around her. "We decided. Alarms are violence."

Raph stretched against her, paused, inhaled quickly through his nose, and sat up. "Mattie, that's the hotel alarm."

"Just shut it off."

"No, it's—" He slid out of bed and Mattie groaned. "It's the fire alarm. Mats, get out of bed."

"It's just a drill. They hate me." She heard the rustle of clothes as he put on the boxers, jeans, and sweatshirt he'd left on the floor the night before. Her covers disappeared in a snap, and she gasped at the sudden coldness. Raphael leaned over and gently cupped her face.

"Okay love, I can see that you need, at best, motivation, and at worst, supervision in the morning. I'd love to let you sleep but with our luck, the time that we ignore it will be the time we're in actual danger. So I'm going to gather your bags and my things, and you're going to put on the clothes from last night as fast as you can, and we're going to get the hell out of this building. All right? Cheers."

He punctuated his speech with a kiss before darting to collect their things. Mattie's adrenaline finally kicked in and she dressed in a panic. The relentless shriek of the fire alarm drove her to move faster.

"We're going to see my relatives again. And Spencer. They're all going to be out there."

"Most likely," he answered from the other room. "Hopefully they'll be as disorientated as we are."

Mattie checked her phone. "Uh. It's after ten."

"After last night, they probably slept in."

"The wedding starts at eleven-thirty."

Raphael stuck his head back in the bedroom. "Then they're in various stages of undress and will be self-conscious about that instead of you. Out. Please. Call Daphne and Rin."

He slung Mattie's bag over his shoulder and held out his hand. They left the room together, cringing at the alarm, louder in the hallway, and shrugged into their jackets. Neither of Mattie's friends picked up. She tried Luke next, but he didn't answer, either. They passed several people in the stairwell—as Raphael had predicted, half-dressed, in undershirts, robes, hair in curlers—and none of them paid her any attention.

As they stepped onto the ground floor, a police officer in front of the elevators gestured toward the lobby.

"Make your way out the front doors, please, quickly, and stay behind the cordon for your safety."

Mattie and Raph glanced at each other. Blue and red lights flashed across the lobby, and they jogged toward the main entrance as more officers entered and yelled instructions.

They had glimpsed the cars, lights, and flurry of activity in the driveway well before they got to the exit, but it didn't prepare them for the wall of sound and motion they entered as they stepped into the madness.

The police had set up a perimeter, with cars and vans closer to the building and red-and-white police tape farther back. Officers directed them to move behind the tape, where they found more vehicles, the rest of the hotel guests, and several people in hazmat suits. Signs on the cars indicated they were with the Ministry of Health.

Raphael gripped Mattie's hand and guided her through the crowd. People in face shields and other PPE handed them face masks and urged them to put them on and maintain a two-meter distance from other people. Unwilling to let go of each other, they held the masks to their faces while they tried to get to a less crowded area.

The yelling of the officers that was prominent closer to the hotel had given way to the yelling of hotel guests—mostly Redgraves. They passed several women openly sobbing, wailing toward the sky, and Mattie's heart sank.

"What the fuck happened?" She asked Raph. Mattie heard her father shouting, the same tone he used to reprimand waiters, though much louder, and Raphael quickly steered her in the opposite direction. "Do you think there was an accident?"

"I don't know," Raphael said grimly. He brought her a little ways into the trees, enough distance between them and anyone else that they felt comfortable stashing the face masks in their pockets. Mattie's phone rang and she let go of his hand to answer it.

"Daph?"

"Oh good, you woke up. I bet that was Raph's doing, huh?"

"Jesus, Daph, where are you? What's going on? Are you okay?"

"Closer to the lake than the driveway. Too noisy. Where are you?"

Mattie glanced around. "On the other side of the driveway, in the forest. Is Rin with you? Luke?"

"Yeah, we're all here. Stay put. We'll come to you. I grabbed some breakfast on the way out. Hope you like cold waffles."

She stared at her phone in stunned silence as it beeped that the call had ended.

"Are they out?" Raphael asked.

"Yeah," she said, shaking her head. "The three of them are coming to us. They are...unperturbed. I think Daphne is bringing us a handful of waffles."

Raphael considered that. "So everything is fine."

Mattie looked at him incredulously, opened her mouth to say something, and burst into laughter instead. "You're probably right."

He grinned back at her. "If Daphne had time to grab baked goods in the middle of whatever nonsense this is, it can't be that bad."

"You severely underestimate her love of breakfast and what she'd risk to get it, but otherwise, yes, she usually knows what's going on and whether it's appropriate to panic."

A woman wearing PPE and a health department badge approached them and asked for their names. They told her, and she made a note on her tablet.

"Do either of you know where I can find someone named Edie Everett or Theodore Payton?"

Raphael frowned. "I know they're staying here, but I haven't seen them outside. What's this about?"

"Have either of you been in close proximity to Ms Everett any time in the past few days?"

"No," Mattie said, before Raph could answer. "We only just got out of quarantine ourselves."

"Ah," the woman said. "Good on ya, trying to keep us all safe. Well, it seems this Edie person skipped her own quarantine, so if you know anyone who's been in contact with her since she got into the country, tell them to contact us, and to go into isolation as soon as possible."

"Sodding Yanks," Raphael said. The woman crinkled her eyes. "Are you looking for Payton for the same?"

She shook her head. "With the state-of-emergency in place, we can't have gatherings of more than ten people. Unfortunately, that includes film sets."

"If you don't mind my saying so, this whole thing seems rather an overreaction," Raphael nodding toward the police vehicles.

"They're not here with us," she said. "They're responding to a different problem. Though we might have to snag a few of them to help with the more unruly guests."

"You might need their help with Edie, too. She won't go quietly."

Mattie's throat was suddenly dry. She'd said what she needed to the night before. There would be no benefit to her pettiness now except to be petty. She heard her father still yelling across the lawn.

"You've put a stop to the filming because it would violate the emergency order. Would the same apply to weddings, then?" She asked. Her heart beat in her throat.

"Oh yeah," the official said, gesturing with her hand. "Right, you said you're a Redgrave. Yeah, sorry, that's been canceled. We'll have the organizers detained if we have to, but the hotel is looking at a very steep fine for even considering going through with it. That'll be enough of a deterrent. Anyway, thanks for doing your part. Stay safe. See ya."

The health official nodded to them and walked back toward the group. Raphael and Mattie watched her go.

"I feel like it's important that I say, aloud, that I did not do this," Mattie said.

"I did suspect you might have, if only because I didn't do this," he replied.

The crowd had grown as more people evacuated the hotel, spilling farther up the driveway and into the woods near Mattie and Raph, though the Redgraves had gathered and stayed just behind the police tape by the health department's most official-looking van.

"Waffle?" Daphne's voice between them startled them both, and they turned to find the rest of their friends had sneaked up on them. Daph offered up a cloth napkin with three Belgian waffles, and Mattie and Raphael each took one.

"We were expecting you to sleep through the alarm," Rin said, Luke at their elbow, an easiness between them.

"I assured them you'd get Mattie out alive," Luke added. He winked at Mattie, and she smiled at him conspiratorially.

"Oh shit," Daph said. They followed her gaze to the main entrance, where the police were escorting out an unhappy, and handcuffed, Mike Spencer. Behind them, more officers guided two more handcuffed groomsmen toward the patrol cars. Someone stopped Kyle from approaching them, and Henry came up beside him to add his protest. Moments later, the cars carrying the arrested men drove past the blockade and down the driveway. Mattie stared as they passed, but Spencer had his head down and didn't meet her eyes.

"Huh." Rin breathed out heavily. "That worked a lot faster than I was expecting."

Daphne gasped. "Rin, what did you do?"

"Well, certainly not *all* of this!" They threw their hands up toward the hotel. "This is sort of a big reaction to getting a tip that there's an American domestic terrorist in New Zealand. I mean, usually they spend at least a few weeks investigating—wait, what the fuck?"

From the back of one of the police vans, two officers unloaded a squat robot with multiple arms and caterpillar treads. A third person was being fitted into a bulky suit.

"That," Luke said, "is a bomb squad. We had equipment like that on *Knuckletracker*. Rin, did you call in a fucking bomb threat?"

"Absolutely not." They all squinted at Rin. "Absolutely not!" They repeated. "Mattie said no violence, but I didn't think Spencer had quite gotten what was coming to him. So, last night, I called the tip hotline and told the proper authorities that the leader of an American hate group was in the country and he was making threats against New Zealand citizens—which he was technically doing by simply being here. But that was twelve hours ago. They wouldn't have moved on him that fast. I promise I did not make a bomb threat."

The group slowly pivoted their focus to Daphne.

"Oh, for fuck's sake," she said. "Why would I call in a bomb threat when I could otherwise be eating these hot, huh?" She waved around the last waffle. A convincing argument.

"But I did call the health department and told them about the wedding today," she continued. "I also mentioned the film project because I figured there was as much chance of Payton voluntarily shutting it down as there was that the Redgraves would cancel the wedding. Which is to say, none. Snitching seemed like the least amount of effort for the maximum desired effect."

"You're both mad," Raphael said. "Mad and brilliant."

Daphne scoffed. "Of course we are."

"Okay, wait," Mattie said, trying to catch up. "The health department person said they shut down the wedding, but they were looking for Payton specifically, and Edie, too. Did you mention her to them?"

"No," Daph said. "But she is a terrorist of sorts. Rin?"

Rin snorted. "Just Spencer."

Luke cleared his throat. "I believe I may have the answer you seek."

"Who are you people?" Raph asked incredulously. Luke just grinned at him.

"Independent of either of them, I, too, took it upon myself to foist our problems onto the most appropriate authority in the hopes of even the smallest reprieve." He lifted one finger in the air as he hid his other hand behind his back, channeling a stage version of Sherlock Holmes. "At the meeting yesterday, Mason said Edie had just met with his daughter in Los Angeles a few days before, and confirmed when I asked that it had, indeed, been earlier that same week. From that, I deduced that she must have flown into Auckland by private plane and arrived shortly before you were released from your quarantine hotel. Payton insisted the car pick you up because it would already be there for Edie. It had to be. Any other transportation out of the airport would have taken her directly to her own quarantine hotel."

"Oh shit," Raphael said, rubbing the stubble on his chin.

"Quite right, dear boy." Luke leaned into the fake English accent. "After she cornered Mattie yesterday morning, I approached her and offered her a deal. If she stayed away from you, Raph, and recanted her claim that she's pregnant with your child, I wouldn't tell anyone about her breach of health protocol. She was unmoved. So I called the health department. Not very clever of me, but, effective, it turns out."

The group considered him for a moment before Mattie burst into tears.

"I..." Luke stuttered, back to his own accent. "Should I not have done that?"

Raphael took Mattie into his arms and shook his head. "You did right, Luke."

"Crying is how she expresses otherwise overwhelming emotions," Daphne explained. "In this case, she's happy that you love Raphael enough to do that for him, and by extension, for her, too. And also that the three of us love them enough to do what we did, independent of each other."

"It's a good thing," Rin whispered to him. "You get used to it."

"God, it is just *so sad* about the wedding being canceled, isn't it?"

With the steadily growing crowd, Edie's approach had gone unnoticed. Raphael's grip on Mattie tightened even as she stepped back with a sniffle, wiping her eyes.

"In how many languages must we tell you to fuck off?" Luke said. "I only know English, so, fuck off."

She ignored him and turned to Raph. "Luke told me how you two were meant to attend the wedding today. What a shame."

"He's not going to leave me for you just because we can't attend a wedding together," Mattie said, her eye roll practically audible. "Is that what you think real people do?"

"Nah, Mats," Rin said. "She just doesn't want Raphael to be happy. Because if he's unhappy, he'll come back to her."

"Jesus, Edie," Raph said, bowing his head but keeping his hands on Mattie's arms. "It's over. Leave me alone."

Edie shifted from foot to foot, blinking away tears. "You didn't give me a chance. We didn't have enough time together, or you wouldn't have left me. But I'm willing to give you another chance. If I'm going to have our child—"

"Edie." He closed his eyes and sighed. His anger hadn't disappeared. It was only eclipsed by exhaustion. "I'm sterile. By choice. Been that way for years. So. You want to try to run that by me one more time?"

"Damn, he just telling everybody now," Daphne muttered.

Edie looked from Raph to Mattie, to the others and back again. "Well, it must not have taken."

"I test annually. It took."

As she stared at him, her mask of hurt melted into genuine disappointment. "You could have told me that before we started dating. It would have saved me a lot of trouble."

"Would have saved *you* a lot of trouble?" Mattie made to move toward Edie, but Raphael held her back.

Out of the corner of her eye, Mattie saw Rin grab something out of Daphne's hand. Daphne stamped her feet and shoved her hands into her pockets, and Rin held her by the wrists.

"Edie Everett!" Luke cupped his hands to his mouth and yelled. "Edie Everett is right here! Who was looking for her?" Out of Edie's line of sight, the health official who had questioned them earlier turned and motioned for a nearby police officer to join her as she walked over.

"I can't believe you lied to me," Edie said with a humorless laugh. "Waste of time. And I could have slept in today, but no, I'm out here in the fucking woods for nothing."

"Are you Edie Everett?" The masked official said.

"What?" Edie turned to them and glowered. "I'm not giving autographs."

"Ms Everett, when did you arrive in New Zealand?"

"None of your business."

"Miss," the police officer said. "Why don't we head over to the van and you can answer her questions. We take public health very seriously, and if you can't provide proof you quarantined upon arrival, you'll have to be detained, and either enter isolation or be deported."

Edie's jaw dropped in her best impression of a fish. "I—I—"

"Come now, miss, they're easy questions," the health official said, holding her arms out to corral Edie toward the vehicle. "Let's have a chat at the van, give you a little privacy."

Edie stepped back and glanced at the cop, closed her mouth and straightened up. "Of course," she said, letting the woman lead her away.

"Hey bro," Luke said to the officer. "Brought the bomb squad out?"

"Yeah," he said. "Haven't found anything though. Someone called it in this morning. American number. Wouldn't have taken it so seriously, but it coincided with a report there was an American terrorist on site. He's been taken in already, so no worries on that. We'll get you all settled back in soon, and you can enjoy the rest of your holiday. Cheers."

"Cheers," Luke and Raph said in unison, as the cop followed Edie, who was complaining nonstop to the health official.

The five of them looked at each other.

"I could still get her from here," Daph said. Mattie looked down and saw her sister's slingshot sticking out of Rin's back pocket, heard the pebbles clicking against each other where Rin clasped her hands.

"Daph," Mattie said with a sigh. "She's getting taken into custody. Don't fling pebbles at her."

"I don't know," Raph added. "Maybe she should."

Daph's eyes lit up, but as she glanced from Mattie to Raph to Edie, her shoulders slumped.

"Fine. Police can have her," she mumbled.

"This day..." Rin said, shaking her head and releasing Daph's wrists.

"And it's not even lunch yet," Daphne added.

Raphael huffed, then let out a longer chuckle. His body shook with silent laughter until it bubbled up, uncontrollable.

"I'd be worried if I weren't one heartbeat away from the same reaction," Luke said.

When Raph caught his breath, he sighed, and said, "Edie. Edie did it."

"Edie's done a lot of things," Mattie said flatly.

"She called in the bomb threat. She has an American number. Spencer didn't have a reason to tank the wedding, but Edie thought we were going, and meant to stop us. Spectacularly."

"Mate." Luke shook his head. "You'd best get that restraining order soon, because that is some scary behavior." Edie's voice carried to them, arguing still, though it looked like she was going to be put in the van very soon.

"I will," Raph said. "For now, I want to take a moment to appreciate everything you've done for me and Mattie." Mattie looked up at him, her face wistful.

"We all took a leap of faith to trust each other," he continued, "and look where we are: the wedding is off, Mike Spencer is arrested, Edie is being hauled off to quarantine as we speak, and the film that would have tanked both Luke's and my career has been shut down. Not because of any elaborate and clever plan, but because...all of you snitched."

"You know, Raph," Daphne cut in, nose in the air. "Not every problem needs to be solved with a bow and arrow."

"Can I get that in writing?" Rin muttered.

"Also," Luke said. "At this point, it was either beat the shit out of several someones or make one quick phone call and let it be someone else's problem." He shrugged. "Work smarter, not harder."

Rin ran their hand up Luke's arm. "Daphne. Mattie. I think it's time to bestow upon Luke his code name."

Luke perked up. "Really? I can join your Honest Mischief Alliance?"

"Mattie's gotta pick your name first," Rin explained. They turned to her expectantly.

"Hmm," she teased. "Luke Maston, you must only use your code name when it's certain you won't be otherwise recognized. By accepting it, you agree to come to our aid when needed, and to call on us when you need aid in turn. So shall you be known as...Harrington."

Luke grinned. "I'll take it."

"So says Vanessa," Mattie said, holding up the last bit of her waffle.

"So says Fran," Rin said, giving the waffle a fist bump.

"So says Betty!" Daphne shouted, crumbs falling from her hand as she slapped it against Rin's fist. They looked at Raphael.

"Oh," he said. He tapped them with his own waffle. "So says Elliot."

"So says Harrington," Luke chimed in, resting his hand atop Rin's.

Mattie grinned at them with tears in her eyes. Her real family. Finally.

Epilogue
Two Months Later

Lena and Cassidy shrieked as their marshmallows caught fire, swelled, blackened, and slid off their sticks into the campfire.

"No, no," Raphael insisted. "You have to pull them out the moment they start to burn, and blow them out, and put them on the graham cracker before they fall off. Here, let's try again. Remember, you want them burned, but you have to take them out before they fall."

"Raphael prefers burnt marshmallows?" Daphne asked, before taking a swig from her beer. She and Mattie sat in outdoor folding chairs on one side of the campfire, facing the lake. Rin and Luke sat a little ways away, watching Raphael try to teach Luke's kids how to make s'mores.

"Nobody's perfect," Mattie grumbled, taking a sip from her own bottle. "He has other qualities."

"I bet he does." Daph wiggled her eyebrows and Mattie nearly spit out her beer.

Rin laughed at something Luke said, their cackle echoing across the lake. Luke was recording the girls on his phone—part of his contribution to their pandemic documentary. The sun had set an hour before, the darkness and the temperature dropping steadily. After spending a self-imposed, two-week "isolation" at the cottage, Luke returned to his own house. He had brought the girls over to the cottage every few days afterward, for his own sanity, and to relieve his mother, who would otherwise be taking care of them.

After watching *Frozen* with the girls for the thousandth time, Rin's own sanity was at stake, and they suggested they spend that evening making a fire on the beach, singing songs, making s'mores, and telling ghost stories. The girls had never been more excited.

Of course, they were also just like their father, and couldn't help causing trouble.

"Oh, no, no," Raph said, watching Cassidy's bloated marshmallow fall for a second time. She giggled as it plopped into the campfire, making him suspect it wasn't entirely accidental.

"Uncle Raaaaaaph!" Lena screamed, as hers followed suit.

"I'm going back to San Francisco soon," Daphne said.

Mattie nodded. "Cinnamon."

Daphne sighed. "Cinnamon. Don't get me wrong, I love it here with my fellow spies and spy babies. But I miss my wife. I wish I could bring her here, but they're not letting Americans in anymore."

The sisters sat in silence, enjoying the contrast of the fire's warmth to the night's chill.

"Spencer was deported," Daph said. "Didn't know if you wanted to know, but, in case you need another reason to stay in New Zealand longer. Him not being here is a good one."

Mattie was surprised she hadn't thought about Mike Spencer since that last day at the Billingstead. Him taking up less of her headspace was a good thing. But she was glad to hear he was gone.

She hadn't heard from any of the Redgraves since that day, either. Of course, she blocked them all, everywhere, so she wouldn't know even if they had tried to contact her. She was a little curious if they thought about her. Probably she always would be. But they didn't have a hold on her like they used to, and the emotional weight that had been lifted from her was something she vowed to never burden herself with again.

Daphne read her silence correctly. "The Redgraves are still around," she said. "I follow them under shadow accounts. Nobody's talking about what happened, but I did some digging—"

"Of course you did," Mattie laughed.

Daphne grinned. "According to the internets, Celeste postponed the wedding indefinitely. From her posts, it sounds like she's upset that Kyle was friends with Spencer. She's reconsidering the type of man who would be best friends with someone like that, and whether she wants that type of man in her life at all."

"Damn," Mattie breathed.

"Right? Mats." Daph reached across and grabbed her hand. "You went in there thinking that if you could protect just one person from him, it would be worth it. And of all people, it was fucking Celeste."

Mattie laughed into her bottle as she took another drink. "Can't pick and choose."

Raphael crawled up to them. "Save me," he rasped, holding his hand out. "They're savages." The children ran up behind him, screaming, waving their sticks in the air before hitting them against each other like swords.

From across the fire, the first notes of "Let It Go" rang out on the guitar, and the girls abandoned their sticks and Raphael to sing with their father.

"I don't hate children," Raphael said, catching his breath. "I just really love giving them back to their parents once I'm worn out."

Mattie saluted him with her beer. His eyes lit up, and she dug out an unopened bottle from the cooler.

"Speaking of," Daph drawled. "I've seen some gossip online, but, how's Edie's pregnancy coming along?"

Raphael laughed, popping off the cap with the opener. "She's dating Clive Chansley, who was the other wanker producer on *Broke*, and I'm not surprised. My lawyers got through to her lawyers and I won't pursue a restraining order as long as she never mentions me ever again. They must know she's a loose cannon because they came to an agreement fairly quickly."

"When someone asks her about the pregnancy, she laughs and says, 'Oh, that!' like it was some big joke." Daphne was always up to date on the gossip. "She said it was part of her method acting for an upcoming role and she was never actually pregnant."

Raphael puffed out his breath in a thin stream. "Yeah, that sounds right."

"She's never going to take responsibility for how she hurt you," Mattie said.

"No," Raph shook his head. "But I never have to think about that again."

Mattie reached over and took his hand. Sensing their need to be alone, Daphne stood up.

"I'd better show them how it's done," she said, stomping over to Luke and the girls and singing as badly and as loudly as she could. Raphael moved into her vacated chair.

"So," he said, putting his arm around Mattie. "Where were we?"

His face glowed in the firelight, eyes mostly pupil, lips quirked into his famously rakish half smile. She smiled back, her contentment an odd but welcome feeling. "I think we were just getting started."

Acknowledgements

Publishing is hard, y'all. I had thought that its solitary nature would be easier than dealing with people all the time. Imagine my surprise when I not only needed but wanted connection and community. I guess that's sort of what this book is about, too. Special thanks go to these stand-outs:

While I leaned on plenty of friends to get this book into your hands, none of it would have been possible without the full and possibly foolish support of my husband. He entertains more of my outlandish ideas than is rational or advisable, and I try my best to make sure he doesn't regret it.

Donna and Ámá read early versions and gently steered me toward coherence when my cleverness grew to conspiracy-theory levels of nonsense.

Once again, May shared her expertise as well as her generous spirit and helped polish this story in ways I could never have figured out without her.

Jerome and Rachael housed and fed and guided me through Aotearoa with the enthusiasm and patience that only true friends can offer. They're also responsible for introducing me to LJ, who did their best to make sure my AoNZ references were correct. Any mistakes here are due to my own failure and not their efforts.

Finally, I want to thank all you readers. I took you on a heavy journey this time, and I hope the joy, freedom, and family these characters found by the end also find their way into your life.

About the Author

Jem Spears (she/they/he) is a queer, neurodivergent writer who was raised in New England, educated in Los Angeles, and embraced by Cincinnati. Somewhere in the midwest, when the sun dips below the horizon, if it's not too humid, you can find her in her natural habitat: napping beneath a pile of cats. The rest of the time, she's at her computer, making characters kiss. She also writes poetry and nonfiction as Jacquelyn Merrill Ruiz, and fanfic on AO3 under yet another pseudonym. *A Courtship in Quarantine* is book two of the International Love and Misadventure series.

***

Find out more about the author online at www.jemspears.com.

Discovery Guide

While I don't often have imposter syndrome, I do feel a little narcissistic offering a Discovery Guide in the first edition of what is only my second published novel. But these prompts are questions and ideas that rolled around in my brain the entire time I was writing, and I think the topics are important enough to ask you all to ponder them, too, if you wish.

1. Why do you think it's so hard for Mattie to decide what to do about her relatives? Do you feel there's a difference between "family" and "relatives"?

2. Do you think Mattie is overreacting about Mike Spencer? About her relatives?

3. Do you think Raphael would have gone through with filming *That Scarlet, Beating Heart* if Mattie hadn't told him it's racist propaganda? Do we have an obligation to point out the biases of systemic oppression in media, or should we just let people enjoy what they enjoy?

4. Raphael describes how strangers feel like they know him and act like they're entitled to his attention and his body. Have people felt entitled to access to you? Have you ever felt entitled to access to someone else? What are some things we can do to set and enforce boundaries? How can we show people we respect their autonomy? What other

examples are there in the book of someone respecting someone else's decisions?

5. Media often show us that people who want to be child-free will eventually change their minds. How are people of different genders treated when they say they don't want children? Has anyone ever tried to change your mind about your decision? Have you ever tried to change someone else's mind?

6. Not all of us emerged from our lockdowns of Spring 2020 with a new romantic partner (despite our best efforts). If you've been in isolation, how did it change the way you approach or maintain relationships? Did some thrive? Did some fall apart? If you haven't been in isolation, how do you think it might change you?

7. The good-looking stranger who sat next to you on a thirteen-hour flight has just slipped a handwritten letter beneath your hotel room door. What do you do?

www.ingramcontent.com/pod-product-compliance
Lightning Source LLC
Chambersburg PA
CBHW050114120726
47904CB00004B/1346